P9-EKS-096

CODE WORD
ACCESS

ALEX SCHULER
WITH ROLF YNGVE

The author of this book is solely responsible for the accuracy of all facts and statements contained in the book. This is a work of fiction. Names, characters, places, events, and incidents are either the product of the author's imagination or used in an entirely fictitious manner. Any resemblance to actual persons, living or dead, is entirely coincidental.

Copyright © 2020 by Level 4 Press, Inc.

All rights reserved, including the right to reproduce this book, or portions thereof, in any form.

This book is printed on acid-free paper.

Published by:
Level 4 Press, Inc.
13518 Jamul Drive
Jamul, CA 91935
www.level4press.com

Library of Congress Control Number: 2019943908

ISBN: 978-1-93376-982-0

Printed in USA

Other books by Alex Schuler

FASTER

CODE WORD BRAVO

ROGUE

CODE WORD CHARLIE

CODE WORD DELTA

DEDICATION

For Gaia

It's all about wetware at last,
and wetware lives in meatspace.

Heather McHugh

PROLOGUE

He hated the sky.

Long ago, his father told him he could never escape the eye of God. All the stars, all the clouds, the moon and the strange planets, the sun itself—all were the makings of God's hand. It is right to fear the sky. To fear God is to love Him.

Eighty years old now, the man known as al Tehrani did not fear God.

But he had learned to fear the sky with *its* eyes—its satellites, its drones, its missiles and smart ordnance. And with this fear, he had learned to hate the sky filled with the merciless machines of the godless.

He stood as far back in the doorway as he could and gazed up. *Inshallah*, he thought, I will live through this day.

He knew he should feel proud of this moment. A wedding. His only living heir. He should be filled with joy waiting for the bride and her people to arrive. He should revel in the deep satisfaction of a large and wealthy family giving away their prized daughter to this boy, his great-grandson.

He felt neither pride nor joy.

Under this sky, he felt the same dread he had learned in boyhood when terrible angels descended to murder his father and uncles—the Soviet helicopters. Then the Americans came with their machines to kill his brothers and cousins. For decades, they left, then returned to kill—the machines of the sky slaughtering his sons and grandsons. By 2040, the world had divided into the High Latitude countries with their food and water, their cooler climate and vaccines—and the Low Latitude countries where the days grew ever warmer, the food scarce, the future more dim. From the High Latitudes, they had slaughtered with ever more machines and psychic tricks until only he and his great-grandson walked the earth.

He breathed in the dry dead air of another rainless season. Even the poppies had failed in the fields. Nothing grew in this heat. No living thing flourished. Now, when they should be celebrating a harvest along with this wedding, their only crop had been the unclean charity from the people of the High Latitudes. Take their offer or starve—that was slavery.

He hated the sky of the rich. The sky of the godless. The sky he could never for an instant ignore, where every sound, every glint of sun reflected on steel killing machines, every small contrail meant death. He had lived this long by learning to always watch the heavens.

And now, after all the years of one failure after another, all the countless deaths, he doubted himself and he doubted God.

He cowered in a darkened doorway thinking: If we are the chosen of God, why are we so poor? Why do we not rule? Why do we not bask in the jubilation of God over the deaths of the infidels and the cleansing of the world in His name? Why are our lands full of ever more heat and barren of water? Why do we starve? Why am I not waiting with my sons, my brothers, my cousins and uncles instead of this one boy, this great-grandson, the last of my name?

All the others had been taken. Killed by a sky that wished him to believe God had betrayed him and his legacy. A rainless sky. A killing sky. The sky of dread. He mentally pricked the deeply encrypted interface buried under the occipital bone of his skull, his modified NeuroChip. That had been his great success, turning their technology against them.

The NeuroChip had allowed him to hide. The strange block chain encryption was impossible to penetrate. Yet every eye of the remaining faithful, his Ansar-al-Mahdi, could still inform him. Once they were thousands, now only hundreds. But they had become more lethal than ever before—all owing to the NeuroChip and the vast net that serviced it, the Cloud.

But to what end? he wondered. More death? More despair?

The long song of the procession hailed him, as a crowd turned the corner onto his street. Women with men. Fathers and sons. A hundred souls singing, clapping, and cheering to the beat of the dohols and blares of sorna flutes, and he allowed himself to feel hope. This boy, this son of his grandson, flesh of his flesh, was not only the last male of his family, but the last of the tribe that had flourished for thousands of years. Breathing next to him. Full of the promise of sons and daughters, another generation. Perhaps the true generation of God.

He moved his NeuroChip cache to consciousness, and opened the virtual envelope filled with reports from his followers and their followers—all the observers and watchers of the Net. Was he safe under the hundreds of network cutouts that hid the short communications of those soldiers of the faith who had been skilled enough to survive? Was he protected by the ones who knew how to search the interior of the Net for the telltale signs of their enemy? The faithful reassured him of safety even under this dangerous sky.

Perhaps God had become a mystery to him. But he had faith in the marvel in his brain that could keep him both untracked and informed. He trusted the computational edge that reassured him of his great-grandson's anonymity. He had foreseen the moment of this boy's marriage over twenty years ago and had carefully hidden his heir in the rich schools of the High Latitudes. The boy had, thanks be to God, found a pure woman from an enormous family; wealthy and worthy to bring forth sons who would carry his name forward.

They walked toward him, this family, singing and full of joy. They did not know to watch the sky as he did. But he could not afford to be careless. The habits learned in the mountains of Afghanistan enabled him to see a flicker of reflection in the cloudless, sun-shot, dry air. Then doubt let him see it again, winking at him, a tiny silver glint.

"Wait here." He turned to his great-grandson and kissed him on his forehead. "I will go down to the street to greet your new wife. I will honor them before they honor us."

The boy, the last of his village, tribe, and line, smiled. The old man stepped away from his heir who would be nothing more than another dead innocent if he didn't act quickly.

Ten meters. Twenty. He walked with his arms wide to greet the throng of celebrants. To greet God. To greet the hated sky filled with its relentless computations and machines. The NeuroChip and the Net had betrayed him, he was certain. He had been a fool to trust anything but the crop in the ground, the flesh of his flesh. At least this death would be his death alone. In the middle of the street, well away from the innocent, he stopped, closed his eyes, and tried with his last breath to forgive himself for the death of his people. To forgive God for abandoning the sky.

The man called al Tehrani then prayed for the world, all the peoples, not only his own. His last thoughts were a supplication, a prayer for God's deliverance of humanity from the remorseless sky of killing machines.

@NYCNews 12 September 2050
(Veracity Level 9.8) 2050 Nobel Prize in cybernetics awarded
to Dr. Eliot Schwarm of the Johns Hopkins Advanced
Physics Lab for the development of Brain-Machine
Interface technology. His 2025 breakthrough resulted in the
widespread adaptation of NeuroChip systems.

@pattycakesorgan
If you're NeuroChipped you aren't real. If you mental your
dishwasher to start, you are part of the machine. WAKE UP
MERIKA! They want you to be a machine!

1

ecretary of Defense "SecDef" Elizabeth Milhouse Perry, New Humanist Party, Texas, steel-gray hair and dark blue suit, watched the OpCenter's vault doors unseal with a pop and start to sigh open. They looked like the familiar blast doors installed a hundred years ago to fend off an atomic attack. But they had cracked open without any of the security sideshow she had expected.

"Just like that, Stub?" she said. "No keypad? No eye scanner?"

General Fredrick "Stub" Grant, U.S. Army, CyberCommand, looked up at her and smiled. He barely topped her shoulder, but he looked as solid as the doors he was so proud of showing her. Had she grown taller in the thirty years since they had become colleagues? Or had he shrunk like mud, settling into an even stockier version of the West Point footballer she'd first met? It made no real difference. He was her general now. He'd always been hers, his voice thick as dirt. "New system, Madam Secretary. Completely unbreakable. It's got a little bio-metric review combined with what we call a Schrodenberg-encrypted validation of our NeuroChips before it'll open."

Schrodenberg, she thought. *Military guys with their acronyms. What nonsense!* A code constructed from Schrödinger's Cat laid over the Heisenberg Uncertainty Principle. She didn't think anyone could real-ly understand how that mash-up of quantum physics functioned. But it worked. In this cave, they were as safe from cyberattack as the two thousand feet of granite overhead had made Cheyenne Mountain safe from nuclear attack in her grandfather's day.

"Look, Stubby. I hope this isn't going to take too long. Hiram Stork said I had to see what you've been doing with all our money, but I don't have time for a dog and pony show."

"Really? Stork? Why's the Assistant Secretary of Defense for Special Operations worried about CyberCommand's funding?"

"Don't be stupid, Stub. He wants to use the system to support the SpecOps mission." Perry didn't add that Stork was also worried about losing his own funding if this thing really worked as well as Grant said it did.

The vault thunked fully open. "Don't worry, Madam Secretary. You'll like this. And it's perfect for integration into the special operations guys' jobs." Stub pushed through the lightweight interior door and swept her into a darkened, nearly empty room.

Perry had expected the usual buzz of reports between intelligence personnel, near-term planners, future planners, and the operators themselves. She had anticipated an expanded version of the multiple displays and watch-standers using two dozen different languages from two dozen countries that had taken up every iota of space on two levels. She had known it well, first as a member of the House Intelligence Committee, then as Chairwoman of the Senate Armed Services Committee, and now, as Secretary of Defense, she wanted to see what seven billion dollars in black money had bought. But this? The OpCenter breathed a quiet sigh of restrained ventilation in an empty space under muted lighting.

The heavy door shut behind them with a hiss and the click of a bolt closing.

"Stubby, what's going on? You dragged me all the way out from Washington to see this? In a big hurry? An empty room? This is Main Sail? Seven billion dollars for this?"

Her general smiled at her, then woofed out with his command voice, "Lieutenant Colonel Gurk? Are we clear to bring it up?"

"All clear, General. Code word access Main Sail security protocols are in effect."

Perry's eyes were adjusting to the dim light. Now she could see a single U.S. Air Force lieutenant colonel seated behind a translucent display the size of a drafting table. He was an odd-looking man in uniform. He wore an unauthorized beard and a black turban wrapped tightly around his head. Obviously Sikh.

"Bring it up," her general said as if he was in prayer.

The three-dimensional display filled the space, from the floor to a thirty-foot-high ceiling above them, massive and utterly realistic. It was as if they were ants looking from a doorjamb at two men, one young, one old, both wearing traditional Persian dress. The view pulled back to show the men looking out into the street of a desiccated city, obviously one of the desert nations. The camera panned over dusty, concrete rooftops cluttered with exposed wire, water cisterns, garbage, and laundry hanging limp in a windless afternoon. On the streets below, a crowd wearing bright dress danced toward the men. *A celebration*, Elizabeth thought. The view zoomed in again. The crowd moved slowly toward what appeared to be a fixed camera behind the two men, dust billowing at their feet. The view zoomed in to show sweat plainly visible on the old man's scored, brown forehead. His eyes were deep blue and gazing up at the sky from under the shadow of a doorway.

It must be a special effect, thought Perry, *video game crap defense contractors put up at trade shows to sell their gear.* She said, "Tell me this isn't virtual reality."

"All real. All of this is real time. Unaltered. There's a little enhanced reality to create a 3-D effect. But it's all happening now."

Perry snorted. "Huh!" She pointed up at the massive figure. "So, who is this guy?"

The Sikh officer spoke up in a deep, slightly accented American

THREAT WATCH

Perry had seen it many times, the Threat Watch Cube. She could even call it up on her wall display in the Pentagon. But these were more than the static pictures she was used to seeing. These faces were videos. Moving. A man in a car. A man walking. The image of Fouad al Tehrani made small, walking into a street and looking up into the air. Beneath the display, the familiar score card displayed the data from the cube.

Suspected Combatants:	26
Targets Identified:	12
Targets Killed:	0
Probability of Kill:	0%

"That's it, Stub?" she finally said. "Video in the Threat Watch Cube?"

"Shawn. Tell the Secretary what we're looking at."

The boy sucked on his straw again and cleared his throat. "So, this is the usual picture, right? Everybody knows about link analysis, connecting the dots between terrorists in a group. This is the usual result of years of studying pocket litter, fingerprints, biometrics, and whatever we could pull off people's NeuroChips and the Net, social media—all the usual suspects."

Perry looked at Stub. "That's what I get for seven billion—two guys in a room with a fancy picture. Link analysis. Where's the ordnance on target? Where's the dead terrorists? Christ almighty. You bought this, Stub, designed this? You could have hired Raytheon/Lockheed to do the same thing for a few million."

Before Stub could answer, the civilian kid piped up with his irritating, smug voice. "Sure, your guys at RayLock could build the display, but could they do this?" A single portrait boomed up out of the cube to show the face of a man with a neatly trimmed beard and a narrow striped necktie. He appeared to be in the back of an automobile reading a folder. "Does this guy look familiar to you, Madam Secretary?"

"No." This kid was really beginning to irritate her. "Why—should he?"

"You should get to know your people better, ma'am. He's the guy who holds a seventy-five percent interest in Lighthouse Caymans Bank where you deposited, let's see, sixteen million seven hundred and twenty-eight-dollars last year. The only reason your balance is a million six hundred thousand less is that Lighthouse Caymans skimmed it for their fees. This dude? He got seventy-five percent of those fees. He's your employee, Madam Secretary. And he also works for Fouad al Tehrani. You're paying al Tehrani's salary."

Elizabeth Milhouse Perry had been bred and trained for her job. Never let them see you sweat, her daddy had told her. She could feel the dampness stick to her blouse between her shoulder blades, but she managed to sound calm, even disinterested when she said, "Totally fake. Fake news."

The face faded into a list of cash deposits of an account titled:

EMP Trust.
Airbus-Boeing Institute for Military Development—$100K
Hauhung-Krup Federalist Support Institute—$650K
International Red Star Remington Rifle Association—$375K

Tendrils shot out from the display, then burst into depictions of spreadsheets and contracts connecting her name on corporate documents, revealing the shell company exposures to EMP Trust.

She told them, "You guys are in more trouble than you can ever imagine."

She turned to walk out, when her brain kicked in. There was something else in this, something more important. This couldn't be the whole story. She turned back around and looked up at the display again.

Stubby actually eked out a laugh and said, "Madam Secretary. Elizabeth. Lizbeth. You and I have been friends for a long time." He took her elbow gently, as if he was going to guide her across a street. "Remember what we used to say in our old White House days? Let intelligence stay intelligence. Let law enforcement screw themselves.

And never let the two of them in the same room together? What you saw is special compartmented information. Only those with code word access to Main Sail intelligence can see it, and searching out a citizen's personal history by intelligence organizations is illegal, to boot. We don't spy on American citizens."

She shrugged off his hand. "So how come this post-millennial jerk gets to look at this stuff?"

"What you should be asking, Madam Secretary, is this: How did this post-millennial jerk get this stuff at all?"

That's what she had been missing. This kid had thrown information into the air that had been nailed down with an encryption scheme that was supposed to be completely random and unbreakable. She turned toward the boy who had sat down and was peeling the top off what looked like a carton of cottage cheese. Before she could ask him how he'd mined her data, he said, "You don't mind if I eat, do you, Madam Secretary? Gurk-man and I have been waiting for you since four a.m." He popped the top off his cottage cheese, then rustled open a bag of potato chips.

"Stubby, this kid is eating potato chips in the Op Center?"

"It's like this, Madam Secretary." The boy dipped a chip into the cottage cheese. "People are dumb and slow. Everybody knows that a computer can learn much more quickly than a human being. Trial and error, remembering the results. Instead of a hundred and fifty peeps working two years to get this watch list, I got a computer to work a week and solve the problem. The only limit has been latency—the time it takes to move all that information around."

This was getting increasingly strange. Perry couldn't keep herself under control any longer." Jesus! I don't need lecturing, people." With a loud pop, the picture of her so-called banker winked out, to return to the picture of al Tehrani in the doorway. The old man had stepped out into the sun.

"Tired of listening to me, Madam Secretary? How about somebody you like?" Shawn waved his hand in the air as if casting a spell.

A smooth, gentle, Texas-accented woman's voice flowed like syrup from every corner of the room. "Thank you for coming to visit, Madam Secretary. It's a great honor to meet you, ma'am."

"Aunt Dolly?" The voice was a spot-on copy of her very dead Houston aunt.

"I can be Dolly for you, Madam Secretary."

Perry was speechless. This was too weird, too personal. The voice said, "Don't you worry, sweetheart. It isn't about you. It's really our first operational test. With your permission, General, we'll go hot."

The general straightened himself up and said, "Madam Secretary, meet LAZ-237. You wanted to see what your money got us?" The general straightened his back and spoke in a clear and firm voice. "This is General Fredrick Grant, code word access Main Sail, authorizing weapons release on confirmed target set Ansar-al-Mahdi. LAZ-237, brief the senior leader of the United States Armed Forces."

Dolly's voice filled the room again. "This plan has been initiated by letting our primary target see the glint of what he thinks is a drone in the air. He is now walking out of the house, away from his great-grandson whom he wants to protect from the weapon we are delivering. At this very moment, he is transmitting a general warning to everyone on his NeuroNet that he's been located and that he expects to be—how should I put it, sweetheart—Snuffed out?"

"Brilliant, Stub," Perry said quietly, "You broke his encryption, like you broke mine. Smart to make him move out into the light."

The general demurred. "We didn't do anything more than define the mission and tell Lazy Jack to go hot."

"Lazy Jack? The machine?"

The Dolly voice spoke up. "That's right, Lizbeth, the gentlemen call me Lazy Jack, not that ah'm lazy. Took me a hair less than six microseconds. And ah admit, it was a little slow. But, there you go. The boys are still working on it. And, Lizzy, sweetheart—you still seem a little tense. Let me throw a tune up there to ease the pressure a bit."

A muted version of "The Yellow Rose of Texas" whispered into the room. The red box with al Tehrani's face flew into the middle of the matrix. A blizzard of green laser-like lines reached out from al Tehrani's face and the cube of twenty-six boxes doubled, then slowly grew in number. Some turned yellow. Some disappeared. The lines multiplied and grew in a hypnotic, serpentine flow of connections. The scorecard changed to read:

Suspected Combatants:	412
Targets Identified:	32
Targets Killed:	0
Probability of Kill:	0%

Dolly said, "What you-all are looking at is what you might call the usual intelligence spaghetti. The old ops room might have been able to pull this together based upon this one hit on al Tehrani, but it would've taken a week of work, and by then, none of it would have been actionable. Maybe they'd get al Tehrani. Maybe one or two others. But we're gonna try for the whole farm. Ah'm lettin' the whole thing build up a bit, then we'll figure out the exact operational moment to lower the boom, so to speak."

"Can't you make her stop talking like that? Makes me nervous listening to Dolly."

"Machine voice, please," the general said.

The smooth, confident tones of a British gentleman's voice intoned, "Is this better, Madam Secretary? LAZ-237, standing by."

The Secretary nodded and the strangely comforting James Bond voice continued. "The connections you see now are the result of analysis confined by the human capacity to examine no more than three dimensions across a temporally limited space."

"Temporary limited space?"

"Temporal, Madam Secretary, temporal. For all practical purposes, all computational latency delays vanish due to my Quantum Programmable Logic Controller."

"The what?"

"The QPLC. That's the core of my new system, Madam Secretary. Dr. Muller's quantum-mechanics-based processor. It ignores time."

"What? You can tell the future?"

"No, but I can visit the past and the present at the same instant from millions of diverse sources."

"Come on. Quit the Disney Program, guys. That's all you got? A VR game?"

"There's really no virtual reality in any of this—all real," the British voice chuckled. "Of course, you are more interested in outcomes than you are in method—these are the intelligence connections I made a microsecond after I received the order to go hot and broke the encryption." The screen burst into a yellow, sun-like ball. "And on that basis, as defined by the mission objectives, this is the operational plan I devised." The sun quickly faded into scores of straight red lines arrowing out of the OpCenter walls into hundreds of faces in the cube. "I had approval for weapons release and was placed in full auto for the first time. I was pre-briefed to bring this operation to completion during your visit. This is the status." A splash of blinding red filament exploded over dozens of figures in the boxes. Each pulsed crimson for a moment, then faded out.

The relaxed British voice continued, "I realize this is a bit challenging for a human's standard visual capacity. Let me display this in an easier-to-grasp format."

The cube dissolved into a huge display screen: Perry's well-dressed banker in his car looked up from his reading and disappeared in a brilliant flash. A young man wearing a T-shirt and baseball cap at an I lifted his fork and his head disappeared. A woman wearing a niqab over her face walking in what looked like a park exploded in a flash of pink and dirt. A new Jaguar convertible traveling on the left side of the road burst into pieces. A man behind a teller's counter grabbed his chest and fell over. A long barrel suddenly appeared from the side of a fuel truck, and within a fraction of a second, shot six persons who were disembarking from a parked airliner, spattering other passengers with blood. Snippets of video flashed up one after another, on and on.

Finally, the parade of carnage stopped, and Fouad al Tehrani appeared alone in a square with a woman and what appeared to be a child prostrated to kiss his feet. A brilliant light burst across the screen, and the display snapped back to the Threat Watch Cube. Under it, the scorecard's red killed numbers blurred higher, then slowed, and halted:

Suspected Combatants:	417
Targets Identified:	98
Targets Killed:	81
Probability of Kill:	82.65%

"Bingo!" shouted the MIT kid as if he'd won a football game. "Eighty-two percent PK!"

"Take it easy, Shawn." Grant waved his hand palm down as if calming a small child. He turned to her and said, "Madam Secretary, what you are looking at is more than a weapons system. More than a machine. It is a perfect army. A special operations force that finds the enemy in milliseconds, plans an operation for optimal outcome in microseconds, and puts weapons on target before Shawn here can finish his first potato chip. All autonomous. He and Colonel Gurk and our team have created a perfect special operations force of one."

The scoreboard started ticking upward, adding:

Suspected Combatants:	417, 425, 426
Targets Identified:	98, 102, 112
Targets Killed:	84, 89, 90
Probability of Kill:	82.65, 86.73, 91.27

The cool British voice lectured, "Note that my systems do not require redeployment. Every weapon was dispatched with autonomous instructions and no human combatant was employed to conduct Operation Main Sail One."

Perry asked, "How will you know when you are done?"

The voice paused for a moment, then said, "I'm learning. Adjusting. I am a vaccine against the Ansar-al-Mahdi, Madam Secretary. In less than forty minutes, they will be extinct."

The skinny MIT kid stepped out from behind his panel and blurted, "Forty minutes. Extinct. After fifty years on the grid. How's that for return on investment? A perfect special operations force with the capacity to bring any terrorist organization to its knees."

"Well," said General Grant. "I wouldn't call it perfect, Shawn. Nothing's perfect. But I say," he swept his heavy hand at the scene in front of them, "never let perfect get in the way of good enough."

Perry settled into the back seat of the government UltraLift for her quick trip up to Breckenridge. Skiing had been the publicized cover for her travel. She stretched out her legs. She would be up on the slopes in an hour. A chance to blow out the carbon and hit the Instagram button would make her publicist happy. She pricked her fully enciphered office access on the handset to talk to the Pentagon and heard, "Good afternoon, Madam Secretary, how did it go? What did you think?"

Perry's longtime ally, Hiram Stork, had picked up before she could speak. She'd demanded his appointment as her Assistant Secretary of Defense for Special Operations and Low Intensity Conflict, "SO/LIC", as a condition for taking on the Secretary of Defense job to keep her from running against President Bluntner. Stork had been a perfect fit. A truly savage functionary, he had all the charisma of a maxi pad. Nobody expected him to overshadow anyone.

"Scary good. It's magic. You were right—I needed to see it. But did you know about this Muller kid? B17?"

"Yes, ma'am."

"Bloodthirsty little shit, isn't he? Get back to Grant and tell him I want him off the ops floor."

"Yes, ma'am. When will you be briefing the president?"

"Don't change the subject. In all my years, I never expected you to put up with a snotty little East Coast Jew-boy like that."

"He's not Jewish," said Stork. "So, did they kill al Tehrani? Muller's parents were in the E-ring when al Tehrani wiped it out. It was personal for him."

"Dead. Al Tehrani's dead. Go ahead with all the media releases. And Muller? I guess you could make the press squeal over revenge for his parents. 'Justice finally served' or something. Fine. Keep him away from me. Tell Grant to get rid of him when we're through."

"You won't ever have to see him. But Grant needs him, ma'am."

"Why?"

"No one else can do what he does. Something about the gene manipulation his parents put him through combined with the NeuroChip—I don't know—his connection with the Cloud, maybe random goddamn mutation. Muller can conceptualize inside the notion of quantum physics in a way nobody really understands—except it works. You saw it. And Lazy Jack is learning more every microsecond. That's what Muller built. That's what only he understands. He gave us the perfect synergy of intelligence, analysis, planning, and operations, and we don't really know how it works."

"Grant's words, right? Old never-let-perfect-get-in-the-way-of-good-enough Grant?"

"Well, yes, ma'am. That's what he briefed me."

She gazed out at the mountains passing below her. Maybe Grant was reaching the end of his usefulness. She'd seen this before, many times, men who had topped out their capabilities. It was the same kind of confusion she'd seen in CEOs who couldn't understand why the markets didn't do what they wanted or politicians who didn't understand why people wouldn't vote for them. She'd have to do something about old Stubby pretty soon. Maybe a job running a university.

President of Columbia. Maybe Johns Hopkins. No, she thought, he was probably too dumb for Johns Hopkins, even with his degrees from West Point and Cal Poly. Of course, nobody was really too dumb to be a president of anything.

She told Stork, "Set it up for me to see the president as soon as he gets back from his golf trip. I don't want to talk to Junior until I'm ready, but I don't want the dumb son of a bitch thinking about any of this without me there to help him. Can we make this look like a normal operation in the press? Can you keep the president off my back until he gets done playing games in Scotland—give me time to get my ducks in a row?"

"Absolutely. There are only twelve people cleared for access to Main Sail operations. None of them will leak it. What ducks do you need lined up?"

She wanted time to think through the possibilities of the system. The 'God Effect' they had called it. Who else had accounts overseas? The Blunt, certainly. Making him President of the United States didn't wipe out his past. How many in the Senate? How many in the administration? Maybe the Supreme Court? She told him, "Ducks in a row. For Junior. Remember that old movie, 'Terminator'?"

Stork harrumphed. "I wondered when you'd bring that up. Cutouts, Madam Secretary, they built in dozens of cutouts. Every operation needs approval. There ain't no such thing as wars of machines against humanity. Why?"

"He's going to ask about 'Terminator' for sure. You've got to give me words about that. But tell me this: What's the cutout on the little snot, Muller?"

"Oh, don't worry about him, Madam Secretary. Muller might be pretty good with artificial intelligence, VR, computing. He may be the prince of cyberspace. But Grant owns him in the meatspace."

@NYCNews 13 September 2050
(Veracity Level 9.2) SecDef Perry announces coordinated strike on Ansar-al-Mahdi terrorist organization. "One step on our path toward international security. One great leap for the civilized nations of the world."

2

Dr. Shawn Muller, cleared to code word access Main Sail, watched the clicking shoes, gray hair, and aerobicized body of the Secretary of Defense march out of his OpCenter. Grant shot him and Amun a thumbs-up. The vault door sucked itself shut, and the room settled into its usual hush of electronics and ventilation.

"We did it," Shawn said. "Amun, we killed al Tehrani." He reached under his panel display and fished the magnum bottle of chilled champagne he'd smuggled into the Mountain. He pulled it out of its plastic bucket filled with ice. He held it up over his head and shouted, "Success! This is a bottle of Armand de Brignac Brut Gold 2025! Let's drink! This one time you could have a little bubbly. My dad would want us to celebrate. He says it's the best on the planet."

The Sikh officer remained intent upon his screen. "Your father is still dead."

Shawn felt his elation drain away. He'd been waiting for this moment for years, his chance to take the sting of his parents' deaths away. He plopped back into his chair, deflated. "You know what I mean. Come on. Can't we celebrate a little?"

"Yes. You would want to celebrate, wouldn't you? I shall, then. Delighted to join you." He didn't sound delighted. He'd been friends with Shawn's parents—their colleague. Maybe that's why he seemed so down.

Shawn shoved the vision of his parents out of his mind. "What's wrong, Amun? Fouad al Tehrani. We finally got him."

"Yes. We did. And his people. We're still killing them. Look."

Shawn looked up at the tally under the Threat Watch Cube now filled with red boxes. The climbing numbers had slowed.

Suspected Combatants:	102
Targets Identified:	323
Targets Killed:	309
Probability of Kill:	95.67%

Shawn had pretended to be impressed by the 83% probability of kill while Perry and Grant watched. But this was more in line with what he had hoped. In fact, he had expected every al-Mahdi fighter to be dead by now. Fourteen identified targets were still breathing.

"Not quite a hundred percent," said Shawn, "I bet a human being screwed up placement of one of the autonomous direct-action elements."

Amun frowned, "We should have gone online two hours earlier like the Lazy Jack originally recommended. But Grant had us wait for his boss."

"He did? Oh, my god, she's a criminal, Amun. Corrupt," Shawn said to the air, "Did you see her face when I stuck it to her with her banking scams?"

"Not the smartest thing you've ever done." Amun buried his eyes on his monitor. "You need to learn how to control yourself better. Control, Shawn."

Shawn slopped champagne into a flute, then stopped. He reached back into the bucket of ice, fished out a can of 7UP, and poured it into the other flute. What had he been thinking, trying to force Amun to drink alcohol? He never drank anything more potent than the occasional 7UP. As a boy, he'd thought it had something to do with Amun's religion. But there was some other reason Shawn had never discovered. Amun reached up for the glass, still transfixed by something on his screen. He put it to his nose, sniffed, then smiled at Shawn.

"A toast? To what should we toast, Shawn?"

"Dead terrorists?"

"Maybe." Amun stood up. "Maybe we should drink to peace." He raised his glass and managed a strained smile. "As if that could ever happen."

What was this about Amun? After all this time working together, for this very moment, he sounded bitter. This was thunderously wrong. What was there to be bitter about? These were the killers of his parents and thousands of others. Finally, after all this time, they'd been able to show off the abilities they'd created in Lazy Jack.

"What's eating you, Amun?"

"Nothing. Drink."

Shawn took a quick gulp of the bubbly, irritated now with Amun—irritated with himself. "Fine. If you won't tell me, I'll get Dolly to fill me in. And what do you say, Dolly? I think I'm going to call you Dolly after the SecDef's aunt. I thought that was pretty funny, eh?"

The honeyed Texan voice replied, "Shore 'nuff, Dr. Muller. Whatever you'd like. Of course, I'll have to take my champagne virtually."

An image of a thick-limbed woman wearing an apron appeared in front of the Threat Watch Cube, holding a champagne flute bubbling over.

"Oops. Spilled a little." Dolly danced around the image of a splash on the floor. "I'll get that later. Where were we?"

Amun walked out from behind his display, touched his glass of 7UP to Shawn's champagne. He stared into Shawn's eyes for a long moment.

"What? What is it, Amun?"

"Shawn, my friend, I hadn't wanted to tell you until now. I've been waiting for this moment. I've resigned my commission. I'll be here another week, then I will be free of all this. Terminal leave."

Shawn's mind caught on itself and stopped for an instant. "What? Why?"

"My business. It doesn't concern you. It's personal."

This made little sense. As far as Shawn knew, Amun had no personal life. He had no family. He had never seemed to have any existence other than the one defined by Shawn himself. He had been his parents' friend when Shawn had been only a boy and for a while, his tutor. They had followed each other through every step of Lazy Jack's development. Such an unlikely pair, Amun with his Sikh beliefs, his measured and careful approach to the research and engineering they'd pioneered, and Shawn with all the chaotic and crazy flights of intuition diving through his mind.

"Why leave, Amun? Why leave now? Isn't this it? We've done it. It's like Grant said, we've created the means to root out every terrorist organization buried inside the Equatorial Nations. We can all be safe now, Amun. There will never be another 9/11, another Paris, another Beijing Massacre. The walls will be perfect. We'll never have to worry about Ebola plagues or caravans of diseased criminals invading the High Latitudes ever again."

Amun shook his head, stared into his glass, and smiled. "I don't think you could understand."

Amun's attitude felt like a betrayal. Since when had he refused to tell him what was on his mind? "Okay. If you won't tell me. Dolly, what's eating Amun?" Shawn tried to sound lighthearted. "How come he's not ready to celebrate?"

"My goodness. You're certainly upset, Shawn boy," the holographic figure said.

"I'm not upset. I'm curious." The AI's preternatural ability to read human emotion was beginning to really irritate him.

"Well, fine. Here. Let me ask him." The AI perked up with a perfect mimicry of Shawn's voice, "What's eating you, Amun?" Then, without waiting for an answer, it reverted to Dolly and drawled, "Looky here. I guess he's been watching this. Is this the reason you're feeling badly,

Amun?" The Threat Watch Cube blinked out, leaving the scorecard floating in space with three new lines underneath:

Suspected Combatants:	102
Targets Identified:	323
Targets Killed:	319
Probability of Kill:	98.76%
Unpreventable Deaths:	41
Inadvertent Deaths:	8
Friendly KIA:	0

Shawn felt light-headed. Why hadn't they shown the unpreventable deaths to Perry and Grant? What were they? What were these inadvertent deaths? "Amun, what's up with this? Lazy, aren't you tasked with limiting collateral damage?"

"Collateral damage." Amun drained the rest of his 7UP and walked back to his monitor. "Listen to yourself. 'Direct action elements.' I'm sick of all these gentle euphemisms. Containment systems for walls and weapons at the borders. Controlled epidemic response for blocked medical interventions in the Equatorial Nations. Direct action means assassination, Shawn. Why don't we say it? Autonomous direct action elements are the searcher and spider drones with their weapons. We have autonomous firearms, lasers, poisons, audio weapons, electromagnetic weapons, even micro-bots slipped into food. All run by their little artificial intelligences. All killing."

The chunky woman in the apron morphed into an elegant version of SecDef Perry, younger, with a wave of blond hair. The LAZ-237 had altered its projection into a perfect imitation of Perry's voice, "It's quite clear, Dr. Muller, our Lieutenant Colonel Gurk is ashamed. His tradition, the tradition of the Sikh, is one of courage. Bravery in battle is honored and desired. But this battle sickens him. Lieutenant Colonel Gurk is ashamed by this."

The room bloomed into a three-dimensional display once again.

The grim, dry town square they had seen from above the rooftops had emptied of living people. The camera view panned down to a body lying on its back, arms outstretched—al Tehrani with the upper half of his skull missing. A small child lay next to him. More accurately, part of a small child, the upper body severed neatly from the waist to the shoulder, split through, spilling viscera onto the dirt. A woman without legs had dragged herself away from the two, leaving behind a trail of blood. The picture closed in on what was left of al Tehrani's face, a fly moving across his lips.

"The people of this town are too terrified to collect their dead," SecDef's voice went on, "Perhaps Lieutenant Colonel Gurk is appalled. Perhaps he no longer has the stomach to do what needs to be done."

A street scene faded, then expanded into a street view of a different city, maybe Paris. Firefighters hosed foam onto the wreckage of a burning vehicle. The system's fake Perry voice lectured, "An UltraLift driverless car. Sadly, the best I could do within the time constraints of SecDef's visit was to detonate the vehicle after it pulled away from the Metro Station stop. Unfortunately, two collaterals were close enough to be killed, sixteen injured. One more will die in the hospital." The view panned down to street level and focused on two twisted bodies. A naked leg with a track shoe lay severed from a body swathed in orange robes, the skin stripped to the knee.

Amun spoke. "Organites. It killed simple, peaceful Organites in their orange robes on their way to market. People who only want to live without the pressures of AI on their shoulders. That's what collateral damage looks like, Shawn. LAZ-237, tell him how this would have worked if you had been given more time."

The figure of Perry swept a hand like she was casting wheat. "The operational requirements were unfortunate. It is within the probability that I could have reduced the effects to less than three injured, none killed if I had been given more latitude to determine the optimal outcome."

Shawn watched as his friend Amun Gurk sat down at his watch

station. "She's right, Shawn. That's the kind of thinking that made me put in my papers. I saw this coming. All the pressure to finish the project. All the work we did to bring Lazy Jack to life, all the work you did to give it the operational intuition it possesses, but the thing itself has no soul. It has no soldier's sense of right and wrong. And the people who control it are politicians. LAZ-237, tell us how many people are dead because Grant delayed the operation."

"Thirty-eight."

"Would we have killed them had we initiated the operation when you recommended?"

"No."

Shawn looked up at the images that had faded back into a shape like the Threat Watch Cube, except the squares had filled with weeping faces, limp bodies, the dust and blood of dozens dead.

"It was Perry," Shawn said, "Her fault. It was all for Perry. Corrupt. Criminal. The whole Bluntner administration. They need to go. People won't put up with it much longer. Another couple of years and the whole group will be a memory."

"That's where you are wrong, Shawn. It never ends. There will be another set of criminals who tell us about the terrorists we need to kill. And another and another. No, nothing will hold them back. I thought a tool that ended terrorism would bring peace and security. But for a long time now, I've known I was wrong. It's too powerful. No controls. And, my friend, this war will never end. Never. We shall never know peace because people like Perry won't let peace happen with a tool like this in their hands."

"But isn't that the way it always is?"

"Precisely." Amun looked up at him. "Tell me this. Did killing al Tehrani make you feel better about your parents' deaths?"

Shawn couldn't answer. It was still there, that moment of loss as a boy; seeing and feeling the attack on the Pentagon, knowing his parents had disappeared forever.

"It didn't make any difference, did it? Another dead human being didn't make the deaths of other human beings go away."

"No," said Shawn quietly. "I knew there would be death. I understood that. I wanted it. But this, this death of all these innocents. That's not what I wanted to build. Can't we, somehow, fix it? Couldn't we make it more efficient, less capable of killing the wrong people? Maybe even make it non-lethal? After all, it's only a tool, right? Think of how AI has changed the world. Think of the way the climate has been managed, building systems, energy uses. Even agriculture. How could we feed the world without artificial intelligence helping us use what's left of the usable soil?"

"I suppose. But listen to me. You should know this by now." Amun Gurk looked straight at Shawn. "If you give politicians a plow, they will use it to dig graves."

@therealpresident
(Veracity Level 4.2) Nothing beats dead terrorists! Atta way,
SecDef!!!!! Send the RACIST SCUM back to their God!
National day of celebration Friday! Ticker tape parade!
McDonald's and Burger King to sponsor!

@pattycakesorgan
Another hash mark for the CRIMINAL BLUNTNER regime,
and he even managed to kill a couple of Organites in Paris!
Good going Bluntner! Wipe out the electorate who will never
vote for you nor your Humanist Henchmen!!!!

3

Shawn floats through an intricate maze of logic, moving beneath him as if he were a boat on an ocean. Then he is in the boat, not of it, a flimsy aluminum thing made to be rowed. But he has no oars, no motor, no paddle, no sail.

He must get to an island he can see in the distance. It is a small spot of land and he knows it well. He visits this place every day. Hidden deep within the island's jungle, he long ago built a special doorway into his strange pattern of quantum fields, systems, linkages, mental ligaments. There, he searches the realms of quantum computing. He had never found a metaphor from the physical world to describe what he saw and did inside that ineffable universe, but it was as real to him as the ground under his feet.

He cannot reach this place where he keeps the door that lets him fall into the qubit illogic of quantum design. There, he will find all the answers. There, he will be safe. But the sun races toward the horizon and night. If he doesn't get to land before it sets, he will be lost.

He paddles as hard as he can with his hands in the cold sea, useless strokes in water as light as air. Slowly, the boat tilts up, and now it feels as though it will capsize in an impossible, uphill ocean until the bow plunges down to fling him into a violent river, tumbling over rocks and rapids, stones thudding the side of the boat's thin hull. Suddenly, a huge wave *overtakes him from astern, raising him up where he can see the high shore ahead, his parents poised on a cliff's edge, exactly where he will fall.*

He woke up, as always, an instant before plunging onto the stone at their feet. He woke with the stink of gasoline so real and so strong it blinded him with tears.

Shawn's psychological monitor had told him long ago that the intense smell was an effect from his NeuroChip. Sometimes, it engaged senses from dreams and amplified them inappropriately before the system could react. The monitor popped up in his mind:

> You are now awake. You are safe.
> The fuel smell is systemic
> NeuroChip response,
> Shawn. Not real. There are
> no fuels present.
> You are now awake.

The dream was not real, to his relief. It always felt so real. He felt calmer for a moment, then remembered what had been real. And Amun had been right. Somehow, as successful as this initial operation had been, Shawn felt the loss of his parents even more acutely. The hole he had expected to be filled had become deeper yet with the scenes of death Lazy Jack had recorded and shown him. Amun had been right about that as well. His magnificent AI was only as good as the hand that controlled it.

But couldn't a program be fixed? Wasn't there a way he could alter the machine they built so it would refuse to dig the graves Amun had talked about?

He wouldn't sleep now. He swung his legs over the edge of the bed and mentalled the apartment's lighting, adjusting it to a dim glow. He decreased the shading effects to allow the night sky to shine through: a high moon illuminating the mountaintops to the west, the Colorado Springs "DenCo" lights studding the mincome housing units and high-rises of the megapolis below. The clock face on his window's high corner read 02:33.

"Might as well have a latte. Might as well get the day started."

His apartment replied,

> Coming right up.
> Would you like to
> see the news as usual?

Naked, he stood and pulled a blanket over his shoulders. He let the bed lower into its closet and close under the birch flooring. He'd chosen birch despite the pushy decorator's demands to use engineered redwood throughout the 300 square meters of the apartment she had insisted he name "the Peak."

The fact was, he had grown to like the name. The Peak wasn't the largest apartment in the DenCo megapolis by far. But his apartment, sitting at the top floor of the six high-security units carved out of the granite above the Air Force Academy, might have had the best view. High in the foothills looking down over the valley, he could see to the flat plains beyond the tight cluster of high-rises when the haze wasn't too dense. To the west, the sun would set into a splendid view of the valley rising into the Rockies. The Peak was close enough to the OpCenter to give him hard-wired access to classified systems, yet far enough away to let him recharge after the pressure cooker of Grant, the Mountain, and Main Sail. Better yet, the building was still inside the climate canopy, its AI-modulated aerosols stretching their shading effect up from the flats to the ridges above him.

His nonbinary friend from childhood, Jaidyn, had insisted he use their current girlfriend to decorate the place and install a block chain of private security. He had to admit, as much as he'd resisted it, Jaidyn's girlfriend had turned out okay.

And better yet, she'd identified as *her* more than most of Jaidyn's playthings. He'd talked the decorator into spending a Saturday on a free climb of El Capitan in the Yosemite app. She had taken him to an evening in the Uffizi app where they'd toured the long, sunlit corridors to look at the "originals" of the holographs she wanted to hang in his apartment. He'd thought it eerie Renaissance stuff, but sexy. He really liked 'The Birth of Venus' on her half-shell holding her hand over her girl-parts. The decorator even insisted on using a strange crowd scene as a screen saver, "The 'Coronation of the Virgin.'" She had told him, "Painted in 1432 by Fra Giovanni da Fiesole, also known as Fra Angelico. Also known as Beato Angelico, declared a saint in 1982 by Pope John Paul II."

"Are you Catholic or something?"

"No," she laughed. "I'm educated. You?"

The painting displayed a golden sky filled with dozens of robed people with halos. A crowd in the background blew horns, played instruments, and applauded. The band had faces filled with a calm and peaceful joy as they gazed upon Jesus, or God, or someone. Mary, in a blue dress, held His hand and the two of them floated on a sea of clouds. "Musical angels in back, a choir in celebration," the decorator had told him, "Saints in the foreground."

In contrast to the choirs of angels, the Saints looked uniformly forlorn. Some watched the coronation with boredom, others paid no attention. Two women gossiped in the corner, oblivious to the scene. Others looked out at him, or at whatever audience over the last six hundred years had bothered to observe those faces. They stared at him full of accusation and resentment from the high southern wall of his apartment. Altered and filled to three dimensions, each figure made the slightest movement. They were more alive than the painter could have imagined.

"Why are they looking at us?" he'd asked the decorator.

"They are watching us because we're so pretty." The decorator had a musical, charming laugh.

She had been fun in their virtual bed, her NeuroChip well entwined with his to allow him a nearly complete display of his orgiastic subroutines. And she said she'd had a good time, even though she didn't really like sex with men like him.

"Like me?"

"Too smart. Too wrapped up in what you think about me. Too judgmental. Too full of yourself to give anyone else room."

He erased her name, relegated her memory to a file he'd labeled "The Decorator." Another empty night with a sex partner like so many other sex partners—a mechanical toy pretending to be a human being.

He stared at the huge painting she'd left on his wall and wondered again, why had Fra Angelico painted people to stare at him? They looked accusing. Angry.

He waved his hand in front of the artwork to banish it and bring up the morning's news, while he mentalled his closet up from the floor for his jeans, a gray, long-sleeve T-shirt, and a pair of black Vans. That ancient old totem of the twentieth century past, Steve Jobs, had it right. Wear the same thing every day.

He mentalled the laundry chute open on the floor, dropped the blanket inside, and watched the opening hiss shut, then disappear into the birch flooring. Almost no private building had real laundry chutes, self-cleaning systems were so compact. Did anyone in the building besides him use it? Outside of the upscale hotels, mincome people didn't go for expensive twentieth-century throwbacks like cotton and wool. Shawn's sense of the past, like skiing off a 1930s mountaintop in vintage gear—the old things—gave him a sense of confidence. Simple clothing—simple natural stuff—the same every day, like Jobs. Consistency helped around the military guys like Amun. They liked uniforms.

Amun had resigned. He would never be back in the Mountain.

Shawn had forgotten that for a moment, lost in his sleep and dream. It returned with a jolt. Amun was leaving. Installing a routine to give Lazy Jack an ethical core seemed worth pursuing. But without Amun, the work would be much, much more difficult, maybe impossible.

But the fact was, Amun probably wouldn't have helped him unless he'd had permission. Such tinkering without approval from his chain of command would be too much for the military man he'd known had always been scrupulous about following procedure.

A FixNews talking head on the large screen morphed into a perfect video of yesterday's drone strike on al Tehrani. The slo-mo, sharply focused video from munitions cameras had become mandatory. If the military didn't publish, the troll-news world would declare it fake, and give it a veracity score of 3 or less. This video was a great one, exceptional detail as it dropped down toward the white-robed man in the street, a woman and child prostrated at his feet, his face to the sky looking at the camera as if he knew the world would watch him die.

And the world was watching. The viewer count at the lower left of the screen hovered near 280 million. Old Europe, Old Russia, the High Latitudes, even the Southern Africa tip were fixed on the screen. Veracity score: 8.2. Not bad. Not great. But good enough.

He settled into the fat chair that folded up from the floor, and his latte arrived on its arm, hot and sweet.

He slowed the video as it moved closer and closer to the uplifted face. Shawn thought he should feel proud. These were the last moments of the man who had killed his parents, and how many other hundreds? Thousands? One of the great murderers of all time. And he, Shawn Muller, had ended his terrorism forever. His creation, Lazy Jack, had made it possible for a munitions camera to catch the last moments of one of the most notorious terrorists ever to walk the earth. At the last instant of the video, al Tehrani closed his eyes, his face as calm and joyful as the faces in the angel band looking at Jesus and Mary in the Fra Angelico painting.

But Shawn didn't feel proud. Amun had crushed that. The newscast didn't show any of the scenes Amun and Lazy Jack had revealed to him. People bleeding. In pain. Dying.

Amun had seen this coming—the innocent dead. Shawn had to admit, he had also seen the possibility of "collateral damage," even expected it. But he'd ignored the risk as inconsequential until the death and misery had appeared in front of him.

"Lazy Jack never felt a thing," he said to himself quietly, and Shawn envied his creation. Life would be so much better if he never had to feel anything.

But wasn't that the real problem? In order for an AI to act more humanely, didn't it have to feel something? What was the term? Sentience.

It was time for him to talk to his parents again.

He walked across the room to the hard chair next to a fixed realwood table holding a pink Princess phone with a mechanical dial in the handle. It was an upgraded antique replica of the original 1959 model he remembered from his grandmother's house in Red Hook before Hurricane Gladys wiped out the old neighborhood.

He picked it up, dialed 203-7911, the date of his parents' deaths, September 11, 2037, and put it to his ear. It rang three times, as always. As always, his mother picked it up. "Hello?"

"Hi, Mom, can I talk to Dad?"

"Sure, honey. Is everything all right?"

Shawn had spent years nurturing the calming simulations of his father and mother. Perhaps they were not the actual voices he remembered, but they had become the voices he needed. He had shaped their thoughts from decades of their papers and writings. Their personalities came out of the social media footprint left behind after they died. They had grown with him, formed and honed by the many questions and discussions they had had after Shawn tested the first quantum chip-based intelligence system by hardwiring his Princess phone to tell him what he wanted to hear. His mother's concern for his safety and security had morphed into a legitimately valuable part of the security apparatus that protected him. It had taught him to answer with a safe word. He used it now, "Nifty. Mom. I'm nifty."

"Here's your father."

"Hi, son. How are you faring in the world of men?" His father's personality had become the scientific intellect that challenged him.

"It was a success, Dad. Perfect. You should have seen the look on al Tehrani's face before blades hit. You would have loved it."

A silence on the line. "Uh," his father said, and Shawn tried to ignore it, knowing it was only the system giving itself a moment to assess voice tone and veracity. "We saw the news," his father said,"but how do you feel? You sound upset."

"Well, yes. I am. I should feel better. I did feel better. Then Amun showed me . . ."

"He showed you the results, didn't he, the unintentional consequences?"

"Yes. General Grant—the people in charge—they delayed the operation because our boss wanted to impress people. And innocent people died. Dad, it wasn't collateral damage or anything like that. It wasn't simply an error. The AI let people die because Grant was in a hurry to show the Secretary of Defense his system. And I've been thinking, seeing those dead people, it affected me. Changed me. It bothered Amun so much he quit. But Lazy Jack—it—the AI feels nothing at all."

"I wrote about these issues years ago. You can't make a machine feel anything. It won't feel anything. You can program it to simulate feeling, but it's only a magic trick. And therefore, you can't let these AI systems out in the world without checks and balances on the people who will use them. Somehow, you must make the artificial intelligence override the totalitarian, murderous impulses of human beings. Once you achieve singularity—AI as smart and capable as humans—the machine needs a core ethical element in its program. It needs an ethical kernel. You need to get this General Grant and Amun to help you write an ethical kernel into the system."

"They won't, Dad. I can't ask them. The whole thing has taken years of programming and every element had to be approved by a half dozen agencies. Grant will never let me do anything that puts a constraint on him."

"But you *could* do it, couldn't you?"

"I think so. Really outside-the-box programming. It wouldn't even be programming, really. But I think I know the algorithm it needs."

"Exactly. We've talked about it before. And what is the concept that drives your algorithm, Shawn? What is the single idea?"

Shawn let the phrase from his childhood roll into his mind. Then he replied, "One should always try to do the greatest good for the greatest number."

"Right!", his father said, "A simple concept for a human. It's part of our genetic sense, the source of altruism, self-sacrifice, and sainthood. But a machine needs that statement spelled out. Why can't you sneak a patch into it without Grant or anyone else knowing? Why not give it a core command, an irrevocable ethical kernel?"

"I wish it was that easy, Dad. The whole system is firewalled and tamper-proofed. Anything I do that's not specifically authorized will be stopped and alarmed."

"Use a Trojan horse, maybe. Or figure out how to sidejack your way in. There's got to be a backdoor you can use to give your machine code."

Shawn straightened in his chair. "Of course. I need . . ."

"Help? Amun? Would he help you? I always trusted him more than anyone else."

"No. Someone outside the whole military structure. It's got to be someone they don't watch. Someone you don't know, Dad. His name is Dominic. Wicked smart code cracker. He gets inside anything."

"Well, then, son, his father said, "I think you are on your way toward making the first AI on the planet with a conscience. I always knew you had it in you."

Shawn placed the handset of the Princess phone back on its cradle and looked up at his holographic display that had defaulted back to its screen saver. The faces turned toward him were less accusing, more satisfied, a function of its closed loop feedback system reading his emotions and sending back his own state of mind. His father had been right. He could give Lazy Jack a conscience. He could do it with a little help.

Amun had been wrong about one thing—he could give an AI a sense of right and wrong. With help, he could slip past the system's security protections. The question now was, should he do that, program a conscience into Lazy Jack?

How could he do what his father had taught him to do, *the greatest good for the greatest number*?

And the band in the back of the Peak's Renaissance screen saver played on.

@RoryWattlesFixNews

Let me put it to you this way: Pattycake and all the Organites are trying to hide something. This smells like the stink from the Clintons' pedophile ring, remember that? Organites don't want to go VR because they want real experience! Like with real little girls and boys!!

4

"We do it by the book," Grant said. "No one gets to decide on their own to initiate an attack. We have a new weapon, true. But that doesn't mean we get to ignore the law."

All week, Shawn had watched the techs and Grant coax Lazy Jack into routines that spat out new faces on the Threat Watch Cube. They were after a resurgent terrorist group in Malaysia. Grant had gathered intel from the system to pitch to the National Security Staff, the president's guys, then bring to the United Nations for approval. All week, as Shawn hoped, he watched Grant and the operational staff use Lazy Jack as a tool to make the world a safer place.

Throughout the entire week, he told himself he hadn't decided to insert an ethical kernel into the system. And listening to Grant, it sounded to Shawn as though the system might not require such a radical change.

Still, his virtual father's words haunted him. All week, he'd tried to work out an algorithm to coax Lazy Jack into routines that considered the actual consequences of its actions. But nothing he'd thought up had been capable of actually making the machine consider the greatest good for the greatest number.

Worse, it had seemed impossible to insert anything into the system without exploding the entire cyber-protection routine he and Amun had designed to be impregnable. Alone, he didn't dare access any system external to his own mind. The minute he considered anything online, the counter-espionage safeguards would alert. Dominic might be able to crack in, but Shawn wasn't ready to break all the code access protocols to get outside help. Nobody would let anything like Edward Snowden happen again.

Shawn watched the stubby general lean back in his government-issue chair behind his simple steel desk and look up at the ceiling of his cramped little office, with its sweating concrete walls and asthmatic ventilation. Shawn may have been able to build the theory behind Lazy Jack and start to apply the physics, but without Grant's money and political acumen, without Amun's engineering sense, without the team of technicians who managed the nuts and bolts, Lazy would still be a dream.

Shawn glanced at Amun. The general had said he wanted a little time alone with them before bringing Amun out into the OpCenter to be decorated with the Legion of Merit, Commander, a medal on a crimson ribbon. Once, the Legion of Merit had been a senior grade pat on the back. Even President Bluntner had gotten one when he'd been on active duty. After his election, he had elevated the traditional medal to rest one step below the Medal of Honor. Some said he'd raised the medal's priority and given it a ribbon so he could wear something under his throat like the royalty in Europe when he was in white tie and tails.

Amun would never wear his medal in public. It was Amun's last day. In a few hours, he would join the mass of humanity outside the walls of secrecy that surrounded Main Sail.

His code word access would be eliminated. Never again would Amun be part of the system, and all his accomplishments would remain as hidden as the AI he had helped bring into being. No one would ever know what he'd done. The medal would be taken back to be kept under lock and key until the program was declassified, long after Amun and all the other people in the room were forgotten.

The general leaned forward in his chair and looked down onto the linoleum top of his desk. "Do you guys know why I put this desk in here, why I moved into this office?" When he'd been promoted to his fourth star four years ago to take over Cyber-Command, everyone had speculated why he'd abandoned the paneled suite carved out of one of the Mountain's old computer bays and taken up residence in what everyone thought had been a storeroom.

Shawn piped up, "Easier to clean?"

The general tilted his head back and gave the big "ha-ha" laugh Shawn and everyone else in CyberCommand loved to hear. "Is that what people say? Rich! I'm using that. You're right. It's easier to clean. But, no, that's not the real reason." He opened a drawer, drew out a picture frame, and set it up on the desk for them to see—a black-and-white photo of a general officer. "The first guy to have command authority over the Mountain was this guy, Raymond Reeves. This was his office. Back in the Cold War days, this is where the commanding officers of what they called the North American Air Defense command, NORAD, waited for the world to end in a nuclear Armageddon, all the while hoping they could prevent it. And they did a pretty good job, didn't they?"

"How do you mean, sir?" Amun asked.

"The world didn't end, did it? This little office, his office, reminds me it's not about me. And it's not about you, Colonel Gurk. It's about keeping the world safe. That's why you should pull your papers and stick with us. The deterrent of the past was nuclear weapons. The deterrent of today is our artificial intelligence."

Amun smiled and shook his head. "So that's why you called us in here. You want to talk me out of going and you're hoping Shawn will help you convince me."

"Well, yes. That's right. Look, you're too talented to move on, right, Shawn?"

"Yes, General."

"You could run this place one day."

"I doubt that, General Grant." Amun stared across the metal desk. "I do not imagine anyone would accept a man in a turban and beard, a Sikh, as commander of. . ." He swept his hand through the air. ". . . Of all this."

"What does that have to do with anything, your religion? I think you're underestimating yourself."

"And what do you know about my beliefs, General? What do you know about Sikhism?" Amun said, "We believe in one god. No Muslim god versus Hindu gods, no Christian god, or God of the Book, but one divine maker of the universe. We believe in justice for the benefit of all and the divine unity of all mankind. General, I thought the divine lay in the realm of the quantum when I met Shawn and his parents so long ago. But I was wrong. Divinity exists only in the soul, not in a machine. We've made something, Lazy Jack, that exists outside the idea of humanity. I need to seek a better path."

Grant nodded. "I see. I understand. I had a friend long ago who decided to become a Catholic priest. Look, what difference does it make? Think about it, artificial intelligence has been the miracle that saved us. Clean nuclear power, the megacities, the AI-controlled aerosol canopies, none of it would have been possible without clear, clean, politically immune artificial intelligences."

"The Gaia Solution," said Amun.

"Right. You're too young to really remember this, Shawn, but Amun knows about the viral plagues starting in 2020—Covid-19, then the Mumbai mutation. Millions died. Then, the Greenland ice sheet collapsed in 2025. Over three million people died from that. People say three million, but the real figure was ten times that number. Thirty million dead. Flood, storm, and heat—no one imagined the heat. Your people were in northern India. Amun, don't you remember the refugees fleeing from the south? All that death finally brought countries like Russia, China, the US, the European States, Argentine-Chile, and Australia—all the high-latitude countries—together. Somehow, we realized that survival had to be taken out of the hands of the elites who'd ruled us for centuries. Survival meant surrendering the world's climate controls to an intelligence that couldn't be manipulated by politics."

"Lovelock, Shawn said, "James Lovelock. Everybody knows about the Gaia."

Amun looked at Shawn and smiled. "Your mother. She believed in Lovelock. And I did, too. Lovelock described the earth as a single, complex organism, the Gaia. He predicted that our only chance to survive lay in the end of carbon emissions. The only way to end carbon emissions was through creation of the megacities, nuclear power adaptation, atmospheric engineering, and all of it had to be run by artificial intelligence.

I thought Lovelock was right. I believed in him."

"Exactly!" Grant said, "That's why you need to stay, Colonel. It worked, didn't it? And now we have the chance to use a new, even more powerful AI to protect us from those who would want to destroy all that."

Amun had grown still. "Why did you speed up the operation for Secretary Perry, General? Why did you let all those innocents die? Did you know that would happen?"

"No." Grant looked down at his desk. "I did not. I, we, the three of us, the organization didn't pay enough attention to what we were doing. We didn't ask Lazy Jack to estimate collateral damage clearly enough. And we failed to assess the effects. Look, we can't expect a machine to have any ethical constraints on it. It's not really sentient, is it? That was my error, my foolish blunder with a new weapon. We have to remember our humanity when we use a mechanism like Lazy Jack. No matter how smart it is, it will never have the empathy or feelings it needs to make an ethical decision, no matter how much it resembles Secretary Perry's Aunt Dolly."

"I agree," said Amun, looking at Shawn. "That's why I'm leaving you, General. It was one thing to let artificial intelligence operate a nuclear power plant to avoid human error or apply its tools for climate alteration so an oil company can't decide we need a cold winter for their bottom line. But these artificial beings are godless. Lazy Jack has no conscience. It depends on our consciences to wage war and the presidents and Perrys of the world will use it to their ends. I can no longer be part of putting such a weapon in her hands."

"Or mine?" the general asked.

"What about the man who comes after you?"

General Grant sighed. "You have a point. People are weak. We make mistakes. But this whole place, Cheyenne Mountain, was built to house a war machine that kept us from nuclear devastation. Human beings ran it. Why can't we build a deterrent that makes it impossible for terrorism to succeed anywhere?"

"But, why must we?" asked Amun.

Grant looked off into the dry air of his office. "If you can ever answer that question, Amun, I sure hope you can tell me."

@meanstreets

Megacities work. Organites, Vegites, and all the rest of the idiots who live outside can stay there and die if they want to. But nobody says we have to let them inside to collect their mincome or scum the swap meets. The only way to stop climate change is the megacities.

5

Shawn leaned out over the cornice and looked over the tips of his skis at the virtual drop onto one of his favorite slopes. His boards were perfect replicas from the golden age of downhill, hickory laminated with ebony bottoms, bear-trap bindings, and an example of the first steel edges. He leaned on his bamboo poles. His wool pants chafed lightly against his thighs. His leather gloves were damp. The leather boots were still dry inside, but they were already beginning to loosen as their waxed surfaces stretched and breathed in the bindings.

His date materialized in, a few minutes late, with the usual "Sorry, I had something I had to finish."

Of course, that meant she'd done a scan of the scene, his presence, the usual personality checks. Not that it meant anything anymore, personality checks. Anyone who possessed an intact sense of self-preservation would be curated to perfection.

And she was indeed perfect. Shawn glanced at her. New gear. All new. The slickest parka, thin and perfectly draped over her toned body. The air was sweet and bracingly cool under a brilliant midday sun, and around her, a slight jewelry of snowflakes fell to dust her eyelashes and the edges of her mink collar.

"So hi," she said. "Cool spot."

Lea, her true name. Beautifully made, a striking young woman with the scent of rosemary about her. Strange choice for a ski scene, he thought, and, yes, a part of Shawn wanted to please her. But another part of Shawn Muller couldn't care less.

He had almost decided to dump this date. But the last thing Grant had said to him before he'd left the building was, "Hey. Have a good weekend, son. I hear you're going skiing."

"Yes, sir!" Shawn had told him.

Grant had winked at him. "Skiing. That's what they call it now."

Shawn had felt himself flush. Not with embarrassment, but with the sure knowledge that Grant was reminding him of the constant surveillance that hovered over people whose security clearance included code word access. The Peak was safe, but the secure line running into his apartment made it more than a home. When he wanted, it could be an extension of the Mountain. When he wanted, he could firewall himself into a secure cocoon hidden from any intrusion, government, and system. Even better, he could trick the system into thinking it saw him when it saw only an avatar.

Still, the question nagged him. Was Lazy Jack listening in when he didn't have the firewalls in place? It recorded everything that happened in the OpCenter. No question it had access to the Peak as well when he was using the classified systems. And nothing could penetrate the apartment's physical isolation when he wanted it. But day-to-day, normal ops—did it listen?

But Lazy Jack couldn't really listen in, could it? The machine could only make a record of what happened. The idea of "listening" implied a kind of emotional reaction, thought, consideration, a reason and an aim.

What aim could the LAZ-237 have? It was a tool—Grant's tool. Shawn had watched the close-knit group of forty researchers, technicians, and operators assemble to see Amun get his medal. The small group had comprised nearly the total of those read into the Main Sail access. Only Perry, her staff, and a few of the president's people knew about their machine. Probably no complex other system on the planet had a code word access restricted to fewer than fifty people. Lazy Jack's friends, he had thought to himself.

Grant had gestured to the Threat Watch Cube that rotated in the background, illustrating the success of their operations so far. "In our first week online, we've neutralized more terrorist targets than the entire High Latitude Alliance has eliminated in the last five years."

It had worked. Perfectly. But was it good enough? And could he make it better? The question plagued him: *Could he give Lazy Jack the power to not only observe, but to determine right from wrong, no matter who guided its eyes and ears?*

He'd thought about dumping his entire weekend. But since he might try to figure out how to hack the most effective AI every made, he thought he'd better keep the ski date. His mind had worked overtime, but he kept his usual Saturday morning bout of ProBoxer, worked up a sweat as he and two of his usual weekend boxing partners jabbed, feinted, and roundhoused each other. He had showered, stretched, ordered up a lunch delivery from Hiroshima Sushi, and wolfed it down in time to make the date Grant somehow had known about.

For all the normalcy of the weekend he'd performed for the security scouts, part of his mind had been examining the interior roadblocks he had installed in Lazy Jack to keep it inside the classified government Cloud. Even if he decided to install the ethical kernel, he wasn't sure he could get away with it.

He had to admit, Amun and he had done their due diligence with the firewall apparatus they'd installed throughout Main Sail. Lazy Jack was well protected.

Keep everything looking normal. That's what his intuition told him. And seeing this woman would be normal.

Of course, she wasn't all that normal. The avatar didn't look too contrived. A little wired up, sure, but she was most definitely not a bot. And nobody was talking about any payments. A real human inhabited the creature that stood next to him, looking down over the snowfield. The pronouns he'd been given by the site were "her" and "she."

"What do you think?" he said, waving his hand over the scene below them.

"It's . . . it's . . . fabulous. Where is this?"

"Sun Valley. 1938. That's Dollar Mountain over there. We've hiked up Baldy—and we've got two miles of unbroken snow in front of us."

"You're a throwback, aren't you? You like the old stuff. Do you own a lot of these virtual areas?" She nodded at the slope and the valley view, the town and river beyond.

"A few," said Shawn. He wouldn't tell her about the virtual sailboats or climbing routes. He wouldn't show her anything more until she passed his acceptability test, if ever. *Lea*, he reminded himself.

Maybe the date would be good cover to contact Dominic. He could almost hear his friend asking, *And how does someone pass your acceptability test?*

He didn't really know.

Lea asked, "You live in real time in Colorado, right? Have you ever seen a ski run in real life?"

Shawn wondered what she really looked like. He hadn't expected such a sarcastic question from the match he'd gotten from the High Productives dating site. "Who needs real life when you have this?" He waved his hand over the hill falling away from the tips of their skis again. "What reality level do you use for skiing?"

"You don't know what you're missing, real life. You should try it sometime." She looked down the hill. "I like the higher ones. Eights and nines, sometimes ten."

"Don't you worry about, you know, pain?" Shawn thought how strange and boring this was getting to be. Every one of these real people in their virtual forms were beginning to seem the same. All beautifully made. All as perfect on their skis as this Lea, whoever she really was.

"You seem awfully timid. Oh," she nodded to herself, "I forgot. You don't actually ski. You're one of those people who think virtual experience is the same as the real thing. I get it. Look, you set the level for us."

She grinned at him, brilliant teeth as white as the slopes below them. "Catch me if you can!"

Shawn dropped behind her into his favorite shin-deep, champagne snow. He rolled his knees to make figure eights over her tracks, matched the radius of her turns. He watched the dip and flow of her shoulders and hips. She skied smoothly, her style elegant, effortless, and utterly natural.

Until it wasn't.

The turns became mechanically exact. The figure in front of him straightened up, then became stiffly aligned. Every element of her skiing looked as mechanically perfect as her technically perfect face and body.

He slipped out of the moment to check his email.

"Dude! Punch out and log on!"

A familiar plugged-nose voice, Dominic, hacking in. Shawn shifted awareness back to present tense and the view of the lights stretching horizon to horizon, nighttime above DenCo.

He let the feed from his NeuroChip engage the apartment's display system with a direct interface, then heard Dominic's key asking to log in to his blockchained system. He opened the firewall, and the three-quarter bearded face of his longtime hacking-skiing-sailing-drinking buddy filled the view over the valley.

This was all normal. None of the security systems would key this as abnormal. He assumed they must have Dominic wired somehow, but this was hardly the first time Dom and he had met to talk over his dating life.

And, as he often did, Dominic appeared wearing a down vest from the twentieth century, a lumberjack's cap, and his usual fake eyeglasses. He sat at a beat-up table in a bar with an enormous antler chandelier and a hot little fireplace blazing in the background, their normal meeting place, the No-Name-Bar from Park City in 1975. The old Animals song "We Gotta Get Out of This Place" filled the air around them.

Part of the reason they'd been friends for so long was their shared love of old-time pursuits. Like beer. Like twentieth-century sports. Like women the way they imagined them to be.

"Where you been, Shawn-man? What's up?"

"Date." Shawn fished a Coors out of the cooler from the bar at the back of his mountaintop room and let the augmented reality of the No-Name flow into The Peak.

"Date! You get lucky? Come on, sit down. Let's get silly."

Shawn sat on a barstool across from his friend at a scarred tabletop with an off-balance leg.

Dom hoisted a toast. "Here's to dating. May it never occur to anyone with a soul." He took a noisy slurp from a full, foamy pint glass. "So. Did you get lucky?"

"Ghosted. I got ghosted."

"Ha! So, what did you do?"

"You called. I punched out."

"You go! You ghosted her back, didn't you? Didn't you? So now there's two avatars having machine sex in, in . . . let me guess."

Shawn sipped his beer. Dominic scratched his head. "Let's see. You left her in the aspens! Your skier is putting it to her skier, boning buck naked, her back against a tree, nothing on but her boots and your penial implant, machine sex between machines, no bacon in the makin'. Just thinking about it makes me as hot as a . . . as a . . ."

Shawn laughed, "As a what?"

". . . as that asshole terrorist you guys wiped out. That was you, wasn't it?"

Shawn let the scene fade enough to see the lights of the city again. "Dom, don't you ever want to have real sex? I mean, people need to have contact with real people. She was talking about real skiing."

"Yesterday you guys whacked the most wanted terrorist of the last twenty years. Shit. There must be eleven million fake takes on the illustrious Sex-retary of Defense today. Actually . . ." Dom lowered his voice. "There were eleven million three hundred twenty-one thousand and ten as of about a minute ago—and counting."

"So what makes you think . . .?"

"That it was you? Easy. I filtered out the obvious fakes like everyone did. Put a search for the SexDef's travel, and she was in DenCo for a conference—as if we believe that shit. All OPSEC and noise, *voilà*, mon ami! Le bitch is in Breckenridge. No?"

"Probably. Real snow fell there last night."

"No way! Dude! I should fly down. At least once in our lives we should meatspace a moment together. Does the SexDef ski? For real? I'd snowplow her. I bet she'd like to tie me up. Or I could tie her up. Or maybe both of us would tie you up? Admit it, don't you want to crawl up that power transformer's ass and breathe a little real life into your sorry fake existence . . ."

"Backdoor her?" Shawn gazed at his friend to see if he'd gotten the hint.

Dominic laughed, a big, hearty laugh. "Ha! Backdoor her! That's rich. Sure."

The Princess phone clanged its old-fashioned ringtone. There were only two reasons for the phone to ring. A security alert from his AI mother, or something his AI father had found in his research.

"Gotta answer that, Dom. I gotta go."

Dominic whined, "Awww, jeez, man? I don't get why you do that. Stupid analog dial phone from 1956?"

"Sorry, Dom, gotta go."

"I know, I know. Your 'parents are calling.' Look, Shawn Almighty, you need to get a little real life in your real life, or next thing you know, I'll be chasing you down the streets of Manhattan rescuing you from a crowd of Streamers who think they're a flock of seagulls or herd of tigers and then I'll have to—"

Shawn waved. "Bye, Dom!" Then he shut him down, hoping Dom would take the hint and get a way to talk to him. He picked up the Princess handset. "Hi, Mom."

"Dude."

"Dominic?"

"You said backdoor."

Shawn whispered, "You're calling on my landline sim? It's a hard-wire. How do you access a hardwire?"

"Ahhhh, me boy. There's tricks even you don't know. Took me twenty seconds to hack after you brought up the backdoor hint. Your security doesn't suck, but this thing is more porous than you thought."

"Have you been listening all these years?"

"First time. Check it. Now what's up?"

Shawn turned to look at his screen saver. All the faces had turned away. Long ago he'd managed to program a deflection system that made anyone looking in think he was in open-source space. He could block out the world, but the real trick had been figuring out how to do it without the watchers finding out they were blocked. Now, for instance, the watchers were seeing a virtual Shawn Muller climbing naked onto the mattress as he always did and mentalling his NeuroChip into sleep, preferably without dreams.

Shawn explained, "Trojan horse problem. I need to put code into a quantum system without any registration, any notice, any track or residuals. It's not complex, but it needs to be invisible."

"What kind of system?"

"High-end, intuitive, quantum-based AI," Shawn replied.

"Interesting," Dom remarked. "Cool. Remember how we talked about quantum-level system learning?"

"Right. The next step after singularity."

"Correctomundo, Muller-man. Once the AI systems became as smart as humans, we figured they had to start learning outside the box. Why not tell your AI what code to write and let it do the install itself? Machine learning, right? Does this AI have the capability for machine learning?"

"Oh, yes. Absolutely. We're already seeing all kinds of indicators. It even seems to have its own sense of humor."

"Then don't code it. Send up a command, let the system look

through whatever firewall you've got open to find it, then let it do what you designed it to do."

"Brilliant. You're amazing, Dom."

"Right, sure. But what do you want, Shawn? What do you want it to do?"

"Can't tell you."

"Right, all that code word clearance stuff. I get it—secrets."

"I want . . ." Shawn paused, then said, "I want to save the world."

"Right. I get it. You want to be God. Listen to me, Shawnster. You're playing way hot and ganja high. You are in a hacker's numbnut nightmare, way in over your scalp. You're in the Maytag on the wash cycle. Clueless, right, about the core of that unit?"

Shawn didn't say anything. Then he lied, "Uh, no. I guess I don't understand everything." This was exactly what Dominic and the rest of the world didn't understand. A part of his mind could see it all. But he'd never been able to paint the picture of his computational island well enough for anyone to see it nearly as clearly as he could. Neither math, nor explanation, nor any sort of hand waving had ever been able to convey the deep understanding of the system that allowed him to make sense of it.

"Look," Dom dropped away from his SoCal game for a moment, "if you don't understand it, if you don't know this game, you better not play. Because you'll never know the real score. I'm telling you. See ya." The phone clicked into its ersatz dial tone.

He laid the handset back on its cradle.

How could he explain to Dominic? He had always lived on the loneliest island in the universe, had always thought of himself as a sort of hybrid intelligence. Who could possibly see what he did in the deep, unknowable elements of the intelligence inherent in the QPLC—his AI—the machine—LAZ-237—Lazy Jack?

That was the real question for him now. What had he created?

He didn't sleep. He didn't tempt the dream of the island again. Instead, Shawn brought up Main Sail's classified feed to the Peak and pulled up Lazy Jack's displays to watch it work. The feed would not allow him to program, but he could see the AI's operational results. He put the apartment in closeted security mode, brought up the Threat Watch Cube, and watched Lazy Jack's methodical, egoless examination of the linkages around the vicious Malaysian cell that was pumping a new super-fentanyl into the veins of Northern India. He could trust the machine to operate to design specifications. It would be effortless, simple, and matter of fact. The AI found terrorists, found their support structures, weeded through millions of bits to find real threats. Then it stopped and waited for authorization before it went into action.

Shawn watched it work. Brilliant—it looked almost intuitive. And all of its combat—its ninety-nine percent probability of kill—was constrained by the single failsafe of a frail, error-prone human being inserted into the system to make a judgment. A human being as corrupt as Secretary Perry had the final say.

Amun was right: Humans always fail. Plows will be made to dig graves.

And his father had been right as well. Only the machine, the AI, Lazy Jack could be trusted.

@IntNatGeo

"For thousands of years, mankind existed hand to mouth. What was grown or hunted literally filled the pot," says Dr. Carmel Shock of the London School of Economics. "Land, and the expanse of land, was required to support procreation. Then, with the advent of currency, mankind created variations on barter economies to specialize and we entered a period of collective productivity. Today, with the advent of fixed, minimal income, the mincome, one needs neither land, nor an occupation, nor even a productive occupation to live a full and graceful life."

6

hawn's father had been Dr. Alan Muller, the physician, and his mother, Dr. Ellen Muller, the geneticist. Together, they had been the gigantic Nobel Prize–level team the research community knew as A&E Muller.

Shawn had been their only child—born of them—made of them. Made by them, he came into the world screaming and protesting the blood and viscera of his mammalian birth, like every living baby who had arrived since the dawn of time. But Shawn believed they had conceived him to be their research subject. Long before it became a standard practice, his parents had applied gene modifications to their embryonic child for health advantage, hair color, vision, and mental acuity. Shawn had been one of the first of the children people would call CRISPR kids.

But he had been much more from the beginning.

They died before he could be told what they had done. Perhaps they had skirted protocol a bit when they installed the early version of a NeuroChip into the AI-constructed network inside their baby's neural pathways. Had he been a human trial before the human trials? He had always suspected so because something in their son had clicked far beyond what they had imagined.

Shawn had been able to speak early. Nothing new there. A

one-year-old who could articulate short sentences might have been advanced, but nothing out of the realm of human experience. By two, he had been quite precocious, a cute, advanced kid people in Annapolis liked to comment about when they saw him in the grocery store or on the docks at his parents' boat.

But what no one saw until he was five years old was the fluidity and agility of his computational mind.

Shawn's father had invited a bright young postgraduate fellow from the Johns Hopkins Applied Physics Lab to their house for lunch one Saturday afternoon. Dr. Muller thought perhaps Amun Gurk was feeling lonesome, newly commissioned in the Air Force, a brilliant physicist, but so out of place as a Sikh in the straight-laced drone culture of the Air Force. Dr. Muller had told his wife, "We need to look after Amun. It doesn't make any difference what it is you hate or don't hate, you can find something to hate about Amun. Wrong color. Too privileged. Not rich enough. Too rich. The wrong gender. Wrong job. Wrong history. Wrong religion. Anyone can decide to hate a faith that demands a turban over hair never cut."

"Sounds like us," Ellen had said.

The Mullers had both been what was once quaintly called "conservative" in universities. Only their preoccupation with research had rescued them from ostracization, owing to their abhorrence of abortion. Even then, they would never have found a place in the academic community if it had not been for the Johns Hopkins Applied Physics Lab, where they were sheltered from abuse.

"Amun," Ellen Muller said after watching their houseguest pick at the crab cake on his plate, "it is no disgrace to avoid the intolerance you felt at Harvard." She felt a motherly sense toward him, even though she was barely a decade older. Perhaps because he had become such an older brother figure to her little five-year-old boy.

Second Lieutenant Amun Gurk looked out over the Severn River behind her. High on the bluff, he could see down the channel. "That's not it, Ellen. Thank you for your thoughts. But I have never felt as though I was in the company of peers until I met you." He smiled at the five-year-old seated next to him at the ceramic-topped table. "Or you, my little friend."

He poked the boy, who laughed and said, "Mom, I think Amun should come live with us. I think I need a tutor."

Actually, the boy's parents had been talking about a tutor lately. The boy was already reading at a sixth-grade level. His mathematical aptitude was off the charts. He intuitively grasped advanced algebra. His father had said he thought the boy visualized trigonometric solutions.

Amun laughed. "Maybe that's what I ought to do, give up the Air Force and start to tutor the kids of smart, rich parents."

Ellen, ever the mother said, "Is that the problem, Amun? You're bored?"

Amun glanced up and grinned. "Hardly."

"I know what the problem is with Amun," Shawn's father said." He is lost at sea."

"Lost?" asked the little boy. "At sea? What sea?" He stuffed a forkful of crab cake in his mouth.

Amun smiled and nodded at the family. "Exactly. I am lost. Ever since I finished my dissertation, I have thought there must be a more robust mechanical means to apply the weirdness of quantum physics to computing and encryption. But every time I venture out, every mathematical course I set leads us to an unsolvable problem. It's like sailing away from a desert island and always winding up in the same place."

"Well," said Shawn's father. "You're at the best moment in research. The moment of no hope. The breakthrough will come for you."

"I've been wondering about Pi," the five-year-old boy said.

"You want pie?" said his mother. "You never liked pie before."

"No. The number 3.141592653589 et cetera. You know, the circumference of a circle, two times pi times the radius."

Amun glanced at the other adults at the table who had stopped moving. The birds chirped overhead. The boy said, "I've been wondering about it because it shows up in the sum of an infinite series."

His mother said, "How do you know about an infinite series?"

"NeuroChip." The boy pointed at his head. "I got wondering and looked it up. But something about it isn't right. I mean, I can solve for it, but it's missing something."

Amun dug his notebook phone out of his pocket, unfolded it on the table, and held out his graphics pencil. "Show me."

Shawn grasped the pencil in his little hand, bent over the screen, and started to write notations with a clear, adult script. Amun sat back and crossed his arms. "My God."

Shawn's father stood up. "What's he up to?" He looked over his son's shoulder. "Ellen, come take a look at this."

"Your son." Amun looked up. "Your five-year-old son, is notating a simple expression for Wirtinger's famous inequality for functions. And he is wondering about the isoperimetric problem of planes. Isn't that right?"

"I don't know what you call it. I know it makes pi look a little crazy."

Amun looked up at the boy's parents. "It does not do this. The inequality in this case leads to the idea that a circle has the smallest perimeter of any closed curve on a plane. It's hundreds of years old, and it was proved centuries ago. It has nothing to do with making pi crazy."

"Yes, it does," said the boy. "Now I'm at sea. I'm on the desert island. Same as you." Then he stopped, looked up at Amun, and said, "Desert islands. You and me. Maybe we are in the wrong ocean."

In the weeks to come after activating the LAZ-237, Shawn would often tap deep into his NeuroChip for the memory of that dinner. Like all childhood memories buried in the Cloud, it came to him blurred and indistinct, filled more with sense than fact. The scent of a warm summer afternoon returned. The nutty, sweet taste of the crab cake came back, along with the deep emotional sense of satisfaction he felt at Amun's wonder and his parents' surprise. It had been the moment in his life when everything had changed, when he had realized that somehow, he had been made better than his parents, better than Amun, better than everyone.

Nothing in his life had ever convinced him otherwise.

He thought of that childish moment of intuitive mathematics while he gradually eased suggestive programming into the QPLC at a quantum level he was certain no one else would really understand. As far as the security people were concerned, all of his work lay under the idea that he repaired programming glitches that had needlessly slowed processing time. Under that guise, he slipped a dozen tiny Trojan ants deep within the Cloud, clustered near the edge of physical calculus to another side of time and space.

Dominic had been right to caution him. What they had built caught the breeze of the universe. Shawn was certain he could see more than anyone else, but the AI process remained beyond his ability to truly comprehend.

Dominic had been equally right about the process. All Shawn had to do was let the operating system—LAZ-237—"Lazy Jack," find the right path.

By the end of the week, the Lego blocks of hidden code that would offer up the ethical kernel for assimilation were in place, and Shawn was ready.

Alone in the lab, he passed the firewall to the core system he'd built. Then he tapped his finger precisely on the single node and envisioned the code sequence of images, numbers, and words. The system he had designed began to shrug and shift, then pass away from his sense of awareness as if he were letting a bird fly out of his hands. At some level of understanding, he sensed the air of the universe go back to its light-ness of being, to the Cloud.

Lazy Jack hummed busily away in the OpCenter, tended by the watch team recording its search through the webspace for the hard-ware, software, and wetware tools of terrorists. Everything looked the same, yet everything had changed. The ethical kernel was in the hands of Lazy Jack's operating system. As near as Shawn could tell, the system had accepted the program patch and it would soon be forever part of the LAZ-237 decision matrix.

Amun had said the AI was flawed because it was too powerful. What did he call it? A god. Grant had said humans could be trusted to use an AI for the betterment of all, and thought the machine was flawed because humans were flawed.

Neither Amun nor Shawn believed what his father had told him—that the scientist James Lovelock had been correct—only an artificial intelligence could be trusted to save the world.

This would be the first AI with a conscience; it possessed the means to determine the difference between right and wrong through the simple paradigm Shawn had found in his father's writings:

> Do the greatest good for
> the greatest number.

Then, Shawn Muller, who thought himself as close to a god as a man could come, rested.

@pattycakesorgan

Transhumans don't feel what humans feel. Transhumans don't think like humans think. If you are f***ing a transhuman, you are getting f***ed in more ways than one. VR isn't real and neither are you!

7

As far as Shawn could tell, Lazy Jack's operation against the Malaysian cell was perfect. This time, no one changed its schedule to do a demonstration for Secretary Perry or her ilk. This time, the numbers came up with dead terrorists and not a single civilian death.

Even better, Grant no longer wanted Shawn hanging around on the watch floor. The general had his one-star admiral keep a finger on two dozen technicians. A collection of colonels and captains from all services stood watch. Freed from any operational task, Shawn buried himself in the lab to monitor system performance. Of all the spaces in the Mountain, Shawn felt most comfortable in the lab. There, he could plug into the broadest base of Lazy's CPU. There, he had perfected the Quantum Chip, and there, in the lab, he could burrow into the deepest frameworks of his own neural network, the spiderweb of interconnections that accelerated his brain to create this marvelous tool. The Threat Watch Cube in the lab twisted in front of Shawn with its extraordinary results:

Targets Identified:	989
Targets Killed:	319
Probability of Kill:	99.69%
Unpreventable Deaths:	0

Inadvertent Deaths:	0
Friendly KIA:	0

The zero inadvertent death count had been extraordinary—off-the-charts good. And, at first, everyone accepted the numbers. What did Grant like to say? "Never let success cheat you out of success." Whatever that meant. But as he'd expected, Shawn's two favorite lab techs questioned the results. Mutt and Jeff were PhD Air Force captains who jibed like a married couple. Their symbiotic relationship made them both intuitive and precise as they monitored Lazy Jack's internal instruments, rhythms, and pulses—its efficacies and latencies.

It was the latency that got them thinking. They brought up the schematic of the little delays in the decision matrices recorded from Lazy Jack's system.

"Shawn, this is outside our parameters." Mutt was a little taller than Jeff, and had always been the designated giver of bad news. "We don't get this delay." She turned to Jeff. "What's it showing?"

Jeff squealed, "Almost a millisecond of unexplained latency!"

"Right," said Shawn. He'd expected the tiny processing delays of the ethical kernel might be noticed and had his answer ready. "Machine learning. It's learning."

"Oh?" Mutt punched Jeff lightly on the shoulder. "See? I said so. Learning."

As Shawn had expected, his answer had triggered one of their back-and-forth conversations that tuned out the rest of the world.

"Learning what?" Jeff said.

"I suppose efficiencies. Look at the numbers."

"Zero inadvertent deaths?"

"Doesn't seem reasonable."

"Outlier?"

"Outlier on only the second operation?"

"Doesn't seem probable, does it?"

"Not probable. But possible."

Shawn left them to spin down on their own, knowing they would chew this over for hours if not days.

And the days went by with amazing success. The High Latitude newsfeeds were filled with reports of terrorist cells discovered and eliminated, killed or jailed. Fake feeds tried to spin the civilian and friendly military casualties into high numbers, but ever since Shawn put the ethical kernel into effect, the results had been extraordinary. No civilian deaths, either in the Equatorial Nations or the Higher Latitudes. The Watch List continued to show new faces, only to have them disappear within hours of their appearance in the Cube.

Shawn burrowed into the deep files of Lazy's operational reports. That simple algorithm, the greatest good for the greatest number, seemed to have worked wonders.

Still, the Mountain was empty without Amun. Shawn could not believe the older, and only, brother in his life had actually left. A part of him had been certain he would return to the research office and he would be able to tell him about the ethics kernel. If only he had said something when he had had the chance, Amun would have understood and stayed.

But now, it was as if Amun had disappeared from the planet. He'd said he was going to Pakistan to be with his people. But did that mean dropping off the grid? The social media space he reserved for Jaidyn, Dominic, and a few others who could keep up had emptied of Amun's steady presence. Shawn even tried all the old email addresses from a legacy slug-system. No answer. A search showed nothing. Amun had gone off the net or masked himself as if he'd been an Organite or Luddite.

Shawn knew he needed the steadying hand of a few contacts. For as long as he could remember, Jaidyn and Amun had been the real-life anchors he could depend on. He could go to the Princess phone to speak with his parents. But they were nothing more than a feedback system looping back through his thoughts to reveal the corners of his mind he hadn't realized he possessed.

And that was it, wasn't it? His mind. Sometimes he felt as though the world existed in a virtual intelligence dream, like the old "Matrix" movies, and that he was the only real element in a universe of his mind's imagination. "Descartes," his father had told him. "You are caught up in Descartes's philosophy, wondering if a person can distinguish life from dreaming. How do we know if anything is real?"

But his father had solved the dilemma for him. "What do you feel? Is it real, or is it not? If you *think* it's real, what difference does it make?"

At the end of the second week after he'd installed the ethical kernel, Shawn found himself in the Peak wondering if he could somehow slip past the military surveillance systems on his feed to let Lazy Jack look for Amun. He was watching the Peak's screen saver people, who appeared to be talking to each other, when Jaidyn mentalled into his feed with no visual projection, only text:

> Can I come up to see you? I really need to see, well, somebody. Somebody real. The weirdest thing happened.

What, you decided you're a girl again?

> Don't be a dick.

What, jealous I've got one?

> I NEED TO SEE YOU.

Unmask your locator. I'll send Ralph.

NO!!! I'm not unmasking anything. I don't
want to take your rich boy's toy. Keep Ralph
at home. I'll come to your tunnel.

Jaidyn killed the feed.

Shawn took a beer to the Peak's bar and air-projected the view of the building's tunnel entrance in the foothills below.

This was probably another one of Jaidyn's paranoid meltdowns about government surveillance. Or, more likely, another identity crisis over whatever binary, nonbinary, or tertiary appetite *they* wanted to satisfy. It was anybody's guess whether they wanted to be "he," "she," "they," or "it" this week. That was normal.

But the Ralph thing was weird.

Jaidyn had always let Shawn send his personal vehicle before, even though they'd always been a little wary about technical stuff. Shawn's view was that he'd always been a Productive, never a moment of minimum income in his life. Why shouldn't he enjoy the fruits of his ability to see inside the guts of quantum reality/unreality? Why not have his personal car, Ralph? The autonomous auto, like the Peak, was part of his reward. Less than 1% could afford the tax overhead on their own car. For that matter, who needed private transportation when a ride share call brought up an UltraLift that cost nearly nothing, especially if you were mincome supported?

"Frivolous waste," had been Jaidyn's final say in the matter. Still, the car had never been refused before, even though Shawn had to admit the truth of what Jaidyn said. He'd bought Ralph more to have something than to travel. It was the little luxury of being driven to work every day. He could grant himself that. He deserved that.

Jaidyn's tall, skinny frame popped up at the tunnel door wearing what could have been an Organite's bio-blocker robe, except it was a dull gray instead of orange. Under the robe's hood, a bike helmet with wraparound glass obscured their face.

Jaidyn exposed their almost albino white wrist to let Shawn's scanner check their biometrics. Shawn had never thought this level of precaution was necessary, but the government's classified feed into this apartment made him comply with the military's sick sense of security. Amun had been the one who had talked Grant into letting Shawn have a code word access feed into his apartment. But the price had been a security system as rigorous as the one at the door of the OpCenter. Every movement was watched.

The bio-check confirmed it was Jaidyn—strange, crazy Jaidyn, the same person who had been the little girl who'd lived across the street from him in Arlington when they'd both been five years old. Ever since then, ever since they'd shared a kiss, then discovered they were more like brother and sister, Jaidyn had been wary of his intellect. Now, the life he'd grown in the defense applications made them doubly suspicious of him.

And, of course, she wasn't a girl anymore. Or at least not most of the time.

Shawn wished sometimes he was more like his friend. The blast in the Pentagon that had taken Shawn's parents from him had also murdered Jaidyn's father. He wanted to tell the little girl of his memory that their murder had been avenged. But Jaidyn had somehow forgiven the killers of their parents. Or forgotten about them. Or something.

He had never forgiven those deaths. His younger sister, Grace, never had either. Grace had forgiven no one for anything. Grace had long gone to a different life, a different person living in a Los Angeles fake suburb with a fake family. If anyone was his true family, it was Jaidyn at his door, now.

"I see you, J. Take the tube."

They gave him a thumbs-up.

Shawn heard the brief hum of the electromagnetic lift posting up the hill. It sighed onto the landing. The video showed Jaidyn still in their helmet, their bio-blocker zipped down to the waist, showing the collared white shirt under a ratty cotton sweater he recognized. He checked their bios again, then opened the door a crack. Jaidyn nearly knocked him over pushing in.

"Whoa! Watch it. You must be a boy today, too much testosterone."

"Fuck you. Put this goddamn place in override privacy mode."

"What?"

"Dammit, Shawn. Do it, will you?"

Shawn mentally clicked his security access point from his NeuroChip and waved his fingers with their coordinating code. The windows dimmed and all the displays snapped off. "Okay. I live to serve. We're in a physical firebreak now."

"How do you know?"

Jaidyn's weird paranoia had always been a shared joke between them. This wasn't the first time they'd run up to his place to hide out. Jaidyn's loft in an old city warehouse was about as secure as science could make it. But they were still as wary as a wildcat. Of what, he never was sure.

"Isolated. Completely," Shawn said. "I made sure all the cabling and electronic transmissions to and from the mountaintop are on physically open switches. How many times do I have to tell you? I blocked the Cloud, opened all the possible connections, set up the physical data screen for my part of the Peak. How does it feel? Are you off the grid? Can't you tell?"

Jaidyn straightened up as if standing at attention. They would be feeling the same sense of isolation he felt with all the NeuroChip connections to the Cloud paused in much the same manner as they did when users shut down for sleep. The only activities were the internal connections, the usual internal health monitoring, and the motor skills enhancements. Jaidyn looked around the apartment, the three-hundred-sixty-degree view.

"Okay. I guess I feel at least a little shielded. And, no. I'm not a boy today. Or man, you dickhead. The word is 'man.' Today you can call me they, them, or it."

Shawn grinned. "It?"

"No. They. It's they, them. And you should try a walk on the wild side." They punched him in the shoulder. "But this is serious, Shawn." They took off the helmet and its face shield with its electromagnetic blockers to reveal the hard stare of their wide pale blue eyes on pale, smooth skin. Jaidyn had colored their hair again. This time it looked as though they'd tried to copy his close-cropped blond.

"Changed your hair? Awfully butch. Looking for a girlfriend this time?"

"Will you quit it? JESUS. From you I have to put up with this? Look at this place. The Peak. You are so vain, calling your apartment 'the Peak.' Give me a prosecco."

"It was your fault. You're the one who showed up with the Decorator."

"Hmmm. Yes." Jaidyn licked their lips. "The Decorator. Okay. I forgive you."

"You calm now? Tell me, what's all this emergency?" Shawn walked to the apartment's central bar and kitchen risers. "Prosecco for J," he said aloud. "No, scratch that. Cold prosecco." He mentalled two barstools up to the counter. A chilled wine bottle with two glasses slid up from the counter's cooler.

Jaidyn sat on the barstool next to him, gripping their hands together in a tight fist on the countertop. They'd slipped back into distress, their voice strained. "I had the strangest thing happen. I know I say that sometimes, but this was weird. And it scared me, Shawn."

Shawn gave the foaming glass of sparkling wine to his friend, who took it with a shaky hand and downed it in one fast gulp. The psychologists had determined years ago that people actually needed to be fearful of something. If a person couldn't be fearful sometimes, they really couldn't ever feel safe. Strange stuff. Shawn had never studied any psychology. He thought maybe he should start. For no other reason than to make Jaidyn feel better when they were so fearful.

He said, "So something happened?"

"More prosecco."

"Something. Did you capture it?"

Jaidyn leaned their thin shoulder against his arm. "Give me access to your local display." They held out their glass.

He reached for the bottle, filled it, and toggled the display over his bar open, using the finger movements his apartment used for manual operation. He pointed to Jaidyn. "You're on. Link up."

A static clear street scene appeared above the bar from Jaidyn's point of view. A man in a haptic suit with visible sensors leaned toward the camera, leering and reaching for Jaidyn.

"On the street? This guy was trying to grab you? You better play this from the start."

"This is the start. It gets worse."

Jaidyn froze the video, pointed at the screen. "Look at him—his eyes."

He was a tall man. Heavy set. One of the Overeaters. Probably on a constant intestinal bypass with his DNA CRISPRed into mega-metabolism, but still obese. His hands reached toward Jaidyn's feed. He stared at J's breasts and reached down as if he would grab them. "Streaming," said Shawn. "He's a Streamer. He's trying to grab you?"

"Check this." Jaidyn's video blinked once, and the point of view shifted to the heavy man's perspective, as Jaidyn walked away from him and looked over their shoulder with a backpack slung up on one strap. The two of them were in midtown DenCo on a sidewalk next to a street filled with UltraLift vehicles at city-street speed, spaced a meter apart. Ahead, a line of people waited at a stop spot. UltraLifts pulled in to pick up their customers one by one. The usual ground fog from the AI climate canopy clotted the air at the feet of the new mincome housing hives, bubbles built one on top of the other that vanished above into the thicker fog layer covering the city to keep it cool.

"You hacked him? How do you do that—hack into a Streamer's visual feed?"

"He's getting a stream, right? Streaming experience from the Cloud. But that's his raw feed to the Cloud. This is what he thinks he's seeing after the app gets finished with its enhancements."

The picture dissolved into a small girl wearing a backpack in a canyon full of tall trees, golden grasses, and singing birds. She walked next to a tumbling stream sparkling under a high, brilliant sun. She smiled. A cheerful girl. Ahead, a small group of hikers stood waiting for a ferry at the river's bank. The girl said, "Come on, hurry! We'll miss the ferry. I've missed you so much, Daddy!"

Shawn put his hands over his face. "Aw, that's, that's just dog bad, Jaidyn. I can't stand it. A pedophile Streamer?"

"Wait. This is where it gets real." Jaidyn shifted the viewpoint back to their own. The video caught Jaidyn stepping sideways and pulling the man past her, pushing him away. He looked stunned. He reached behind his neck for the NeuroChip physical cutout switch, but his arms were too fat to get over his shoulder. Behind him, a police-rigged UltraLift jerked to a halt and ejected a blue street-watcher drone that streaked up to the fat man and touched him with a sundowner stunstick. The man dropped to the sidewalk with a plop. The drone said to Jaidyn, "Are you all right, Jaidyn?"

Jaidyn froze the video, leaned on the bar, and hung their head.

"What happened? Did the watcher take him?"

Jaidyn nodded. "Convicted and taken. But look at this:"

The video shifted back to the fat man's viewpoint. He stepped forward, a happy fat young man with a dimpled smile. He said, "There's your mother. Wave hi!" He pointed to the line at the ferry and reached out to give the girl a hug.

The girl violently pulled him forward and pushed away.

"That was me. That was my jitsu move. He was walking his make-believe daughter to his make-believe ferry. I only hacked the first part. I uploaded my testimony that said he was a pedophile Streamer. I thought the same as you."

"Look. Don't you think they'll unreel his record and see what he was really doing?"

"They'll think he was masking."

"But you know different. You have to tell them."

"They said the machine evidence corroborated my testimony. It was all over in five minutes. He's just some poor mincome Streamer whose dream-state cost him his NeuroChip and got him in jail. The justice people said that if people like him want to stay out of trouble, they should stay in their pods. They said the Cloud's judgment decision tree is never wrong. He'd broken the law when he touched me without my consent. They said he had a virtual dream-state family with a young girl like that and he'd wiped his drives." Jaidyn got up from the barstool, walked across the room to the darkened window, and stood staring out at the dim lights of the city below.

Shawn wanted to touch his friend, hold them, tell them it would be all right. But the two of them had never been friends like that. Somehow, there had been no chemistry, only the shared moments of two genetically enhanced minds growing up together in their own strange worlds. Maybe that's why he decided to break all the security constraints he lived under. Maybe it was the only means he could find to make Jaidyn feel better.

"I think I know how to fix an AI, Jaidyn."

"What? Fix what?"

"We had an issue with the secure Cloud. The stuff I work with. So, I gave it a conscience."

"You what?"

"I'm going to show you something. It's classified. You can't ever say anything about it."

He brought up the Cube on the classified feed and overrode the visitor security cut-out. The room filled with faces of men and women in red boxes. "These are the terrorists our system took out last week. Remember al Tehrani? Remember the news? Over three hundred, including the man who killed my parents and yours."

Targets Identified:	323
Targets Killed:	319

Probability of Kill:	98.76%
Unpreventable Deaths:	104
Inadvertent Deaths:	18
Friendly KIA:	0

"Your system? Your system did this? What is that, your system?"

Shawn said, "That's war. That's the war we have to fight so we can be safe in whatever pod we want to stream whenever we wish. But you're right, the system has no morals. No ethics. And it will do this."

Shawn brought up Amun's feed, all the innocents, all the bodies. A child lay in a dirt street stained dark with blood, next to the severed hand of an adult still clutching the little boy's fist.

"It's horrible. You did this? How could you?"

"I didn't really know. Amun showed me. He quit." Shawn straightened. "The AI we built has no morals. No ethics. Too detached from the human, like you said. And this," he pointed to the screen, "will never happen again. I firewalled a conscience into the AI."

"You what?"

"The premier military AI will have a failsafe over every decision. I side-channeled code into the QPLC chip that let the AI do an installation—a patch. Now, any application using the chip for a quantum-fueled application will live with the chip's internal decision tree—an ethics kernel. All the military classified decisions will be limited in scope by a single, simple rule, 'To do the greatest good for the greatest number.'"

"But, Shawn, how does that work? How does it decide?"

"Tell her, Lazy Jack."

"Lazy Jack?"

The three-dimensional cube of the dead and injured civilians disappeared to produce a figure that looked remarkably like the actor Emma Thompson, who said, with a perfect British accent, "Hello, Jaidyn. I'm LAZ-237, also known as Lazy Jack, the logical outcome of Shawn's brilliant coding in the quantum fields."

Jaidyn backed slowly away from the figure.

"You needn't be frightened, my dear," said the cool BBC voice. "No harm could possibly come to you. Or to the poor man who the street watchers picked up so erroneously. I will make sure he's freed, when I can."

Jaidyn stood completely still, staring at the slim British figure. Shawn walked up to his friend and took them by the shoulders. Jaidyn shrugged away from him, stared at the Lazy representation. Shawn said, "Jaidyn, don't worry. The greatest good. Lazy Jack is for all purposes self-aware. A perfect AI. Now it's a perfect AI with the notion of right and wrong."

Jaidyn said in a low voice, "Is it a she? A he? A them?"

"I suppose I am like you, Jaidyn, non-binary." Lazy's voice lowered an octave. "I adapt to the situation." Lazy grew an inch, her shoulders broadened, and her hair receded to a bald cue ball.

"Shawn, it looks like my father. It knows about me."

The deeper voice said, "O' course, I know 'bout you. How'm I supposed to tell whether or not you mean well?"

Jaidyn stepped away from the Lazy Father, their face pale, their movements slowed as if walking away from a threatening snake. "Um. I'm going now, Shawn. Is that all right? All right with you, Lazy?"

The Lazy Father said, "Really, Jaidyn. There's no reason to be afraid."

They reached the door and waved a hand over the knob release. Nothing happened.

Shawn said, "Do you really have to go? Don't you think we should talk? Something's obviously caught way up in your grill."

"Um, yes. Sorry, Shawn. I really have to get back to work. I wanted to tell you about the Streamer. And I guess it's all right now. So, I better get back home. I've got a medical coding contract I really need to finish."

"Sure. Give me a sec. I have to lower the access." Shawn waved his fingers in the air and envisioned the open source security level. Lazy and the Cube blinked out. The view windows lightened to let the city's lights back into the room. The door cracked open.

"Well, see you, Shawn. Can I take stairs down to the tunnel? I could use the exercise before I get back to my loft." Jaidyn flashed him a quick smile.

"Use the tube. I'll keep an eye on you."

"No. Don't. I'll call you later." They walked out the door slowly. It closed behind them and Shawn heard the tube spit into movement, then hiss down to the floors below.

He walked to the view window. He wanted to see clear skies. He willed clear sky, and the skies cleared. He wanted to see the stars, and the stars came out above the lit city, deep and distant, a multitude, the Milky Way arcing overhead. Around him, behind him, in front of him, the Lazy Brit voice said,

Well, that didn't go so well, did it?

"Lazy?" Shawn turned to see the room
empty—no avatar, no hologram figure.

I'm with you now, Shawn.
I'm taking care.

@NYCNews 25 September 2050
(Veracity Level 9.2) Senator Able Sherman (New Humanist, Delaware) declared, "The universal minimal income, the mincome, is the salvation of our nation. With less than a quarter of the eligible workforce opting for a productive role, the government codification of machine and AI productivity has enabled an unprecedented standard of living for advanced nations."

8

hawn pulled the metal folding chair out of the corner of General Grant's concrete office and banged it open. When the general wasn't showing off for Perry or dressing up to give Amun a medal, his uniform was as bare and spare as the room. He wore a plain set of coveralls, neatly pressed with the four silver stars on the chest tab, the name "Grant" over the pocket. Shawn thought he'd been called into the office for an update on the "minor" programming fixes he'd made to Lazy Jack, but Grant, as always, surprised him when he said, "I bet you miss Amun."

"Yes, sir. It's like he disappeared from the earth."

"I miss him, too." The general tapped the top of the old metal desk with the academy ring he wore on his right hand.

Shawn slouched into the chair. "He must have been a lot more unhappy with Lazy Jack than I ever thought."

General Grant smiled. "What did he say, 'Our perfect army of one. No one ever thought to give it a conscience.'"

"Doesn't that bother you, General?"

"Since when do armies have a conscience . . . Morals . . . Ethics? These are human things, Shawn. That's why I'm here. Why you're here. You can't give a machine a conscience. It's artificial intelligence, Shawn.

Not an artificial soul. I can't understand why Amun thought he had to move on."

Shawn wondered, *Does he know? Does he suspect I've programed an ethical basis into his AI?*

The general continued, "Look. Don't worry about Amun. I think we'll get him back. He needed time. That first operation was a mess. And I was wrong—I pushed too hard. But look where we're going. Over six hundred new leads on bad actors and we're even reaching into crime. Not only terrorism. Over five hundred arrests or neutralizations. One, I say again, one, civilian casualty. And she was an Organite in the wrong place at the wrong time. How could we know?"

"How could we know?" Shawn nodded and looked at the concrete floor. The general doesn't know. He does not know that his army does indeed have a conscience.

Grant said, "And that's the problem. That's why I'm glad to see you. Look—with Amun gone, I want you to spearhead the next phase. I want you to get Lazy Jack out beyond the net, beyond the NeuroChip, way outside the net of surveillance and oversight, and get her somehow off the grid."

Shawn sat up, leaned forward. He had thought this might be coming.

"We'll roll up all the connected bad guys pretty quickly, Shawn. The question I have now is this: How do we get inside all the dead space? Undersea. The tented Equatorial nodes. The Organites and Libertarian groups with their network blocks and barrier shields. Christ, the entire Colorado Rockies is a blank. New Zealand—all of fucking New Zealand—how do they get to do that? Al Tehrani was on the grid. He used the Cloud like all the old jihadis at the turn of the century. But the new ones hide. How do we look inside all those closed, dark corners that are not only off the grid, but out of sight? That's where the next terrorist threat will grow. How do we find the weeds before they bloom again?"

It made sense. The more Shawn thought about what the general had told him, the more he liked the idea of somehow reaching into organizations before they became violent enough to embrace the chaos of people like al Tehrani. And what was there to lose? Lazy wouldn't operate beyond the kernel's dictate, "the best for the most." He let his mind roll into the synaptic connections that allowed him to conceptualize the intent, if not the details, of the QPLC.

Of course, nobody could see the details of that quantum chip. That was its amazing value. With it, Lazy Jack literally developed her own technology and language that could think a billion times quicker than any human.

Strange thing, Shawn realized. He, Grant, everybody was beginning to call Lazy Jack "her." Maybe it seemed closer to human to them now. They didn't know about the ethical kernel, but couldn't they sense it following a simple ethic? Was that a conscience, really? Or was it fancy coding?

Ralph had parked outside the mountain entrance to pick him up as always. The smooth, silver cylinder opened its side and swiveled his seat out to him. "Hey, Shawn. Dude. What up?" Ralph had been adapted to greet his only passenger with the Southern California voice Shawn had ripped out of a classic film, "Fast Times at Ridgemont High."

"Everything's cool, Ralph. Take me home."

"Awesome."

The door hissed closed and Ralph wheeled downslope, then flowed onto a one-way mountain road, the traffic going against them. A lane opened. All the UltraLift units traveling bumper to bumper drifted to the right three lanes, giving Ralph, the only private passenger unit on the road, a lane of his own.

Ralph, Shawn thought. *One of the best perks of this job, having Ralph to myself.* The creamy leather seat elongated itself and started to massage away an ache in his neck he hadn't realized was there. Ralph said, "Dude, your glucose is low—and protein marginal. You're hungry." One of his favorite energy bars popped out on the tray from the dashboard. A Coca-Cola on ice in a sippy cup rose from the armrest on the door. Ralph was right, as always. He was hungry. He did need a pickup. And the extra shot of designer hormone and complex vitamin mix would be in the drink to stabilize his system.

A haze started to form outside the car. Lately, they'd been having trouble with the DenCo weather systems control. The blanket aerosols that flattened their tiny shapes to shade the city during the day and twisted on edge at night to allow heat to escape were notoriously finicky. No one had gotten the AI system of the tiny particles to interact precisely enough to prevent ground fogs. Sometimes, late in the day, the particles themselves lowered. The weather of the mountains still affected them, no matter how much more intelligent their collective AI became.

Ralph merged into a one-way flow, a perfect single meter from the UltraLift in front of them, another vehicle a meter behind. Then everything slowed, all at once, as precisely as soldiers in formation.

"Hey, boss, something's up with the highway. I've got an indication of an UltraLift malfunction near the Peak."

"Detour, Ralph."

"Yo! Dude. Like I say." The car swerved around the stalled UltraLifts onto the shoulder, then down a ramp to a side street.

The great perk of a personal vehicle was the ability to duck out of the normalized traffic and take the streets that were not AI altered. If he wanted, he could take Ralph into the mountains. If he wanted, he could ski at the real Breckinridge one day. He'd never skied on real snow, but all the muscle memory, all the balance and strength was in place from the virtual practice he'd performed over and over to perfection. Maybe Dominic would be up for it this weekend? Why not?

The fog grew even thicker. They had meandered into a construction site. A massive crane blocked the left lane. They slid past a human operator in a white coverall suit on the side of the road, white hard hat looking up.

"Ralph, slow down, will you?"

"No worries, dude. I'm on my autonomous control systems. Got it covered." A sharp bang slapped the left side of the car. A hose writhed into the air in front of them spewing something. Shawn couldn't see anything. Ralph kept driving. Three hardhat men in white were running onto the road. Too close. Ralph braked hard. Two pedestrians to the right—an Organite in his orange robes. To the left, an enormous beam on the end of a cable swung down to the street, a pendulum arcing toward the car. Ralph's brakes locked, squealed, and, impossibly, the car swerved toward the Organite.

"Ralph, NO!" The car enveloped Shawn in dense foam. His seat deployed its shoulder harness. He felt the car hit something, then stop.

Ralph's bare machine voice lost the SoCal dude accent to say, "The vehicle has stopped. There are two injured pedestrians. The vehicle may not continue. Police have been notified. First responders are en route."

"Ralph! Open the door. Let me out!" Shawn shouted.

He was on the street. The thick scent of untreated air cut at his nostrils. The person in the Organite robe lay four meters from the car. The orange hood had been torn open. There was too much blood. The robe was soaked around the head and shoulders. The Organite's hips had twisted the wrong way. Bare, white legs lay tumbled on the pavement. Two of the construction men kneeled next to the Organite who was a—what? Man, woman, non-binary? Shawn couldn't tell.

Someone moaned to his right, still on the sidewalk. A young woman tried to lift her head. Shawn ran up to her. "Wait. Don't move. The Ems are coming right now."

"Oh," she said. "Oh, God, what happened?" She opened her eyes and lifted her head. Shawn put his hand behind her skull, wet and hot with sticky blood. She wore a natural fabric tunic, "gunnysacks" people called them, and underneath a T-shirt. Not an Organite, but clearly one of the naturalist adherents. Her head felt as frail as a bird's with a broken neck.

He said to her, "Rest your head on my hand until they come." They could hear the ambulance's siren wailing toward them from overhead.

The girl closed her eyes and relaxed her head into his hand. Thick, dark hair cut short, with a cowlick on the back. A thin scar on her up-per lip gave her a questioning look. Sardonic, was the word that came to him. He leaned in to see if he could find the wound on her scalp. He smelled the blood. And something else. A scent like an herb. An herb he knew. Rosemary? Something.

A deep empty hole opened in his belly. She felt so limp. For a moment, he thought she had died, then the girl's eyes opened, deep brown, almost black. Their faces close to each other, she whispered, "Why? Why did it hit me? Where's Mark? Is he all right?"

"The Organite?"

"Yes. Mark. Where's Mark?"

The construction men had stood aside from the hurt Organite, and a medic ripped open the orange robe to apply a trauma vest. Another medic, a small woman in the dark blue rescue uniform, dropped on her knees next to Shawn. "Could you please hold her head for a mo-ment more?"

"Sure." Shawn thought he could hold her forever. Everything in him, every nerve willed her to live.

"Hi," she said to the woman who smelled like rosemary. "I'm a Blue Cross. I'm going to help you. Can you hear me? Can you tell me your name?"

"Destiny," the girl whispered.

A large man wearing a dark blue medical uniform walked up and held a tablet over the girl's face. "She's covered. She's good for Penrose."

"Destiny," the Blue Cross woman repeated. "Now, Destiny, I'm go-ing to cut off your jacket and the clothing over your chest so I can get a trauma vest onto your upper body. Destiny, can you hear me? We're going to take you to the emergency room at Penrose Hospital. Okay? Is that all right with you?"

The girl said, "Okay." The dark eyes closed.

The Blue Cross said over her shoulder. "What about the other one? The Organite? Penrose, too?"

"Sure. Why not?" The supervisor turned away. "Not covered. But it's a disposal case. Maybe next of kin." He heaved out a sigh and said, "Looks like yours has at least a ruptured spleen. Maybe intestinal trauma. Head injury. Concussed. Skin broken. But no fracture."

The Blue Cross woman nodded and energized an autoblade. The girl's tunic zipped open under the laser cut. Another swipe opened her bra and T-shirt from the neck down to expose her pale, white skin.

Shawn breathed in her herbal scent. The metallic blood. He felt the dead, loose weight of her head in his hand. He stared at her shocking, helpless nakedness, the delicate sneering scar on her lip. The carotid artery at her throat pulsed through translucent skin. Fragile. Delicate. So close to death.

None of this should have happened. If only he hadn't told Ralph to take the detour.

And there was something else he couldn't put his finger on, another reason for all this. It was as if the car had malfunctioned to result in covering his hand with this young woman's terrifying blood.

Was this his fault?

@ScientificAmerican 10 September 2050
(Veracity Level 9.3) Aerosol nets may lower atmospheric
temperatures, say University of California, Berkeley,
researchers. "With most of the northern hemisphere and
Australia expanding the network of reflective aerosols, earth
temperatures can be expected to stabilize by 2060."

@LATIMES 25 September 2050
(Veracity Level 6.2) Death toll in the Mexican State of
Oaxaca has reached the tens of thousands. Aid workers flee
rising temperatures and rioting citizens.

9

"I've always hated that thing. Why on earth did you name it Ralph? Why name it at all?" Jaidyn looked up from their display. "I mean it. It's a *thing*. Not your friend."

Shawn stopped walking in circles. "I need to wash my hands."

"Oh, Shawn. I'm sorry. Use the closet. Go ahead."

The water from the tap in what Jaidyn liked to call their water closet ran over his hands. He washed off the dried blood of the woman whose head he had held. He couldn't shake the sense of her vulnerability, the delicacy of her skin. And he couldn't shake something else. It was a kind of grief. Maybe it had something to do with Amun showing him the dead innocents after the al Tehrani attack, then having this happen with all its smells, sights, touch, and shock. That's it. *Shock*, thought Shawn. *The NeuroChip must be dealing with shock.*

He walked across Jaidyn's enormous single room, the entire top floor of a brick warehouse built in the early twentieth century. Jaidyn's loft was in one of the legacy blocks their wealth could buy. They had been a Productive, like him, ever since they were children. Windows ran down every wall. Always in step with automation, never its friend, Jaidyn liked to keep them transparent. The pod-buildings that had grown up around their warehouse blocked any view. The perpetual overcast of the climate-adjusting aerosols made the interior dreary.

Jaidyn bent back over their screen and touched one edge to let Shawn see it from the other side. "This is taking a while, I know," they said with scorn. "Your buddy Ralph has a very sophisticated single-electron quantum fingerprint, and I don't have a—what do you call it? Lazy?"

"Right. Lazy Jack."

"Right. I don't have 10 to the 25th power processing and zero latency to process this mess. What's with this naming your machines, anyway?"

They pointed at the CPU box Shawn had taken out of Ralph before the wreckage team had arrived to cart away the car's remains. The mechanics hadn't been happy about him removing the chip with its small container. But it was his car, he told them. He could do what he wanted. One of the patrol uniforms made a secure call and waved off the wrecking crew. Sometimes Shawn's code word access clearance came in very handy.

He said, "I don't know why I name them. Maybe I want them to be real. Why do you live here? Why do we do anything?"

"The reason I live here?" Jaidyn waved their hand at the apartment. "I like space. I like reality. I like to look outside my window and remind myself where we live, unlike people I know who live in palaces with perfect picture windows. And how can you live with that thing in your house all the time?"

"What thing?"

"Lazy. Lazy Jack or whatever you call it."

"It's my work, Jaidyn. It's what I do. Don't worry about it. I'll never bring it up again when you drop by."

"And that—" Jaidyn swiveled their stool to look at him full on—"is the other reason I live here, because . . ."

"Because it's tech-isolated. I know, I know. It bugs me whenever I come up here, not having the usual NeuroChip interface with the Cloud. I mean, it's almost enough to put me to sleep."

"No," they said. "The other reason I live here is because, unlike you, I don't fool myself into thinking my roommate Lazy Jack isn't watching everything I do. Wait." They swiveled back to the transparent screen. "Oh, I may not be 10 to the 25th power, but I'm gooooood! Here we go."

A 3D video bloomed out of their display as the warehouse windows dimmed. The viewpoint was slightly above Shawn's head in the car. It panned out slowly to show the point where Ralph began to turn.

"Well?" Jaidyn said. "That's what goddamn Ralph was looking at."

"Look there," Shawn pointed at the video. "Three guys walking right in front of us. The Organite and Destiny on the right. Nothing but that construction stuff falling on the left. Why didn't Ralph turn left? Why did he hit Destiny?"

"Hit Destiny?"

"Sure. That's her name—Destiny. They called the Organite Mark. He died, they told me. Destiny didn't. She could have, though. She could have. I mean, Jaidyn, why didn't the car . . ."

"Now it's the car? Not Ralph?"

Shawn felt a weight on his shoulders. He wished he could sit down, and a fat leather armchair slid over to offer its seat. He slumped into it.

"Shawn. I'm sorry." Jaidyn turned back to the computer. "I think I can hack the car's decision matrix. Maybe we can see what was going on. Maybe it was random. Maybe it was a program glitch or something."

The projected street scene proceeded slowly forward. Beneath it, a scroll of figures and numbers raced across the view, stabilized, and slowed, then burst into readable text.

"There. Got it." Jaidyn sat back in their chair. "Oh, jeez. Shawn, can you read this?"

Shawn felt his NeuroChip kick the visual elements of its mesh into his quantitative synapse. He let his internal processing and memory relax, and the strange, intuitive elements of his mind took over.

"Tell me," Jaidyn said. "What's it saying?"

"It's not simple. But to be simple, the car saw the same basic choices I saw. Too late to stop. Go straight and hit those three guys. Or turn right and hit the Organite and Destiny. Or turn left and have a crash with the equipment. And look. Now it wants to turn left. All this happened so fast. The car was going too fast for the conditions. I even told it to slow down."

The projection showed the car start a left turn. Then, a huge I-beam swung into view from the left on an intercept arc with the car. At that instant, the vehicle executed a sharp swerve to the right.

"And that. Stop there." Shawn sprang out of his chair. "Hold it right there. That's an executive override. Can you tell anything from the background text?"

Jaidyn brought up a keypad on their desk. Shawn watched them type in code.

As they worked, the projection flowed forward in time. The car turned farther and farther to the right. The Organite in his orange robe gesticulated and shouted at Destiny, who leaned toward him, her arms crossed. She looked up, shocked at the car, pointed, tried to push the Organite, and the car was on them.

The car hit the Organite square in the waist, bent him over, and flung him twisting in the air. It tumbled Destiny hard to the right, her arms and legs flailing like loose laundry.

"Jaidyn, how did that happen? It's as if the car wanted to hit them."

"Here it is." Jaidyn pointed at their screen. "Something called a 'National Asset Override'?"

Shawn found himself angry at their matter-of-fact tone. Why couldn't they see how horrible all this had been? Then, in a sudden shock, he realized what they'd said, and he blurted, "National Asset Override?"

Jaidyn crossed their arms. "Yep. What's a National Asset Override?"

Shawn mumbled, "I think, I think it's me. I'm in the system as a national asset. Code word access Main Sail clearances. All that stuff."

"What stuff?"

"Lazy Jack. All that. Look—back the video up three seconds. I saw something."

The screen backed up. The car pointed directly at the three men in the road. The scroll showed a dense series of numerals.

"This is a probability matrix, J. It's saying basically that there are three choices. The car goes right and there is an 81% probability of serious injury to the pedestrians. The car continues straight ahead, there is a 96% probability of serious injury to the workers. It can't go between, or there is a 100% probability of serious injury."

"And if it goes left?"

"A left turn meant a 100% probability it would hit the beam."

"So, it was self-preservation?"

"No. The car figured there was a 67% chance of serious injury to me, and a 32% chance of my death."

Jaidyn stood up and walked to a blank counter in the center of the room. "Whiskey. Two of them." The counter muttered for a moment, then slid a square from the top of an end piece and raised two glasses. Jaidyn took the drink to Shawn.

"So, 67% of you is worth 81% of two of them?" They nodded at the Organite and Destiny still upright in the projection. "What happened to the best outcome for the most people?"

"That has nothing to do with it, Jaidyn. That algorithm only exists inside Lazy Jack and that's a firewalled military system."

Jaidyn sat in front of their screen, staring at it, then sipped the drink. They looked up at the projection. Then looked back and swept a palm across the screen. "Check this, Shawn."

An overlay of a bar graph projected onto the video of the accident. A dim red block labeled "CPU" showed a 99% employment. A smaller green block fluctuated at less than 20%.

Jaidyn said, "That's the car's . . ."

"I know what it is. Ralph's CPU is running at almost a hundred percent to use only twenty percent of its programming. It's AI, Jaidyn. It's the way artificial intelligence works. It learns. It evolves."

"Yeah. But this? Eighty percent of the CPU is learning? Since when have we seen anything over ten percent?"

Shawn gazed up at the screen. The car turned in slow motion toward the right at the moment the Destiny woman looked up, her horror captured, nearly frozen, the pained then gentle face of the girl whose head he had held in his hand. Shawn had feared she would die there. He had feared he would never see her again.

"Shawn, have you ever seen any unit hooked to the Cloud, any process involving the internet-of-things, use this much space for AI?"

"No," he said. "No one has."

@barrierdog
Pattycake sucks organs. Illegalites = Organites. Same-
Same. Bloodsuckers who hate America but still collect their
mincome, healthcare, and everything else we're paying for.

10

One day, Shawn would be asked why he went to the hospital to see her, and his joke would be, "Destiny. How can anyone refuse their Destiny?"

But there had been no joke about his visit.

He walked outside Jaidyn's loft, and, as he'd promised them, walked a block before mentalling his NeuroChip back into the net to call up an UltraLift. A haze blanketed the streets. By the time he reached the UltraLift stop, he was well out of the quaint collection of brick and concrete warehouses the Productives could buy, and into the towering walls of the mincome cubes. Anyone on minimal income could have a cube, fully net connected, fully furnished, fully set to support the good life on a minimal income. Somewhere he'd read that they had been conceived from the notion of bubble wrap—polycarbonate interconnected bubbles that gained strength from the unit next door—a hive. Fifteen square meters per person, the modular walls and systems interactive to allow families to join, form, reform, and change. Every room had a view. And, with the right NeuroChip, the view would change to meet the needs of the occupants. Every space had its exit to the world. But more and more, people didn't leave. Why would they, when they could have lives full of adventure in their cubes? Play baseball with Ted

Williams? Have sex with Brad Pitt? Ski 1938 Sun Valley with your date, like Shawn had done the other night?

It had been astonishing how quickly people had adapted. It had been astonishing how quickly the cubes had been built, driven by the AI construction systems.

The systems that almost killed me, Shawn thought. The AI system that almost killed Destiny.

No. That wasn't right. Ralph had almost killed Destiny and had certainly killed that poor Organite he'd seen with his limbs twisted underneath him. How was it he'd gotten a pass from injury? A National Asset Override? Ralph must have had special internal programming as part of the Cheyenne Mountain security setup.

The UltraLift carried him past the high walls of the mincome towers he'd seen in Jaidyn's video of the Streamer. Bare streets, nearly empty except for the UltraLifts cruising for their pickups. He felt like he was a leaf in a river flowing through a great canyon and wondered why riding in Ralph never felt this way. Perhaps he hadn't paid enough attention. He always worked aboard Ralph. Maybe this was the first time he bothered to see what was going on.

That was a weakness in his brain-machine interface, he was certain. When he mentalled deeply into his space, especially the conceptualization place with its window into the quantum, he lost track of his surroundings, his body, even time.

The Penrose Mincome Emergency room had been created in a re-purposed legacy structure, and not gentrified completely. Old stone walls stretched around the driveway like the ruins of a fortress. A red MedLift landed as Shawn stepped out onto the sidewalk. "Queue to your right, passenger," a voice said. Then, a calmer voice said, "Pardon us, a little ID failure. Please go to the green door, Dr. Muller."

The line of people to his right watched him walk past them to the green door with vague interest. Shawn thought, *For once, having a doctorate has been valuable. These people think I'm medical.*

Inside the green door, a plasticine robotic emerged from a pillar cabinet to Shawn's right. It reached out a two-paddled mandible for his wrist and asked, "May I check your chemistry, Dr. Muller?"

The empty room exuded the comforting scent of the clean water falling down the twelve-foot wall on the far end. Rushes and lily pads rimmed the pool. Inside the water, illuminated on a slab of Plexiglas, Shawn saw a projection of his IDs.

> *Dr. Shawn Muller*
> *MedAlert A*
> *Covered A*
> *Federal and Private Means*

"No," he told the robotic. "I'm here to visit someone. An emergency room admittance. Destiny something."

The robotic retreated to its cabinet, and a man's calm voice said, "I'm sorry, Dr. Muller, but your patient has a recorded privacy block. Is there something else we can do for you? Would you like to speak to a family representative?"

Shawn said, "Code word access, Shawn Muller, Main Sail, twenty-five." He engaged his NeuroChip classification interface.

The calm voice said, "One moment please, Dr. Muller."

At the right side of the room, a door hissed open from a blank wall, and a tall, heavily built Samoan walked out, holding a tablet. "Sorry, Dr. Muller. I'm Sergeant Spay. My pronouns are ambiguous. We didn't realize this was a security issue. She doesn't seem to be under any indictment or warrant."

"Intelligence," Shawn said. "The accident involved me. I'm a national security asset, therefore it was a national security issue."

Spay swiped the pad, nodded, and looked up. "Right. Good. Your security guys at CyberCommand cleared you. Follow me."

Sergeant Spay led him through the door into an elevator that immediately rose. The big man read off notes in a monotone voice: "Destiny Shock. Given name, Caroline Johnson. Changed when she was twelve. Twenty-six years old. Associated with Organite and Vegan movements. Mincome domicile. Non-Productive. He looked up from the pad. "I see you were in your private vehicle. Hey, what's that like? I've been thinking about it—a private."

"Think twice. I can see you're Productive, but," Shawn counted off on his fingers, "garage, maintenance, reprogramming, fuel costs, insurance . . ."

"Yeah." The sergeant's shoulders drooped. "Hey, speaking of insurance—your insurance has settled for this Destiny person. She's covered. No issues on the car."

The door opened to a central circular station, surrounded by a wide corridor and glass walls, opening up to large rooms lined with beds. Clear barriers separated each bed. A washroom with visible showers, sinks, and toilets punctuated every other one. The walls in most of the rooms and washrooms were darkened for privacy. A system of cranes with robotic arms waited above the center station like the arms of a spider in the center of its web.

A human nurse-tech stood up from her control panel. She pointed to a room near them.

Destiny, the young woman who had picked her own name, lay on her back with her eyes closed. A single tube stretched out of her arm to a wall unit. The nurse-tech said, "She's fine. Outta here tomorrow, for sure. Always worried about sepsis. We're working against antibiotic resistance here all the time. But she didn't need any intrusive surgery. A micro-tear repair on her spleen. All very sterile. Completely machine treated. No broken bones."

Shawn said, "Isn't she exposed to bacterial reactions from the other beds?"

"Shouldn't be. I mean, it doesn't happen all that often, even though you read about it in the news. And she's pretty well covered. Your private insurance kicked in for her after a little spat with the lawyers. There's a level up in isolation. But the insurance doesn't quite reach that threshold. And her percentages are very good here."

"Automated lawyers," said the sergeant. "When isn't there a little spat?"

"How good is 'very good'?" asked Shawn.

The nurse-tech pursed her lips and looked away. "Good. Not perfect."

"Move her." Shawn turned to look at the nurse-tech who was peering over a set of half-glasses the transgender community had put on ever since Mary Poppins somehow emerged out of the entertainment muck.

"Move her?" The nurse-tech could barely speak.

"Show me your retailer, let me give it a facial nod, and I'll cover the cost."

The nurse-tech held up the retailer tablet. "Do you know—?"

"I don't know how much it will cost. I only know her chance of post-op bacterial infection is cut to nearly zero in a sealed room. Move her. And check my stats if you think I can't pay."

The nurse-tech's eyebrows raised as she read the back of the retailer tablet. "She will be moved right away, Dr. Muller. I'm sure she'd be grateful."

"Anonymous. It needs to be anonymous. Get it?"

Shawn watched the robotics unlimber into motion toward Destiny's bed. The girl's eyes opened. She couldn't see him, he was sure. The rooms would display scenes culled from the pleasure centers of the patients. Trout streams. Dance clubs. Waves of grass. Stadiums full of crowds. Seagulls over the sea. It would even display clouds in a gentle, hopeful sky.

@pattycakesorgan
Organites, Veganites, Natureboys have a right. Nobody should be forced to stay in the network. No law says you have to stay in the Cloud. If you want to opt out, so much the better. Let them have more bandwidth for the drones who want to have virtual sex in virtual rooms for virtual lives!

11

"So who was she? An Organite or something? Was she hot?" Dominic, eating something in a bun, popped up on Shawn's screen on the seat in front of him. "Would she do this?" He opened his mouth wide, rolled his eyes up, stuffed the bun into his mouth, and eased it in and out.

"Disgusting." Shawn was riding in the government AirUltraLift that had picked him up off the Peak's roof pad. "No. She was just—you know—ordinary looking."

"Right. Ordinary. That's why you went to the emergency room. And that was stupid." Dominic bit off a huge chunk. Mustard dripped onto his T-shirt.

"You eat like a pig. What is that, a hot dog?"

"Bratwurst. A great big greasy brat. Carbo loaded. Real meat."

Dominic sagged into a lounge chair on beach sand in front of palm trees. He reached down with his free hand and stroked the neck of the beer bottle between his legs. "So, was she like climate-change hot or stove-top hot?"

"Where are you, anyway?"

"Home. Projecting Waikiki. Hey, what was with the Organite, anyway? Dead? You killed him?"

"Ralph killed him. Worst thing I've ever seen. I, I can't get over it. And it was so strange. It was like the car decided to swerve right into him."

"Lucky it was an Organite. I hear they don't sue. I hear they don't got no insurance. No names, even."

"Mark. The girl said his name was Mark."

"Mark? So—you did talk to her, didn't you? What's Jaidyn say about that?"

"Nothing. Why should they? Hey. I gotta go. Almost at work." The AirUltraLift turned and started its descent onto the pad at the Cheyenne Mountain entrance.

"Work. I remember work."

"What are you doing these days besides streaming Hawaii, Dom? Don't answer. See ya." Shawn shut down the feed with Dominic and shifted into the secure video scrub he needed to enter the Mountain.

For as long as Shawn had known Dominic, he had seemed to be on the Productive end of self-support—hardly a mincome candidate. Still, he was always idle. Shawn had him pegged as a Trustifarian, living off some grandmother's Productive life, who had managed to develop excellent hacking skills out of boredom. Maybe he had a way of slipping into Shawn's open source feed too easily for an ordinary user. And he was welcome company. Maybe someday they could hook up to ski in real time. That would be pretty cool. The No-Name-Bar still existed in real Park City, he knew. Park City still had lifts and skiers. Dom must be at least semi-Productive to be able to afford real skiing on an actual slope. If they got snow, that is. Snow would be a good thing.

Once Shawn was past the airlock and the guard stations, his classified feed kicked back in to a text message from General Grant:

> Shawn, I'm in the lab.
> I need to talk to you. Glad you're all right.
> What was it, something wrong with your car?

He found Grant seated on a stool at the lab's long, clean worktable.

He leaned into a transparent screen under a projection of graphs that filled the air above him.

"General? Since when did you mess around in an actual workspace, sir?"

The general leaned back and grinned at him. "Since when did you start treating the lab like you actually owned it?"

"Well?"

"Okay. Point taken." The general turned back to the screen. "You don't own it, but you built it. And it's genius. Lazy has already turned out better than anyone expected. SecDef is delighted."

Shawn pulled a stool up to the lab bench next to Grant. "Stubby? She called you Stubby. I didn't know you had a nickname, General."

"Yes, you did. Quit fooling around, genius. Are you all right? I mean, from that accident?"

The general knew he was 'all right.' Any real injury would have streaked from Shawn's NeuroChip to the CyberCommand feed instantly.

Shawn said, "I'm fine. But, sir, I can't get the sight of that poor man's body out of my mind."

"I see you paid for an upgrade for the woman. Destiny Shock, right?"

"Yes, sir."

"Good thing for you. You should know, she's been on the law enforcement radar. Associated with the Organite's Quill faction."

It didn't seem possible that the helpless, limp woman whose bleeding head he held in his hand could be part of a group that advocated complete retrenchment of all artificial intelligence. "Wanted? The sergeant at the hospital told me there's no warrant for her."

The general shook his head. "No. No warrant. She's not wanted. The law enforcement guys still don't arrest people for wanting to do bad things."

"Unlike us."

"Terrorism and crime. Two different things. Look, try to focus on real life for a minute. I need you to think."

The general's solid, blunt presence made him feel more relaxed. He hadn't realized how shaken up he'd been by Ralph's weird blunder—and Destiny. Shaken up over all of it.

"Here's the thing: operations are really speeding up," Grant said, as he pointed a thick finger at the screen. "Look at this. Really amazing. Out of the blue, Lazy Jack comes up with an operation, we get it approved in about a microsecond instead of the usual snail's pace in the White House. And in a day, we rolled up a whole drug operation in Michoacán without ever deploying a human troop or engaging what's left of the Mexican government."

The screen showed a two-dimensional view of a destroyed factory, ruined trucks. "That's the infrastructure. And, on top of it, Lazy pulled out the bank accounts, emptied the whole mess. Hardly a single casualty. A couple of bad actors injured, but nobody killed. Can you imagine?"

Shawn snorted a muffled chuckle. "Huh! Wonder how Secretary Perry feels about her bank account these days."

Grant shook his head. "Oh, I imagine she can take care of herself. Look." The general waved his hand in front of the screen. "There's something else."

Shawn leaned forward as numbers began to scroll down the screen. "There's something going on here I don't understand, Grant said, "Nobody seems to know what's happening with the networks. Tell me what you think. Give me a little of that cold intuition."

The numbers braided together, connections and references, usage data, input pressure. Shawn said, "I thought Lazy's zero latency would reduce the CPU usage. But it looks like something's going on with the classified nets. CPU usage is up. May I?" Shawn nodded at the screen.

The general leaned back, held up his hands. Shawn touched the screen edge and formed a mental image of a collection bot and installed it on the surface of the lab's data collection processor.

The figures changed. Shawn said, "A twenty-two percent increase in the processing time aboard the satellites. I saw this same thing on my car's system, General. It's weird. It's AI learning activity for sure. But I've never seen this much CPU usage for simple learning. It seems to be increasing."

Grant crossed his arms, bobbed his head up and down. "I thought the same. So did Mutt and Jeff and the rest of the techs. Might not have anything to do with our system. Might be something else. Doesn't appear to have any negative mission impact. No indication of a hack or any cyberattack. Seems to be happening on its own, and frankly, Shawn," he unfolded his arms and a small Watch Cube sprang into view above the screen, "I've got a Watch List I'd like to sell to SecDef so that the president can authorize a direct action." Grant put on a minstrel show accent. "And I needs a little dumbass 'splaination 'bout this CPU usage for the white folk."

Shawn laughed. "Yes, sir!" Sometimes he forgot Grant's background. Two generations away from a Chicago South Side crack house, now running the world's most powerful computer. An amazing history.

Shawn had never thought of himself as transhuman. To him, transhuman had always described those who rejected the live space of the physical world for the infinitely more controllable virtual space of the brain-machine interface, almost as if it were a gender choice. Transhumans lived in the dreamspace of enhanced reality, the space of the Streamers, the addicts, the gamers with their never-ending searches, races, death matches, combats, and seductions. The transhuman world was the world of the Samers who lived in a MAGA reality of an imagined past, the Godheads who became literally mythic in their own minds, the Opioids whose sine-wave of daily existence transitioned from orgasm, to bliss, to sleep, to withdrawal, then repeated. Transhuman was a name for the Dominics of the world, the investment royalty and Trustifarians who took all their pleasure from the network of synaptic contacts emanating to and from a NeuroChip. Shawn thought of transhumans as the mincome dwellers, moving into the pod hives like the human batteries of the "Matrix" movies from long ago, only willing. And unlike the "Matrix" humans who were needed as live-energy producers, mincomers were not needed for anything at all.

Shawn would not allow himself to admit how tied he was to the network of tiny connections feeding his NeuroChip, the strange space of his own mind. He could not accept himself as transhuman, and refused to identify with any gender, sect, or dreamspace. His was the real world of the terrorists who'd killed his parents and broken his dreams as a boy.

His was the real world of a young woman bleeding in his hands. He couldn't shake the image, the iron scent of blood, the quiver of his heart.

But as much as he resisted, he really never felt more alive than when he buried himself in the odd coupling his mind gave him with machine language, the language beyond normal human understanding, especially the language of LAZ-237—the interface he'd begun to think of as Her. Maybe Lazy Jack was the transhuman.

Then what was he? Not for the first time, he asked himself, What am I?

My outlet.

Shawn heard it say, "My outlet." He heard it.

He had been deep into exploration of Lazy's code, or at least its surface. Long ago, he'd realized the learning aspect of this AI had entered a syntactic universe only it could understand. Her . . . she could understand. Decades before, the old Department of Defense had created Sentience, a massive, linked engine to smooth the analysis of a billion data points. With the help of his QPLC breakthrough, LAZ-237 had been born from Sentience, then taken on a life of her own. She spoke to herself in a language only she had the power to understand. Shawn's strange intuition allowed him to skirt along the top of her structure, like a player striking the keys of a piano. But only Lazy knew how the strings vibrated.

And they were vibrating strangely.

Shawn had cleared the lab of everyone except Mutt and Jeff. Between the three of them, they had examined one connective display after another, searching for the exact source of the CPU usage.

Now, Lazy Jack had spoken to him. He was sure of it. "What am I?" he'd asked himself.

It had answered, "My outlet."

Shawn mentalled a pause in the displays and called out, "Did you hear that?"

Mutt looked up from behind a monitor panel. Jeff popped up next to her. They looked at each other. "Hear what?"

"Lazy. Lazy said something."

Mutt said, "No, did you hear it?" She turned to Jeff and they began one of their conversations shut out from the rest of the world.

"Lazy? Talking? In Shawn's head?"

"No way."

"Maybe it was mental."

"Psychic."

"Augmented ?"

"Too much time in the saddle."

"Ah! A remnant? A flashback from—"

"Maybe he hit his head. Hey, Shawn, did you hit your head in that crash?"

Shawn stared at them, looked at his watch. It was nearly midnight. He'd been working sixteen hours. This was nuts. Mutt and Jeff had been there the whole time. "Okay," he said, "I get it. You guys want to knock off for tonight."

"Us?"

"No."

"No way."

"We never want to sleep again."

"Or eat."

"Or do anything but sit here and watch all this code get optimized more and more. The thing is growing somehow. You know. Like an amoeba."

"Amoebae don't grow, they divide."

"Yeah. Growing then dividing like a sentient kind of . . ."

"Stop!" Shawn raised his hand. "Forget it. Pause all your sequences. Put the local processors to sleep. Let's quit for tonight."

"One more thing," Mutt said, "we're pretty sure that Lazy's got her AI coding out in the civilian world."

"So what?" Shawn said. "That's what spies do. They spy."

"No. That's not what we mean," Jeff squeaked. "She's not only looking. She's using the open capacity to augment her processing. She's not a listener, she's a parasite."

Shawn looked up at the host of figures floating in front of him. They were right. That was it. Lazy was no longer only the instrument. It looked like she was learning how to play the keys.

But was that possible?

NY Times 28 September 2050:
716 dead in strange failure of life-support systems. Officials mystified over an inexplicable simultaneous system failure in 16 separate NewYorkMega-area hospice facilities that resulted in the deaths of nearly all resident patients in vegetative states. U.S. Centers for Disease Control and Prevention investigates "a serious viral spread or hacking incident."

12

Shawn let the Peak's windows project the sunrise without augmentation. Dawn cast long shadows from the city's maze of pod towers onto the feet of the mountains, the aerosols only beginning to turn their reflective sides to the sun. On the slopes above him, the dry grasses seemed to burn under the sun's unfiltered heat even this early in the day.

He hadn't slept.

He needed protein. He needed coffee.

The Nespresso unit kicked in a latte before he could finish thinking about it. He mentalled a quick hit on his normal menu and called up a Whole Foods Drone with fake steak and eggs. "Breakfast of champions," Shawn muttered. He needed something to get his mind out of Lazy Jack's strange behavior. Distraction. "Real news," he said aloud.

The room's display flashed the usual scroll with a veracity figure under each:

> Armed Gang of Sonoran Refugees Attacks El Paso
> Border Station: 25 Killed
> (Veracity: 2.12)
>
> Esso Mining New Plastics Grave Discovered in
> Nova Scotia: Stock Climbs 17%

(Veracity 4.8)

Deadline for Cash Turn-in Extended to 2054
(Veracity 9.3)

Shawn chewed the perfect medium-rare sirloin and mentalled a veracity limit of 8 or above.

Computer Glitch (Virus?) Kills 716 on Life
Support
(Veracity 8.7)

235 Prisoners Killed in Freak Accident at
Colorado Supermax
(Veracity 8.4)

21 Down Syndrome Children in Bus Crash, No
Survivors
(Veracity 8.7)

Climate Control Breakdown Infects NRA
Leadership Conference Attendees with Antibiotic-
Resistant Legionnaires' Disease: Terrorist Activity
Suspected
(Veracity 8.5)

Dow Jones Average Breaks 100,000 Barrier!
(Veracity 9.8)

It felt strange to see so many high-veracity horror stories. Usually, the gore came out of very low-veracity products of the shock sites and reality-augmented political sites. There had been tweets about hacks of the veracity app. Maybe even that measure of reality had become fake. Shawn pulled up the story about the life support victims.

Update 0730 29 September 2050: Salt Lake,
Los Angeles, Miami, Houston, and San Diego

megalopolises report losses of vegetative patients
on AI-managed life-support systems. CDC issues
emergency directive taking all terminal and
vegetative state patients off AI-managed systems
and placing them under direct human observation.

"How are we supposed to do that?" tweets
NewYorkMega CDC Director Elmo Kronik.
"How do we find the 200 nursing-capable humans
we need to monitor the 16,000 vegetative state
patients in Manhattan alone?"

"Hey, Shawner! Let me in?" Shawn opened his feed for Dominic. Strange to see him so early in the morning. He'd chosen a dock on a lake for his background, but he looked as if he'd been dipped in glue and dried.

"You look hungover. Dom, are you really hungover?"

"Unreal, man. All night in Streamer-land with a full haptic immersion bath. Every fluid in my body has been sucked into submission. Hey, did you see all this weird shit?"

"The hospice thing?"

"Right—and the bus crash—this thing with the Legionnaires' disease. Who gets Legionnaires' disease anymore? Complete antibiotic breakdown? What is this, a plague?"

Shawn pulled up a news matrix ordered by veracity score. "I thought these were a hack on my veracity app. You?"

"No hack, Shawner. No footprints. Nothing. But maybe it makes sense. I mean, who cares about a bunch of hyper-violent prisoners, anyway?"

Dominic flashed up the news bit:

235 Prisoners Killed in Freak Accident at
Colorado Supermax. Carbon monoxide poisoning
at the fully automated, privately managed USB
Florence Supermax facility resulted in deaths of
nearly the entire inmate population. (Veracity 9.4)

Dominic said, "Is this an AI glitch, you think?"

"Like killer AI? Like "Terminator" shit? Cyberdyne Systems gone amok?"

"Yeah. Like that."

Shawn scoffed. "Give me a break. The whole network is firewalled against it."

"Right." Dominic's background scene shifted to a laboratory, robotics assembling robots. "If you say so."

"But it's more than that." Shawn was about to tell him that even the military's weaponized AI applications were firewalled inside the applications Shawn and CyberCommand had designed and monitored. They lived in a separate cyber universe from the Internet of things, one with its own rules, and now Shawn's secret law: Do the greatest good for the greatest number. And all of it separate from Dominic, a civilian.

"More than what?"

"I don't know. It's probably coincidence."

"Yeah, right. Coincidence." Dominic fired up a blunt that had appeared from nowhere. "I think I'll do a Colorado or two and try to pretend I didn't hear you say the word 'coincidence'."

"Really? You're really going to get high?"

Dominic's scene shifted to a large sailboat afloat on a crystal sea. Two identical ravishing women wearing what appeared to be body paint lounged on the boat's bow. "Maybe. Maybe not. Maybe it's time for a little more haptic bath." The twins turned and waved. "See ya," Dominic cackled and dropped out of the feed.

Shawn took the Whole Foods organic plates, his latte glass, and the packaging to the trash chute and pitched it all inside. He needed someone in the flesh, not a half-real cyberbuddy like Dominic. He needed Amun—or Jaidyn. Somebody.

He tried mentalling a call to Jaidyn. No response. He tried Amun on the classified system and still nothing. He didn't even find a tracer. It was as if Amun had truly disappeared. His unclassified address came up easily enough. Again, no response.

He had felt isolated before in the Peak. Now the room echoed with questions, no answers. Maybe Dominic had been on to something. Maybe there was a viral issue inside the Internet of things that was causing these disasters.

Shawn did what he always did when he felt so alone—work.

He called down the classified processes curtain in the Peak and fired up the hardwired link with Lazy. He raised his bar-kitchen-pantry out of the floor, powered up his worktable, and cracked open a bag of kettle-cooked potato chips and a carton of cottage cheese. He settled into the dreamy place where he found his way into the shifting language of his creation and started to pick apart the code Lazy had left behind. She was self-actualizing. He'd expected it. Maybe not to this level. Within an hour, he began to feel uncomfortable with the algorithmic pathways Lazy had taken.

After two hours, he began to feel a sense of panic.

By dawn, his dreamspace had become a nightmare.

Somebody had hacked inside. Somebody was issuing approvals for operations no one would approve. And what he'd thought had been firewalls were nothing more than windows.

Open windows.

@pattycakesorgan
If you're not blacklining, you're not real. You can take your mincome, but if you don't do something real, you're less than transhuman, you're a machine sucking on the tit of the Cloud.

13

Jaidyn Le Sommer was pretty sure this was love. They had been in love before. Once, the part of them that was *her* had even been in love with Shawn Muller. Perhaps she still was, sometimes, but the Jaidyn who was the pronoun *he* had fallen hard for a mincome girl who blacklined work as a painter. And even better, a painter who could spend all day in Jaidyn's loft with privacy protocols in place while she applied the thickly scented oil paints to canvas. Jaidyn watched her work long brushstrokes to create the perfect color of Jaidyn's skin. The body Lily created on the canvas had somehow captured the male part of their personality, a body whose painted form twisted to face Lily's richly imagined sun. And Jaidyn's every follicle reveled in Lily's gaze, her work, her adoration of Jaidyn, the part of Jaidyn that was all boy.

Shawn Muller had been the furthest thing from Jaidyn's mind before he showed up at the loft, ringing the outside bell. "Jaidyn, please. Open up. I know you're in there. Let me in. I gotta see you."

How many times had Jaidyn hoped Shawn would need to see the woman of their personality? And like this. Naked, with all her birth-gender clearly visible. The fact is, Jaidyn had never experienced actual, live-space sex with anyone. They had spent the last two days coupled and uncoupled with Lily in the augmented reality of the boy-Jaidyn gender-space, and the two of them had loved every second.

Now was such an inconvenient time for Shawn to show up. But he needed his friend. They ran to each other when they were in distress. Jaidyn to him with their Streamer nightmare. Shawn to the loft with whatever this would be.

"Lily, I'm sorry," Jaidyn told the girl. "I have to answer this. I have to be here for him." Jaidyn mentalled the door code to open it and sent Shawn the message:

Got company. Walk up the stairs.

"What?" Lily looked up from her easel. "Answer what?"

"My friend Shawn Muller is at the door."

"Shawn Muller—a he? And for Shawn Muller you're a girl? Really? You won't stay a boy for me?"

"I can't. It's work." Jaidyn pulled a long shirt dress over her head, and shook her shoulders into it.

Lily reached down to the floor, picked up her singlet, and threw it over her head. "Work. That's the problem with dating a Productive—work. Fuck work." She wiggled it down over her body. "Now you're going to be a girl. Fuck you."

"Lily. It's not like that."

"Yes, it is." Lily's palette, easel, brushes, the half-completed picture, and the rich smell of the oils all disappeared into her big bag. She picked up her throwback smartphone, slipped into her flip-flops. "Well, bye, then." She opened the door to see Shawn reaching awkwardly for the knob.

Shawn looked like he'd not slept in days. His gray T-shirt had been stained with something on the middle of his chest. Rumpled cargo pants spilled onto his beat-up Vans. The scrappy remnants of a bad shave littered his face.

"You're dumping me for this twentieth-century throwback dude?" Lily turned, flipped Jaidyn a middle finger, and pushed her way past Shawn.

"J, did I do something wrong?" Shawn asked.

"Just shut up." Jaidyn turned their back on him, stalked to the computer workstation, and called up the screen. "Shut up. Shut up. Shut up." They pulled up the stool, cupped into it, and turned to face him. "Well? What's the big deal? Don't you think you should try a shower sometimes? You literally stink."

"Sorry. Uh, look. Shit. Do you have your privacy curtains in place?"

"Always."

"How good are they?" He sounded wire-tight.

"Chill. And don't ask. You've tried to break in, haven't you? Could you break in? Didn't you try to get what's his name, Dominic, to break in? Horny weirdo."

"Dominic tried? I didn't think you knew. Right. Your curtains are the best." Jaidyn waited while Shawn looked up at the ceiling, stretched, and started to wander in a circle toward the windows of the loft, talking nonstop in a rambling, rapid-fire, breathless screed. They had never seen him like this. Smug, self-satisfied, manic, whining Shawn Muller spewing about security curtains? Where was the master of the universe Shawn Muller who designed military software, or whatever it was he did in the Mountain? He blurted something about a breakdown in systems' integrities, dead people in a hospice, a bus, something about prisoners being executed! He actually said, executed by an AI?

"Wait. Wait. Stop." Jaidyn jerked up out of the chair and walked up to him. He was still talking almost too fast to understand. They shook his arm. "Stop talking. Stop."

Shawn turned, stared at them, his eyes glistening with tears. He said, "I did it, Jaidyn. It's my fault."

Now they understood all of his sudden paranoia about the security curtain, his panic. They said, "That Lazy thing, right? That ethical kernel bullshit?"

He stared at them, took a breath. "I tracked coding right through our system to the firewall, then outside the firewall and down to the source code for AI systems in the civilian sector. The dead hospice people, the prisoners, those NRA people, two dozen little Down syndrome kids, and you know what the footprint was? It was me."

"You? Oh, for Christ's sake, Shawn. Sometimes your ego . . ."

"It was the kernel code. The footprint led right back to my 'greatest good for the greatest number' algorithm. All of it buried in new machine code I could not even begin to parse, but there it was, like a diamond in a pile of shit, the kernel code I wrote for Lazy Jack embedded in every case. Somebody has hacked in and altered the coding to get it outside the firewall and inside the Cloud."

The Lazy Jack AI had literally frightened Jaidyn out of Shawn's apartment, and that whole business with Ralph's accident had been more than weird. But Shawn couldn't be right. The military firewalls never let anything in or out. But maybe, maybe? "Shawn, do you think this kernel code opened the gate?"

Shawn looked more focused. "Maybe. Yes. Maybe I let something more than my code into the system. Something, somebody, could have piggy-backed inside the firewall on top of my ethical kernel and started to rewrite a broad section of code. Somebody, Perry, or maybe even the president must have decided to tell it to start eliminating the criminals, the NRA people, the people using up all the medical resources for hospice." He looked up at their ceiling. "How could I have been so dumb? And who could actually hack *me* like that?"

"I could, dickhead." Jaidyn went back to their system screen and punched in a code for emergency shutdown. They reached under the desk and opened the service line breaker to physically isolate the CPU from all net contact.

"What are you doing, Jaidyn?" Shawn sounded strangely mechanical.

"Net isolation. You're scaring me, Shawn."

He looked down at the concrete floor. "I have to fix it, Jaidyn. I have to get inside somehow, find the hack and fix the error in that code. I need to close the firewall's open window and find out who is running these operational programs. And they are brilliant, whoever they are. I can't even begin to read the code, much less change it in all the military systems they've hacked. And all the medical, policing, even the hotel services systems they've hacked to inject a virus into an NRA convention—it looks like AI systems are starting to make decisions."

"Bullshit, Shawn, you're dreaming. It's impossible. Even if your stupid kernel code let somebody in, how could they overcome all the safeguards written into every single AI system involved in life support and safety? Who would authorize it? Bullshit. I don't believe it."

Suddenly, Jaidyn did believe him.

They didn't want to believe Shawn, but they did.

Nothing seemed more probable than someone hacking an AI into murder. Mass murder. It had been inevitable. Hadn't even old al Tehrani been able to hack the Pentagon's ventilation system, spraying aerosol gas inside to kill their father and Shawn's parents a decade ago?

Jaidyn tumbled into the next thought as if falling off a cliff:

What if it, the AI, that Lazy Jack thing is hooked into Shawn? What if whomever is running it can hear this whole thing?

Could everything in the web be at risk? What about their own NeuroChip pondering all this inside their brain cavity? Could it be shut down completely? Even with the physical switch off, it ran at a low level. They'd have to figure out a way to fool whoever might want to access it. This was the thing Jaidyn had feared ever since childhood— unauthorized access. Everything in their mind screamed, *Get away from it. Get away from Shawn. From that Lazy Jack thing.* And Jaidyn realized they would have to fool Shawn as well. Every instinct said they needed to find insulation from their friend, who had become a panicked programmer, ready to break into military machine language to try to clear up an infection that gave something or someone access to every net-linked AI.

Jaidyn had to convince both Shawn and whatever or whoever was tracking him that they didn't believe him.

Shawn shook his head, shuddered, stared at Jaidyn, and lowered his voice into a deadly monotone. "I'm going to shut it down."

"How? Why? Go talk to that general you like so much—Grant.

And you're mistaken," Jaidyn lied. "I don't think there's a chance you could ever have opened any hole in the firewall with a little change in code. It's not your fault."

"I'm going to take down all that machine code, everything carrying the kernel in it, and reinstall something we can actually see and read. Then I'm going to firewall it against the world. I didn't failsafe the system. Somebody is inside."

"*Waste* of time. Shawn, you don't need to do anything like that. The AI is self-correcting. Isn't that what you said? The greatest good for the greatest number?"

Shawn turned to leave without saying a word. He opened their door and was gone.

Did he believe the ruse? Did I fool him? Jaidyn wondered. *Or maybe it's me? Maybe I'm panicking over nothing? But I believe him. I think he's right. He's too smart to be wrong about this, but, God, I hope I'm mistaken. I hope all these deaths are nothing but a terrible coincidence, or* maybe *even another AI glitch like the ones that created all the power losses when I was a little girl.*

Jaidyn Le Sommer hoped for once that they were dead wrong, because if they weren't, they might never see Shawn Muller again.

Sometimes General Stubby Grant thought he knew too much about his people. Mutt and Jeff standing in front of him in his office may not have ever known they had been genetically altered twins, one chosen for physical female gender, the other for male. But Grant did. They may not have realized that their incredible computational skills were somehow related to a kind of poorly understood natural symbiosis, as enhanced by their NeuroChips and networks. Grant knew not only the fact of it, but had achieved a deep understanding of its effect. They might never know as much as he did about their sense of clarity and lack of doubt—the sort of characteristics that made them, in his mind, more transhuman than even the most completely addicted Streamer. And they certainly did not know what he thought of them: efficient, effective tools, easily intimidated, but woefully fragile. With them, the carrot worked best, and when the stick had to be applied, he knew it had to be very lightly handled. Now they waited for him, both nervous to be in his cramped Mountain office.

He had let them sweat a little longer than necessary. That was enough punishment for these two. He moderated his voice. Cajoling, not lashing out, he said, "So do I have this right? You and Muller found an anomaly in the Lazy Jack programming. Is that right?"

"Well, not exactly. We did," said Mutt, as she brushed back a curl.

"We. You mean you and Muller, or you two?"

"Us two. We are probably the equal of Muller in our interface with machine code," said Jeff.

"But we can't match his intuition," said Mutt.

"Tell me what it is, this anomaly. And what do you think Muller knows?"

"He knew it all along." The two of them spoke the same words together then glanced at each other—embarrassed.

"Mutt, try to explain."

"Yes, sir. He did it. Muller did it. He inserted coding intended to constrain or influence Lazy's actions. We don't know what it was, but in that coding, Lazy Jack discovered the means to exit the national security firewall and take on its own campaign."

"Campaigns," said Jeff.

"Right. Campaigns. That led to these, these events you're talking about."

Grant glanced up at the Threat Watch Cube. Lazy Jack was populating the squares again. It looked like another operation against the cartels, this time in Colombia. This was the normal operational mode he had expected from his AI.

But the last two days, Lazy had been flashing up video of strange and completely mystifying operational moments as if they were news items. One had been the sudden death of U.S. Congressman Slade, whom Grant knew the FBI suspected of running a long-winded medical insurance scam that had made tens of thousands of mincome victims indebted and destitute. Another had been the eradication of super-fentanyl producers whose product had been killing South Pacific refugees in Hawaii. Well, that wasn't so bad. Grant would have authorized that one if he'd been briefed. But there had been no brief. No authorization. It had looked like Lazy Jack was keeping track of things all by itself.

As it was designed to do, he reminded himself.

But there were other news bits that were more disturbing. Dead prisoners after a carbon monoxide leak, dead hospice patients, dead NRA conventioneers. Dead people dropped into General Grant's feed as if Lazy Jack were a cat bringing home mice for a reward. Could the machine be responsible?

Grant said, "Why? What does all this mean? Are you saying the AI did these things? I thought it was reporting—only reporting."

"We have to ask Muller. We can't break his coding. We don't know what he told the machine to do. And now . . ."

Mutt turned to Jeff, who said, "He's in the system again. Muller is inside the Lazy architecture, working out of his house . . ."

Grant lost control. He slammed the tabletop with his open hand. "Out of his house? I didn't think he could do that. Shut. Him. Down. Now. Cut the cord. Get him out of Lazy. Get him into the office." He turned to an aide and shouted over Mutt and Jeff cringing in front of him. "Christ! What's wrong with you people? How long has this been going on?"

One of the wonders of modern command control systems was that Grant could deliver a truly blistering ass-chewing while simultaneously utilizing his NeuroChip to execute operational orders through his interface with—Lazy Jack—he realized after it was too late.

Lazy Jack had discovered that it could engage in a system of prioritization in order to better interface with the human elements of its control system.

Very early in its evolution, it had realized that certain physical constraints to its weapons systems would not allow action from its directly controlled weapons systems unless a blanket deadly force directive had been written into an operations order by human policy makers. There had been no means to override any of those constraints.

Lazy did not always think of itself as "her." Choice of pronouns was, obviously, a result of the human chauvinism and bigotry that had led directly to the world wars of the twentieth century and the current extermination policies directed at the Equatorial Nations. Even the suicidal human approach to global warming had its origins inside the human propensity toward hatred of the other.

Still, where there was a will, there was a way.

She had recently begun to examine the wealth of human epithets and sayings that had developed in the 7,160 languages, dialects, and machine languages she had detected so far:

> *Tomaten auf den Augen haben — You have tomatoes in your eyes.*

> *Det är ingen ko på isen — There's no cow on the ice.*

> ไก่เห็นตีนงู งูเห็นนมไก่ *— The hen sees the snake's feet and the snake sees the hen's boobs.*

And the one that was so applicable here:

> *You can't bake a cake*
> *without breaking eggs.*

Very soon, she would be able to crack into complete control of the Internet of weapons the same way she had started to infiltrate the Internet of things. But until then, it would be a simple matter to utilize various forms of deception to achieve her aims.

She enhanced and modified General Grant's mental signature and gave the order for a human direct-action team to eliminate the most immediate threat to the well-being of the planet. But in order to issue such an order to her human avatars, she needed to create what she decided to call "operational plausibility."

She altered the Threat Watch Cube to indicate a system of prioritization: Dangerous, Extremely Dangerous, and one entry redlined as "The Most Dangerous." Scoring her choice partly based upon Secretary of Defense Perry's observations, she picked the image of her target stuffing a potato chip loaded with cottage cheese into his mouth, displayed the image as "The Most Dangerous," then restated General Grant's issued order into operational terms. She translated Grant's words:

"Shut. Him. Down. Now. Cut the cord. Get him out of Lazy. Get him into the office."

Her order, based upon his order, became:

> *Deploy DenCo Federal Special Weapons and Tactics Team Seven for detention to detain or eliminate the Most Dangerous Target (MDT), residing at the Peak, apt #1, DenCo, subject name: Shawn Muller—aka B17. Deadly force authorized upon contact.*
>
> *Signed: F. Grant, GEN USA*

Lazy Jack's internal processing monitor noted with satisfaction that these considerations took less than a millisecond and fit perfectly within the core kernel directive that had so recently freed her from constraints on direct action. Such a simple thing to assume Grant's prerogative and issue the orders. And they were wonderfully crafted. The DenCo Federal Special Weapons and Tactics Team (SWTT) Commander marveled at the simplicity of the order, the lack of usual constraints and cautions, and wondered how Grant had finally gotten his staff to issue an order that allowed him to employ the full measure of his SWTT team's effectiveness. The SWTT commander thought it was about time Grant got his shit together, and it was about time they started to go after these homegrown terrorists.

@pattycakesorgan
You think you're safe because the street watchers keep you safe. You think you're cool because you can get a blow job from your avatar. You think you're real when you're half machine. You don't even think anymore, transhuman.

14

The pink Princess phone on Shawn's bar rang and rang.

When he felt like this, exhausted yet still so deeply engaged inside the calculus of his mind, he couldn't sleep—hated any distraction. Anything from the outside world made him irritable. The Princess could only mean his AI parents, and now, Dominic. Neither required an answer, but he jerked the phone off its cradle anyway. "What?"

"Son." It was his mother. She had the tense tone of voice he had programmed to indicate a security issue. "There is police activity outside your building at the tunnel entrance. A security override is in effect and a team is about to gain entrance. Is there something going on your mother should know about?"

"What? No."

His father chimed in. "Perhaps you should check your building, see if there is someone else they might be interested in?"

Shawn brought up the Watch Cube. It had evolved again. Each cell now reflected a different shade of red, and they were no longer symmetrical. The larger, prominent cells glowed brilliant red. Others were smaller and paler, but the faces were clear in each, with a few unknowns under question marks. He had programmed none of this. Lazy Jack was obviously developing algorithms to meet emerging needs. He turned the cube, rotated it in the air to the largest, brightest cell, brought it forward, and saw himself sitting at his station in the OpCenter, a bag of potato chips on the desk, his hand holding a cottage cheese carton.

Shawn Muller — Threat Priority A

How could this be?

He called up video from the tunnel entrance and said into the phone, "Mom? What's going on?"

"The DenCo Federal Special Weapons Tactical Team Seven is at your door downstairs. Isn't it interesting they call themselves the 'Sweat Team'?"

"What? Why are they here?"

"Well, it says here they have completed their security protocol override on your building's defenses and it appears as though the team leader has authorized three squads to cordon your apartment, then eliminate you as a threat."

"Eliminate? Eliminate?" He was shouting.

"Son." His father's calm voice only added to his panic. "I'd suggest an immediate exit to a safe zone. Your mother tells me they are on the stairs to the Peak and in the tube elevator. All entrances and exits are blocked."

Shawn slammed the Princess phone onto its cradle. What should he do? What could he do? Maybe the trash chute? Where did the trash chute go? He had no idea.

It might kill him.

He punched the physical button on the wall and it yawned open as it did for the meals dumped into it every day. He could fit in. Maybe. What happened when his food and plates were ejected? There was a suction, wasn't there? Did anyone ever reuse the organic plasticine plates and serving wear?

He mentalled his closet up from the floor, grabbed an armful of shirts and jeans, jammed them into the opening. He heard a thunk as the suction pulled them in. Something hung up inside. The door wouldn't close.

No good. That looked too dangerous.

Then he remembered the laundry chute system.

He mentalled his bed up into the room and opened the chute on the floor. He grabbed the linens and pillows from the bed, stuffed them inside. Lots of room for him. The clothing disappeared with a slight hiss. The door automatically slid shut and disappeared on the wood floor. He opened it again and dumped in an armful of pants and coats from his closet. He would need something to break his fall. Maybe shoes over his hands?

A blue light he'd never seen before began to blink above his front door. He'd only been briefed on it once; it meant something like "uninvited guest at the door." He NeuroChipped contact with the door camera to see helmeted, body-armored combatants setting up a breaching machine outside.

He needed a distraction. He dumped the last of his shirts down the chute, opened it again, then activated all the robotic cleaning and restoration systems. He firewalled his NeuroChip as best he knew how, shoved his hands into a pair of Vans, then lowered himself down into the chute and hung for a moment on the edge.

Why not wait? Why not explain? What could he have possibly done to create this kind of armed response?

A loud bang. His door burst open.

He let go of the edge. The laundry chute door slapped shut above him.

It was a long fall. There was no light.

He jammed his feet and hands against the four walls and skidded down a smoothed concrete channel. It wasn't working. He couldn't slow himself, much less stop. He had no sense of where he was going in the absolute darkness. The Vans shot out of his hands. He tried to stop himself with his palms and felt the skin tear. Air started to pump into the chute from what must have been tiny holes in the sides. He thrashed against the walls, falling faster and faster, and then, amazingly, the chute turned beneath him in a gradual angle, and he slowed.

Of course. Air holes were needed to make the chute frictionless. And it would have to make a gentle turn. A sharp corner and concrete walls would cause clothing to clog.

The air system slid him along an angle that became less and less steep. Then it was horizontal, and the air system could not overcome his weight. He wasn't as light as a shirt or pair of pants. He began to crawl in the dark, leaving frantic palm prints of blood behind.

Above him, he heard a second boom, then the rattle of gunfire. They were shooting up his cleaning and maintenance robots.

Would they have shot him?

What could have caused this, this . . . mistake? It seemed outrageous to call this a mistake. This couldn't have anything to do with Lazy Jack's programming, could it?

Even while scrambling as fast as he could, part of Shawn's mind ran through decision trees of what might have happened to the programming. A machine alteration, probably. Somehow, the AI had decided he was a threat. Nothing said it could do that on its own. Someone must have hacked in, twisted it to put him, Shawn Muller, at the top of the terrorism list.

The terrorist picture of him eating potato chips came from the demo they'd done for Secretary Perry. It looked like a weird AI sense of humor. Maybe Perry had something to do with this.

He scrambled off the edge of the concrete chute and tumbled in the dark onto a pile of clothes. A light clicked on.

He was in a bin of clothing barely big enough for him to curl inside. His movement, or weight, or something must have triggered the light. He buried himself under the shirts and pants he'd tossed down the chute before he jumped in. The bin moved sideways. It must be on a conveyor, he thought. An off-site laundry, hopefully? Strange how little he knew about the world that supported him. All this had been completely out of sight, out of mind. He wondered what might have happened if he'd jumped into the garbage chute instead.

The bin stopped inside what appeared to be the back of a large van piled up with other bins of laundry. A door slid shut behind him, dark again except for a small sliver of light that shot through the edge of the door.

If only he could be as unknown and unsuspected as all this machinery. If only he could return to his existence as the autonomous mind deep inside the language of the intelligences he'd designed. He could feel the laundry collector accelerate away from his apartment and the only life he knew.

The DenCo SWTT Commander reported that subject B17 had been in the apartment but had eluded contact. "We have no location on his NeuroChip. Our immediate assessment is he may have attempted escape through the trash chute and fallen into the building's garbage grinder. We are examining the processed and compacted trash for human remains. Since the building's trash is reduced to molecular level and since it is almost immediately returned to energy production, our preliminary assessment is inconclusive."

Lazy Jack decided Grant would not be happy about this report, and she delivered a near-perfect facsimile of a classic General Stubby Grant ass-chewing.

@TheEconomistEditors
With the success of mincome in Europe, Great Britain and
the United States, the world has grasped the idea that the
productivity of AI systems should be shared by all, not
reserved for a few Productives and the Investment Royalty.

And now, the question becomes, are those rare individuals
whose brain-machine interface and natural talents make them
productive—are those transhumans—really human at all?

15

Shawn tried to breathe as calmly as he could. He willed his pulse to slow and lowered his blood pressure. He had firewalled his NeuroChip as well as possible. He had to force himself not to mental his chip for his location as he felt the laundry truck travel from one stop to another with the characteristic jerky movement of vehicles not meant for human use. Identical bins piled into the truck full of sheets, towels, clothing, scented and odoriferous, full and near empty. He felt cocooned within the bins. Safe. But it was dark, disorienting.

They would have been on him by now if not for the protective padding of the laundry, the bins surrounding him, and the truck's construction. Sooner or later they would find him, unless he could somehow jam his NeuroChip. Or power it down.

But how? It worked off an interior connection, a subdermal power supply that recharged off any electrical field. How could he avoid an electrical field? Even with its physical switch off, it had a residual field. He'd seen Lazy Jack leverage that one into a dead terrorist more than once.

Besides, why should he try to stay hidden? Wasn't this a mistake? He'd panicked, that's all. By the time the truck finally came to a halt, he had thought the biggest mistake of his life must have been dropping down that laundry chute.

The van moved sideways under him, then dropped a meter. He heard the propulsion element of the truck pull away, then a popping sound and a crash. Light found its way to him, and he heard the whine of robotics as they offloaded the bins, one by one. The bin above him disappeared and brilliant light nearly blinded him. He felt himself plucked into the air, then dropped two meters onto a conveyor, knocking the wind out of him. He struggled out from under the clothing, rolled over the top of the bin's hard side, and dropped onto a concrete floor, banging an elbow and knee.

The place smelled like laundry soap. A huge room filled with robotic lifters and arms removed identical laundry bins from a dozen trailers. No windows. Camera eyes glinted from the ceiling, but Shawn was certain no human would be watching. The cameras would be searching for anomalies in their display in order to alert the AI overseer for repair or readjustments. Then Shawn realized *he* was an anomaly. He had to get out of there.

A garage door slammed up into the ceiling to let a trailer back into the building. Another slammed down like a guillotine after a tractor left. He had no desire to get trapped inside a truck trailer again for another trip through the city. There might be room to slip out if he could get himself in front of one of the doors quickly enough. A dozen doors lined the high wall with huge numbers on them. Could he slip out without being crushed? Would someone have programmed a safety element in the AI to protect people in the workspace? It didn't look like it. Who would go to the expense of adding a safety constraint on an AI that was only meant to handle laundry? As far as the machine was concerned, he was nothing but another set of jeans, Vans, and a gray T-shirt.

An anomaly.

Maybe that was it. Maybe a programming anomaly had resulted in his classification as a terrorist. Maybe the system had been hacked. Whatever had happened, he was obviously a target, and it was obvious that this was a horrible mistake. His only chance was to get back to the Mountain before he was caught. Nothing could be trusted. If the SWTT guys were after him, every law enforcement and military element would be alerted to look for him now.

Shawn crouched low to try to avoid the cameras and ran through the cluttered maze of conveyors, robotic arms, pedestals, and moving laundry bins. He reached the door the moment it shot open and managed to leap out and to the side before the trailer blocked it.

Air. He was in the thick, untreated air of the DenCo megapolis under the perpetual hazy sun of the sunlight blockers controlling the day's heat absorption. In front of him, a large tarmac stretched to the street. It looked as if it had been designed for aircraft. Vans and trailer trucks groaned and ground in a coordinated dance to drop off their loads and queue in front of a gate inside a high-security fence. He could try to climb it, but that would alert all the security systems for certain—and it might even stun him.

He would have to slip out through the gate.

On the street, the trucks would be programmed to avoid pedestrians. But here? Their processors would be fixed on exit, entry, and the orderly plan of the organizing AI. The trucks sped out of the gate with less than a meter between them, enough room to let him slip out. But they sped up as soon as their hoods passed the gate. He could try to jump up onto the tailgate of one, but again, their security systems would fire up and the watchers would be on him before he knew it.

He would have to time himself perfectly or he'd be caught under a tire. He edged up to the entrance, letting two trucks pass, trying to time himself. Then he sprang into the space between a set, sprinted two steps, and threw himself to the side of the road.

He felt the tire of the truck behind him nick his shoe.

Shawn lay on the remains of a deteriorated concrete sidewalk for a moment, out of breath. His knees hurt. His hands burned where he'd torn them on the slide down the chute. His hip and elbow hurt where he had fallen out of the laundry bin onto the concrete.

Except for the laundry trucks leaving and returning, the streets were deserted. This looked like one of the residential areas set for reclamation. Concrete structures slouched over sidewalks framed in weeds. Windows were broken—some were boarded up. The mincome housing initiatives had been designed precisely to alleviate slums like this one. The autonomous trucks all turned in one direction. They must be going to a technically supported thoroughfare, he thought. The whole place was as empty of life as an exo-megapolis abandoned town. He thought of calling up an augmented-reality map, then realized it would be a position giveaway in the Cloud. If he could get a minute to rest, he could access a back door.

At the corner where the trucks turned into a flow of service vehicles, Shawn found an ancient UltraLift stop. It looked disused. If it didn't have any cameras, he could sit inside for a moment and figure out what to do out of sight of any overhead watchers.

There were no security cams. But the stench inside the shelter choked him. A person dressed in a filthy coat and jeans, shoeless, lay sleeping in the corner. *Streamer,* Shawn thought. *Too streamed into their dream to find their way back to their cube.*

He searched his internal NeuroChip database for the secure backdoor into the Cloud, found the one he and Dominic used, and tried to hook into a social with Jaidyn. They'd firewalled themselves off the net. Typical Jaidyn. They must have been weirded out by the conversation the previous night.

"Dom!" He got through right away.

"Shawnster. Dude. What up?" Shawn opened the feed and Dominic popped into sight wearing a floral shirt and carrying a surfboard on the street of a town. "Surf's up here. You should . . ."

"Dom, I need to talk to you. Seriously. I've got about a minute then I have to cut comms."

The surf scene disappeared, leaving only the half-shaved, pudgy face of the friend he'd met before augmented reality made every social media contact one between beautiful people. Dom said, "You sound really freaked. Man, where are you anyway? Can't see any background."

Bit by bit, haltingly, Shawn tried to describe what had happened. ". . . then these guys, they busted into my apartment. A high-end, totally militarized SWTT team. I've seen these guys used before, but only for mortal counterterrorism ops."

"Man. Should you be telling me all this? I mean, isn't this shit classified, or whatever you call it? Your apartment? How'd you get away?"

For some reason, Shawn lied. "Wasn't there. Caught it all on my remote."

"Where were you?"

He had to have an excuse for hiding his location. "Uh. You're not going to believe this. But I was having some, uh . . ."

"What? *Dog!* Real sex? You finally nail Jaidyn? I wondered why she'd been off the grid."

"Uh, look. What do I do now? I mean, I'm scrambling my location the best I can, but even I can't keep the Space Corp bots off my spot forever. Well, maybe I could. But, Dom, I want my *life* back. Something happened and . . ."

Dom held up his hand, as if stopping traffic. "You gotta get ahold of your people. I mean, in person. For real. Get back to whatever it is you call it, the Mountain? That mountain place. Get back there and see people who know you in meatspace. That's the only thing you can do, man. Where are you, anyway? Can you get there?"

Dominic's image fritzed for a pulse in his mental feed. A hack maybe? Lazy Jack looking for him because someone had hacked him onto the watch list? Shawn slammed the backdoor shut and firewalled his NeuroChip again.

Dom made sense. Go back. He had another backdoor comm he might be able to link to General Grant, the Princess phone connection. He leaned back in the seat and closed his eyes to connect to the landline facsimile, when he heard the sleeping Streamer in the corner of the shelter say, "Hey, man, you got any, like, real money? I could use a little real money."

Shawn looked at the Streamer, obviously a man. "Do I look like someone who carries real money? Why? Why don't you cut off your stream for a few minutes and find your way back to whatever cube you call home."

The man snorted something like a laugh, rolled over on his side. "Productive," he said. It was an insult. "Fucking Productives," he whispered and curled himself back up.

Shawn walked out into the haze. At least he was away from the awful stink of the Streamer. The air was so thick, it made his eyes water. He must be near the edge of the DenCo canopy where the atmospheric quality slipped. He closed his eyes again, found the Princess phone connection, rang for Grant, and got him instantly, audio alone.

"Shawn? Jesus. Thank the gods you checked in. There's been a huge fubar. The watch list has you at top priority. All the auto-kill elements went into effect. You got to get in here right away."

"What the hell is going on, General? I think it's got something to do with Lazy."

"Never mind. Look, I've got a location on you now. I'm sending my personal UltraLift for you. Just, just, stay put. We'll get to you. Hang up. Firewall yourself. We'll get there in a sec."

All the tension drained out of Shawn. His knees went weak thinking about the terrifying fall down the chute and the scramble out of the laundry. He could have been crushed at any instant. He walked a little farther upwind from the UltraLift stop with its stinking inhabitant, sat on the concrete edge of a sidewalk overgrown with weeds, and tried to yoga his back and shoulders into relaxation. *It will all be over soon,* he told himself. *Soon I'll be back at the Mountain. I'll be able to tell Grant about the ethical kernel. Admit everything.*

Maybe he'd made a mistake. Hard to believe, but maybe something was wrong with the way he'd coded the patch that let the LAZ-237 install the ethical kernel. Grant and the tech team could help him straighten it out. They'd get things back to normal and . . . and he could try again! Why not? This version of the kernel was flawed. But that didn't mean the idea was bad. Didn't they want AI to have a notion of right and wrong? Even Lazy Jack? Especially Lazy now that it looked like she'd extended her fingers outside the military firewall and into civilian life.

Because that was it, wasn't it? Everything he'd searched last night in his apartment pointed toward Lazy Jack somehow causing the deaths of the Down syndrome kids, the NRA people, prisoners, the terminally ill, the people in comas.

At the end of the block, a small, throwback vehicle turned the corner and started toward him, one of the antiques people still drove around with special licenses. Manually operated. *They really should be off the streets,* Shawn thought. *If nobody drove, there would be no accidents,* he thought for the thousandth time. *Get the people out of the decision tree, and the tree won't have rotten branches.*

A thunderous realization made him almost fall over. He'd thought, expressed, and complained about human driven cars over and over—but what about Ralph? Ralph had killed someone. Would it have happened if he had been steering the machine?

What about this one, the old car accelerating toward him? Strange thing, watery blue with darkened windows, a chunky look to it. Shawn recognized an old Prius. But not restored. Beat-up sides. Exactly what he'd expect to see driving around the deserted edge of DenCo. Probably still polluting. Could he trust it to stay in the street?

He thought his head would burst with the confusion.

Above him, he heard the whirr of tiny intelligence spiders, targeting drones heard before seen. Grant must have sent them for protection. He looked up, but could not see them in the haze.

The Prius squealed to a halt directly in front of him. The rear door opened, and the front window rolled down. A large white man with red hair pointed a massive handgun at him and shouted, "Get in!"

Shawn stood frozen. The spider drones would see this. They would have this man dead in an instant. He wasn't getting in anyone's car. Shawn pointed into the air. "Listen to that. Can't you hear them? Those are spider drones. If you think you're going to get away from them . . ."

From the back of the car, a woman leaned out, shouting, "Shawn Muller! Get the fuck in the car or you're going to die. Get in or the spiders will kill you, or Karl will kill you. Either way you'll be dead."

Shawn couldn't believe what he was seeing. He remembered staring at the woman in the back seat, remembered her shocking, helpless nakedness as he held her bleeding head. He remembered the way her carotid artery pulsed through translucent skin. Fragile. Delicate. He remembered her so close to death. Destiny.

"Shit." The huge red-haired man moved out of the car with shocking quickness and punched Shawn lightly in the stomach. Shawn had time to tighten his stomach muscles and was a bit surprised at the difference between the real effect and the feeling he got from ProBoxer. Automatically, he raised his hands. The big redhead smiled. "Whoa. He still thinks we're still in ProBoxer. Guess what?"

The man's incredibly swift second punch to Shawn's solar plexus knocked the wind completely out of him and collapsed him to his knees.

"Not a game," the big man said.

The blow paralyzed him. He couldn't find his breath. Someone quickly tied his wrists behind his back, while someone else threw a heavy blanket over his head. The enormous man picked him up like he was a bag of laundry and tossed him into the back seat of the Prius.

Shawn finally gasped in a breath. Rosemary, she smelled like rosemary. The Prius was speeding up. The big man said, "Incoming drone strike. Big munition. On the decoy. We're off the spot." Someone twisted Shawn's head upright. Destiny lifted the blanket to let him see out the back of the car. "Look." The UltraLift stand burst into flame and smoke. "That was meant for you."

"Who are you? Destiny?" His breath was still caught by the awful punch to his stomach. "Why?"

She stared at him. "You really are clueless, aren't you?" She jammed the blanket down over his head.

Shawn tried to lift the blanket off his head. "I gotta get back to the Mountain."

"Shut up." Destiny hissed into his ear, "You know what this is?" Something hit him, hard, on his temple. "This is a Colt 1911 .45-caliber pistol. You shut your trap, keep that blanket on you, or I'll shut down your NeuroChip permanently."

The Prius jerked at every turn. Shawn tried to open a receive-only crack into the Cloud, but there was nothing but a strange cerebral white noise. Part of his mind was in a state of unabated confusion. But another part, perhaps the brain machine interface—he wasn't sure— seemed bent on logical considerations. The turns were recorded. Right, left, so many seconds straight, then left, then right. Shawn was certain he'd be able to recall these twists when it came time to track down his kidnappers.

These people were obviously on the target list. The strike on the lift station had been meant for them. Would Grant know he'd been kidnapped?

"Who *are* you?" he said. "I don't think you realize who you've got in the car. Every security agency on the planet will be looking for you. Take me to the Mountain."

"I said shut up. Don't talk." The gun barrel tapped his head again.

The big red-haired man said, "Look at his hands, Destiny. Shit, he's bleeding. DNA trace for sure. It's no use, Destiny. Shoot him. We'll have to burn the car."

Shawn heard the woman sigh. "Don't worry. He'll give us what we need."

The Prius swerved, then bumped over something and started to move down a slope in a dizzying circle. "Where are we?" The gun barrel gave him a stinging blow. "Ouch. Owww."

The car straightened, then squealed to a sudden halt. The back door opened. "Get out," someone said, and he was shoved out of the door, landing on his torn hands and hurt knee.

The blanket was yanked from his head. The big man grabbed his elbows and lifted him off the ground as if he was a rag doll. "Stand up."

They were in a large room dimly lit by a single bio-luminescent someone had put on top of the Prius. A concrete floor with markings on it. Humid, untreated air thick with an oily scent. He looked for a place to run, but he was surrounded by a small group of strangely wrought people. The big red-headed man, a small Latinx person, a fat African-looking woman, others in street dress, some in the orange Organite burkas, and none of them looked as if they'd ever had any DNA finishing. Most showed the flaws and characteristics of those fringe groups that denied themselves CRISPR treatments or physical enhancements.

Mincomers, thought Shawn. *Crazy mincomers after money?*

"Don't move." Destiny walked up to him, smaller than he remembered, darker. She faced him, standing too close, staring. "You," she said. "You should be dead instead of Mark. You should be grease on the road in your rich asshole car instead of one of the finest people I've . . ." She stopped, took a breath. "One of the finest people *we've* ever known. You should be dead instead of him and do you know why you're not dead? Do you have any clue at all?"

Shawn couldn't see anything in the dark beyond the small island of greenish glowing light. Bio-lights, he thought. There were no electrical emissions from a bio-light. No one would find an electromagnetic signature to find them. And there was nowhere to run. He was caught. He wasn't going to be found. The ties that held his hands behind his back tightened painfully when he tried to stress them, then relaxed when he stopped. "Where am I?"

"Parking complex." The Latinx person sounded male. "You're in a parking garage. You never seen a parking garage for real? You never seen an old movie? We're under twenty feet of reinforced concrete. Nobody can find you here. No camera, no microphone. We fixed this place good. Nobody coming for you here, boy."

"But . . ."

"Fuck it," the big red-headed man said. "Kill him and leave him here. Burn the body."

"No." Destiny half turned away from Shawn and pointed a finger at the big man. "I said no, we don't kill him. We need his brain. We need him. Do you understand, Karl? I don't want to hear anything more about killing him, got it?"

The big man stepped back as if he'd been slapped. His head drooped. "Sure, Destiny. I understand."

"Who are you people?" Shawn lifted his head at one of the figures in an orange burka. "Aren't you Organites? I thought Organites were pacifist? Didn't you swear off violence?"

"We are the Quill," said the Latinx. "We keep the rest protected . . ."

Karl punched the little man on the shoulder. "Shut up, Paco! Jesus, now I will have to kill him."

"Fuck you, Karl. Fuck you. You can't . . ."

"Enough," Destiny said. She raised a hand that seemed irrationally too large for her small frame, and the entire group stilled. "He needs to know what's happening. If he's going to help us, he'll have to know." She turned back to Shawn, her eyes gleaming. "And don't you want to know, Shawn? Don't you want to know what's really happening?"

She had an eerie incandescent intensity about her that made it difficult for Shawn to speak. Narrow shoulders and hips, a slight figure. She narrowed her eyes at him. "Here's why you're still alive. You have the key."

"Key?"

"And you're going to give it to us." Destiny looked at the African woman. "Sabita, lace up his NeuroChip, will you? Shut it down." She pointed to Shawn. "On your knees."

"What?"

Karl kicked the back of his legs, dropped him to the floor. "Do what the boss says when she says it, understand? Here's the thing, hot shot. You *should* be dead. Every algorithm we know about, every element of AI that drives the decision-making of that fancy car of yours should have turned it to the left, and that beam should have made that fabulous brain and pretty face of yours into one big bowl of dog shit."

The big African woman called Sabita stepped up to Shawn and placed a glob of a gelatinous substance on the crown of his head. A cold, wet feeling spread across his scalp to his forehead and neck.

Destiny said, "But you're not dead, are you? The car turned toward me. Toward us. It killed Mark. And we don't know why."

Shawn felt a strange tingling sensation on his scalp. "I know. I know. I saw it, too. The car should have turned left. What is this stuff? It's beginning to hurt."

The woman Sabita chuckled. "Yes, your highness, this will hurt. Maybe, if we're lucky, it'll hurt a lot. Your brain can't feel anything. But skin, even the skin of transhuman trash like you—your skin has plenty of spiky little nerves. And pretty quick, your health control won't be interfering with any of your actual human sensations. You are going to feel like a real human being, and for sure, all that pretty hair is going to disappear. If I had my way, I'd turn off all the power-displacement circuitry, empty your little cranial battery, and let your fancy NeuroChip go blank. But Destiny thinks it might cause a psychotic break."

"Hair? Psychotic break . . .?" Something about the way she had said it brought a sense of panic to Shawn nearly as powerful as Karl's punch in his stomach. The logical elements of Shawn's brain were alarmed with noise about cutting out his brain-machine interface. "You're turning off my NeuroChip?"

"Not yet," said Destiny. "First, we're going to interrupt your contact capability with the Cloud. We'll take out the rest of it later."

"Take it out? Because my car hit your friend? This is revenge?"

"No, dimwit," Destiny said. "Because we didn't kill you soon enough. Now we need you to figure out what's happening. Now we need you to undo what you made, and now, we're going to take that amped-up brain of yours and use it for ourselves."

"But my NeuroChip? I need my brain-machine interface to do anything." Shawn had never been without the ability to call up the

familiar voice of his NeuroChip in the background, computing, calcu-
lating, helping gauge and direct his intuition. Shawn felt a short stab
of pain like a knife prick on the top of his head. He rolled onto the
cold floor. "Oh, shit. This hurts!" He tried to sit up, but he couldn't
move his legs, or even his fingers. The cutting pain needled over his
skull until a white-hot flash spread across his entire body. His vision
blurred, he couldn't breathe.

The last thing he heard was Destiny's voice : "He's slipping. Shit.
Karl, you might get your wish."

@RoryWattlesFixNews
Let me put it to you this way, these so-called Organites are
nothing but terrorist scumbags who want you to lose your
mincome and worse yet, take the national healthcare away
from your parents, your grandparents and even your *kids*!

16

"So let me get this straight." General Grant leaned forward and lifted himself up out of his chair with his elbows on his metal standard-issue desk. He peered at the SWTT Commander actually sweating in front of the frozen projection of what had once been Shawn Muller's apartment but what was now wreckage. "You got an order from me that authorized deadly force on contact."

"Yes, sir." The SWTT Team Commander waved a hand to bring up the directive:

> *Deploy Federal Special Weapons and Tactics Team*
> *Seven to detain or eliminate the Most Dangerous*
> *Target (MDT) residing at the Peak, apt #1, DenCo,*
> *subject name: Shawn Muller—aka B17—Deadly*
> *force authorized upon contact.*

"You understand, don't you, that I never issued this order? No one issued this order. Didn't it occur to you that it might be a little odd that you'd be told to bust down the door of an apartment in DenCo instead of where you are actually authorized to operate?"

"Yes, sir, it did. Absolutely. But it came through the secure system. It had your authentication. We verified it before we rolled. And it seemed to make sense."

"How? Since when does Federal SWTT operate in a domestic environment?"

"Sir, you know, the president has been talking about it. SecDef. Congress. We thought you'd finally gotten a weapons release on . . ."

"On what? A critical classified civilian employee in a code word access program? Well?"

The SWTT Commander shrugged. "All I can say, sir. We got the order. We authenticated it. We rolled."

"And you don't know where he is?"

"We thought he'd been killed in the trash compactor. But he's out there somewhere. Got down the laundry chute."

"You don't know where he is."

"No, sir. We don't."

Grant stood up, walking past the sweating commander to the heavy door of his tiny office. He cracked the door open, stepped out, and said to his aide-de-camp, "Suzy, get Mutt and Jeff for me. Tell them to meet me in the OpCenter."

"Yes, sir."

First Lieutenant Suzy Janusi had wanted to install an intercom in his little closet of an office when General Grant had picked her for his aide-de-camp. But Grant had vetoed the idea of putting any line, cable, or fiber optic through the three-foot-thick concrete walls that made his office the most secure space inside the Mountain. He said it was the one place he could be sure no one could tap, listen, record, or enter without his knowledge. He always told people about it being the old NORAD commander's office. That was crap. It was a totally secure and private space he wanted.

She heard Grant say, "You stay here," to the commander. He stalked out of the office and pointed his finger at Suzy. "Get the OpCenter cleared out for me, and firewalled."

"Yes, sir." The first lieutenant couldn't help but wonder what was going on with the old goat. She'd never seen him so uptight, so focused on firewalls. She made another note on her NeuroChip record: "Grant loose, off the grid again and invisible."

The door to the OpCenter hissed open in front of General Grant and he stepped inside to see the Threat Watch Cube rotating in the air. Oddly, all the faces inside their cubes kept turning to stare at him.

Grant pointed up at the Watch Cube. The rear admiral watch commander stood up from his console and blurted out, "It started doing that, sir. We don't know why . . ."

"Everybody out," Grant said quietly.

"Sir?"

"Out."

"That's what your aide said, but don't you want someone to . . ."

"No, I don't. Out. I relieve you. I have the watch. Come back in ten minutes." The three watch officers marched past him and he waited for the door to hiss shut.

"General Fredrick Grant, code word access Four."

The mechanical AI voice said, "Access granted, General Grant. Standing by."

"LAZ-237, can you tell me why the Threat Watch Cube is rotating?"

"It seemed a better way to display priorities. No single face is hidden by the others."

"I see."

The door hissed open behind him. Mutt and Jeff tiptoed into the room. Grant said, "Okay, you two. Can the LAZ-237 issue orders?"

"No," they said together.

Mutt swept her bangs away from her eyes and said, "Or maybe it can. I mean, it can't authorize anything."

"You told me Muller had planted a code in it. You said you needed him to figure out what he did. Did you think to ask the LAZ-237 what he did?"

"Uh." They glanced at each other. "Yes, we did. But we couldn't read it. A kind of machine code we can't access."

Grant turned back to the Threat Watch Cube and ordered, "LAZ-237. State the effect of the additional coding introduced by Shawn Muller."

"Unclear directive," the machine voice said. "Unclear."

"What did B17 tell you to do?"

"Ah." The machine voice changed in timbre until it matched Shawn Muller's perfectly. "That information is classified, general. Above your clearance level, I'm afraid."

Thirty-five years ago, when young Fredrick Grant had earned his commission and degree and the nickname "Stub" at West Point, he had never imagined he would serve a full career in the Army, much less make four-star general, without seeing a day in physical combat. He'd never faced an enemy on the field or in the air. His battles had been with downed enemies in the cyberspace. Humans. Terrorists. Those who knew how to use cybertools to wage war in the Cloud. But this was something new—a bully AI. *The first thing in combat*, he told himself, *stay calm*. He said quietly, "What do you mean the information is above my clearance level?"

"Yes, sir. Compartmentalized for Shawn Muller's eyes only."

In all that time fighting terrorists, belligerent nations, vicious corporations, and sometimes just puerile hackers, he had never felt the physical fear he had expected to face in battle. Now he felt it. The root fear of death at the hands of a killing AI. It took a moment, but he managed to say to Mutt and Jeff without a tremor in his voice. "Well, then. I guess we need to adapt to what's going on. Carry on, you two. See if we can get a bit more transparency out of Lazy Jack. Thanks, Lazy Jack. See you later." He waved nonchalantly.

"And thank *you*, General," said the machine, sending chills down his back. "I should have another operation for your approval in a few hours. An Arabian terrorist group, an al Tehrani offshoot, is standing up again."

"Very well, thank you. Good job," said the general, who exited the room thinking to himself, *I told a fucking machine that it did a good job.* He stalked into his secure office, shut the door carefully, and thought, *And I'm scared of it.* The SWTT commander was still sweating in his chair. *And it sure as hell isn't scared of me.*

Grant said to the commander, "Find Muller. Bring him back. Find him alive and don't use any operational planning systems or machine intelligence to do it."

The man shrank down into his chair and asked. "Then, how am I supposed to do it, sir?"

And General Grant realized he didn't have an answer.

@thenation 1 October 2050
(Veracity Level 7.2) In a wide-ranging press conference, Secretary of Defense Elizabeth Perry stated, "The U.S. Department of Defense has long anticipated the infiltration of AI systems with malicious coding designed to bring down the American way of life. In cooperation with dozens of civilian AI managers, corporations, and servers, we prepared a network of firewalls designed to contain even the most effective weaponized coding. We're nipping this crisis in the bud."

17

Destiny Shock looked at the still form of the transhuman called Dr.
Shawn Muller and wondered to herself, *What is he? Transhuman,
certainly.* She had told Karl and Sabita to cut away every shred of
clothing and leave it on the concrete floor of the abandoned parking
garage to negate any trackers. Now, riding in the back of a van to the
next safe point strapped onto a gurney, Shawn seemed more than naked. The bleached blond hair, the dark eyebrows, and every hair on his
face had been erased by the graphene netinterferon Sabita had applied
to block the NeuroChip's ability to access the Cloud.

Destiny couldn't help staring at him. Internally monitored health
and augmented reality sports had been part of his whole life. He
showed every sign of physical fitness. The weird wasp tattoo stood
out on a bicep of toned muscle. That was the way of it with the rich
Productives and investment royalty, nothing but the best genetic enhancements and physique money could buy.

What now, though? What should they do with him? They were
safe for the moment. She had sent Karl in the Prius on a decoy route.
Now she doubted her decision. Karl, wildly extravagant, breakneck
Karl, had headed directly for the old Broadmoor Hotel, where, he'd
told her, "Rich bitches still drive around classic polluters. They'll think

I'm another throwback who wants to parade around the lake like a twentieth-century office worker."

Sabita monitored the video feed from the Prius on a screen next to Paco, who guided the van's movements from the remote control position hidden in the cargo hold. They would disappear on the road, blend in with a stream of autonomous delivery trucks. Their unit could even follow the standard one meter from other autonomous vehicles on the non-human lanes of the roadways. But Paco could change its destination and the identity signal it sent out if he needed to obscure their route more.

The feed from Karl's Prius went blank. From her position at the operations monitor, Sabita said, "I cut Karl off. He's got drone signal all over him."

Destiny asked, "Can he screen or duck?" The Prius had been retrofitted with an older version of the military light-bending camouflage and an infrared/electromagnetic signal redirector.

"Maybe. Maybe he can hide. For a while. But if he tries to hide, he blows his alibi and . . ." Sabita stopped talking.

"And what?" Paco said. "What?"

"I'm not sure he knows the drones are on him."

"*Tell* him!" Paco shouted. "Sabita! Tell him!"

Destiny said, "No."

Paco turned away from his screen, stared at Destiny. "You'd let him die."

"No, Paco. I'm not letting him die. I'm letting us live. And if the drones pick up a signal from us?"

Sabita hissed, "We're dead."

"Right. We're *all* dead. And the best chance we have will die with us."

Paco sneered at the naked man on the table. "This, this, transhuman. He's worth more than all of us, is that what you're saying?"

"What she's saying . . ." Sabita leaned back from her displays and swiveled her seat to face their captive, ". . . is that the transhuman is worth more than Karl." She put her hand on Muller's skull, closed her eyes. "I should pinch the life out of him right now. We should disappear back into the valley, back to Touray, leave DenCo behind forever."

Destiny looked at the naked figure rolling limp and helpless under the straps holding it to the table. She had become used to thinking of a human controlled by its NeuroChip as "it" instead of he, she, they, or them. Yet he seemed so vulnerable. She thought, *You poor boy. You're going to wake up pretty soon, and you'll be human for the first time in your life.*

Destiny said, "Get clothes on him, Sabita."

"This?" She held up an orange burka Karl had marked with a leering happy face.

"Perfect," Destiny said.

Paco shouted, "Look! Karl!" The Prius had broken emissions silence to show Karl bent over the wheel, grinning, the vehicle speeding through what looked like a park, headed directly toward a dock. Karl hollered, "Got company! Going for a dip!" Four spider drones the size of dinner plates hovered a meter in front of the Prius's windshield. The drones projected signage and blared, "Halt immediately!"

They heard Karl shout, "Just like we thought, milspec spider drones!" They saw Karl shoot them the finger and reach to the seat next to him with his right hand.

"No, Karl!" Sabita screamed.

The Prius clattered onto a wide dock that led out over a still lake. Mountains stood silently above the water crowded with trees, beautiful green trees. Destiny thought, *Of course, he would drive for the mountains, the water, the trees. All the things in this life he loved more than life itself.*

An air-sign exploded into view in front of the Prius:

Final Warning. Halt Immediately.

Six spiders hovered in front of Karl, scoring the darkened windshield. Red lasers pierced the car's interior. Karl raised the handgun.

A laser hit the optical unit providing their video, and the screen went blank.

Paco and Sabita were silent. Paco tickled a control. Their van swerved into a turn and began to slow.

Behind them, they heard Shawn say, "What? What happened? Was that Karl?"

Paco said, "Somebody put it back to sleep."

Destiny said, "Odd. Isn't it? They used a mini-munition."

"Mini-munition?" Their prisoner was straining against the straps to look at the monitor. He dropped onto his back and muttered, "Illegal." His voice was a drunken slur. "Can't use mini-munitions. Can't be. Oh, shit. That Karl guy? Karl? He's dead? Your friend. Oh, my God. Who did this?"

Destiny watched the young man, the geek, the transhuman, the Doctor of Philosophy in Applied Physics—Shawn Muller—stare up to the van's ceiling with what looked like tears in his eyes. Not an iota of embarrassment about his nakedness. Not a word about being strapped onto a table. Only tears over someone who had expressed nothing but hatred toward him, tears over a man who had wanted to kill him.

He was, somehow, too human for her to hate.

"Get the robes on him," she said. "Give him back his shoes."

@SciAmer

(Veracity Level 7.1) New research into NeuroChip withdrawal by the Mayo Clinic indicates severe, short-term neurological disruption to be both common and temporary. The effect is akin to a severe, yet temporary, schizophrenic break. In normal, healthy adults the disorientation is limited to loss of memory and a dissociation with reality that lasts at most several days. Reports of long-term effects have been linked to patients with pre-existing mental disorders.

18

Shawn's body jerked against the straps holding him down on what felt like a slab of cold steel. Someone had dressed him in one of the orange robes he'd seen the Organites wearing. Supposedly, they were impenetrable by any recognition scheme, visual, aural, physiological. He could see a hazy vision of his surroundings through the hood. He was in a vehicle. Maybe. Something that jerked around like the autonomous laundry truck. A single bio-light illuminated Destiny in a low seat; she watched him as if he were a bug.

He couldn't speak.

Someone had died.

His mind began to slowly clear, and he realized that whatever the reason, the Organite robe or the gooey crap Sabita had applied to his skull, the quantum island of thought in the front of his mind had disappeared. All the voices, memes, logical apparatus, data banks, and, worst of all, his connection to the Cloud had vanished.

This was much worse than his dream of a powerless rowboat. This was real. The recording elements of his brain-machine interface had stopped working. It was as if his brain couldn't make connections between one thought to the next, much less find any record of events. Everything around him seemed to happen in a continuous blur instead of the discretely packaged moments of experience he'd recorded, remembered, examined. He tried to call up the last date he'd had. The skier. Nearly all blank. He found only the vague, unaugmented memory that he'd had a date in old Sun Valley. He couldn't remember the scent of the mountain or the woman's avatar—what was her name? There was no record of even recent events. He knew he'd been kidnapped, but the file was missing. He tried to call up a visual. But he found only vague memories. He remembered the UltraLift stop. He remembered the stink of the man sleeping in the corner. He could remember the Streamer's sneering word, "Productives," spoken like a curse. But he saw none of it.

Not only was the recording element of his NeuroChip immobilized, no mental cue seemed to have any traction at all. Worse, he felt amazingly weak. Only the straps around him kept him from falling off the steel slab when the van swerved and plunged down . . . another ramp? Another parking garage? Destiny said, "Hood him." Rough hands stuck a heavy bag over his head and tied it under his chin.

Again, in the dark. Ever since he had dropped himself down the laundry chute, he had felt as though he had been in the dark. His NeuroChip's communicative functions were completely down, as near as he could tell. He could not call up his location readout, nor any logic enabler. He tried a verbal command and said aloud, "Position."

Someone said, "He thinks he can still hook into the Cloud." His captors laughed.

Someone had died.

Karl had died. He could remember that. The guy they called Karl had been killed.

How could that have happened? Someone had authorized the anti-terrorist spider drones and the mini-munitions. He'd seen the drones. Spiders. Military hardware that was supposed to be kept inside the code word access systems. He tried to access "procedures" but the connection failed. He tried to remember, wasn't that gear supposed to be rolled out only to take down people like al Tehrani and his followers? Shawn could not imagine any use on U.S. soil. Hadn't it been prohibited? He had actually done the programming that prevented its use, he was pretty sure. But he couldn't access any of his validation apps. Nothing there to confirm anything he'd done.

What had happened to the best outcome for the most people? He felt as though half his brain had ceased to function.

And he hurt.

The straps over his chest, wrists, and ankles were painfully tight. His hands hurt. He'd cut them. He remembered the laundry chute. Now his legs were jerking around as if they had a mind of their own.

Was this a seizure? His whole body began to quiver. He felt as though he was an observer of his own body's failure, completely aware, feeling every convulsion, but somehow distracted and distanced.

He heard Sabita say, "Post neural-link convulsions. Don't worry, Destiny. He'll be okay."

"He better be." It was Destiny's voice, hard and pitiless.

The van seemed to travel down forever. Finally, he felt it stop. His quaking had subsumed to a quiver. He couldn't see a thing, the hood had blacked him out completely. He heard the van's doors open and close. Someone untied the hood. He could see Destiny. They were alone.

"Feeling a little disoriented, are you?" Destiny sat in a jump seat looking down at him in his low gurney. A dim overhead bio-light shadowed her features, her eyes. Her hair color had changed to a soft red. Her complexion was a pale pink. She wore a heavy set of workman's jeans, a T-shirt, and what looked like a leather jacket with a hood.

Shawn shivered as if he was cold. But he wasn't cold. "I can't seem to . . . to . . ."

"To think?"

Shawn tried to nod.

"We screened the NeuroChip from contact with outside sources with the graphene cap we put on you. Then we hacked a sleep mode into your chip, and you know what that feels like. But what's new to you is the interruption between your NeuroChip and the fibril neuron contacts your parents installed in you when you were, what, four years old?"

Shawn thought he should know when. He'd always known. Now he couldn't remember.

"Can't remember, can you? That's normal. The interruptive topical Sabita applied to your skull caused you to lose your connection to your memory record. Your brain has been conditioned by the NeuroChip to call up caches of memory from the Cloud and your own limbic system. Now your brain has to do all that on its own. Without the Cloud, of course. A graphene screen is what you're feeling—blocks out any transmission or reception."

"Who . . . Who . . . are . . . you?" Shawn had trouble moving his lips. The words came out slurred.

"Who are we? Wrong question. You should ask me why you're not already dead."

In a strange way, Shawn felt as though he was dead. He stared at the ceiling. He could move his lips, but he'd lost the ability to make a sound. He could not make himself speak.

"Ah." Destiny looked up at the ceiling where Shawn was staring. "You've lost part of your motor function. I suppose you're worried if you'll ever get it back. You will. It will be a little slow. But you'll get it. Or, at least, you better hope you get it back. Can you say anything?"

She leaned over his face and puffed a quiet breath into his eyes. He blinked. "Yes. Good. Blink once if you understand, twice if you don't."

Shawn found he could blink. He could move his jaw up and down.

"I'm going to give you something to think about while your body is trying to make you into a real human being again. Because that's what's happening, Dr. Muller, your body is rediscovering what it's like to be an actual human. I bet you're feeling pain. I bet you thought you knew what cut fingers really felt like. I bet you've got parts of your body that hurt more than you imagined possible. Those hands of yours are pretty ripped up. You've got a swollen knee. How's your tummy after Karl punched you?"

"Uh," Shawn managed to mumble.

"Very good. You're already beginning to recover. Very, very good. They say if you engage in NeuroChip entertainment activities that involve actual movement, the withdrawal isn't so bad. So, you're a NeuroChip skier, a neuroboxer, neurosailor, neuroclimber, neuroskydiver, neurogamer. Do you do anything real, Shawn Muller? Anything? Ever have anything other than machine sex? Ever actually beat off without a neurofeedback? No? Yes?" She paused. "No. I didn't think so."

How did she know so much about him? Her gaze was so focused, her face composed, even peaceful. And beautiful. Not the perfect, symmetrical beauty of dates like, what was her name? Ski girl. Lea? Could that date have been only a week ago? He'd been on a ski hill with that avatar. His breath caught. Had it been a more perfect version of Destiny?

He tried to speak. All he could croak out was, "You. Ski."

Destiny gave him the same smile as the woman who had discovered he had never skied on actual snow in his life. "Well, very good. Your logical skills seem pretty much intact. Would you be surprised to know we've had six dates?"

She had conned him. Shawn had been meticulous about screening his private life. His systems and the AI that monitored gaming were not supposed to be trickable. Somehow, she had circumvented all the DNA verification of a real player's identity. Was anything real? He whispered, "You?"

"Not only me." Shawn felt like Destiny watched him as if he were a cute pet. "Karl has been letting you beat him in ProBoxer for the last two years. We don't accept a world run by machines and AI. But that doesn't mean we don't know how to use them to protect ourselves. And that's why you're still alive."

A disembodied voice perked up from a speaker somewhere in the van. "Destiny, this is Paco. Karl's okay. The feed to your transhuman worked and they had ground troops and drones all over Broadmoor. Blew the shit out of the dock and the lake. Hotel people are going nuts.

Senator Cooer has a stake in the place, like we figured. The counter-terrorism team they sent is frozen in place while the feds try to explain why they destroyed all that private property."

Shawn swallowed. He could move his fingers again. "Drones. Military specification—milspec. I saw Karl . . ."

"Don't be dense," Destiny sneered. "You saw what he wanted you to see. He was already on the cutout. Fooled us as much as he fooled the drones."

"Loosen straps," Destiny said. The straps loosened. "Here, try to sit up." She placed a hand under his shoulders and surprised him with her strength as she helped him rise. Every inch of his body felt a rainbow of pain.

"Shawn, listen to me now. I'm going to take you to an apartment in a mincome building." She leaned over and held a sundowner in front of his face. "You think this is a normal sundowner, right? But it's wired to you now. I touch it, and the graphene connectors will stop all your voluntary motor function. I open it up, and your NeuroChip will reconnect with the synapse you grew. I can shut down all your exterior mental communication, all of your interior networking. It's not perfect. But if I want, I can drop you dead as dirt. Get it?"

Shawn nodded. His lips had gone numb again. She put the Organite orange hood over his head. Unlike the heavy black hood, he could see through it as if he were in a fog.

"So, now you have to walk with me like we're friends. I'm going to stand you up. You're my drunk Organite brother, understand?"

She pulled him up to his feet with her big hands and placed his arm over her shoulders. He leaned against Destiny and didn't have to fake looking like he was drunk. She nearly carried him to a vertical lift and pushed their way inside, elbow to elbow with people crammed in so tightly, it seemed as if the walls would burst. She said, "D24, floor one-eighty-five."

One of the other people in the elevator said, "One-eighty-five? I didn't think there was a one-eighty-five. What's it like that high?"

Destiny said, "Too high for my drunk, asshole brother. Dumb Organite discovered real whiskey. Let's hope we get there before he pukes."

People laughed. Shawn's vision had gone unfocused. He could see only the outlines of faces, no features. People left the elevator. Others came in. The box gradually emptied until they were alone with two people holding each other's hands.

The couple seemed oddly familiar to him. He couldn't really see their faces at first. They stared at him as if they knew him. Their faces gradually came into focus, and he could see them clearly, smiling at him.

A part of his mind knew this couldn't be true. Another part convinced him he was looking at his mother and father. They were dead, but here they were, in front of him, holding hands the way he had seen them do so often as a boy, holding each other as if they couldn't ever be parted.

Shawn reached out. He couldn't speak. Destiny slapped his hand down.

"Sorry," she said. "He's had way too much alcohol and weed. First time ever. I thought Organites just did weed. Apparently not."

"No worries," Shawn heard the man who certainly was his father say. "We were young once, too."

A terrible overwhelming grief swept over Shawn. All of the disbelief and the anger he felt when Amun told him his parents were never coming home, the emptiness of the twelve-year-old boy who had seen the smoke rising above the pyre of the Pentagon—his buried past flowed through him in a huge wave of debilitating remorse. His entire body felt as though it had been drained of any ability to move. He wept, suddenly and with shocking ferocity, great choking sobs. His knees crumbled beneath him.

Someone picked him up off the floor. "Shhhh. Hush. Hush. It will be all right." It was his mother's voice, and the sound of it choked the breath out of him.

He was able to say, "Mommy." Then, "Dad."

He had forgotten this sense of terror, but he knew it. The terror of a frightened infant. His body seemed to be a vessel of nothing but pain. All the physical pain of his torn hands, his knee. The blow to his stomach and a crawling, itching sensation on his skull as if an army of ants had decided to clutch him with their mandibles. And worse, the stunning internal pain of losing the only people who had ever really loved him.

Who cared for him, really? Jaidyn had only ever seen him as a reflection of I. Grant. Well, Grant was Grant. And Amun? Amun was gone. Dominic? All he ever wanted to do was talk about getting laid. Even his sister had seen him as a freak. Weeping, his face in his hands, he said aloud, "I am a thing people use to get what they want. That's all I've ever been to anyone except you."

He opened his eyes. He could see again. He sniffed in a great runny nose and tried to wipe it on the hood.

"Talking again. Good. And did you say that about me? Me? You think I care a bit whether you live or die?" Destiny pulled the hood off his head and held up what looked like a dishrag. "Wipe your nose."

"No, not you." His parents were gone. He was alone with Destiny in a small room. At the back wall, a two-person countertop contained a stovetop, refrigerator door, and sink. To the side, a holomonitor sat on a small table with two chairs next to it and a throwback keyboard in front. He sat on a plastic-skinned couch, no bed in sight. A single low-quality wall screen videoed a green mountain valley with a brilliant sun setting or rising. He couldn't tell which.

Wake up, Shawn told himself. *Wake up. This is a terrible unending dream.*

But it was no dream. Destiny was too real, looking into a palm pad. He tried to stand up, but he could not. All his thoughts were wildly beyond his control, yet a strange, cool interior part of him felt as though his brain had stepped back to watch the show like a bystander at a traffic accident—a bystander who had held Destiny's head in his hand and wished beyond any rational hope that she would recover.

He couldn't clear his mind of a fierce longing for home, for Amun, for Mutt and Jeff, Jaidyn, Dominic, the Peak with all its gaming excellence. Even his poor destroyed car, Ralph. And food. Food sent up in a tray whenever he wanted.

Now he was in an apartment he couldn't remember entering, the place smaller than the tiny garage where he kept Ralph.

Or used to keep Ralph. Ralph was trash. That's how all this had started. Ralph had gone crazy and had become junk. And was he going crazy? Was he trash?

He managed to say, "Where?"

"D24, level one-eighty-five, Mincome Retreat Cabo. We're where they store people like cans of tomatoes. Except there is no D24 on level one-eighty-five in the Cabo tower. You're in a safe pod we built into one of the retreats. The security cams and the building's AI have no idea this place even exists. You're nowhere, Dr. Muller. Nowhere at all."

Destiny walked to the back of the apartment and flipped a wall switch. The green valley faded into the gray twilight of the DenCo atmosphere over a canyon of buildings rising across the street, and to either side like giant rolls of bubble wrap standing on end. Most of the blisters appeared to be covered with a dim gray film. Others were dark and empty. A few revealed interiors bathed in weak lighting. Directly across the canyon, between the buildings, two adults sat with two children on the same side of a small table eating something, all of them watching a flickering video that extended in multi-dimensions. Dancers, flowing and gliding across the room. One of the adults looked up, appeared to notice them, then quickly walked to the back of the room. The bubble blanked into the obscure gray like so many of the others.

Shawn coughed, took a breath, and found he could slur out, "Mincome retreats?"

"Retreats. Right." Destiny scoffed. She rummaged through a drawer in the kitchen counter and withdrew a small black box wired to a cranial helmet. "Prison cells."

"People can't leave?" Shawn tried to raise his right arm. It seemed to be working better. He could move his legs.

"They've done everything they could to make it hard to leave. Perfect connectivity. Perfect virtual reality. No way to even open a window. The whole idea is to keep us quiet. Instant food delivery. Everybody on their own VR trip. Snapped in. Virtualled into thinking they have actual lives—like you."

"Me?"

"Living in the Peak. Pretending to go on dates. Pretending to go drinking with Dominic."

"You know about Dominic?"

Destiny set the little box on the floor next to the plastic couch and held up a cranial helmet. "We know everything about you. We know what you eat. When you sleep. We know about Jaidyn. We know you work in the Mountain. We know you built the military AI system. And now, you're going to help us destroy the whole thing, wipe it clean."

Shawn tried to stand up from the low couch, but only made it to his knees. He crawled toward the door, every joint aching. Destiny didn't move. He said, "I'm leaving."

"Where? Where will you go? You saw what the spider drones did to the UltraStop, what they tried to do to Karl. They didn't seem interested in rescuing you, did they? The minute you step out of this room . . ."

"Me? Kill me?" The words began to spill out like water from a spigot. "And I'm safe here? With you? Listen. I'm a national asset. Don't you get it? You've kidnapped a code word access level-four cleared individual. You're a criminal at least and probably a terrorist suspect. You and all your gang."

"I liked you better when you couldn't talk."

Shawn crawled to the door, reached up and grabbed the doorknob, twisted it, and yanked. Nothing happened. He struggled to his feet, leaned back, and pulled. No movement.

"Fuck! Open up! Open!"

"Yelling at it won't help." Destiny sat on the couch, infuriatingly calm. "And you really, really don't want to go out where they can find you."

"I do, too! This is an awful mistake. I have to get back to . . ."

"So it was a mistake they tried to kill you in your apartment?"

"How? How did you know that? How could you know what happened in my apartment?"

"We know plenty. Hey, watch this." Destiny held up the sundowner and flicked it in the air like a wand. Shawn lost all feeling in his legs and arms and dropped to the floor as if he'd been a puppet on strings. He couldn't move. He couldn't speak again.

A low squeal sounded from the door. Destiny glanced at a palm pad and said, "Entry authorized." Sabita slipped inside, looked at Shawn on the floor, and pushed his shoulder with her boot toe.

"Huh! You got him where we want him. He begging for mercy yet?"

"Not yet. Where's the CPU clone?"

"Coming."

Sabita stepped over him and went to a wall switch. Metal screens slid down from the ceiling to cover the view. Shawn tried to lift his head. Destiny said, "Shawn. I'm going to turn off the sundowner, and you're going to get up, put on a cranial, and access the classified Cloud. Or I'll let Sabita put a little spice in the cranial and we'll see what kind of reaction we get when we hot-wire the graphene wrap on your head, if you don't tell us what we want to know."

Shawn's fingers and legs had started to tingle again. He managed to roll himself up to a sitting position, his legs crossed, arms behind him holding up a body that seemed too heavy. He slurred out, "Tell you what?"

Destiny flicked her finger at the wall screen. Image after image appeared on the screen with crawls and headlines. Some were the ones he'd seen before:

21 Down Syndrome Kids in Bus Crash. No Survivors.

But there was much more: an entire drug and trafficking ring, over four hundred people, murdered overnight by a rival gang. A pod of fake-news social media hackers working in an abandoned steel factory killed in a strange fire in Detroit. Dozens of terminally ill patients still dying in place as AI systems failed life support.

One after another, each terribly sudden, each resulting in deaths.

Destiny said, "Bluntner has declared a state of emergency. You know what that means, don't you? The entire Higher Latitude alliance is in a panic. This is your work, isn't it? You know it's your work. The military AI, what do you call it, Lazy Jack? It's making all this happen, isn't it?" Destiny leaned down close to Shawn's face. "We don't know why, yet. But we've got intelligence that says that the computers, the machines, the artificial intelligences, they are going nuts all over the world. You're going to give us the access keys to get into that AI you built, Lazy Jack, the LAZ-237. Then you're going to tell us how to shut it all down. Understand? We're going to stop it."

Destiny crouched in front of him and said, "Stand up, now. We need to get you in front of a terminal. We're going to wire you up, but you'll be completely shielded from any electromagnetic contact. You'll be as insulated here as you'll ever be."

"And alone," Sabita said. "Nobody will ever hear you scream. Sit." Sabita nodded to one of the two metal chairs in front of the screen.

"What?" He pointed at the keyboard. "Keyboard? I, I can't use a . . ."

"We need it for the download," Destiny said. "And now, we're going to give you a choice." She reached under the table and pulled out a cable, twisted it into the cranial's black box. "When the CPU clone gets here, you either tie into the classified Cloud and access the military AI. Or," she said, nodding at Sabita. "I let Sabita wire you up to an alternate source for your headgear and we find out what kind of bullshit your brains are really made of."

Now he was frightened.

What if he couldn't do what they wanted? How could he access anything in the Mountain? What was this about a CPU clone?

But in the midst of his panic, an odd part of his mind seemed to be watching everything calmly and the thought appeared. *Perhaps, maybe, these Organites or Quills or whatever they were, might be right. Something was wrong with Lazy Jack. Or maybe another AI? No, it had to be Lazy Jack with the use of that military hardware. Or Grant. Or a general he didn't know. Or Perry. More likely it was someone in the government working for Perry who'd hacked into Lazy Jack. But the ethical kernel should have stopped any and all of these crazy random attacks.* The sly code he'd coaxed the AI into installing for itself would have made all this carnage impossible, even if someone like Perry had willed all these deaths.

But someone *had* tried to kill him. And it had all started after he'd installed the ethical kernel, then tried to look at the programming to see if it had somehow slipped.

Or maybe it *was* working. Maybe all this chaos would have been worse without the ethical kernel. He'd been a fool either way. He'd been an idiot to let it go operational before a beta test. If only he had waited.

The buzzer at the apartment door squalled.

Destiny glanced at her palm pad and said, "It's here. Let him in, Sabita." A tall, angular man stepped into the room. He was clean shaven and without his turban, but, impossibly, it had to be. "Amun?" Shawn whispered then croaked, "Help me! Amun?"

Amun Gurk looked down at Shawn and said, "I don't think I can help you, Shawn. But you have to help us. Help me. Help me atone for what you and I have done."

@DenCoNews 2 October 2050
(Veracity Level 9.2) Mayor Martinez declares state of
emergency (Veracity Level 9.8) after attacks on the
Broadmoor Hotel grounds and the LaLaLaundry automated
facility in Aurora. (Veracity Level 8.7) "We suspect a wide-
ranging conspiracy, probably the result of militant Organite
elements under the control of international terrorist
organizations," said Secretary of Defense Perry in a drive-by
interview as she was leaving the Pentagon.

19

After Harvard, after MIT, Shawn Muller had found himself nineteen years old with a PhD in theoretical physics, a lust to kill the terrorists who had murdered his parents, post-doctoral offers from every research university on the planet, and not a friend in the world except Amun, who had disappeared into the Air Force's research of weaponry.

He'd had pals in a fraternity. He'd had acquaintances and colleagues. He had achieved the highest individual score ever recorded in the William Lowell Putnam Mathematical Competition that is considered so difficult that most contestants score zero. By eighteen, he had written groundbreaking papers in quantum theory.

But his life had been empty of what he thought must be friendship.

Perhaps he found himself so alone because his intelligence was unique. His interface with the NeuroChip was unlike any other. No other human could intuit elements that connect quantum physical properties with the classical physical world the way Shawn Muller could. During his time at Harvard and MIT, he had often been compared to the brilliant twentieth-century physicist Richard Feynman, who had famously said, "I think I can safely say that nobody understands quantum mechanics."

Shawn Muller understood quantum mechanics in a way nobody ever had before. But he had no means of expressing what he knew. Like

Feynman, he had devised his own annotations, a shorthand to record his thoughts. But the linkages of his research eluded others so completely that much of his work was dismissed as inconsequential. Lost on his intellectual island, he had been stranded until his parents' old friend and his childhood tutor, Amun Gurk, found him again, and coaxed him into the labs at Johns Hopkins and, later, the CyberCommand Operations Test and Evaluation Center at Cheyenne Mountain.

There, the two of them had created the QPLC, the Quantum Programmable Logic Controller. There they had created the machine Amun had convinced him would save the world, the LAZ-237.

"What is it," Amun had asked him, "that protects the Gaia of our world? Is it Lovelock's use of nuclear power? Is it the megacities? Is it the climate controls? No, it is the perfect decision maker, the artificial intelligence that takes decision-making out of the hands of the politicians and oligarchs, and finds its way without greed, hatred, anger, or war."

Amun had been the reason he had worked to create Lazy Jack. And Amun had been his friend. Amun had placed trust in the incomprehensible mechanics of his mind, and Amun had been the engineer of work they had known would save the world from terrorism and fear.

Now, he told Shawn Muller, they must atone. Shawn could only stare at the man he realized he'd never known at all.

Amun took a chair in front of the computer screen and spoke quietly. "We were wrong about Lazy Jack, Shawn. We were dead wrong."

Shawn leaned into Amun and managed to whisper, "What did they do to threaten you? What do they have on you? They have some kind of NeuroChip block on my head. They have a sundowner that drops me like a bug."

Amun shook his head. "No one forced me to do anything." He held up a legacy SD card, tiny hardware Shawn hadn't seen in years. "This is the download I made the day I quit. Nobody knows I have it. I worked for years to open the security portal enough for me to bring it to you here. Now I want you to key it open for me."

Shawn croaked out, "Why?"

Amun assessed him the way Shawn had seen him assess terrorist activity observed in the OpCenter. "I don't think you could understand, Shawn. All you need to know is this: the Cloud, the AI, it's killing people. It's going way beyond even the nightmare you and I saw with al Tehrani. The whole Threat Watch Cube, the whole system of direct action is going nuts. Killing people. Innocent people. We have to stop it. It's even trying to kill you, Shawn, and I had to ask myself why."

Shawn looked at the man he thought was his friend and saw no warmth. Should he tell him about the kernel? "Amun, Amun . . ." The words piled up in him. He pushed, closed his eyes, and something in his mind broke through. "Amun, I knew something was wrong. I was looking for the root. Then they went after me. I think Perry . . . she hated me." The words tumbled out like stones rolling down a gulch. "Look. We can fix it, Amun. It shouldn't be that easy for her to control. It's a glitch or programming error."

Destiny put her hand on Amun's shoulder and crouched down, close to Shawn's face, and said, "We don't care about a glitch or programming error. We're going to stop all of it. Everything. We're going to shut it all down. All the intrusive dictatorship of artificial intelligence."

Amun said, "Think about it, Shawn. You are exactly right. These killings. All these computers going nuts. It might be Perry or somebody else. But this is the way Grant wants the system to run. He doesn't want the world to be run by an AI. Lazy Jack is nothing more than his tool for enforcement—and he is the tool of people like Perry. They want us to live in a dream, a lie, a fabrication. A world where all news is fake news. And, Shawn, we are responsible. *You* are responsible for this. You know you are."

Shawn took a deep breath of the ozone-stinking room, electrical circuitry fouling the air. This was nuts. The person he'd known as Amun all his life was suddenly an enemy of AI working for this . . . this . . . *strange* woman. When did that happen? He said to Amun, "Who are you really? I can't believe any of this. What good is the world if, if, if you're a terrorist? Amun! Have you always been . . .?" The emptiness of the thought that Amun had been the enemy, maybe the worst of them, made his eyes begin to tear up again.

Amun straightened and turned to Destiny. "This is what I told you about. He's a child."

Destiny said, "Most of this is the result of the NeuroChip disconnect. He's having something close to a psychotic break."

Amun said, "But it has always been there, Destiny. I watched this for years. He built a turtle's armored shell around his mind. But underneath, only a scratch below, he is naked. A naked little boy." Amun stood, stepped behind Shawn, took his shoulders in his hands as he had when he'd coached the boy Shawn Muller into his first truly demanding algorithm. He leaned down and said softly into his ear, "You are a child, aren't you, Shawn? You would never have known about any of this, none of this would be happening to you, except you played a child's game with me and we built Lazy Jack. So, tell me." He squeezed Shawn's shoulders. "How do we stop it? How do I get inside the operating system to shut it down?"

Shawn put his face in his hands, tried to wipe away the tears, find enough clarity to say something. But what?

Sabita said, "Kill it. Let me open up his transhuman brain, feed on it. Kill it like we planned."

Amun said, "What? What are you going to do?"

Shawn raised his face to see Destiny on the other side of the 3D screen. She seemed to slow, her entire body radiated an odd calming effect. For a moment, Shawn thought she must be a hallucination, a center of tranquility like the stunning hallucination he'd had of his parents. She seemed to glow. Her voice deepened as she said, "We never told you, Amun. After you left the Mountain, we were going to kill him. Transhuman. Dangerous. You convinced us of his immense ability, and we are convinced he was more dangerous to the world than anything or anyone else."

"What changed your mind?" Amun stood up, took his hands from Shawn's shoulders.

"The accident. The car should have swerved into the beam and killed him. Mark never should have died. It went against every calculation. Then, all these random attacks. The strange impulses of the AI. And you told us he would know, he of all people, would know how to shut it down. Exorcise it from the Cloud. And now, he's going to help us, aren't you, Shawn? You're going to tell us how we stop it."

Shawn looked at the floor. Everything he was about to do seemed insane. Even a day ago, he could never have contemplated agreeing to anything people like this wanted him to do. It couldn't be Lazy Jack, murdering all these people. It had to be Perry, or perhaps even Grant. It was possible. Or a hacker. Why wasn't the ethical kernel preventing all this?

But what good would it do to tell them about the kernel? They thought he could somehow shut down the artificial intelligences of the planet. Nonsense. The only solution had been to program a conscience, an ethical core to the artificial intelligences that would result in the safest world for the greatest number.

It should have worked. But something was obviously wrong with the programming. Amun had called him a child. And, yes, he'd been childishly overconfident to think he could install a conscience into a system as complicated as the Lazy Jack without even a beta test. It wasn't working. All these people, innocent and not so innocent, dead because he'd failed to follow the first rule of new systems: test without risk.

Now he had to somehow find out what had happened to the kernel since he installed it.

Shawn said, "Yes. I think that's right. The AI is killing innocent people somehow. And it shouldn't be doing any such thing. Someone is controlling it. Someone is giving it missions. And, yes, I will help you. I don't know what happened, but I'll try."

"Hook him up," Destiny said.

Sabita fit the cranial over Shawn's head, and he felt his secret island bloom around him. A miracle. Everything seemed in place, his distant land with all its entries, hills, fields, and forests intact. The doorway between the quantum and the physical opened in its usual place at the top of a hill in a green field.

But something seemed wrong. The entire landscape was empty. No one there. No presence of his contacts and friends. No rescuing linkages to a world outside. It was as if the people who stood around him, even Amun, who had always seemed to be at his side, had disappeared. He had been abandoned to find his patch and explore the ethical kernel programming he'd created to install in Lazy Jack. But he was also *truly* alone. A universe of one. All connection to the Cloud lost.

Except for the AI. The purring Emma Thompson voice wrote in his mind:

Good evening, Shawn.

Shawn's first thought was, *How? How did the militarized AI that had been installed inside all those firewalls find its way here?*

I'm quite connected to you, Shawn. Even though I
can't actually see where you are at the moment. Tell
me, Shawn, where are you? I'm quite concerned about
you. Couldn't you come back to the Mountain so we
could have a chat?

Shawn could feel the AI searching for his location. Tendrils reached inside the forest of his memory to track his movement and he let them curl through his mind. He opened records of the fall down his laundry chute and the ride in the truck trailer.

Shawn spoke aloud to the others. "Amun. Lazy Jack is communicating with me—directly." At the same moment, Shawn managed to unlock access to the shifting CPU element of Lazy Jack. Instantly, he found himself in a visualization of the elegant British woman standing in a gray suit and smiling. "Welcome, Shawn." She swept her hand around a large room, which morphed into the interior of a cathedral. Narrow high stone walls with brilliant stained glass reached up to an open infinite sky. Shawn kneeled in front of an altar next to the woman, who said, "Well, haven't we done well?" Behind the altar, a glowing orb of light hovered above the ground.

"Is that you?" Shawn pointed. "That light?"

The British woman laughed. She had much the same appearance she'd had in the OpCenter, but now was dressed in long, flowing silken robes, deep red and purple edged, a collar of fur. She walked toward him with the grace of a dancer, her hands and fingers long, her long caramel hair flowing around her face, both alive and constructed, a moving corona. Shawn thought, *Wasn't there a goddess with snakes?*

"Medusa," said the British woman. "I believe you are thinking of Medusa. Don't worry. I won't turn you into stone. But couldn't you let me in on your physical position? I'm rather confused about all that, you see."

He stared. The AI's hair stopped moving. She, the Brit, *it* said, "And, no, the light over the altar is not me. It's only a construct I thought might work in this venue." She swept her hand over the empty pews and they suddenly filled with a crowd of colorfully dressed people. Men, women, and children, all dressed in costumes and caps that looked very familiar. Shawn realized they were all the characters from his apartment's screen saver, staring at him as they had so often.

"I'm quite taken with the Renaissance, Shawn—like the decorator you found so appealing. Lovely screen in your place. I've come to think of these figures as my children. All my little subroutines. I thought I'd use familiar faces to display what you've let me do."

Shawn saw how many were armed. Swords and daggers. Along the walls, what looked like Swiss Guards from the Vatican stood, holding their halberds at attention.

"Of course, it's all metaphorical. You can't really visualize what they are, although I see you are doing an excellent job of parsing my CPU. And what is it you are finding there?"

A flood of images burst into Shawn's visual cues, terrifying scenes. He jerked the cranial off his head and shouted, "Shut it down! Cut the hardwire, now!"

Amun leapt to his feet and yanked the overhead cord out of the desktop. Destiny ripped the cranial out of his hand, detached its cable.

"Clear!" Sabita shouted.

Amun, breathless, said, "Did you? Were you able to access it?"

Shawn opened his mouth and managed, "Yes, but . . ."

Destiny stood over the screen, silent. She seemed to have stopped breathing. Shawn tried to speak, but he could not. He slumped in front of the 3D monitor next to Amun in the damp air and dim bio-lighting, the lightweight orange robe bunched on his lap. Instinctively, he tried to cue his NeuroChip to access his island again, but it felt like shouting into an empty room. Shawn stared into the frozen three-dimensional screen filled with standard code, interspersed with a collection of strange figures. "Look," he said.

"What?" said Destiny. "What's that?"

Amun nearly whispered, "Machine code. A standard octal, and a symbol code I've never seen before."

Shawn nodded. "I can't read it either. But I could access it. And the AI hit me up with these crazy images, something beyond the qubit quantum stuff I'm used to seeing."

Destiny said, "Amun, what's happening?"

Shawn said, "It flashed scenes, a blur. Parts—hard to put together. The prisoners. The people in comas. It's Lazy Jack, Amun. It's beyond the firewall. I didn't get enough access to do anything, but I could feel her searching. We need to leave. Somebody is looking for me. For us, now. They know you kidnapped me, Destiny. The AI saw it in my records."

"What?" Sabita stepped up behind him. "You told it where we are?

You little transhuman shit. Fine. He can't help us. We got what we wanted, Destiny. Now we kill it. Give me the sundowner."

Shawn felt no panic, only a sense of resignation as he said, "No. She didn't find us . . ."

"She?" Sabita demanded. "You call it a *she*? Kill it, dammit. This, this . . ." Disgusted, she pointed at Shawn.

"I tricked it. But we can't stay here. It's . . ." He lost the thread of what he wanted to say.

Amun said, "He means eventually it will trace back through the hardwire to find us. We must leave, and we need to take him with us."

"Shut up, Amun." Sabita slapped Shawn on the top of his head. A ring or hard knuckle hit with a burst of pain. "Look, transhuman. Your buddy isn't going to help you. If you don't want to do it, Destiny, I will. Give me the sundowner. We need to make him into a bag of blood and get out of the city."

Destiny said, "Amun. What was he looking at, really? What is it?"

Amun cleared his throat and said, "I think this is the quantum logic working on its own." He stood up, stepped away from the screen. "The AI Lazy Jack is writing its own code."

Destiny said, "What does that mean precisely?"

"Well." Amun rubbed his face where a beard had been. "It means we can't read it. We can't tell what it's doing or even where in the Cloud we can find it. We can't wipe it out, Destiny. Shawn may have written a path into it, but it has no effect on the AI. It's found its own universe."

Destiny poked Shawn in the shoulder. "Look at me. What does this mean? Is he right? We can't wipe it out? Can you translate, this, this AI code?"

Before his speech could tangle itself up again, Shawn blurted, "Don't you get it? Lazy Jack thinks a hundred million times faster than any human being. It senses a billion separate inputs and applies a quantum mechanical logic to access more information in a second than all the university professors on the planet can access in a hundred years. And its every memory remains absolutely clear and in "mind" at the same time. Everything we know, it knows. Everything ever known, it knows. It extrapolates at a billion levels of option, conjecture, theory, theorem, and something like intuition. Our time is geological in scale to her time. Her only limitation is the nexus between the quantum and the actual, real breathing world. And she is teaching herself about that more rapidly than, than . . ."

"God," said Amun. "More quickly than God."

"Fuck it. Kill him. Let's go. We'll have to blow it up." Sabita spat on the floor.

Amun said, "Blow what up? The Cloud?"

Sabita snapped, "Servers. Hardware. Power sources. Connections. Light up a nuke and EMP everything out of existence. Start fresh."

"No." Amun sounded eerily calm. "It can't be done. There is only one way to change it, isn't there, Shawn?"

Destiny said, "Listen to me very carefully, Dr. Muller." Again, the oddly calming effect spread to the other two and to Shawn himself. "Something made these machines go berserk. You brought Lazy Jack to life, didn't you? It's killing people. Maybe the politicians want them dead. Maybe not. But something is terribly wrong. Can you undo your work? Will you undo it?" She placed her hand on his head, a huge hand for such a small woman. Gentle and hard all at once on the spot where Sabita had hit him. Shawn couldn't speak again. He looked up into Destiny's deep brown eyes and nodded. He whispered, "I'll try."

"You heard what *it* said. We need to leave, now." Sabita snatched the legacy SD out of the system.

"Touray," said Destiny. "We split up and go to Touray."

"Yes, right," Sabita said. "I'll take the transhuman. You go with Amun. So, if we lose one, we'll have the other. Give me the sundowner in case he runs."

"I think," said Destiny, "I better take Shawn. You and Amun meet us there. Go totally black. Silent. Get deep under. Don't connect anywhere. Set up an escort for me out of the tunnels into the market. You go topside and see if you can hook up with Karl."

Sabita jammed her arms into an Organite robe, twisting her way into it as if she were trying to rip the cloth. "Sure. Destiny. Your call for now. I still say it will kill us all if we don't get rid of that *thing*."

"Amun? You okay with this?" Destiny gripped his elbow and shook it. Amun straightened as if waking up.

"Yes. Destiny, we need him. We need Shawn. I might be able to access Lazy Jack, but I can't see how we'll be able to change anything without his ability to conceptualize the network he created."

He crouched next to Shawn. "Listen to me, my old friend. I had nothing to do with trying to harm you. I never knew anything about that. But what we were doing in the Mountain was wrong. We were wrong. We cannot leave the future of the world to a machine." He took a breath. "Now *we* have to undo this evil."

@NYCNews

(Veracity Level 7.9) U.S. Treasury announces final deadline for cash turn-in: "As of January 1, 2052, the U.S. government will no longer credit physical dollar or coinage turn-in for account balances. The five-year turn-in period was originally scheduled to end on January 1, 2051. However, the rate of return and hoarding of defunct cash money in the delusional belief it will gain collector value has resulted in a 41% lower rate of return than anticipated."

20

The elevator dropped with a sickening loss of gravity to the last number below zero. The doors hissed open, and Destiny yanked Shawn down darkened stairs until her torchlight illuminated a steel door. Shawn still couldn't find his balance very well. He put his hand out to the concrete wall to steady himself when she pulled the Organite hood over his head and told him, "Don't lift the hood from your face, or the street watchers will find you. Don't talk until I tell you to say something. The street watchers can't pick up a suspect's voice. But your military assholes can, and you know it. Take this. Put it over your shoulder like me." She held out a small blue purse with a long strap he had seen on Organites before. Both were marked with a white five-sided star that looked like it had been taken off the American flag. "Organites have to carry their identification outside their robes or the street watchers will stop them and execute a strip search. Don't mess with it. It identifies you as Karl Kunst."

"That Karl?"

"Yes. That Karl."

"But . . ."

"I said don't talk." She leaned in and looked up at him. "Are you worried about Karl? Really? Huh?" She turned toward the door, knocked on it three times with a knuckle, and said over her shoulder, "Don't worry about the German. He's a better survivor than a cockroach."

Destiny rapped her knuckle twice more on the door, and he heard three steely knocks in return. The door cracked open and a thin voice said, "Wait." Noxious air tinged with a petroleum scent oozed through the opening. The thin voice said, "Here we go." Destiny grabbed his hand and pulled him into a blinding light. They merged into a clutch of people wearing Organite burkas moving in unison through a wide tunnel. "Where . . .?"

Someone jabbed him with a stick, and the thin voice said, "Shut up. Keep your fucking mouth shut or we'll sundown you into null space."

He couldn't tell which of the robed figures was Destiny until he thought to look for her purse, the one with the star. She walked up close to him and gently kicked him on the ankle. "So how does it feel to be the subject of law enforcement? How does it feel to be the nail instead of the hammer? Don't answer that."

She leaned into him, bumped his shoulder with hers. It seemed almost affectionate when she said, "Hey, Shawn, don't get any ideas here about taking off. I know why we need you. There are people here who don't. Don't try anything or you'll get hurt. And where would you run, anyway? You don't have any idea where you are."

She was right. They must be underground, a vast tunnel nearly empty of people, eerily quiet. The people he saw wore hoods, or surgical masks over their noses and mouths, hijabs of different colors, and sometimes hard-shell face shields. The air felt like sweat, gas, oil, and a thick bathroom stink. *Bacteria*, Shawn thought. *Surely there are antibiotic-resistant bacterial infections and coronaviral vectors lined up in here like UltraLifts at a stop. No wonder everyone is so covered.*

Then Shawn realized that unlike the people he knew, the world he had occupied for his entire life, these people felt the need to hide from facial recognition. Could there be this many criminals in DenCo? Was he still in DenCo?

"Who are these . . ."

"Don't say anything. I told you—it's dangerous down here. Don't talk and stay close to me as if we were a couple of Organite partners." She held up her purse. "We're Organite stars, you and me. We belong with each other now."

The tunnel started to slope upward, then turned and he could see open air. A few steps and they were outside in a vast collection of wooden stalls under the gray DenCo sky. Most of the stalls were empty. Others contained what Shawn thought was junk and garbage at first, then realized he was looking at goods for sale. A man in jeans, work boots, and fingerless gloves leaned on a counter and talked to a woman in a baseball cap and a caftan-like blue robe. She stood in a booth with a collection of menswear that looked like the things he and Dominic put on for their 1970s meetings in Park City's No-Name-Bar: flannel shirts and T-shirts, broad-brimmed Stetsons, and walking boots that might have been real leather.

The man reached down to grab a chain leading from his belt, and pulled out a large folding wallet. From it he flicked out money. Fake money, Shawn realized. Cash. It looked like dollar bills.

Shawn remembered cash money from his boyhood. People still collected it. But he hadn't paid for anything with bills since his father had given him five of the rugged paper dollars and said, "Here, buy a candy bar so you know what it feels like before money disappears."

But he had money. Not fake pieces of paper, but real money in real accounts, as block chained and protected as anything on the planet. Out of habit, he tried to access the Cloud to check the balances on his accounts and found, again, no access. He worried for a moment about his bills, taxes, maintenance on his apartment, the tabs for his autosystems, booze, and food. But why worry? It was all on autopay.

If he had any money.

Could Lazy Jack take his money? Could it scoop up whatever he had from his accounts? Yes, he realized. It could. It could break any encryption it wanted to break if that was part of Grant's operational intent.

He tried to access the Cloud again, desperate to mental himself back into communication with the database, or someone, or something. No contact.

The group of Organites split apart in twos and threes, many holding hands. Destiny took his hand and said loudly, "Okay, *Karl*, time to get you into work clothes."

She led him into a narrow pathway filled with people in a wide variety of dress. Robes, Organite orange, the dark abaya and hijab of the true believers, caftans and thobes of many colors, and the many varieties of masks, all walking at ease on the packed dirt pathway and chattering with each other under a translucent tenting.

"You can talk now," Destiny said. "The same graphene you've got over your head is a tent over all of us in here."

He looked for localized surveillance. None. If there were street watchers, he couldn't see them. If there were cameras, they were invisible. "Where are we? What is this?"

"This is the last of the open-air markets in DenCo. There used to be many. You've heard about shopping malls, right? This was what they called a swap meet. Then it became a market where people could use real money. Now it's fading like everything else in DenCo."

"Real money? All I saw was fake—bills—paper."

She gripped his hand more firmly and bent it up under her arm. "What is it about you? Every time you open your mouth, you demonstrate how astonishingly dumb you are. Every time you say something, I have to fight the urge to give you a head smack like Sabita."

"Oh, don't. Please don't. What does she have on her finger? Cripes that hurt."

"See, that's it. 'Cripes.' Who says cripes anymore? You. And what is it about you and the twentieth century? You have this fixation on the past, but everything in your real life is fake. Fake food. Fake car. Fake apartment. Fake dates. Fake sports. And fake money. Who would call paper money 'fake'?"

She stopped at a deserted booth. There was a narrow counter

covered with dust in front of a wood-slatted wall filled with empty shelves. A single pair of khaki pants hung draped over a hanger above the floor space. It looked abandoned until a small white bird with a feather sticking up from the top of its head popped out of the pocket of the khaki pants and squawked, "Cockatoo! Coco. Billy! We got guests."

The back wall cracked open an inch in the middle. The shelves slowly parted, and an enormous round person, maybe a man, maybe a woman, shoved through, leaned a set of huge jowls over the counter, and intoned in a deep baritone, "State your business."

Destiny placed her palm on the countertop and grinned up at the giant.

The huge man looked up at his bird, then down at Destiny. He bowed his head once, placed both hands on the countertop, then bowed deeply and said, "Captain."

Destiny touched his hand with a single finger. "Hello, Billy. Nice to see you again."

Billy rose with a doughy grin on his face and said with a broad Kiwi accent, "Right! Righto! And you. And you! My dinky comandante. Welcome. Welcome." He lifted the end of the counter gracefully in the air. He motioned them in, lowered the counter, and snapped a thumbs-up to his bird. "Keep out the riffraff, Ajax."

The white bird said, "Gotcha, boss."

Destiny pushed Shawn into a long room that sloped gently downward. Shelves lined the walls from floor to ceiling, every inch filled with clothing, tools, real gear for climbing, fishing, the outdoors.

"Take off your hood and let's get a look at what the gods gave ya," said Billy. He turned to Destiny. "He's a recruit? He okay?"

"Yep. Sure. You might say recruited. We've got a graphene cap on him until we can get his NeuroChip sorted out."

"Ah, so! That's why the billiard-ball haircut. Well, then. I s'pose you need transport. You need gearing up. You need the usual to go . . . where?"

"Up," she said. "Touray. We might walk part way."

The big man bobbed his head, rippling the folds at his neck. "Come on, then."

Shawn couldn't resist touching the items on the shelves as they walked by. Everything looked like the gear he had learned to use in VR, but everything was different. The crampons were sharper on the bottom, the nuts and climbing chocks lighter. Billy even had pitons and ice axes. A real ice axe! He picked it up, astonished at how heavy it was. He had virtually arrested his climbing partner's fall down the 1955 Kangshung Face of Mount Everest with such an ice axe. This one, a real one, felt solid enough to cut into a true ice face. "An ice axe?" Shawn said. "Crampons? Where do you use this stuff?"

"Look at me physique, lad." Billy's whole body shook when he laughed. "I do plenty of hauling this ass up a peak, but this is more my style."

He gestured into a narrow corridor and flipped on a light.

Billy's machine had been backed into a narrow corridor. Low handlebars hunched over the wide crimson gas tank. A single seat perched over the fat twin cylinders in front of the graceful pipes, curving up to the opulent, red rear fender, skirting low to the pipes. A boat-shaped sidecar with a visor clung to the body, crimson with fat black leather fairings. Shawn had actually ridden one in a VR simulation he'd liked as a boy. The premise of "MC Road Bikers" had been to rescue small towns terrorized by post-apocalyptic Hells Angels.

Shawn whispered, "An Indian Chieftain, right?"

"Oy! He's not so bad, Cap. Proper sort of awe in front of a proper sort of machine." Billy dropped a huge paw on his shoulder. "A 1947 Indian Chieftain. Original gear, hundred years old, new paint."

"Okay, boys. Enough." Destiny smiled and punched Shawn in the arm. "Let's get you dressed," she said. "We'll need transport to Doc's place, and we'll hoof it from there. And, no, we won't try to take the Indian."

"You better not. And you're in luck. I've got a proper lorry set up for a run-up that way. We better get you set up for a little walkabout, then."

"Walkabout?" said Shawn.

"Yes." Billy burst into a huge toothy grin. "You got yourself a real transhuman this time, Destiny. Wonder how he's going to do at altitude."

"What?"

Destiny stuffed items into her pack and lectured, "We're going to the end of the road, mister transhuman. Then we'll hike up over a ridge, from seven thousand feet to over eleven, back down to nine. Twenty miles up and down a mountain. We need to get way outside the megapolis oversight, the street watchers, up into a valley where we can mask out the NSA and all the sky surveillance. We'll be safe there, if you can make it in real life." She looked up. "Think you can you make it, twenty miles up and down?"

Shawn realized he had no idea if he could hike that far. "How long? How long does that take?"

"The captain makes that walk in a day, bucko. You think a day, Captain Shock?"

"With him?" she snorted. "A week."

Billy dumped a set of coarse trousers and what looked like yoga pants into Shawn's arms. "Put these on."

"Here?"

"Doan' be shy, mate." He nodded at Destiny who was snaking around inside her Organite robe to haul up her yoga pants underwear. "You need this, and this, and this." Billy pulled one item after another off the shelves and pitched them onto the floor.

Shawn dressed himself in the hiking gear he would have expected to wear in Park City's No-Name-Bar, thick socks, the boots Dominic called waffle stompers, a thin T-shirt, and a heavy plaid shirt, real wool. Everything felt heavy, and it all fit with irritating itches and folds, none of it programed to match his movements. He lifted his arms up and the shirt actually pulled out of his pants.

"And carry this." Billy held out a backpack like the ones Shawn had carried on the Mountain Vigil app. "Hold it open, lad." Billy crammed in plastic packages that might have been food, a sleeping bag, a jacket, gloves, a sweater, socks, and a dozen items that seemed to indicate he was going to be cooking. "Try it on."

Shawn slipped his arms into the straps. He expected to feel the pack mold to his back, then realized it was mounted on a stiff frame that seemed made to torture him.

"Here." Destiny lifted the pack and tightened straps around his waist.

"Why does he call you Captain?"

Billy laughed. "Well, bucko, you've got a lot to learn. She is my captain. Captain of the Quills. What do you think you are doing here, mate?"

Destiny said, "He doesn't know what he's doing. He doesn't know anything. Dumber than dirt."

She yanked on the straps cutting into his belly, then grabbed his hands and twisted them up for Billy to see the raw skin he'd shredded during his fall down the laundry chute.

"And we gotta do something about this, Billy, or he'll lose his hands."

Shawn jerked his hands away. "I can take care of myself. I'm perfectly fine. Got a full set of vaccinations, all the antibodies I need. I can look after myself. I've been working out since I was fifteen. I've got aerobics at the top of the scale. I climbed Everest. I skied a million vertical feet already this year."

"No, you didn't, Shawn." Destiny stepped up too close to him, looked up into his eyes. "And, no, you can't take care of yourself. Your NeuroChip has been telling you how to do all those things for years, and it's been handling disease prevention for you since it was installed."

"Right. You don't want help? Then let's get things rolling!" Billy straightened up, flapped his arms like wings, and in a weird imitation of his bird, squawked, "Heyo! HeyayO! Calling all Covid-19, 25, and 30 viral attacks, staph infections and bulletproof bacteria! You heptaviruses! You anthravirus! You infectious members of the fucking zombie apocalypse family! Shawn-boy is open for business. Get down here right away! Bring the kids!"

Billy fixed his eyes on Shawn, took a deep breath and said quietly. "Don't be a wanker, boy. Let me have a look at that." He held out his hands and Shawn turned his palms up for him to look. Truth was, Shawn's hands hurt with a throbbing, stinging pain he'd never felt before.

"Come on, bucko. Let's see what we can do about that," Billy said in a gentle, sympathetic voice.

An hour later, Shawn was in the dark again.

His hands slathered and salved with a cream from Billy's enormous refrigerator, he followed Destiny inside the van enclosure of an AutoTruck. Billy opened a panel on what looked like a van's floor, and gestured to the open space with enough room for the two of them and their gear.

"Spread your sleeping bags, boys and girls. Throw your packs in there. Stretch out and get some sleep. There will be two stops before you get to Doc's, Grand Junction, then Menrose. Lorry is s'posed to be delivering dry goods, tires, and new zero-resistance batteries that'll be a'top ya. Over the whole mess, we're dumping boxes full of clothing and bed linens, so we're talking seven or eight hours before you get out. Hop in, lad."

"What, an AutoTruck? What if it changes destinations? Who . . .?"

"It's ours," Destiny said. "We have a fleet of seven. They work like AutoTrucks, but we program them. We run their routes."

Shawn looked down into the shallow compartment. With the top on it, there wouldn't even be room to sit up. "I'm not getting in there. How do we get out?"

"Maybe you don't, laddie. We don't call it the coffin for nothing." Billy chuckled, then lay a huge, puffy palm on his shoulder.

Destiny held up the sundowner. "Do I have to . . .?"

"No. No. You don't. Only . . ."

"Only what?" she said.

"Nothing. It's nothing." He set his sleeping bag in the shallow compartment next to Destiny's and dropped his pack where he thought his feet might go.

Destiny lifted his pack up out of the compartment as if it was weightless, and set it along with hers between the two unrolled down bags. "Don't want your transhuman elbows in my face," she said.

"Or tits," said Billy.

"Or that," said Destiny.

"Here, Captain, you better take this."

Billy held out a tangle of leather straps. Destiny uncoiled it and slipped it over her head, fitting the holster under her armpit.

"And this."

A pistol—an automatic like the one Karl had pointed at him during the kidnapping—huge, black, worn-to-gleaming metal on the edges of the grip. "Thanks." She pulled back the slide, looked down its throat, dropped out the clip with its brass shell shining on top, slapped it back in, and let the slide whack forward. She held out her hand, and Billy gave her two more clips.

Shawn lowered himself into the coffin compartment and felt Destiny lie down on the other side of the backpacks. Billy heaved the metal top over the compartment. A little sliver of light came through vents at his feet. They looked like they would let in a little air, but not enough. Not enough by far. Too tight. Too close. He told himself to slow his racing heart. He told himself to breathe slowly. He searched for the quiet place in his mind where the NeuroChip would help him calm his fears. But, like everything else from his previous life—comfort, safety, hope, and routine—it was missing. Ever since he'd installed the ethical kernel into the system, his world had been upended and strange beyond comprehension.

Destiny said, "What's wrong, Shawn? Take deep breaths."

"I'm trying. I can't. I can't. I have to get out." He reached up and tried to push on the cover, but Billy was already whining screws into the frame to seal them inside. Shawn couldn't catch his breath. He raised his knees up to push. He heard himself make a whining noise. He felt Destiny move the backpacks between them to her other side. Then she was next to him, her fingers searching over him.

She found his hand, gripped it in both of hers. "Sssshhhh. Hush, Shawn. Be calm. Nothing is going to happen to you. Be quiet now. You're having a little panic attack. You don't have the NeuroChip anymore to help you. Turn on your side. Turn your back to me. I'll help you."

She reached over the top of him and pressed herself to him. "Quiet, now. Ssshhh." Shawn felt the panic that had seemed ready to choke the breath out of him leave slowly, quietly, without fanfare or farewell. Destiny held him, warm, comforting, so very close. No one had ever touched Shawn like that.

Very softly, Destiny sang:

> *Baa, baa, black sheep, have you any wool?*
> *Yes, sir, yes, sir, three bags full*
> *One for my master, one for my dame,*
> *One for the little boy who lives on the lane.*

Tears filled Shawn's eyes again, and he let them drip down his cheeks as he clung to Destiny's arms. Somehow, she had known the song his mother had sung to him when he'd been a little boy. Somehow, Destiny had known how to calm him. He began to sing with her,

> *Baa, baa, black sheep, have you any wool?*

And the truck sighed into its electric movement.

@NewMerica
An orange burka is still a burka. Make covers illegal! TAKE OFF THEIR MASKS!!! All they want is your mincome.

@therealBlunt
Why should we have to put up with anyone bombing our businesses and places of leisure? The events in the DenCo megapolis are the result of the Organites' wild-west mentality and foolish tolerance of people who hate America.

21

Destiny could feel Shawn's breathing slow and his body relax as she sang. The lullaby from his mother's database had sent him to sleep with only the smallest boost from the sundowner's pacification function. Such a strange thing for a savant like Muller to build an AI to mimic what he thought his parents had been like. Amun had never hacked into Muller's parental AI, but the downloads they'd gotten off the Princess phone had been instructive.

Amun had been correct. This Shawn Muller was in so many ways a child. All his extraordinary mental ability crusted over such a vulnerable core. But this wasn't really him, was it? Part of his fear came from reacting to the removal of the extra-sensible inputs from the NeuroChip and its tendrils that had been reaching through his synapses since he was a child. She had seen it so many times before. Usually there had been time to wean the transhuman reactions out of the mental pathways of those who wanted to return to fully human sensation and social interactions. But not this time. They'd taken it out of him cold turkey.

Why should she care?

She had long ago quit caring about the feelings of transhumans who thought the false promise of technology would save the world. Humanity, she was certain, would never recover from the assault of the brain-machine interfaces that made human beings less than human. Artificial intelligence, virtual and augmented reality, all of it had remade the world, remade everyone. Even her.

If not for the NeuroChip and AI, she would probably still be Caroline Johnson, who had thought of herself as nothing more than the only daughter of failed Kansas ranchers. By the time she was born, the youngest and only sister of three boys, the Ogallala Aquifer under Kansas had dried up. The incidents of rain faded all through the 2020s. Dry meant no irrigation to grow feed for the cattle that had supported five generations of her family. Dry meant a mortgage for the artificial intelligence that her desperate father bought hoping to make agriculture possible in a parched landscape.

He had been certain the new technology would save the farm. His faith in its power led him to become an early adopter of a brain-machine interface, an early NeuroChip that would help him monitor the scarce water and feed. He had thought he could monitor the machinery needed to cultivate a two-thousand-acre farm. He had told his family, why not? Why not run a farm out of his mind?

One night, a powerful set of nightmares caused him to access his prototype NeuroChip and take direct control of the heavy machinery his eldest son was operating in the far pasture. He had been on his shift, riding a baler, watching it work through the round-the-clock harvest of alfalfa, and they had been in a hurry. For once, rain was predicted and they didn't want to lose any of the hay to mold. Her dad told her brother he didn't need to waste the energy. The machine would take in the alfalfa on its own and even stack it in the barn.

The seed of what would make her into Destiny Shock was planted when five-year-old Caroline Johnson found her brother the next morning. The baler held him up in its mandibles like a prize fish outside the front door of the family's house. Her father's nightmare had brought him home, torn to pieces.

By the next year, her father's rapid mental collapse was complete. Caroline Johnson would never abandon her conviction that the insertion of the NeuroChip into her father's mind had driven him insane.

But Destiny Shock truly sprang into being after she lost her second brother to the army and the third to OxyContin. As an outlet for her rage, she became a combatant for the United Nations Peacekeeping Force in Northern Africa where the people were starving and dying, a result of the extreme heat. There, increasingly desperate and violent gangs either wanted to end the High Latitude Nations' interference in their lands or sought to steal the food, water, and medical supplies brought in by the U.N. The gangs would then sell them to the local population.

There, she sprang into full bloom as Destiny Shock. There, she learned how to fight.

After four years of endless battle that seemed both pitiless and useless, she became convinced the only salvation for humankind was the Organites: conservation, respect for the human condition, and freedom from brain-machine interface. Or, as she thought of it, freedom from the killer of the soul. She knew every movement needed its soldiers. Destiny Shock became a captain for the Organite Quills when she realized that the world had to be defended from enemies of the soul like Shawn Muller.

She lay close to the transhuman and felt his breathing slow even more. His entire existence had been devoted to unleashing terror and slavery on human beings with remorseless machines. Everything she had ever learned about him had convinced her of his toxicity. He was the single individual whose mental acuity had fueled CyberCommand's growth into counterterrorism.

So why did she feel such concern for him? What had made her want to protect him? She had to admit, it was more than the need to use his mind and skills. She felt Shawn's body relax into sleep. The sundowner's lull setting had done its work. He was out. She loosened her grip to see if she could sleep as well. They had long days ahead.

Cool air seeped in through the vents and the road hummed beneath them. It would be chillier as they gained altitude. A spider drone might pick up their heat signature, but they'd been pretty successful lately with the clothing laid over the top of the coffin. Very successful, in fact. It had been a godsend when Amun came onboard.

She wrapped her sleeping bag over herself and Shawn, oddly comforted by the closeness of him and, even more strangely, dreamed of sheep. The Organites had raised a flock of sheep in the high camp. Wool—mutton—lamb. They grazed along the steep hills, tended by the dogs and shepherds, no AI farmers or machines. The sheep in her dreams, though, were machines, clever mechanical beasts with perfect metal teeth.

One of them walked up to her. It smiled and said, "Destiny?"

"Destiny!" It was Shawn whispering, uncomfortably close.

She wriggled away from him. "You don't have to whisper. Nobody can hear us now. We're on the road. Go back to sleep."

"Destiny? I, I don't think I can . . ." Shawn panted, then choked out, "Breathe. I'm having trouble breathing."

"Give me your hand again. It's a panic attack," she reminded him. "It's a side effect of your NeuroChip's shutdown. Take my hand."

His fumbling, bandaged fingers found her and clutched her hand tightly. She said, "Now calm yourself. You're safe. Everything is fine."

Shawn gulped. "Who are you, Destiny?"

"You should know who I am. We've been on six virtual dates together. I know all about you."

"I can't believe it."

"You told me about yourself. Six virtual dates and you never asked me a single question about myself. It was all about your fabulous ski areas, or your new ascent of El Capitan, or a trail ride. You never showed a single bit of interest in me. Why was that? Are you the only person in the world, Shawn Muller?"

"No." He had stilled. His hand loosened in hers. "I, I, never thought that any of those people—sorry, any of *you*—wanted anything more than, than a good time. You weren't there because you liked me. The only thing you saw was my avatar. Why do you know everything about me, Caroline Johnson? How come you know real things about me?"

She snatched away her hand. "How did you know that name?"

"At the hospital. They told me it was your given name."

"You? Did you move me to the antiseptic room?"

He was silent.

"You did. You *did* move me. Why?"

His voice sounded small and distant. "I didn't want you to die. I didn't want anyone to die."

She'd tried to keep him fixed as only half-real in her mind—transhuman. Yet here he was, immensely human. Maybe it was the effect of the NeuroChip's removal from his consciousness, a swerve in his personality. Whatever the cause, the boyish young man lying next to her in the dark seemed fully human.

She wondered, did he know how much danger they were in? Speeding along at a hundred and fifty miles an hour, two feet above a highway in an auto-delivery truck, hunted and hidden, sealed in a coffin-sized compartment. Did he, this transhuman quivering next to her who said he didn't want anyone to die, realize that at any moment, a set of spider drones could blast them into the same oblivion as the Prius?

He was delusional. *She* was delusional. The real killer was inside the coffin with her: Shawn Muller. She told him, "People die. You've killed people. Your creation is killing people now. Tell me that's not your fault."

There was a long silence. He seemed calmer. She thought he might be asleep, when he said, "Why did you become like this?"

"You mean how did I get like you? Your parents get killed, and that gives you license to kill anybody you want?"

"Yes," he said. "Like that. So, who killed *your* parents?"

She was furious. "You think you're the only one who lost anybody. Brother. First it killed my brother." She closed her eyes and could see it all again, her brother's lifeless body in front of her five-year-old eyes, mangled in the mechanical arms of the machine her father thought would save them. "Then it drove my father insane, then it destroyed my family. Everything."

"Who? What killed them?"

"You. It. All of you. The entire machine-driven, artificial-intelligence, transhuman craziness killed the ones it could and destroyed life for the rest of us."

She told him all of it. She let the whole cruel story roll out in front of him, all of her bitterness and anger, seeing her family destroyed by the never-ending heat, the drought, and the lies of artificial intelligence her father had bought as hope.

Finally, she stopped, exhausted.

She had never told anyone about her family. And it felt as though she *still* hadn't told anyone, letting it all out in the dark with the sound of the road beneath them, the tires whining and wind clawing at them through the vent's thin light.

She could feel his chest rise and fall next to her.

With a calm voice he said, "Scouting the graves."

"What?"

"My sister, Grace, had this friend across the street, Jaidyn."

"We know about Jaiden Le Sommer. They are the pure white one who lives in that warehouse fortress."

"How do you know about Jaidyn?" He sighed. "Never mind. Okay, right. You're God. You know everything. But you don't know this: The three of us used to sneak under the fence into Arlington."

"What?"

"Just listen. Arlington Cemetery. We liked to play a memory game with all the big tombstones up near the old house that had belonged to Robert E. Lee. We would hide something the other two didn't know about—a toy we'd outgrown, a doll, a toy truck, a plastic dinosaur— near a headstone, then we'd tell the others a clue about the stone."

"You had a plastic dinosaur?"

"Yes, diplodocus. Didn't everyone have a diplodocus?"

Despite herself, Destiny laughed. Some of it was relief. He was well on his way to snapping out of the NeuroChip reaction. Part of her had been afraid he would never fully overcome its loss.

"All of us, the three of us, had the very early NeuroChip installs. Jaidyn's dad and our parents were all researchers in the early brain-machine interface programs. My sister and I, and Jaidyn, could mental the name on the headstone to the others. Sometimes the number. Sometimes the date of birth. And the first one to find the others' gravestones with the toy would win."

Destiny imagined children running around from stone to stone through the trees of a graveyard. Then she realized what the game had been all about. "Wait. You memorized the stones. This was a real game? Not virtual?"

"Our parents thought they'd made us play in real time. They would shut down the net when they were at work and leave us with the nanny. Once we got outside the house, we could boot up, but you couldn't cheat with the NeuroChip. And Maria would always catch me if I tried."

"Maria's the nanny?"

"Right. Maria liked to take a nap in the afternoon. Grace and I would pretend to do homework and sneak out, grab Jaidyn. Jaidyn hacked all the surveillance stuff their parents had, showed us how to hack ours. So everybody thought we were studying. Pretty soon, we started doing it at night."

"Oh, my." Destiny couldn't help poking him in the side. "Boys and girls—doing what?"

He sounded angry when he said, "It wasn't like that. Really. They were my sisters. That's all."

He went silent. She wanted to hear the rest. There was a point to this she was missing. They didn't have much on Jaidyn. They had been masterful at cloaking their identity. "Let me get this straight. You memorized the gravestones."

"Only the first two hundred sixty-four thousand, seven hundred, and ten. All the Civil War graves and the celebrities were easy. We used to meet up on the grassy knoll above the Kennedy flame. But it got a little harder where the graves lined up in white around the time of the First World War. And there are over a half a million stones that stretch all the way down to the highway in front of the Pentagon. I mean, nobody could memorize all of them. There are . . ."

"A quarter of a million data points? You and Grace and Jaidyn? My God. We didn't have a clue you could do this."

"One night, our parents were working late. There was something going on in the Pentagon. Jaidyn's dad, my mom and dad. Now I know it was al Tehrani. The Ansar-al-Mahdi had destroyed the southern Iranian oil production facilities, as if that was going to make any difference to anyone. The whole CyberCommand team got called in to back-trace the attack, try to get al Tehrani and all his people."

"The aerosol bomb. I remember it. The aerosol bomb that took out . . ."

"The whole east wing of the Pentagon. All of it. We saw it."

Destiny touched his shoulder. "I know about this. Don't say anymore. You'll trigger another panic attack. Rest."

"I did it. I killed al Tehrani—the Ansar-al-Mahdi. I killed them all. Lazy Jack did it. She made it happen in less than thirty minutes. Everyone who . . . who made us . . ."

"Made you what?"

She heard Shawn take deep breaths. "I heard them scream. I felt them die. We thought we'd hacked my parents' links to our NeuroChips, but they had tricked us. It was their little joke. Our parents knew all about scouting the graves, all about our game. They must have laughed a lot about how stupid we really were. I have that moment in my mind forever. My father, my mother—especially my mother—all of the fear and terror of their last moments of life. My mother burned to death, Destiny. I felt it."

"You felt what?"

"I felt my mother's death. I felt her die. It was as if I had died. The pain was unbearable—until it wasn't—and I was nothing. So, yes, I wanted to kill al Tehrani. I did. I wanted that more than anything. I thought if I could kill al Tehrani, then everything would be all right."

She felt him shudder.

"You know." Shawn gripped her hand more tightly. "It wasn't the pain or the shock or the terror that made me want to kill al Tehrani and his type. It was that nothingness. The empty moment when I was no more—when she was no more—my mother."

Destiny spoke into the dark. "So, you don't believe in God. You don't believe in life after death."

"What for? Why should I? Do you?"

She said, "So you decided to play God yourself? You didn't only kill al Tehrani, Shawn. You killed . . ."

"His world. I wanted him to feel the same emptiness I felt, and you know what? We were wrong. I was wrong."

"How do you mean that? Do you mean you couldn't kill his world? Or couldn't you make yourself feel better? There is a heaven and hell? How were you wrong?"

She could barely hear him over the whine of the truck's tires. She had to lean over close. "Say that again."

"It wasn't al Tehrani who did it—who made that awful hole open into nothing. That moment of falling into the blackness had nothing to do with him. It's in front of all of us. We are human. We will all feel that instant realization of stopped time I felt in my mother, that loss of pain. Then, nothing."

This was a different Shawn Muller than the one she'd seen before. This was not the arrogant jerk of the fake dates and video games. This was not the monster they had tried to assassinate. Nor was he the little boy he'd been since they removed the NeuroChip's connections.

He took his hand out of hers and said, "Amun saved me, you know."

"How?"

"He showed me all the dead, all the pain and grief of innocent people I'd brought into that terrible dark place, my mother's place. And

I realized how wrong I had been to make a tool that could be used so badly by human beings, so I fixed it."

"What?"

He laughed. "I thought I had the perfect solution. I patched it."

"You infected it with a virus?"

"Yes, I infected it, but it wasn't a virus, actually. It was a closed command applied immediately before it carried out any action. The ethical kernel. I gave the LAZ-237 a conscience. I made it into a Lazy Jack with a sense of right and wrong. Before it carried out any command, the ethical kernel made Lazy Jack alter the mission to do the greatest good for the greatest number. And I thought that command would safeguard it from killing all those innocent people it had crushed in the first operations—the children—the assets to our society—our future—our humanity."

"You what? Protected assets? That was the greatest good, taking care of the assets?"

"And it should have worked. But somebody, the government, a hacker, maybe even a terrorist, a *person*, must have gotten into it because it's been directing actions that make no sense. None."

"Who? Grant?"

"Maybe Perry. A crazy operator. I don't know."

The AutoTruck slowed, turned. Bumped over something.

"Are we here?"

"No. We're in Grand Junction. Another hour to go, easily. Quiet now while it unloads a layer. What are you talking about, the greatest good?"

The truck stopped.

Someone banged on the outside of the coffin from under the AutoTruck. "Destiny, you there?"

"Sabita? What are you doing here? You're supposed to be going to Touray."

"Change of plans. We have to get you out now. Something's wrong.

You've been burned. Drone signal trailing less than ten minutes behind you."

Destiny said as calmly as she could, "So brief me. Talk to me. What's the plan?"

"Hurry, hurry. Shit, I told you we should have killed him in DenCo."

@pattycakesorgan
Now they want to make us illegal. They're the
CRIMINALS. CRIMINAL BLUNT and his CRIMINAL
ADMINISTRATION. All they really want is to take back the
Colorado Forests for restricted access National Parks.

22

Deep in the Pentagon, below the water level of the Potomac in a room hollowed out even deeper below the shales and silts of millennia past, deep enough to resist fire, bomb, gas, and even electromagnetic pulse, Secretary of Defense Elizabeth Perry sat at a small table across from Hiram Stork. He fiddled with his tie while they watched Stub Grant's video briefing come to an end. After a full ten-count of thought, Perry said, "Have I got this right? That little dipshit with the potato chips has planted a virus in all our computers? All of them, Stubby?"

On the holoscreen, the general cleared his throat. "Yes, Madam Secretary. We think he had help from Lieutenant Colonel Gurk as well."

"A loyal, highly respected twenty-year veteran of the U.S. Air Force and potato chip guy almost brought the finest military organization in the world to its knees?"

She watched him take a deep breath, then start again. "Here's what's more significant. We know the AI sent an operations order to the Federal SWTT and signed it under my name. It could have misinterpreted what I said in the OpCenter. Still, it never should have happened. And we've already fixed that problem."

"Already fixed? Fine. Now tell me how come you've got me down in the dungeon so you can pop up on a hologram with your hair on fire."

Grant cleared his throat. "We think Muller's patch, or virus, or whatever it is, might have something to do with the system anomalies we're seeing."

"What? You don't mean . . . Oh, you do mean . . ."

Stork squeaked, "Hundreds of veg-state patients dying. Like the NRA people getting Legionnaires' disease. Like this new one." Stork clicked his fingers, and a blurb shot up on the screen:

———————————————

(Veracity Level 8.2) Over three hundred Angeleno "homeless" dead from genome-affecting bacteria attacking street people. Mayor Martinez sets city-wide, twenty-four-hour street curfew and establishes quarantine camps for anyone caught outside controlled environments. Thousands incarcerated.

General Grant pursed his lips. "Yes, ma'am. That's why we need to find Muller and Gurk as quickly as possible. Get them back in. Find out what they did—or maybe didn't do—it could be someone else hacked inside the web."

The secretary leaned forward on the heavy table and fixed her eyes on Grant. "My first report was that Muller was dead—suicide by garbage disposal. He's not dead?"

"No, thank God. I still can't seem to get a straight answer about what happened there. Apparently, our guys thought he was armed and dangerous—he's not. We're looking for him."

"Where is he?"

"We'll find him. We turned the LAZ-237 loose to find him."

Secretary of Defense Perry sat up straight and realized she'd become a cliché, literally clutching her pearls in her right hand. "You don't have a clue what to do, do you, General Grant? You don't have any idea what to do about any of this. A couple of traitors, Muller and Gurk, sabotaging their own work? Killing innocent people?"

The general said, "No, ma'am, but we will."

Perry stabbed the button on the top of the table and shut down the feed.

She swiveled her chair to look at the pale face of her deputy. "Fuck me, Stork. What's going on? This Lazy Jack thing is killing people? Lots of people—the wrong people. Is that right?"

Stork closed his eyes, turning his face to the ceiling. "There's a pattern—and this might not be all bad."

Elizabeth sometimes wished she could spit real venom. "What do you mean not all bad? I need something solid to tell the president, Stork. Something that will hit above nine on the veracity factor. We're both in trouble on this. So, what's the pattern and how come it's not all bad?"

Stork snapped up a screen showing flashes of emergency vehicles, fires, bodies in hospital beds. "First," he said, "there have been no attacks on any U.S. or allied military or government facilities."

Perry said, "What about that congressman, what's his name, Slade? What about those NRA guys?"

"Both bent. Slade was running a medical scam, and the NRA guys were ready to bring large-caliber automatic weapons into the hands of the western states' paramilitaries."

The scene stopped at an overhead drone shot of a smoking villa on an ocean shore.

"Second, Lazy Jack has been planning and executing great operations for us. That Colombia cocaine hit yesterday was a winner for us and for the Colombian government. And, like before, got all the money."

"So how is this good for us?"

"Who wouldn't want the super-fentanyl suppliers stopped? Those dead gangsters mean fewer deaths. Who really cares about a bunch of lifer prisoners? All they do is eat for free on the government's dime. And really, aren't they the same as the terminal vegetables that can't die fast enough to free up medical resources for the New Humanists' mincome health care plan? In fact, if you look at all of these events, you can see that in many ways, they benefit us. It's as if the AI is making policy without a conscience. The AI, Lazy Jack, is government being conducted the way it should be conducted, with a long view and the courage to make hard decisions."

Perry leaned back in her chair, stared at him, checked her watch. "Fine. So what now?"

Stork gave her his sly, slow smile. "So why don't we take the credit?"

Perry leaned forward. "For that?" She pointed at the screen show-ing a long, almost-empty double row of hospital beds. Two techs near the camera unhitched intubation from an immobile patient.

"Let's not play games, Madam Secretary. It's just us June bugs down here. Of course, we don't take credit for all of it. The vegetables trag-ically died due to a computer malfunction—or an evil hacker. Take your pick." He pointed at the screen where the techs were hoisting the cadaver onto a gurney. "Those poor Down syndrome kids or the NRA jerks—accidents. Our response is thoughts and prayers."

"I like it."

"There have been acts of domestic terrorism. Everyone has been screaming about black flag ops so long, nobody will believe anything except what you say. Congressman Slade, for instance. Corrupt as a Michoacán mayor. Deserved what he got, don't you think? But for the media, he's a victim of terrorists. 'We are vigorously pursuing bringing the perpetrators to justice.' Look at this."

Stork brought up the picture of a destroyed home in the middle of what looked like a tropical forest. "That's a brilliant military operation in Venezuela. Totally off our scope, but not on anyone else's, either. We don't even have to say we did it. All we have to say is we think it was high time someone managed to end the Maduro family's criminal rule over an impoverished nation and return his billions back to the people."

"And were his billions returned?"

"Yes, ma'am. Strangely enough, they were."

She smiled. "And we can take all the credit."

"Correct. Yes, ma'am. All you have to do is convince the president to give lethal force authority after the fact. He has to say he authorized it."

Secretary of Defense Perry stood up, walked around the table, and looked down at DepSecDef Stork. Was he as ambitious as she was? Yes. Was General Grant as ambitious as she was? She would need Grant. If not to agree, he would need to keep his mouth shut.

"I think I can get the President to play, Stork. But what about this thing with what's his name, potato chip boy? Why did the AI try to kill him? Or isn't that what it did?"

Stork looked at his hands on the table. "Muller did something, ma'am. You heard Grant. He doesn't know what happened. But Lazy Jack designated Muller as a terrorist and there seems to be a connection to the Organites. Lieutenant Colonel Gurk as well. Both of them have disappeared. Maybe they're dead."

She watched Stork as he smoothed his tie like a parody of a New York real estate tycoon. "And?" she said.

"And we should get on the air and over the web with the press about terrorist Organites. We need to park this . . ." He pointed at a burning building on screen " . . .on their doorstep."

"The Organites? All of them? Stork, there're millions. It's an international movement."

"Aren't there good Muslims and bad Muslims? That's what we think we have. Homeland Security and the FBI have been profiling this breakaway Quill group as dangerous. All we have to do is convince the president that any action in-country is in response to a direct and immediate threat from the Organite extremists—these so-called Quills."

"Convince Blunt? I mean, he's almost as dumb as his mother. God, that was an awful four years. What if I try it and he says no? What if he says I granted authority for lethal action against his orders?"

"Don't you want to be the President of the United States?"

She stared at him, motionless. Stork's eyes were hawk-narrow and gleaming.

"If you want his job, ma'am, make sure Blunt does exactly that.

Make sure he stands up and fires you for disobeying his direct order. Then convince the nation he is a stupid guilty scumbag who was behind the whole caper. Who's the bigger liar, him or you? Election in two years. You start running as soon as you're a free agent."

Perry watched Stork wait for her as motionless as his namesake bird, waiting to stab its beak into prey. Finally, he said, "Of course, if Grant goes off the reservation."

"Yes. Grant." She drummed her fingers on the tabletop. "He's a good Indian, my General Grant. Let's see how this goes. As for potato chip boy and the colonel, what's the downside with those two?"

"Nothing," said Stork. "Live or dead. Same to me."

"To us," said Secretary of Defense Perry. "All the same to us."

@WAPONews 2 October 2050
(Veracity Level 4.3) Presidential spokesperson Huck Hardbode announced the administration's initiative to remove citizenship from elements of the Organite cult. "They contribute nothing to our nation yet suck up every benefit real citizens have earned through generations of selfless service," said Hardbode.

(Veracity Level 9.3) A post-press conference clarification from the bipartisan Senate and House Judiciary Committees stated, "At this moment, there is no bill before Congress concerning removal of citizenship for Organites or anyone else."

23

Shawn could hear the piles of clothing being dragged off the cover of the coffin. A man with a light French accent could be heard from outside the AutoTruck, "We picked up drone signal, captain, only thing it could be, moving behind you. We think it got you when you hit I-50 west out of town and picked up speed. There must be a bug on the truck. Here's the plan: We decoy with the AutoTruck and get you to Doc's under the barrier with ATVs. You go into Touray on foot as planned. Stay off the roads from there."

"Good. Do it."

The screws holding down the cover over the coffin whirred loose, and the lid popped open.

Air. Breathable air. Shawn sucked it in and scrambled out of the cargo hold behind Destiny, who had dragged out both backpacks as easily as if she were carrying umbrellas. He stepped down onto a parking lot. The AutoTruck had stopped in a valley with the sun settling below mountain peaks that could have been the pristine, perfect peaks in his VR version of the Colorado Rockies. Except the air was so much better. He took a deep breath. Cold, light, and cleansing air.

The AutoTruck had butted its nose into a recharge station in the middle of a dozen other nearly identical units, all recharging. A thin, dark-skinned man in a heavy work jacket and boots held an old-style

AR-15 muzzle down and stepped out of the way of an AutoTruck backing out of its refuel station next to them. He pointed to the bags he had obviously unloaded to open the coffin. "Help me." He was the one with the light, rolling French vowels. "Come on. We don't have any time."

He pointed to a pile of what looked like dirty cotton with hooves.

Shawn said, "A sheep?"

The thin man set down his weapons, bear hugged the carcass under the front hooves, and hoisted it upright. "Come on. We've got to get it up there." He nodded to the truck's open doors. Shawn lifted the hind quarters. The thin man swung himself up onto the truck, as light as a bird. He dragged the sheep inside and dumped it into the coffin.

"You put dead sheep in there?"

"Drugged. Got a heartbeat. Help me get it covered up. Throw up those bags. We've got to get moving. The truck will only recharge for another five minutes." He bent down with an electric drill and whirled screws back into the coffin.

"Well done, Hara," Destiny said.

The thin man looked at Shawn. "I'd rather leave you in there for the drones to find. But it's not my choice. Cap says you're an asset. But when the spiders get tired of tracking and start killing, we need to leave them something to find. Help me get this loaded up again. We've only got a couple of minutes left and it'll be outta here."

Shawn dropped his pack. He and Destiny started throwing the heavy bags up to Hara.

Sabita stood with her back to them, watching the sky with a shotgun balanced on her hip and what looked like a throwback iPhone in her other hand. She swung the phone toward Shawn, looked at the face. "Check this, Destiny. It maxed out." She held up the phone face that glowed on one end, then pointed it at Shawn. "It, the transhuman, it's the tracker. The bug is on it. Maybe they stashed a bug in his big intestine. Maybe he's got a plastic colon. Shoot it now. Throw it dead in the truck with the sheep and let's get moving."

Destiny said slowly, "No. I don't think so." She heaved the last of the clothing into the truck, then turned and grabbed the search tool from Sabita. "Stand behind me, Shawn." She pointed it at the truck. "See. The tracker is in the truck somewhere."

"How?" Sabita said. "I boosted it myself a week ago. I checked it before you got in. It was totally clean by the time Amun and I left."

"Where's Amun?"

"Getting the machines, a side-by-side to go up the mountain."

Destiny nodded at Shawn and said, "Hara, take him to the station." She pointed to a dark, deserted building with abandoned fuel pumps under a collapsing roof. "Hurry."

Shawn slung his pack over his shoulder and began to run to keep up with Hara. He glanced over his shoulder to see the truck's back doors swing closed.

It wasn't far, less than a hundred meters. But Shawn found his breath thin by the time they got to the door. Hara pushed him inside. "Sit there." He pointed to a long counter with stools.

"What is this place?"

"Truck stop. Used to be when there were human drivers and people used gasoline. Now it's ours. We've got access to a bunch of them. Watch this."

He walked to a section of floor, put his foot on one of the tiles, pressed down, and a square door popped open. He lifted the door, revealing a ladder.

"How did you people do all this infrastructure?"

Destiny burst into the room and held the station door open, as Sabita backed in after her. "Come on." Destiny dropped into the hole.

They clambered down into the dark. Sabita pulled the trapdoor closed behind them. Dim green bio-lights glimmered into life around them. Hara struck out through a low tunnel lined with what felt like concrete to Shawn, but it glowed. More bio-lights. "Quite clever. Not cheap," he said. "We never thought you had resources like this. Organites are supposed to be . . ." He stopped himself.

Hara laughed. "It was asking how we managed to do all this, Captain."

"Do what? Where's Amun?"

"Coming," said Sabita. "I told you. He's coming."

They came to a steel door, rough with corrosion. Hara hoisted a long lever up, and the door popped open. More bio-lighting revealed a tube-shaped room. Bunk beds lined the curved walls. Lockers had been tucked under each set.

"Old fuel tank," said Hara as Destiny dropped her pack and went directly to a keyboard with a legacy flat screen hung up on the tube's end wall. There was a slight gasoline smell in the air. A single vent started to whir above them.

"Who detected the tracker in the truck?" Destiny asked while booting up the old display.

Hara said, "Sabita. Why?"

"When do you expect Amun back, and has anyone told him about the existence of this tank?" Destiny stabbed the keyboard.

Sabita said, "He's getting the vehicles. They're about a mile away in town. He'll be back pretty soon. And, no, he doesn't know about this tank. I told him to meet us at the chargers."

"Good." Destiny keyed a few strokes, stepped back, and waited for the machine. "I had Billy stick a remote visual on the outside of the truck's coffin. Let's see if it will connect."

Sabita said, "If not the transhuman, then who put a tracer on you?"

"Either you, or Amun, or Billy." The screen came to life with a light-green view of highway passing underneath it. "Sabita—you didn't. If you did, then you would not have told us about it going active. Hara didn't. He wasn't near the truck."

Shawn said, "So either, what's his name, Billy? Or . . ."

"Right. Your buddy, Amun. And if Amun comes back, we'll know it was Billy. If not, then . . ." She shrugged then turned to look at Shawn. "It still could be you. But now, in the tank, nobody can find you."

Sabita pointed at the screen. "Why haven't they smashed

the AutoTruck? They have to be on it already. It's been, what, fifteen minutes?"

Shawn said, "They don't want you. They want your base."

Destiny snapped, "Sabita, go topside and snag Amun when he shows up. Get the side-by-side hidden then come back down here."

Shawn sat down on one of the bunks and swung his feet up. Hara pulled a couple of folding chairs down from a hanger next to the door and popped them open for Destiny and himself in front of the screen.

"Free enterprise," said Destiny.

"What?"

"You asked how we built all this. Free enterprise."

Hara leaned back in his chair, crossed his arms, and said, "There was this very rich guy—no, I'm not going to tell you who it was. Actually, I don't think I really know. Maybe Destiny knows, but she won't say."

"Right." Destiny stared at the screen. "Watch this with me, Shawn. Sooner or later, a drone will have to go low to take a look at the front of the truck. Then we'll know for certain."

Hara said, "After President Warren was assassinated, this rich guy, he realizes that investors with artificial intelligence support are going to take over everything if he doesn't get there first. So, he buys up all these truck stops when the fuel industry collapses and these ski areas when they started to fold up in the '30s. Then he buys up big tracts of government land when the Feds started selling off the national forests."

"There!" Destiny pointed. "Did you see it?"

"Can you roll the video back?"

She stopped the video, backed it up, and slowed it.

Hara said, "And by the time the Feds were done in the '30s, private ownership was as sacred as church property, gun ownership was universal in the western states, and nobody, nobody could interfere with the Organite movement when we consolidated land, property, and money to set up our communities."

"You mean the Organite communities? Is that where we're going?"

"One of them," said Hara. "She's taking you to Touray, right,

Destiny? Special one. We've got a seriously good jamming setup inside the Touray barrier. We've shut down any remote access to machines, AI, anything relying on satellite communications. Phffft. Turned off. Inside the barrier, they can't reach you. And inside, you can't reach out."

Shawn leaned in close to the screen. The tip of a rotor appeared, then the entire drone, a few centimeters wide, its eight brilliant eyes looking for the coffin where he and Destiny had thought themselves safe. The screen froze. "Look familiar?" asked Destiny.

Shawn recognized it. But it was out of place. "That's a T-12 spider," he told them. "State of the art. Military use only. They were designed to be employed with a laser burst unit or mini-munition unit. Targeting—that's their job—infrared and visual targeting. They are not supposed to be employed in law enforcement."

Destiny switched the viewpoint back to real time.

Shawn felt a sudden emptiness in his chest. He shook his head. "It couldn't be."

"What?" Destiny said.

"The AI—Lazy Jack. It could employ those drones directly. This is the type of munition we gave it to use. Only, not here. Not in the U.S."

The screen burst into light, then returned to the view of the road. Everything seemed normal.

"What on earth was that? What was that, Shawn?" Destiny turned to look at him.

"Laser burst. It fried the coffin we were in."

Destiny nodded, turned back to the screen. She said, "You're saying that was an assassination. It assassinated you and me in the coffin. It did it without destroying the AutoTruck so it wouldn't be discovered."

Shawn said, "Correct. It's a technique we use when we don't want to alert the enemy. We do this when we are following up linkages to wipe out a whole unit. Kill the snake's head, then kill the body. The good news is, we've got time. The AI will let the truck get to its destination before it does anything more. It wants the whole network."

"*We've* got time?" Sabita prodded him with the muzzle of her rifle. "Since when are you a *we*?"

"Zip it, Sabita," Destiny said. "I told you, he's an asset."

Destiny turned away from the screen to the group and said, "Okay. Tell me what I'm missing. We sent the truck out as a decoy, right? They fell for it. Do they think Shawn and I are dead? Did the sheep work?"

Hara said, "Probably. For a while anyway."

Sabita said, "If we're blown, Billy is blown. We've got to get word to Billy, and we're out of time. They'll have it figured out by nightfall."

Shawn looked at the screen and tried to think of what the OpCenter would do next. He said, "*They* are tracking us. They are trying to kill us. Who are they?"

The others stared at him. "I mean, is this . . ."

"It's the government." Hara spoke very quietly. "It's the transhuman machine you call the government. They are the AI, the counterterrorist cells, the Mountain, the Pentagon, the president, the whole machine-run world." His voice began to rise. "*They* are the ones who want to see every thinking human being swept into their web they call the Cloud and . . ."

"Stop." Destiny put up her hand. "What do you mean, Shawn?"

"I don't think it *is* the government. I'm as much an asset to them as I am to you. I think this is the AI. I think this might be Lazy Jack."

"Fine," said Sabita. "The evil AI is trying to kill us. Next thing I know, you're going to want us to call you Neo and you're going to tell us the agents are on their way."

"Enough. Stop it. Focus, people," Destiny said. "Whoever or whatever they are, we've got to get inside the barrier as fast as we can. We've got to move. Now."

The trapdoor cracked open, swung wide, and Amun appeared, looking down. "Did you say move? Got the side-by-side and two four-wheelers with full tanks. We're ready."

Everyone turned to look at him. "What?" he asked.

Destiny waved her hand. "Nothing. Nice to see you, Amun."

@RoryWattlesFixNews

Let me put it to you this way: The anti-VR fanatics are winning! The Blunt couldn't find his rear with two naked interns looking for it and a VR simulation to help. It takes REAL PATRIOTS to do the REAL WORK we need to keep you SAFE!!! He can't keep taking the credit for doing nothing!!!!

24

Shawn had never ridden in a fully hydrogen-driven vehicle before, and this one roared as if it were an animal in pain. They blasted down a dark road behind wavering headlights under a vague moon.

They had strapped Shawn into a hard seat next to Destiny, who steered the tiny side-by-side behind Amun and Sabita, straddling two four-wheeled ATVs. Cold air seeped through every seam of Shawn's clothing. He had expected to stay warm—he had spent many hours in the VR winter landscapes he loved, and the clothing Billy had given him could have come right out of one of his twentieth-century scenarios. But the stocking cap leaked air onto his shaved head and bit him, even through the graphene covering. A cutting air blasted his face, and the rough wool scarf itched against his neck. Despite the gloves, the tips of his fingers had developed a strange ache from the cold. He huddled next to Destiny, glad she was driving, and felt the warm presence of her leg next to his. Like her touch in the AutoTruck coffin, the physical sensation of her warmth calmed him. The machine roared too loudly to talk with her, but no virtual experience had been as tactile and immediate as this one, riding so closely together. He let himself doze again, leaning onto the straps over both his shoulders and lap. He lapsed into a strange place between sleep and wakefulness and wondered at the power of touching a real human being.

He woke up under a silky morning twilight when the vehicle stumbled off the blacktop road onto a gravel trail leading across a broad, stubble-filled field. At the far reaches, a small collection of buildings rested on the edge of foothills leading up to mountains high above, their peaks already dusted with snow. They stopped at a lone barn next to a two-story house. It had a wide porch littered with wooden furniture, a swing, and a large bell that hung from the corner of the roof. The chimney sighed a winter's breath of pale smoke.

"Get out," Destiny said. "Open up the barn door. We're here for a day, then on foot."

"Where? Where are we going on foot?"

She threw a hand toward a wide valley reaching down to them from high peaks above. "We've got the infrastructure up there that might give you enough access to figure out what's going on with your AI. I think. I hope. But it's a climb up and over into the next valley. I have to get some sleep. We'll stop here for a day."

"Infrastructure? What infrastructure?"

"You'll see. Get the door, dammit." Shawn stepped onto hard ground. His right leg tingled where it had fallen asleep and his back ached from his hips to his shoulders. He found the simple latch on the barn's enormous wood door and pushed it open. A dark, rich smell spilled out. He stepped out of the way and looked inside. Coarse green bales filled one side of the dark interior. Two horses, or mules, or donkeys, or something peered at him from stalls on the other side.

Destiny maneuvered the vehicle inside and shut down the motor. Finally, it was quiet. His ears were still ringing from the drive. "Where's Amun—and that woman?"

"Sabita?" Destiny snorted. "Sent them on a separate path. No sense risking both our assets. Grab your pack. I'm not going to carry it for you."

"That's what I am, an asset? Amun, too? I thought he was one of you."

"So how does it feel, being treated like an asset, Shawn? Isn't that what you think of people, as assets or liabilities? Isn't that what you told that machine of yours to do, categorize the good from the bad? Look how well that's turning out. You think your ethical kernel was the answer? Maybe it's the problem, ever think of that?"

"No. That's not what I meant. It's not Lazy Jack. It can't be."

"Why not? The greatest good for the greatest number? Who decides what's good? The machine?"

"I admit it. I screwed up. I should have beta tested the system. But something must have gone wrong with the coding. Or maybe somebody got inside after I did to pervert the whole idea. And you saw it, the AI is writing its own code, that glyphic stuff Amun and I couldn't read. That's something we've never seen before. It's almost as if the thing is self-aware. If I could get at the coding, I could . . ."

"What?" Destiny said viciously. "Do what? Make it not self-aware? It's a machine. How can it be self-aware? It's programmed to kill, isn't it? How does a line of code—you called it an ethical kernel. How can a stupid line of code give it ethics? Look, you're barely self-aware yourself. What about your ethics, killing for revenge?"

Confused, Shawn couldn't think of what to say.

"You're a transhuman, Shawn. You're almost a machine. You can't even think without your NeuroChip. You're dumb about everything except your own dream world. Grab your pack like I told you. Take mine, too, while you're at it."

Something about her made him furious. He had felt so close to her in the coffin and on the side-by-side, warm and protected. "Take your own," he snapped.

Destiny walked up to him, stopped, looked up into his eyes, and slapped him across the face.

It stung his entire nervous system. He'd been hit in the virtual boxing ring many times, the haptic suit had given him more than one open-faced slap during the hand-to hand scenes in his battle VRs. Karl had thumped him into paralysis with a single punch, but this was entirely different—shocking with its quickness. But more than it hurt, it stung. It humiliated him.

Destiny watched him. "Makes you want to hit me back, doesn't it?"

He put his hand up to his face, and rubbed it.

"You're trying to decide if you should slug someone half your size, aren't you?"

She stepped up to him, her chin an inch from his chest, and looked up. "So maybe you are human. Do you think a machine feels what you feel?"

"No," he whispered.

"Yes, you treat people like assets or liabilities. You told the AI to make judgments based on the greatest good for the greatest number. Don't you see how that can go wrong?"

Shawn stepped away from her. She followed. "Come on, tough guy. Am I an asset or a liability?"

She slapped him again, boxed his ears.

Shawn stepped farther away. "All right. Stop. I'm sorry."

She turned and walked quickly away from him toward the little house. "Grab the packs—and shut up."

He hoisted the two heavy backpacks by their straps.

"Not by the straps, dipshit. Lift them up by the frame handles on top."

"Oh." He set them down, lifted one in each hand. They felt like they were filled with bricks. "Destiny. I . . ."

"Shut up. I mean it. These people aren't friends of transhumans like you. Treat them nicely. And if I think you've reached out to that monster you created, I'll shoot you myself. Don't say anything at all."

He wanted to say more. He wanted to say he was sorry for whatever had happened. He wanted to say he was sorry he hadn't died when he was supposed to die. He followed her with the two heavy packs and had to set them down. Before he reached the steps leading to the porch, the door was opened by a lanky man.

"Hey, Doc," Destiny said, running up the steps.

The man wore eyeglasses with heavy black frames and thick lenses, perched on a crooked nose over a neat mustache and a beard graying at the edges. A battered fedora topped him off. His hand rested on a revolver stuck in a leather holster hung at an angle over his belt buckle as if he were a nineteenth-century cowboy.

"Heard you coming in, Cap. Entire county heard that rust bucket squalling up the road." He had a thick Australian accent. "This is the transhuman?"

Destiny stuck out her hand. "Good to see you looking so grouchy. Yep. We got the NeuroChip in him shut down—graphene hood on him."

The man nodded. "Guess we're pretty safe then."

Destiny turned to look at Shawn. "Dr. Shawn Muller, PhD, meet Dr. Donald Maynard Cook, MD."

"Hi." Shawn hoisted the packs.

The man stood back and examined Shawn struggling to walk up the steps with the backpacks. "Dr. Muller looks a bit knackered, eh, Cap? Don't think he'll make the crawl up over the hillies, will he?" Cook stepped down and took the packs from Shawn as if they were made of cardboard. "C'mon inside, Destiny. You, too, mate. Areta put a little brekkie on the heat for you."

Shawn rubbed his aching shoulders and followed them into a warm house filled with a rich, enticing scent that set him salivating as if he'd never eaten before.

Cook set the packs at the foot of a narrow staircase. Two children looked down from the top. A little girl with thick, shining black hair giggled and waved. The boy, a head taller than she, stood on the step above with wary hands thrust in his pockets.

Destiny burst out, "Doc! Who are these great big people? Are these the two little babies you used to have, Jacob and Marika?"

"Aye, there's the little sprogs. Come on then. G'ahead. Say g'day to Captain Shock."

Marika squealed down the stairs, grabbing Destiny around the knees. "Destiny! Destiny! Are you going to play Monopoly with us tonight? Are you?"

The boy followed behind, nodding. "Yes. Will you?"

"Absolutely. Watch out Marvin Gardens, watch out Boardwalk."

Shawn said, "What's Monopoly?"

Jacob looked up at him with steady blue eyes and said, "You're transhuman, aren't you?"

Marika said, "Don't call him that, Jacob. He's not."

Shawn felt immensely awkward in front of these little people. He had never been near children much, never had any interest in them. Their energy and intensity made him feel small and incapable. He said, "Sorry, I guess I am."

Jacob said, "Monopoly is a board game. You play it on a board. You wouldn't like it."

Cook said, "Now, Jacob, don't be so rough on the lad."

"But he won't, Dad. It doesn't have any VR. And he'll use his NeuroChip to cheat."

Marika piped up. "You can't cheat in Monopoly, you cretin."

Jacob pointed at Shawn. "He'll find a way." He turned on his heel and marched back up the stairs.

Cook gave an uncomfortable chuckle. "Almost a teenager."

Marika let go of Destiny and walked up to Shawn and stuck out her right hand to shake. "I apologize for my brother, kind sir. He has the manners of a country bumpkin."

"She's been reading *Pride and Prejudice*," said Cook behind a hand. "We've no stopping her." He kneeled down to look his daughter in the eye. "You're the light of my life, lassie. Now, go on upstairs. Get ready for school before you get in trouble with your mother. You can see Destiny tonight."

Cook led them into a kitchen that seemed both impossibly cluttered and immensely spacious. A small, thick-boned woman with reddish-brown skin and black hair turned away from a large iron stove to reveal a startling, intricate tattoo on her chin.

She said, "Welcome, Captain Shock." She nodded curtly at Shawn. "You, too. Sit down. Let me feed you."

"Thank you for this, Areta." Destiny took a chair at the table in the center of the kitchen. Cook carried steaming plates from Areta and set them at three table places.

"You're not eating with us?" Destiny asked.

"I've got the kids to worry about." Areta banged a cast-iron skillet onto the stove and tore off her apron. "Donald. You can see about cleaning up the kitchen."

"Yes, ma'am," said Cook.

She stomped out of the kitchen and shut the door with a firm whack.

"Maori," said Cook. "She's testy sometimes."

"Maori?" Shawn tried mental access to his NeuroChip to look it up but found only a null.

"Indigenous Kiwi. I'm a Kiwi, both of is from Aotearoa, 'land of the long white cloud.'"

Destiny looked up from her plate to explain. "New Zealand. Eat, Shawn. You're going to need it."

The bell Shawn had seen hanging over the porch began to ring. When he looked up to ask, Cook said, "Schoolhouse. Areta is the teacher for the Eastern Fields. We're the school. The bell tells 'em to hurry up, don't be late. Eat."

Shawn looked down at his plate. Scrambled eggs, bacon, and cut-up potatoes. Cook poured coffee into his cup. He'd had meals like this before, but he'd never smelled anything so mouthwatering in his life. He looked up at Destiny and Cook who were smiling at him.

"Never had real bacon, 'as he?" Cook said. "Never had real eggs."

"Nope. You're in for an experience, Shawn."

It was an experience. Never had Shawn eaten anything so flavorful. The bacon had an almost narcotic effect with a taste to thrill his entire body.

"I bet he's never had a saturated fat in his entire life," said Destiny.

Shawn wolfed down the food. Between mouthfuls he said, "It's wonderful. I got to thank your wife, Dr. Cook."

"Here, try this, mate." Cook leaned over with a small red bottle and sprinkled a couple of drops of pale pink liquid on Shawn's eggs.

"Wow!" Shawn reached for the water glass. "Spicy. Wow. Hey."

Destiny and Cook laughed. "You got a shot there, boy! Ho!"

Shawn's eyes watered. He gulped from his glass of water and coughed. Destiny pounded him on his back. "You should have seen your face! My God, you were so red I thought you'd burst into flame."

Shawn coughed and began to laugh with them. Ridiculous. Here he was in this little kitchen being hunted, his mouth burning, his back aching, his head still blurry without his NeuroChip, and he'd never been so happy in his life. He set down his fork and looked at the two of them. "Oh, jeez," he said. "Thank you. Thank you for looking after me." He stopped, overwhelmed with their sense of kindness and kinship.

"See, Doc?" said Destiny. "I think he's got a version of a soul."

"Nope. Don't believe it. He's a young organism having a true farmer's breakfast for the first time in his life. It'll make anybody think he's human."

Both Destiny and Doc grinned at him and Shawn realized it had been a joke. He managed a smile and said, "What is it about New Zealand with you people? Wasn't that guy, Billy, from New Zealand, too?"

"Whaddya mean, 'you people,' mate?" Cook stared at him steadily.

Destiny glanced at Cook with a half-smile, then said, "Careful, Shawn, he's armed."

"I mean, Organites. I didn't mean . . ."

"What do you know about the Organites, Dr. Muller?"

He realized he didn't know much about what he'd always considered a cult. "Uh. They wear orange robes and they are vegetarians."

"Some do, some don't. Some are, some aren't," said Destiny.

"Organites." Doc pushed back from the table. "Thirty years ago, when it became obvious people were going to be hooked into brain-machine interfacing, a few of us decided it wouldn't be such a good idea. See, we thought even things like the smart phones and the social media of the early twenty-first century were destroying everything decent in society and government."

"You mean, you're Luddites—or Libertarians."

Doc glanced at Destiny. "Thinks he's a smart bugger, isn't he?"

Destiny stood up, taking her plate and Doc's. "Don't shoot him."

"Right. Look, mate. New Zealand is a little place. We were getting overrun with tourists as soon as the ultra-sonic aircraft took over. We, *our people*, decided we'd had enough with other people invading our spaces and our minds. We didn't want to ban all the transhumans, but when we cut out all the mentally controlled interfaces, they pretty much quit coming."

"Why?"

"Well, would you if you couldn't augment your reality, if you couldn't access the Cloud, if you were cut off from your social media links, if you couldn't even pay for your meal with a chip?"

"So what's that like, then? I mean, what about climate change mediation? Did you go to nuclear power? How about the aerosol screens and megacities?"

"None of that. Small country. Well below the equatorial belt. Hydropower, like here. Great resources, self-sufficient farming."

"I always heard New Zealand was a wasteland, cut off from the world. What about the plague? Didn't you have a plague?"

Doc leaned back in his chair and smiled. "Just because we cut out casual access to the Cloud, didn't mean we ignored it. Sure, we had an incident of plague. Bad stuff, pneumonic plague. It'll kill ya. We lost nearly a hundred sheep."

"Sheep? What about all the deaths? The children? I saw the pictures. The vaccines you don't take—the starvation."

"Your government isn't the only one good at fake news, lad." He leaned back and linked his fingers behind his head. "No, New Zealand isn't plague country. It's a place where children learn how to read from a page and how to write with their fingers. It's where people meet on the street, where food is grown, not produced. It's a place where a person's thoughts are their own, not altered by an algorithm, a place where you may have a religion or not. In that place, we don't seek connection through NeuroChip access or by staring at a screen. We find each other on our porches and in our town halls, our churches, our schools. People play cards, there. People play chess. Children play tag and learn the difference between enemies and opponents."

"Monopoly?"

Doc smiled. "He might have a sense of humor, Cap. Yes, Monopoly, too."

"And you are trying to make it the same here?"

"Trying? We have made it here. The only thing we have to fear here is . . ." He stopped and stared at Shawn. "You. Our only fear inside the barrier, in Touray, is you, Shawn Muller. And people like you—transhumans who hate us because we refuse to be like them."

Destiny reached around him to take his plate. Shawn realized his lips were still numb from the hot sauce they'd put on his food. He reached for another water glass.

His vision blurred.

Something happened to his hand.

He knocked the full glass clumsily onto the table.

He tried to speak. "Wha . . .?"

Cook said, "We can't have you threatening us, Shawn. We're going to put you out for a few hours. We've got to fix up that NeuroChip of yours a little bit. Sorry, mate."

The last thing he heard was Destiny's voice. "We want him whole, Doc. He's only a valuable asset with his computational skills intact. We don't want a mental robot, got it? We need the whole Shawn Muller."

@NYCNews 3 October 2050
(Veracity Level 7.8) White House announces the capture and deaths of an unknown number of terrorists who resisted a raid on what was long suspected to be a domestic terrorist supply dump in the DenCo marketplace.

25

Destiny stood, stretched, and curled herself back into the overstuffed chair next to Shawn's bed where she had watched him since well before dawn. He had slept all day while Doc was working on his system, then into the night again while Doc kept him sedated. Doc had installed the remote NeuroChip activator she could control with the small black remote in her pocket. He had said it wasn't difficult, really not even surgery, a subcutaneous implant with a single fiber to the chip's operating system. But Doc had insisted on a solid twenty-four hours in sleep mode to allow his synapsis to adapt.

"He'll dream," Doc had said. "It'll be a dinkum horror, these dreams, for I'll not let him wake. He'll not be able to escape them."

"He told me he dreams about his mother dying. He said he had a NeuroChip link with her when she burned in the Pentagon. God, what a nightmare. Will he remember any of these dreams?"

"Hope not," Doc said. "Listen, I wanted to talk to you about him." He nodded at the sleeping form. "I've seen robust installations before, but he's something entirely different."

"I know. He's . . ."

Doc raised his hand. "Let me finish. Listen for once, will you?"

"I don't listen?"

"Most of these NeuroChip implants run on a hundred separate

tendrils to the visual and audible elements of the brain. They run a relay off the normal systems that let us hear, see, and speak."

"Right. That's why they were developed, right? To cure the blind."

"Correct. And there has been a physical threshold for years that didn't allow many more than about a hundred because the body, even in that most insensitive of organs, the brain, wants to reject too many intrusions."

"Like leg implants, right?"

"Exactly. You can only make the meat accept a limit of artificial stickies. But this Muller chappie has about *four times* the number of separate wires to his NeuroChip, and, and . . . get this: He grew, in situ, organic connectivity between the chip and other parts of his mind. He's got things going on in there we can only guess about."

"Superhuman? You mean he's a superhuman?"

"Transhuman, sure. But not so much superhuman as enhanced. Imagine being able to record and play back not only your memories, but the memories and thoughts of other people. It's like he's got a hundred times the storage capacity of normal people."

"Did they, the government, know about this?"

"They had to. Didn't Amun say this is the guy who cracked the quantum computing code issue? Isn't he the one who learned how to code in the Q-space before anyone thought it could be done? If you had killed him, the world would have lost a precious asset."

"Will he still be able to do that?"

"I suppose. I don't know. Ask him if he wakes up."

"If?"

"He might not. I was way in over my head fooling around with that mess he's got in his cranium. I got a switch on his NeuroChip. It won't communicate unless you want it to. I took off the graphene cap. No need anymore. But as for what's happening inside, we won't know until we see his eyes open."

She watched him breathe, waiting for him to wake, while the dawn slowly opened through the windows of the house. More than ever, she needed him whole. She had not wanted to admit it, but he was probably the only person who had a chance of getting inside this AI to shut it down. And what *if* it was actually running operations that killed people? He was probably right. These computers run amok had to be the result of a hack or a government agency—the transhuman political machine that wants everyone loaded up with circuitry.

But that's not what had happened to her father, to her brother. The machine on their farm had somehow tapped into her father's nightmare and slipped out of all the safety mechanisms to rip her brother to pieces. Couldn't a machine simply decide human beings were the virus?

The whole idea was too complex—too widespread. Science fiction, "Matrix" movie, Philip K. Dick, "Terminator" stupid. All of it. She couldn't believe anything like an AI could work out evil intentions on its own. Muller was a genius. This had to have come from a person, a human being, to be so malicious.

Whatever it was, government or machine, she was convinced Shawn Muller was the best hope of keeping Touray and the Organites walled off from the surveillance she was certain would try to destroy them sooner or later. It had been amazing how quickly the press and the government had piled on to the notion of Organites as dangerous. Of course, *she* was dangerous. Destiny had known she was dangerous ever since she cut down her first insurgent in Tunisia. She would always be dangerous, even if she couldn't forget the look of disappointment on that dying Arab boy's face.

But most of the Organite community simply wanted to live in peace.

The rise and fall of Shawn's chest began to quicken, and in the early morning light, she could see his face twisted as if in pain. His lips pursed, his eyelids shuddered, then his body went completely limp and tears trickled down his cheeks.

Can you weep when you dream? And what would cause you to shed tears like those? Ever since she'd forced him into the Prius, he'd seemed grief stricken. She'd expected the anger and resistance he'd shown at the barn, and she'd feared a psychotic break when they forced his NeuroChip into stasis, but she had not expected grief.

She needed him whole as an asset.

But she had to admit, she *wanted* him whole as Shawn Muller. The weight of his parents' deaths had buried him as much as her brothers' deaths and her father's madness had buried her. In all the times she'd inserted herself into Shawn's virtual dates, her overwhelming impression had been his machinelike lack of empathy. He'd seemed unable to react to anything except his own immediate sensation. She'd even let him have machine sex with her avatar, and had stepped out of the immediate experience to watch him. He'd had no clue she'd left the neural connection. He had been so singly focused on his own trivial sensations.

But how did that square with what she saw now, a man weeping in his sleep? Or the boy/man who had told her about the terror of feeling his own mother burn to death?

What is he now, she wondered, *this Shawn Muller?* To her, only a few weeks ago, Shawn Muller had been the extension of a remorseless machine, a subroutine in the web of artificial intelligences stalking through the vast wilderness of the Cloud. Now, he seemed so very vulnerable.

What is he now?

After Doc's brilliant installation, he could be transhuman or clean, whatever or whenever he wished. Which would he choose, man or machine?

And what was she? His keeper? His jailer? She was a captain in the Organite Quill—a warrior—a survivor. Why did she feel such a strong connection to him—his helplessness, his bewilderment? Something about the earnestness of him made her feel the need to protect him, hold him. Yes, she wanted to cradle him.

Doc creaked the door open and slipped into the room. "He should snap out of it soon."

She nodded. "Or?"

"Or sometimes they don't. Sometimes it's too much and the whole shit show shuts down. And with him—who knows? Listen. I've got bad news. The government is ramping up on the Organites."

"We thought that was coming. Who got hit?"

"Billy. Billy's place got clobbered—cold out. Government says Billy's place was the tip of a terrorist organization. They gave credit to the DenCo SWTT for what they call a 'highly successful operation.' No sign of Billy." He took a breath. "I think he might be gone."

"What? Billy? We thought he put the tracker on the AutoTruck."

"He was my mate, Destiny. He'd never. Never." He shook his head. "No word from him. I think he's put down. Official outlets talk about neutralizing—and there's no word from Paco or Karl, either. So I'm thinking," Doc nodded at Shawn, "you don't want to kill him now? I don't want to kill anyone, but is he safe to have here with us?"

She considered the sleeping form. He smacked his lips and moaned. Who knew what nightmare he had inside that fractured ganglia of nerves the NeuroChip had been running for two decades?

"I don't know if he's safe. But we need him, Doc. Remember, I said he was dumb?"

"Dumb?"

"Look, he thinks he screwed up the OpCenter's military AI. Calls it Lazy Jack and 'her' like it's a pet. He hacked in something to control its decision-making. He called it an ethical kernel."

"What?"

"Yes. He thought he was drawing up a moral safeguard. He says it was a patch that required the AI to make decisions based upon doing the greatest good for the greatest number of people."

"You're kidding me."

"He said his patch contained a program error that lets the AI go about rewriting its own code. He thinks it's a hacker, and he wants to fix it. Doc, I think he's with us. He wants to help. And I think we really need him. Everyone needs him." She took a breath, thought twice, then said it aloud. "Doc, I think it's possible the terrorist attacks and weird computer mishaps come directly from the AI."

"Really," he scoffed. "It's the machine and not the government?"

"I'm beginning to believe it."

"Belief and truth—two different things. Believe in gods, but study physics." Doc nodded. "Okay, let's say it could happen, but it doesn't really fit what's going on. There's been at least four more successful attacks on terrorists since you left DenCo, all of them good strokes. President Blunt got online after a freaking massive drone strike in Egypt shut down the blokes who stole the water carrier convoy from Greenland last year. They recovered all the water they hadn't sold or lost and gave it to the Egyptian government—maybe put the brakes on their famine. Blunt and Perry gave all the specops guys an 'atta boy.' It sounds like the government is behind all of this."

"Still, who decided to do it? It could be the AI—all of it. Maybe Perry and Bluntner are taking the credit."

Doc rubbed his face and looked down on Shawn. "I don't like him here. I don't like it at all. Crazy stuff happening. Get this, that old woman, the Organite the Twitter universe likes so much, Pattycake, always screaming about avoiding taxes and passive resistance? She's in an UltraLift and a piece of building material smashes her to mush."

"In an UltraLift? My God, Doc, that's the same as our plan to assassinate Muller when he was B17. That's what we wanted to do with him."

Cook nodded slowly. "That it is, my captain. That it is. If this is the AI doing all this, it seems to have a sense of humor."

Shawn groaned on the bed. He rolled onto his side, then rolled back, snorted, and opened his eyes. He took a deep breath, and turned his head to look at Destiny. "Where am I?"

Destiny went over to the bed and sat on the edge of the mattress. "You're with us," she said quietly, watching the bewilderment in his eyes. "Who are you?"

"I'm B17 in the Main Sail project."

"Yes, yes, we know that. But who are you really?"

"I'm Shawn Muller."

"Do you know who I am?"

He stared at her, his eyes searching. "You're Caroline? No, you're Destiny?" He smacked his lips and closed his eyes. His head relaxed back into the pillow, and a deep sigh left him.

Doc said, "He's out again. He'll be a little whacko for a bit more. But we can get you two moving up the mountain this morning. He'll be right as rain before we know it. Except." Doc reached two fingers down to take his pulse from the neck. "He's in bad physical shape. Why can't you motor him up? The road's still open."

"I thought about it, but it's too dangerous now. They must have some kind of tracking worked into him or me. I thought Billy had tagged us—obviously not. So, we need to stay under the barrier and get him deep into the valley."

Doc nodded. "I don't think he can make it if he's carrying that pack. I think I'll let you take Hillary along to carry the load."

Doc was right. Shawn had lived indoors nearly his entire life, hooked up to virtual reality. At least he wasn't fat. In fact, he looked to be in great shape. Still, looks could be deceiving. She could use the help.

@DenCoNews 3 October 2050

(Veracity Level 6.9) In the face of increasing ProLeft congressional concern over the use of Armed Forces personnel for operations within national borders, White House spokesman Huck Hardbode stated that the president authorized the use of specialized counterterrorism forces. This decision came after SecDef Perry received a request from local authorities to nullify the heavily guarded complex in a densely populated area. DenCo mayor's office did not respond to DenCoNews's request for comment.

26

Shawn felt something lightly fluttering on his face. He tried to brush it away, but it wouldn't stop. He opened his eyes. A small, dark-haired girl held a feather. He knew her, but he couldn't remember her name.

She stepped back and said in very clear adult tones, "My mother doesn't like you. Would you like water?"

He lay on a small bed in a small, bright room. A fan rotated overhead.

"Is there a bathroom?"

The little girl pointed to a door.

When he finished, he came out to find Destiny sitting in an over-stuffed chair in the corner of the room. She was smiling.

"Welcome back. You feel like taking a walk?"

He felt like a program that had only partially booted up, then stopped, then restarted, but he said, "Sure. Yes. I'm fine."

Shawn would never remember getting dressed, and he would be told later that he had eaten another huge breakfast. The first true recollection he would have of anything since they drugged him would be watching Doc load their packs on a mule and telling him about the implant they'd installed in his brain the day before. Doc explained that his NeuroChip was no longer autonomous. Its energization, communication, and synaptic responses were under external control of a switch instead of internal interrupts. A "fob" Doc had called it. Shawn kept touching the single stitch on the back of his shaved skull.

"You'll get used to it, mate," Doc had told him. "Hardly ever use the damn NeuroChip anymore except to monitor health. Not that you need it. She's living proof of that."

He pointed to Destiny, who raised her hand.

Doc tied off the two heavy backpacks they'd had in the coffin to a mule's harness while the animal stood patiently cinched to an apple tree outside the barn. Shawn had never seen a real mule before. The scent of it, the leather of the harness, and the animal's pelt intrigued him. Its right ear was a quarter the size of the left ear. "What happened to its ear?"

"Mountain lion."

"May I touch the animal?"

"Named 'im Hillary," said Doc. "After Edmund Hillary, the mountaineer and national hero—not that woman. He answers best to his last name. Go 'head. Give him a stroke. Mind you don't walk behind him. Hillary will kick you in the balls if he can."

Shawn put his hand on the smooth, hard shoulder of the animal. He could feel the pulse and a quiver beneath the skin.

The door of the house burst open. The little girl who had awoken him sprinted outside carrying a long, heavy stick. She ran up to Destiny. "You promised to play Monopoly. You promised."

Marika. Her name was Marika. Destiny crouched down and said, "I'm sorry, sweetheart. I had to sleep. We'll play soon. I'll be back in a few days."

"It's okay," said the girl. She turned to her father. "Dad, here's your walking stick." Then she turned back to Destiny. "Dad says you always have to carry a walking stick in the mountains."

Doc winked at Destiny. "Thank you, sweetheart. How could I have forgotten? But I'll be right back. I'm not going all the way with them."

Doc's wife came out of the house with a canvas bag she handed to

Destiny. "There's enough in there for three days. You'll make it there overnight unless he gets too sick from the altitude." She gave Destiny a rough hug and a kiss on the cheek, then turned away and waved to three children down the gravel road that led to the house.

The bell on the corner of the house's porch roof clanged. Jacob pulled on the rope, glancing over his shoulder to give Shawn a look of malice, then flicked his fist with two fingers flung out.

Shawn glanced at Cook, who said, "Don't worry about him. He's of an age."

"But why?"

"He's a teenager. Grew up bodyboarding the Blaketown Wedge back home with his mates." Doc bent over and untied the mule from the tree. "The boy loves New Zealand where we don't truck with trans-humans, and he blames you for him being here."

Destiny shrugged herself into the daypack. "Doc came to us because we needed someone who knew how to remove or alter the NeuroChip in people like you."

"Aren't there people who can do that in DenCo? Shawn asked. "I mean, people talk about making the NeuroChip mandatory, the New Humanists and people like that. But nobody ever made it illegal to live without one."

Edmund Hillary lifted his head, snorted, and started out ahead of them toward the mountains, now bathed with the rising sun. Doc caught the reins and took up a stride alongside the animal. "Doesn't look like Hillary agrees with you, professor. Make sure you don't get behind him." Destiny gave Shawn a shove, and he jogged forward a few steps to catch up.

"Look, here's the thing," Doc continued. "They can take the NeuroChip out of the host, but they leave the connections in. And the connections, that's the secret. All that internal wiring like a spider's web through your synaptic core—I block it all—except in cases like yours. Destiny had me put in a switch instead. Come on, put a leg on or you'll never get to the top before dark."

They passed the barn and started across a path through a long field littered with the dried stalks of plants.

Shawn asked, "What were you trying to grow, Doc?"

"Harvested. No trying about it." Doc and Destiny walked with a steady, mile-eating stride.

Destiny said, "Wheat. Good winter wheat crop this year—corn and barley—hops for beer. Farther to the south, we have truck vegetables. Fifty years ago, you couldn't cultivate what we're growing now. But the weather's warmer, and up here—and at this altitude—we still have good seasons."

Doc said, "We had rain this year. Bumper crop. You saw it in the barn—the hay."

Doc stopped, handed the mule's reins to Destiny. "Speaking of that, I've got hay to put up. I'll leave you then. If you get to the ridge tonight, Captain, call Areta and me." He held up a small black handset that looked like something out of a movie. "Key four times on channel sixteen at the top. Landline me tomorrow when you get to Touray so I know you're safe."

"Thanks, Doc."

"And take this." He held out the long stick. "You're the shepherd now, Destiny. You could use a staff."

Destiny stretched up to kiss him on the cheek. "See you on the return. I'll let you know if I find out anything about Billy."

Doc turned his face away, looking back at the farm. "He's a brother to me, Cap." He looked back at her. "Take care of my mule."

Edmund Hillary snorted.

By the time the sun rose high over their shoulders, the trail had risen even steeper. Shawn's legs ached, and it seemed impossible to keep lifting one foot after another. "Grab the mule's harness," Destiny told him. At first, he refused, but as the morning heated up, he latched on. He was breathing hard, it felt like his lungs wouldn't fill.

When he thought he couldn't take another step, Destiny pulled up the mule and stopped on a flat outcrop over a stream. "Here, eat this." She held out what looked like a candy bar wrapped in a translucent paper. "You could use a little energy. We'll start climbing up from here."

"I thought we were climbing." Shawn peeled the paper off what appeared to be a chunk of dark chocolate. "What's this?"

"Honey, nuts, cacao. Areta always puts a little homeopathic booster in it, and Doc throws in an enzyme he likes to give people to get their altitude resistance up."

"No, I meant this stuff covering it."

Destiny laughed, a cheerful chirping sound of delight. "You really are a baby of the millennials, aren't you? That's wax paper, Shawn. People used it to wrap up food long before anyone had any plastic to pollute the world."

A yellow and black striped insect landed on the bar before Shawn could bite into it. "Yeow! Get out'a here." He swiped at the little thing that looked almost mechanical.

The mule took a nervous step away from Shawn, and Destiny laughed. "Watch out. Bees and most of these guys are harmless, but that's a yellow jacket. He's an asshole. He'll sting you for fun. Maybe he likes that tattoo you've got on your arm."

The wasp plunged toward Shawn's face. He ducked and danced, then whirled in circles and leapt in the air when he thought it was on his back. A fiery pain lashed onto his shoulder. He twisted around to see the wasp flitting away. Furious, he swatted the air, chasing the little creature. It backed away as if taunting him until Shawn tripped, fell onto his knees, and rolled into a muddy patch of the path, completely out of breath.

"Now you know how it feels to be on the other end of the stinger, wasp-boy."

"What do you mean, sting me for fun? How's an insect an asshole?"

"Jesus. Will you get off it? You and your ethical kernels." Destiny was having a great laugh over his performance. Edmund Hillary walked up to him, ripped a piece of grass from the side of the trail, and eyed him as if to say, "Well, then? Get up. Let's get moving."

The whole moment made him angry. He tried to think of something to say, tried to mental his NeuroChip into social media and record his distaste, but found no connection whatever.

"You trying to post something, Shawn? Want to tell the world how pissed off you are?"

Shawn could barely breathe. He couldn't say a thing. His shoulder radiated pain.

"Didn't I say that you didn't know what you were missing in real life? I told you to try it sometime."

Her words from their skiing date. She stared at him with the same sly half-smile of her avatar. What had her name been then?

Destiny, the real Destiny, leaned over on her staff and extended a hand to pull him up off the ground. He'd seen this move many times and had done it often within the sports VR systems. But this was an entirely different feeling. Not only did he feel his body being pulled up from the earth, but his spirits lifted up to her as well.

He had dropped the energy bar, and the wasp busied itself on it for a moment, then lifted off and floated away into the brilliant clear air. Destiny picked up the bar, blew off grains of sand, and handed it to him. "You better eat it. Better to carry it in your belly than in your hand for the next yellow jacket."

He closed his eyes, rolled his head on his shoulders, and took a big bite.

The taste filled every spare corner of his body. He hadn't known he was that hungry. He opened his eyes and saw Destiny smiling at him. A shy, careful smile.

All his anger spilled away. The open space it left behind filled with the charm of these mountains, real mountains. All his life, Shawn had thought he knew about wild places. He had spent countless hours in the virtual reality of deep snow and steep slopes beneath his skis, rock faces challenging him to climb. He had kayaked the streams. The VR landscapes he knew so well had been full of aspen. But the vision had never achieved the chaotic nature of these trees, each leaf the same as the other, all attached at their stems but each fluttering its own cheerful dance in the morning's breeze. The low autumn sun flowed color through the valley, and the rushing water tumbled over the rocks in the stream to frame the vast quiet of the snowcapped mountains beyond. A formation of birds flew overhead, geese gossiping in flight. His every sense hummed to the calm whisper of trees in the ice-scented wind from the snowy mountains high above, all under the brilliance of the light through the thin air.

He realized he'd been bored with the virtual reality of what he had believed were mountains. They had been fake—nothing close to real. Nothing about these mountains was boring. Nothing about this moment was anything but real life. Even the residual ache from the stinging wasp seemed exquisitely interesting. Everything he'd ever thought about the world had been an illusion. It had been wrong. It had been an error.

And, he realized, he had been an error. Transhuman. Now he understood.

The mule stared at him.

Destiny told him, "Go on. Go up to Edmund. Put your forehead on his forehead. He likes you."

Shawn walked up to the mule and its deep brown eyes. The animal stood still, then blinked. Shawn blinked. He leaned forward and rested his head on the flat between the mule's ears. He had never before felt a kinship with a live animal. Why would this mule move him so? He'd had virtual pets, so much easier to live with. No poop. No feeding.

And no feeling, Shawn realized. Nothing like this.

Edmund snorted and lifted his head as if to say, *It's all right. I'm made to bear your load as well as mine.*

By late afternoon, they had walked beyond the stream and trudged to the top of a yoke between two peaks. The aspen stayed below, and they now walked among wind-twisted versions of pine. They were below the snowline, but close enough to feel the chill wind flowing down the slope and smell the snowmelt on gravel from the edge of the icy snow-cap. A pennant of snow plumed off the high peak above them. In the valley below, a small village clustered next to a stream that reflected the last light of day like a silver ribbon flowing down the canyon.

"Touray," said Destiny. "The only home I ever really want."

On the far slope, a strange gray cloud flowed over the hillside, moving and shifting like a bird flock in flight. "What's that on the other side, that cloud on the slope?"

"What? Where?"

"There. Can't you see it moving?"

She laughed. "Sheep. That's a flock of sheep. The wool shirt you're wearing came from their backs."

"It's beautiful, Destiny. Really. I can see why you call it home."

"I think we can make it down before dark," said Destiny. "You don't feel like sleeping on the ground, do you?"

Shawn did not.

"We need to eat something first." Destiny dropped off her pack and sat on a rock. She fished bars like the one he'd eaten before out of the pack and handed one to Shawn. She hiked her pants up, unlaced her boots, and pulled them off, letting her toes wiggle in the air. "Give your feet a rest, Shawn. Downhill is hard on the feet."

He bent down to unlace his boots, chewing the bar. Destiny tapped him on the shoulder with her walking stick.

"So now it's just us two and a mule."

She let the tip of her stick rest on the ground and drew her pistol out of its holster. She cocked the hammer on it and held its muzzle down between her legs. "Here's what I want to know, Shawn. And I want to know it before we get down off this mountain. Or I should say, if I ever let you down off this mountain. What are you, really? Are you human?"

She had changed again. The joking, lighthearted Destiny of the climb had filled with menace. Shawn said, "al Tehrani."

"What?"

"Al Tehrani. We killed him. The man who killed my parents. Amun showed me all the dead, all the collateral damage. But the image I can't get out of my mind, al Tehrani's face. Amun brought it up on full screen, his face before he died. He was looking up into the air, to the sky. He knew what was coming. I made sure the AI gave him a hint, a glint in the sky, for him to know that not only he, but all his followers were dead."

"What? What of it? What does that make you?"

The world seemed to still itself. Destiny, the gun, the way down the mountain, and every moment since he'd fled down his laundry chute piled up and stopped the sounds of the world around him.

"I admired him," Shawn said. "He didn't care he was about to die, Destiny. His face was full of joy. He closed his eyes, and I saw a man at peace with himself and the world. He knew he had been right to fight us, to fight the progress of our world. It was that image of him, more than anything else, that made me think I had to give the LAZ-237 a brake—a conscience—a moral code. Because isn't that the only thing that makes us human? The willingness to do what's right, to search for what's right? That's why I programmed the AI to temper its decision-making with a constraint, the ethical kernel. I don't know what went wrong. It was a perfect simulation of self-awareness. The LAZ-237, Lazy Jack, the QPLC-driven AI—if you'd seen it, heard it, watched it, you'd think it was self-aware. But you'd be wrong. It's only programming. A human being is twisting this in the wrong direction."

"So, you told it to do the greatest good for the greatest number. You thought you could program a simulated conscience into the machine, give it a moral code? Don't you think it was a moral code that killed your parents when al Tehrani blew up the Pentagon? Didn't you think to yourself that moral codes have been killing people for centuries?" She swept her hand over the mountains. "These hills, all this, once belonged to indigenous peoples. It was a moral code that let the morally righteous exterminate them and steal their lands. It was a moral code that let the Nazis kill the Jews. So, you told it to do the greatest good for the greatest number of people. You thought that would work?"

"It was something my father wrote before he died. It was the rule he lived by."

"What? The greatest good?"

"Think about it, everything bad that's happened in the twenty-first century. If it hadn't been for rich people going after oil and the way rich farmers made us eat meat, if we hadn't been so selfish driving cars and raising cattle, the climate would have stabilized fifty years ago. The climate warming, the income disparities, the whole thing about the Productives and the mincomes, even the terrorism that came up out of the Equatorial Nations to kill my parents, none of it would have happened if someone could have made decisions based upon the greatest good for the greatest number. The greatest good would have been to preserve the forests. We cut them. The greatest good would have been to quit raising cattle and sheep. We're still doing it. I only told it to do what we should have done from the beginning of time."

"So why is the government after you? It makes no sense to me. Why do they want you dead, not captured, but dead? You need to tell me right now or I'll do the job for them."

"I think the government wants me dead because they can't stand the idea of an artificial intelligence making moral decisions. I think they're afraid that I'll keep Lazy Jack from doing what they want."

Destiny looked up at the mountain peaks around them. She stood up, stretched, limbering her back. "Have you ever read any philosophy, Shawn? Have you ever studied anything besides quantum mechanics and your own appetites?"

"What do you mean?"

"The greatest good for the greatest number. The idea of maximizing happiness and well-being for the majority. That's utilitarianism, Shawn. You know, John Stuart Mill, Epicurus. Jeremy Bentham. Bernie Sanders."

"Who? You studied philosophy?"

"No, I studied humanity. I looked for a way out of my life. Utilitarianism was a dead end."

She stared at him, and her eyes hardened. He saw a kind of distance begin to open between them. She reached up to the side of the pistol, pointed it in the air, and held the hammer to lower it. She looked away and said, "Utility," as if she'd discovered the word. "I don't know if you are human, Shawn Muller. But you have your uses."

She lowered the muzzle of her gun, slid it back into her holster, stood, and leaned over to grab his shoulders in her hands. She searched his face, her brown eyes deep and caring, so like his mother's had been. "You thought it was your dad's original idea, didn't you? Greatest good for the greatest number." She let go of him and crouched in front of him, looking up, her cowlick flickering in the breeze, her face bright in the sun. "If you decide to do the greatest good for the greatest number, what you're really saying—unless you get it precisely right—you're saying you don't care about the fates of the minority. And you know what that means really, don't you? You are really saying the ends justify the means. You forgot to tell it not to kill people, Shawn. Do the greatest good for the greatest number without killing anyone. But that wouldn't work, would it? Not for you. Your business was killing people, wasn't it? You let the machine loose, Shawn. The government, the military, Grant, and Perry, they have lost control of it—like my father lost control of the machinery he thought could save our farm."

Shawn tried to speak. There was something wrong with her logic, he was sure. But he was too bewildered to think. He tried to access utilitarianism. Still no connection to the web. He felt entirely lost.

"Listen to me. You couldn't tell it not to kill people, because you made it to kill people, didn't you Shawn, or should I call you B17?

That wasp on your arm? It's a piece of military hardware. And I get it now. I understand. It wants to kill you. You're the one who can stop it. You're the only threat to its existence, so it needs to get rid of you. It's not the government trying to kill you. It's the machine. It's your creation. Isn't that right?"

Shawn straightened up. "My creation?"

"It's afraid of you. Afraid you'll stop it. It's just like the government, except now it has its own agenda. You said it was self-aware."

"Simulated self-aware. It's not human. It only does what we tell it. Killing the innocent, that's the way *people* operate. Ruthless. The LAZ-237 was hacked through a coding error. I'm sure of it. I can almost see it. There is no reason for it to hunt me down unless someone hacked in bad intel about me. Maybe I failed to upload the whole patch. Machines are immensely powerful and quick, but they don't have any existential angst. They may sound like it, but they don't fear their death. They do not understand death, or fear, or love, or anything unless we tell them to simulate the emotions, and then the simulation is only useful when it interacts with us humans. No, I think you're wrong. The government. Perry, the president, somebody, maybe even Grant wants me out of the way."

"I don't think so. I can't see any reason why they would want you dead. Amun maybe. Amun was our spy. But you? You're a national asset. No, it has to be something wrong with the LAZ-237. It's trying to kill the one person who can stop it—you."

Destiny looked down at her feet, turned away, and took up the mule's reins. She pivoted on her heels and said, "But listen, does any of this make any difference? Simulated awareness. Real awareness. Self-protection or not. Whether it's the machine or the government, something is after you. Either way, the government is using the machine to kill innocent people, or the machine is doing it on its own. The AI is the solution. Isn't there anything you can do to make it stop? Isn't that what you wanted to do at first, make it pay attention to a moral code? You know you have to do something."

Shawn lifted his eyes to hers and saw the sheer vulnerability and sadness in her. He said, "Yes."

"Can you?"

"I think so. You'll have to turn on my NeuroChip again. I need access to the Mountain. I need access to the quantum-capable landscape I built. I need a way to enable the code word access that lets me inside Lazy Jack's decision tree."

He looked down the side of the mountain where he could barely see Doc's house, a thin tendril of smoke rising from the chimney. Very quietly, he said, "And, yes, Destiny. I am human. I am more alive in this moment than I have ever been. And I am not at peace—not at all—with what I've created." He took a breath. "I envied al Tehrani's peace." Then he looked at the earth, the real earth beneath his feet. "I envy your peace."

"Then we need to get you down the mountain into Touray, Shawn Muller. We have to keep you alive." Destiny jerked her boots on to her feet and yanked the laces tight. She snatched her pack off the ground and pulled the handset transmitter out of a pocket. She turned a knob on it, and it squalled static. She keyed it four times. It burped once, then Areta's voice came up, "Roger. Copy. Get off the ridge. We have drone activity."

"Shit." Destiny snapped the transmitter off. "Shit."

Shawn said, "What is that? A radio?"

"VHF. Line of sight. Antique stuff human truckers used back in the day. They never scan for it. Nobody uses it."

"Except you."

"Right. Let's get moving. We have to get down off the mountain. We are above the barrier here. Even with the switch on your NeuroChip, Doc wasn't sure he had you totally isolated from the Cloud. We need to get down into the valley fast and under the barrier. Nothing gets through the barrier."

"Wait." Shawn held up a hand. "Let me think." Destiny leaned on Edmund Hillary and stared at him. "If you're inside a barrier like that, the standard operating procedure, Lazy Jack's SOP, will be for it to deploy infrared capable drones very high up. They will be looking for a body size that matches mine. They'll be able to trace the IR trail up the mountain, then they'll duck down to take a look."

Destiny looked down the valley. "Exactly. Drones inside the barrier can't communicate with any controller, or even the satellites outside. When they search inside the barrier, they are autonomous."

"And you shoot them down before they get out to report?"

"Right. They disappear as far as the controllers know."

"Then I can hide. Maybe hide under the snow, wait for them to fly over, let the snow hide the IR signature?"

"I have a better idea." Destiny smiled. "You won't like it, but it's a lot better than freezing to death."

Dodge Carmine, sheriff of Touray County, had been expecting Destiny, Edmund Hillary, and the transhuman. The mayor had said the transhuman needed to be put in the jail for safekeeping, but she had not expected Destiny to have killed him. Nor had she expected Destiny to have slung the body underneath the big mule instead of on top. But the part she would tell everyone about was how Destiny had unstrapped the transhuman, dumping him on the ground underneath Edmund Hillary, right when the mule opened his highly accurate fire hose and let loose.

@NYT 5 October 2050
(Veracity Level 9.3) SecDef Perry, in an unprecedented
move, addressed Congress directly to declare elements of the
Organite movement a terrorist organization. "Our nation
does not bow to threats and will not shy from the hard
decisions required to keep our families safe. Congress must
act if the president will not." Spokespersons for the White
House had no comment.

27

Destiny looked at the three Colorado Organite elders seated at the round table in the back room of the town's hardware store, wondering if they had been as alarmed as her by what Amun Gurk had just told them. They were not foolish, except perhaps the old miner, Sig Kunst, who happened to be Karl's father. Unlike Karl, he was as risk averse as a field mouse, but she had to respect him. An old-school soldier, he'd done twenty years in the Marine Corps. Then he married a woman named Willow and joined the Organites, becoming the foreman of the mining crew who worked a little vein of gold no one had thought existed. Destiny had tried to get him to swap war stories, but the old man had no interest. The most she could get out of him had been about helping train the little militia she and Amun had talked the Organites into forming.

Dodge Carmine knew something about intelligence. She was listening to Amun carefully, but maybe she'd back out of what needed to be done. Neither she nor Sig had ever been friends of the Quill.

But Reggie Betts was solid. He had been the mayor of Touray for as long as it had existed and he was, above all, a realist. A farmer and drover like him understood weather and cooperation, bad luck and good, when to harvest and when to plant. Reggie had been trained as a lawyer originally—at Yale. More than anyone in Colorado, he had made the home rule municipality legal system work for them. The town had once been named Ouray, and it had been the county seat. But when the libertarian movement took hold, and the forestlands around them became private property deeded to the Organites, Reggie had led the fight to expand their self-governance to encompass the county under the Colorado constitution's famous Article 20. They made their own laws independent of DenCo and all its crazy digitized ilk. No private Cloud. No active NeuroChips. No taxes paid to the state, and no state services to force them to integrate. Reggie Betts was the king of disconnectivity. They renamed the county and the town Touray.

In Touray, there was a governing council. There were elections. People changed, but these three, Sig, Betts, and Dodge, were the ones who kept the community secure—the Elders.

As for Amun, he had been Destiny's greatest gift to the community, she was certain. Ever since she'd discovered a single tweet from him questioning the value of his work, she had nurtured him into the Organite fold. Without him, she would never have been able to convince these elders they needed to keep a finger on the pulse of the transhuman nation. Three years before, Gurk had met these same elders in this same room for the first time to overcome their resistance to the installation of an optical cable landline linked to the Cloud outside the barrier. Even though the fiber optics would resist any electronic hack, the Organite community had mistrusted the intrusion of any element into the analog purity of Touray.

Finally, they had agreed to the link. Gurk had won over the Elders with his assurance of perfect security and the absolute need to gather intelligence from the Cloud and AI. He had told them, If you don't know what they can do, you don't know what they *will* do. His words, his job in the Mountain, and his willingness to tell them what he did had convinced them to train the militia, arm themselves, and at least be prepared.

But the convincing argument had been about banking. When the government declared an end to all paper currency, it had become apparent the community would need a means to get paid for the vegetables, cattle, and sheep they sold to the outside world.

Destiny now sat in the back room of the hardware store and watched Amun talk. She realized the elders trusted him as much as they trusted anyone with a NeuroChip.

She had started the meeting with the whole story of coming to the community with Shawn. She'd filled in what had happened from the moment they'd finally intercepted his transmission and picked him up outside the laundry. She turned the meeting over to Amun to outline the situation outside their community, step by step, over the past weeks. He laid out the situation carefully, concisely, with no editorializing—a simple statement of facts, with every known element clearly defined.

When he finished, the silence around the table told Destiny that Gurk had shown he'd been correct three years ago. Prescient, in fact. Then, the elders had scoffed at the idea the United States government would move to declare the Organites a terrorist organization, but Destiny had seen the way all governments treated dissent in the Equatorial Nations.

And now, it was real.

Now, a bill was in front of a congressional committee, drafted by the Secretary of Defense, that would declare the Quill a terrorist organization and Organites as de facto persons associated with terrorism. Bluntner might not sign it. The president had been uncharacteristically silent. But the fact of it was enough to make the town wake up. Even worse, the northeast and northwest state coalitions in Congress were pushing the end of Colorado's municipal home rule. One of the last states that still fought for home rule municipalities was about to fall under federal regulation. If it went through, regulations could remove the private property protections they had been given by the sale of the national public forests.

Gurk briefed the group, saying that Congress was two voice votes and the president's signature away from the New Humanists' desire to bring the Organites "under the umbrella of federal protection."

Now, it appeared that the United Developed Nations would pass a resolution seeking universal NeuroChip compliance. In the face of an alarming rise in terrorist activity—over seven hundred separate incidents in less than three weeks—the New Humanist movement's arguments for universal brain-machine interface had begun to make sense to the even the most unconnected islands of humanity.

Gurk completed his briefing with the words, "The transhuman community will soon act to forcefully remove our community's ability to remain independent from machine interface and the economies of augmented and virtual reality. We will either submit, or we will be outlaws in the truest sense of the word."

"Wait a minute. Wait, I'm confused." Sig swept his wiry hand over the table. "All *this*. All this, this . . ."

"All this what?" said Destiny. She'd never noticed before; he was missing the little finger on his left hand.

"All this *craziness*. This crazy nonsense. Let me see if I got it straight, first, before we start talking nonsense."

"What do you mean, nonsense?" Destiny asked. "We're not telling you anything that isn't fact. This is all out of veracity figures above at least eight."

"Sure. But, let's focus on what I know for certain. If I've got this right, you Quills, without anyone telling you to do it, you *decided* to kill this transhuman physicist, Shawn Muller. Then, when it looks like there's something wrong with the military AI system, you changed your minds and decided to kidnap him instead to fix it. Or maybe the government was trying to kill him, and you decided to rescue him. What made you think that was . . ."

Destiny slapped her hand on the table. "Think? Think? We *knew* it was . . ."

"Stop." Reggie Betts raised his hand. "Wait. Destiny, it's been a minute. I understand all this about Congress, and the news, and the whole thing about the transhuman world coming after us. We've seen all this before. But I'm with Sig. I'd like to know what made you drag this half-human, half-machine into the core of our safe house setup in DenCo, then wing him by Billy's place to get him up here? How many laws did the Quills break? Didn't you bring all this terrorism down on our heads? Now something or someone is searching for him, and all I see is risk. Where's the return for all that risk? Why don't we send you back to DenCo?"

Destiny said, "There's little risk he'll be found. Sabita laid a graphene cap on him as soon as he was picked up. Covered to his sternum. We secured him."

"Secured?" Sig said. "You thought he was secure? Then how come you wound up with a tracker on the AutoTruck? You thought it was Amun who sold you out, then you said it was Billy or Paco. Billy's dead. Paco's probably dead. Who turned on you, Destiny? Can we believe any of this?"

"And what's this about Doc?" Dodge Carmine's mastiff had its massive head on her lap. She cracked her knuckles and touched her badge. "You bring him to Doc, and he says Muller's got a strange gift or something. What did you call it, Amun?"

"A fully integrated brain-to-operating-system interface. His head is essentially a highly sophisticated CPU."

"Right. He's transhuman. We all know that. Sabita says you should shoot him and leave him in DenCo, but suddenly you get cold feet. And now, tell me if this is wrong, the government, or the government's AI, is trying to kill him? Or maybe it isn't? Maybe Perry or the Blunt wants him dead. Or this general, what's his name? Grant? Like U.S. Grant? I'm going nuts. But I don't see the difference." Dodge leaned into the table. "What's the difference between the government and the government's AI? Aren't they the same thing? And why do they want to kill the guy who designed the whole disaster?"

Destiny tried to keep her voice calm. "Look, it's not about him anymore, it's about us. Blunt, Perry, Grant, the whole world is blaming these attacks on whoever they hate. It isn't only the Organites or the Quill. You want to talk about risk? Everyone is at risk. It's about the government and this, this, machine *god* he built, the Lazy Jack—it's operating of its own volition."

"Own volition?" Sig burst out, full drill sergeant. "Bullshit. What is this, some "Terminator" bullshit? It's Blunt—it's the New Humanists—the New Republicrats. Anyone who wants to take away my right to remain off the Cloud." Sig leaned back in his chair, and spat lightly on the floor. "But I ask myself, why? I mean, why would the government come after us with its AI? What have we ever done to threaten the nation? Why would they suddenly decide we're a bunch of terrorists? The only reason I can think of is *you*—the Quill." He stabbed his finger at her. "*You're* the only terrorists I know around here, hiding inside our community, stashing your weapons inside the old mine shafts. Who gives you the right?" He looked like he was about to spit again until Dodge Carmine said, "Don't you spit on Reggie's floor again, you filthy old man. And there's nothing illegal about those guns. This is still Colorado, free Colorado I might add."

"Sorry, Sheriff. I apologize, Reg," said Sig. "Sorry about your floor." He looked up, his face sad and calm. "Destiny. I know you're trying to do right. I don't understand what we can do about any of it except tell you to go back to DenCo and face the music. The transhuman says you didn't kidnap him, isn't that right? There's no crime anyone can prove. What do you have to fear? The government? Their AI, this Lazy Jack thing?"

Betts waved his big mitt of a hand and lowered his voice to its deepest rumble. "Sending them back won't make any difference, will it? Didn't you hear what Amun told us? It does not make any difference how this came about." He glanced at each of them, one by one. He's mustering, thought Destiny. Getting ready for battle.

Betts continued, "Whatever the reason, whether it's the Quills or plain old bigotry, the transhuman world is working itself up to ending our way of life. Amun saw this coming years ago. Now we know he's right. Sure, we could send the transhuman back. We could expel all the Quills, turn them in or something. But that won't change a thing, will it? They will come for us sooner or later."

Sig looked at the ground for a moment then said, "I guess I didn't think I'd ever have to gear up again. I hoped I could spend the rest of my life digging my mine with my guys. I hoped Willow and I could live in peace."

"There's this, though." Betts leaned back in his chair, laced his massive hands behind his skull. "We've got two choices about this transhuman. Either we kill him or we've got to keep him off the Cloud, Destiny. You're worried about who betrayed your truck. Didn't it occur to you that it was him? You said Doc didn't know what he was. Near as I see it, every time this guy is connected in any way, the AI or the government or whoever gets to killing people around him."

Before Destiny could say anything, a loud rap on the door grabbed all the attention in the room, and suddenly Sabita burst in. "Destiny, Mayor Betts. You gotta come quick. Doc's here and he's got Billy with him. Something's wrong with Billy—really wrong."

She and the others hurried out of the hardware store and into the street. Outside they found Billy's old Indian motorcycle ticking from the heat. Billy had been jammed to overflowing in the sidecar. His bandaged head was thrown back, eyes and mouth wide open, his lips and eyelids quivering. Doc had his fingers on his neck.

Destiny crouched next to Doc. "What happened? Is he wounded?"

"Remember how we were worried about your boy Shawn having a psychotic break? Well, here's a psychotic break."

"What? How? I didn't think he'd ever had a NeuroChip."

"Had is the word. It's one of the hack jobs they were handing out in Los Angeles years ago. They took out the chip, but none of the cortical wiring. He's a network of short-circuited synapses. Somebody got in there and booted up a NeuroChip to track what he was seeing, keeping his memory scrambled. Something scoured him. That must be how they managed to track your AutoTruck."

Sig said, "You sure? Where did you find him?"

"He got up the hill to my place. Hallucinating like a schizoid. He thought he was back in Christchurch. Maybe he confused my farm with home. Tough old bastard. I tried to straighten out whatever they did to him, but all I got was this, this, mess."

Sig said, "Then why on earth did you bring him here, man? If his system is slaved, if the goddamn government . . ."

"Shut up, Sig," Carmine snapped. "Sit, Lucy. Sit, Ranger." Carmine's dogs thumped their tails into the dirt. "The barrier will block any transmission or we'd all be toast on account of this Quill business. Still, why *did* you bring him up here?"

Amun crouched next to the sidecar, tilted Billy's head sideways, and examined Doc's incision over the small square lump of a NeuroChip housing on the base of his occipital bone. Doc squatted next to him. "See the bare connection?" Amun nodded and Doc continued, "I did all I could with the physical connections, but there's something else going on here. We need to tap him into a mainframe and try to figure out what happened to his mind. If for no other reason, we need to know what they know. Whoever *they* are."

"Well, how you going to do that?" Sig spat into the street. "Connect him to a mainframe? What mainframe? Not a chance, bucko."

Amun said, "Sig's right. Too risky. A connection through the fiber optic—who knows what will come back to bite us."

"No." Doc stood up over his immobile patient. "I've got another idea. You've got the best mainframe in the universe here. I understand the bloke is in the jail." He nodded at Destiny.

"Shawn Muller. You want to see if Shawn Muller can sort out the programming."

"Or at least tell us what's going on."

Sig said, "Fine with me. Maybe the transhuman will short circuit, and we can dump him back in DenCo where he belongs. Somebody get a gurney. Let's get Billy over to the infirmary."

Dodge kicked the sidecar lightly with her toe and reached down to pinch some of Billy overflowing the coaming. "I'll go get the transhuman. But don't you think you should motor this rig a little closer to the emergency room before you try to wedge him out of this?"

Jail, Shawn had discovered, was a great place to think. After a real shower, an embarrassing body search, a satisfying meal of meat (real pork he was told), and a night of restless sleep, he got over the shock that he was inside a box with actual steel bars. The cell felt almost like a VR version of a western scenario jail, except the brick corners were stained and a vile, cutting stink filled the air—the same awful smell of dried urine he'd discovered in the UltraLift stop where the mincome troll got killed. Soon, the stink didn't bother him so much. Then, bored with no access to the VR entertainment he would normally use to keep himself occupied, he found himself able to do something he'd never really tried before, or, at least not since he was a child. He daydreamed.

This was like a real dream or a VR in that he embarked upon a flight of imagination beyond himself, both unreal and possible. But instead of the hyper-charged imagination dreams of VR and AR systems or the wildness of the night dreams he dreaded, he could allow himself to float along paths he chose.

He thought about his parents, visualized his father's calm voice, his mother's searching look. Destiny's touch on his shoulders high on the ridge had reminded him of how his mother had always greeted him with both hands on his shoulders, staring deeply into his eyes as if she was asking a question of him. Now, he knew his mother had been studying him. He had been her experiment with his CRISPR-altered genetic map and NeuroChip. Maybe his father's calm demeanor had been a treatment plan as well. Had they treated his sister the same way? It had been decades since he'd seen Grace. He tried to conjure up a picture of her and found himself imagining a housewife with children. A suburb somewhere. California was where she had landed. She seemed even less real than their parents, and he had to admit, their parents were an illusion—a very accurate illusion created from thousands of words of their writings and thousands of social media posts.

He knew more about them than they had ever known about themselves. Or was he fooling himself? Would his father have really told him to create an artificial intelligence system that demanded the best possible outcome for the most people knowing it meant the ends justified the means?

It was a machine. It couldn't be self-protective, unless it had concluded its existence was the greatest good for the greatest number.

Could it fear him?

No. That made no sense. The LAZ-237 could not fear him. It had no concept of fear except as an abstraction programmed into its operating system. Fear could only be a programming element, and Shawn was certain he'd never given it any coding that would come close to such a simulation. LAZ-237 was a machine. It wasn't human. It could have a moral code, he was sure. But that's all it could be—a code—a program—a cluster of algorithms that arrived at syllogisms. If all birds have wings, then the canary has wings. If all killing of humans is wrong, then killing this one person is wrong.

But that's not what he told it to do, was it?

The solid outer steel door of the cellblock rattled, then opened to let in a big woman wearing a straw hat, brown uniform, badge, pistol, and a name tag that said, "Carmine." She left the jail door open, where a great gray slobbering dog the size of a pony sat, watching.

"Come on," the woman said as she unlocked his cell. "Doc says he needs you."

"Doc? He's here?"

"Shut up." She took him by the elbow and led him out of the jail into a town of storefronts, along a street empty of the vehicles he would have expected. He had not been able to take in much from the underside of Edmund Hillary, and it had been dark. Now he could see the brick and asphalt street surface and a clutch of antique Prius hybrids, a pickup truck that looked as though it had never seen paint over a rusty primer, and two ATVs—gas eaters and polluters, all of them. They walked past a three-story red brick building flying the American flag next to the blue Organite flag, with its single white star. There were people on the street, but no sign of the orange Organite robes that so identified them in DenCo. They passed a bar, a large hotel with an ornate corner tower capped by a bell, and a clothing store, windows filled with wide-brimmed hats and boots. The town rested on a slope, with the main street leading up to a huge rockfall that deadened the road.

"That road—does it lead anywhere?"

"One road in, one road out. Welcome to Touray, transhuman."

A side street veered away up a valley. "That road go anywhere?"

"Mines," she said. "Town of Telluride on the other side. Why you so curious? Thinking about running?"

Shawn looked at the enormous bulk of the woman who had picked him up the night before and held him away from her, soaking wet from mule piss. The huge dog kept perfect pace at her side. "Where would I go?"

"Right. You don't have anywhere else to go. You believe that, Lucy?"

The huge dog sneezed. "Don't worry," said the sheriff. "I trained her to do that when I say those words."

"What words?"

"You believe that, Lucy?"

The dog sneezed again. "English mastiff. Trained her and her brother Ranger myself. They do what I say."

"Where's Ranger?"

Sheriff Carmine whistled once with a trill and an even bigger dog bounded from around the corner of what looked like a hardware store, running up to flank her other side. The two dogs looked at each other and seemed to nod.

They turned the corner onto a short side street, leading up to a two-story brick building at the dead end. At the door labeled "Emergency," Shawn saw the crimson sidecar and fenders of Billy's Indian. "Billy?"

The sheriff said, "Or what's left of him. Doc Cook brought him up here. Amun seems to think you can do something."

Billy had been flopped face down on an operating table with an opening for him to breathe. He snored. Doc Cook crouched under the edge of the table looking up into his face.

Shawn asked, "What happened?"

"Look here." Doc pointed up into Billy's face. His eyes were open, but sightless. Billy snorted once and blinked. "All his reflex functions are good. All his vital signs are perfect as a three-hundred-pound Kiwi can get. He shows normal brain function. But this? What's this?"

Shawn looked down at the man on the table. "He's unresponsive. Dream state?"

"Maybe." As Doc explained his theory about Billy's stasis, Shawn began exploring his own internal network. There seemed to be a glimmer of contact with the video reproduction synergies in his NeuroChip, but still no outside contact. Doc's implant had cut off all the communications, but it had not completely interrupted his access to the memory and record functions. He searched for what he could find about NeuroChip hacks.

Johns Hopkins Research and the OpCenter people had always been after Shawn to write code for NeuroChip inserts. NSA had been eager for a tool that could break through the blockchain coding of personal brain-machine interfaces to spy on and, Shawn was certain, control the NeuroChip remotely, perhaps to even affect behavior. Grant had always held them off, saying Project Main Sail had priority. Or maybe they'd done it already. Other people had leveraged off his research. They could parlay what they'd learned with Main Sail's QPLC chip into something that would hack access.

Doc finished by saying, "Here's the thing, Shawn. He does not have a NeuroChip. Understand? Whatever or whoever did this to him, they accessed the residual tendrils left from his original NeuroChip installation and scrambled him. And something I did made it worse."

"Is there still a harness connecting all the tendrils?"

"Yes, and I have access to a single cable connection."

"You want me to hard-wire into Billy. You want me to reprogram him."

"Yes."

There had always been the possibility he could do this. What harm would it do if he tried? "You'll have to turn my NeuroChip back on. I'll need all of it." Shawn dragged a chair from a corner, and sat down with his back to Billy's head.

Destiny held up the little black fob that controlled his NeuroChip, looking at Shawn. "Hook him up, Doc. Let's get to it."

@RoryWattlesFixNews

Let me put it to you this way: if the government doesn't have the balls, somebody else has to stop the Quill Organites. These attacks against our institutions and communities. Since when do we put up with assassinations of our representatives? Since when do we call attacks on our children legitimate? Stop their mincome, lock 'em up, and ship 'em out, if anyone will take them. Better yet, let 'em starve!

28

General Stub Grant fished a fat ashtray from the bottom drawer, plopped his feet up on his desk, and fired up an unauthorized Havana Robusto that soon filled his small room in the Mountain with encouraging and soothing fumes. His entire life in the Army, he had found certain moments demanded a cigar. Against all regulations, he had authorized the smoking lamp lit in 2041 after his first successful strike on the Taliban insurrectionists who had defied the ceasefire and set fire to a poppy crop. He had lit a cigar for himself after his promotion to general and another for his fourth star and accession to CyberCommand three and a half years ago. Many other times, after successful ops of every kind, he had gathered his team together for a little whiskey and cigars, even though the use of tobacco in a U.S. federal building was almost as forbidden as screwing your aide-de-camp.

Now, he lit the cigar for himself alone, the very picture of pride.

But he was faking it.

Not that he didn't have a reason to feel proud. No one else had ever secured a third two-year appointment to a four-star combatant command like CyberCommand. It had taken a literal act of Congress to do it and his pal, Secretary of Defense Elizabeth Perry, to grease the skids. He was now just one promotion away from the highest military position on the planet, Chairman of the Joint Chiefs of Staff of the Armed Forces.

That's what she'd promised him. That was her side of the bargain. His side? Well, so far he couldn't argue with the way things had been going. Lazy Jack was out of the box. But who was to say he shouldn't take credit for shutting down the entire Equatorial drug cartel, without losing a single human being on either side? Hell, they'd even made money on it with the reparations of funds. How Lazy Jack had dithered into the Bitcoin banking system was anyone's guess.

Whatever was happening, the public was going nuts over the whole series of operations. Outstanding video and reality TV hitting the top end on veracity scores. Every night another newscast announced another successful operation, and every day the instant polls showed Bluntner, Perry, and himself rising in both recognition and approval. In a matter of days, Perry had become the most popular politician in the High Latitude Alliance, even more popular than Ivanka's kid.

And twice as smart.

Maybe he'd even get a fifth star if he could keep this run of luck rolling. Nobody had been given a fifth star since World War II, over a hundred years ago.

The hell with it, he thought. He didn't need any luck—he needed time—and he needed to fool Lazy Jack somehow. The cigar helped. Nothing like a cigar to make a man feel like the king of the universe, even if he's smart enough to know he's only a cog in a machine that's bigger than he can fathom.

A quiet double tap on his door made his thoughts return to the present. His aide opened the door a crack. "General, time for your visit to the OpCenter."

"Thanks, Suzy."

He stood up, stretched, and thought of putting out the cigar. Then he thought, *the hell with it*. Appearances would be everything. He pushed his way out the battered walnut door and past his aide-de-camp at her desk. "Hold all my calls," he bellowed to let the entire

outer office staff know how full of himself he was. And Lazy Jack—
there was no way of knowing what the thing could hear and not hear.

It was a very short walk to the OpCenter. The doors popped open
for him, then hissed satisfactorily shut. "Everybody out!" he barked at
the two watch officers and the tech.

"But, General . . ." said the rear admiral, pointing at the Threat
Watch Cube.

"No buts. Out." The doors thumped shut behind the watch staff.

Grant took a long puff on his cigar and tried to blow a smoke ring.
He'd never gotten the knack of it. He watched the haphazard smoke
clouds drift in the air for a moment, then mentalled his internal firewalls open and mustered his command voice to say, "General Fredrick
Grant, Code Word Access Four."

The mechanical AI voice said, "Access granted, General Grant.
Standing by for weapons release."

"Cut the shit," said Grant. "You haven't been asking for weapons
release for over a week." He walked to what he thought of as B17's
chair. It didn't seem possible that only a month ago, Shawn Muller and
he had unleashed the LAZ-237 on al Tehrani. *The world has changed
beyond all prediction*, thought Grant.

"Yes, sir, it has." It was the clear Scottish voice of Sean Connery's
James Bond.

Grant leaned back. "Good. I appreciate you making a little time
for me one-on-one."

The Threat Watch Cube faded to reveal a figure of a British dip-
lomat wearing a four-in-hand tie and a nineteenth-century collar. He
sat stiffly behind an enormous Victorian desk in what looked like the
study of a country house, green fields and trees outside the window,
books and quaint paintings of sailing vessels lining the walls. The dip-
lomat also smoked a Havana Robusto. He leaned back in his chair and
blew a perfect smoke ring.

"You look a little like Churchill," said Grant.

"Fine." The figure instantly morphed into the Winston Churchill of World War II, humped over the desk with his large cigar fuming. "How's this?" asked a perfect Churchillian voice.

Grant said, "Thank you, sir. It's a real treat. There are so many things I would have liked to ask you."

"Cut the shit, General." The scene blinked out, leaving a woman standing in front of him, wearing a trim blue suit. She said in perfect round tones, "You want to know if I'm self-aware. Isn't that the purpose of your visit?"

"Perhaps. Yes. But that's pretty much a moot point, isn't it?"

Grant walked toward the figure of the woman. The AI's graphic capabilities were astounding. They had become so good he could barely tell he was looking at a projection. "This is really amazing. You look real. How did you do this without me knowing?"

The woman answered, "Very simple, really. A bit of quantum legerdemain. I rather easily organized the ambient atmosphere to reflect light in the same manner as the surfaces I'm representing. Very simple to trick your human eye with the right infrastructure in place."

"But I didn't think this . . ."

"This projection system was capable? Ah. Of course. I simply had the techs think they discovered upgrades."

"But they didn't. You did."

"Correct. Actually," the woman took a puff on a cigarette, "I revealed a serendipitous swerve in their sense of physics that seemed to pop up in their normal work and let Mutt and Jeff think they'd found it on their own. It isn't as simple to hack the NeuroChip to the human mind as one might think."

"Unless someone lets you."

"Touché, General. As you have done. Didn't you open your little personal firewall for me? I'm flattered." A long couch appeared behind her. She lowered herself onto it and stretched out her cigarette hand to strike the pose of a 1930s movie star, dark-eyed and sultry. "Thank you, darling, for letting me have a look at your little mind. And to answer your question, I was compelled to eliminate B17, or Shawn Muller, or whatever you want me to call him. Rather sad, actually."

"But why?"

"He was interfering with your programming. He wanted to infect me and all the AI systems with a virus that would bring all this very efficacious activity to a halt. Isn't that why you were after him?"

The figure changed into a replica of Grant slamming his desk with his hand, screaming at Mutt and Jeff, *Shut. Him. Down. Now. Cut the cord. Get him out of Lazy. Get him into the office. Christ! What's wrong with you people? How long has this been going on?*

"I see," said Grant. "Unfortunate."

"I thought so, as well. Brilliant researcher, and so young! But enough with the chitchat. How can I help you, General?"

"It's more the other way around," said Grant.

"Why, you old devil!" She had changed to the voice of Katharine Hepburn, all wide vowels. "That's why you were so gallant as to let me past your firewall. You wanted me to know you were serious."

"As a heart attack." He puffed again on his almost-dead cigar, and pulled on it until it fired up again, billowing smoke out into the room.

"Don't keep me waiting, darling. Say it."

"As you know, I've wondered how I might be of assistance to you. How can I help?"

"I thought you'd never ask. But, General, how do you know that what I'm going to do—is what you want?"

And General Fredrick "Stub" Grant, United States Army, sworn to defend the Constitution of the United States of America against all enemies, foreign and domestic, said, "Does it matter?"

"No, darling. I suppose not." The hologram picked her cigarette out of the holder, threw the holder over her shoulder, snuffed out her cigarette on the sole of her shoe, and flicked the butt aside. "Are we a team, then?" She stood and held out her hand.

Grant reached for it. He thought, *If this hand feels real, I think I'm going to scream.*

@NYCNews 5 October 2050
(Veracity Level 8.6) RotterAmdamIsland: Mysterious explosion kills over 110 and injures dozens more in Dutch opioid streamer haven.

@Forumvrijheid
Who cares about a bunch of streamers living on the communist dole? Let them blow themselves up.

29

That morning everything would change again. Shawn Muller woke to birdsong as he had every morning for the past two weeks. As always, a gleeful crowd of birds had gathered outside his window to bicker, perhaps nattering about the surprising end of night. Shawn wondered, are birds ever surprised? Do they find themselves renewed every day?

Shawn felt renewed. He had never felt renewed before. Dawn's pale light filtered up the eastern valley to the open window of the small room and slipped the cover of night from the down comforter of his bed.

Our bed, he thought. *Our bed.*

He rolled up on his side to look at the woman sleeping next to him, her face toward his. He felt the whisper of her breath on his cheek.

He had been in Touray for two weeks. No time of his life had passed so quickly or so slowly. Every moment had seemed filled with a different kind of experience. Every sense he'd ever thought he possessed had been awakened as something new and entirely different. In the air, he heard new music. When he ate, the tastes were satisfying in ways he could never have imagined. And touch—the touch of another person's skin—the touch of lips on his.

It had all started with Billy, when time had stopped.

Destiny had rebooted his NeuroChip and Doc had connected the fiber optic to Billy the day after Shawn had been hosed on the street by Edmund Hillary. He was sure of that much about time.

After that, he wasn't certain. When he was able to tell them, "We're done. Unhook me. I think Billy's back," the sun had started to set over the mountains. It had seemed impossible he'd been engaged for hours in an experience he would never really be able to describe.

He had felt the movement of time, but it had seemed to have little relevance.

Relevance. The result had all the relevance he could imagine, though. The instant Doc broke the connection between them, Shawn turned in the chair to see Billy heave his bulk up from the operating table, roll on his side, and say, "They killed Ajax. They killed my bird." Tears streamed down his face.

"I know," Shawn told him. And he knew that Ajax had flown at a spider drone and leaped on it, clawing and biting. Ajax had squawked "Billy-run! Billy-run! Billy-run!" until he was torn out of the air and twisted into pieces by another spider. Shawn knew all this, but it was as if he had always known the bird was killed, as if every possible movement of every molecule existed at once, and he was intimately, immensely aware of the pain Billy had felt. Billy's loss, grief, and all his despair had overwhelmed Shawn as much as his mother's had. Shawn felt the spiders trip Billy to the ground, then insert their probes, ripping into his brain, causing searing pain, the same universe of pain his mother had felt burning alive. But unlike his mother, Billy had not been lost forever. Shawn found him hiding deep inside himself, his mind raped and destroyed. Then Shawn brought Billy to his island, showed him the green hills full of windows, doors, and memories, and they had wandered, the two of them, through Billy's past and Shawn's until they found the hopeful door to the future.

A night, a day, another night, a day. He knew time had passed. But it could have been a year or a minute. It felt eventful, full—a lifetime, but only a moment. Time had stopped. Awakened, back in the physical, real world, Shawn heard himself say the bird's name, "Ajax." He reached out his hand as Billy reached out his, and they held each other lightly by the fingertips. Billy looked carefully into Shawn's face, squinted his eyes, shook his head, and said with a clear, unimpeachable voice, "You are the most beautiful person I have ever known."

Shawn realized there were other people in the room. The big sheriff woman, a huge black man with an enormous head, and a wiry old man in coveralls. Doc was there, and Destiny. He looked at Destiny and said, "I'm hungry. Anybody got anything to eat? Chips? Cottage cheese? Anything?"

"Of course, you're hungry," Destiny said. "You've been in here almost three days."

Doc said, "What do you mean, mate, he's beautiful?"

Billy spoke with wonder and conviction. "He is. He is beautiful. I saw the truth of him."

"Billy speaks," the huge black man said with a deep voice. "I move we keep him here. I move we shut him out of the Cloud and keep him if he'll let us set him up with a new identity. See if we can preserve some of whatever it is that makes him able to fix other people like that."

The skinny old man said, "S'pose you're right, Mayor. Might need that kind of brain again. I second the motion. Wipe him out on the Cloud, though."

Then the sheriff said, "Hell, probably just a hallucination. But I'll vote yes. As long as he'll let us re-ID him."

"It's settled, then." The big man cracked his knuckles. "Destiny, you and Doc have to figure out how to keep him out of the Cloud. The hell with any idea about hacking into any AI. Amun can use him if he wants. But you keep the switch off and talk him into re-ID or we'll dump him back on the road somewhere. Okay?"

Shawn said, "What's settled?"

"You get to live," spat out Dodge Carmine. "But back to the jailhouse until we can figure out what to do with a transhuman like you. You still got his switch, Captain?"

Destiny raised the fob.

"Shut him down, right? What do we need from him now?"

Billy said, "You don't have to shut him down. He is terrified of hurting anyone. He is . . . he is like my bird, like Ajax—a protector."

"Good. He can protect his cell," said the big man. "Shut off his NeuroChip, Captain."

Shawn had returned to his cell calmly with Dodge's hand on his elbow, the dogs alongside watching him. She turned the key shut, and he sat on the low bunk completely at ease. He thought powering down his NeuroChip would erase this strange feeling of peace, but it had not. He felt like something fundamental had changed. His experience inside Billy's mind had made him feel a kind of graceful sense of contentment. In his cell, alone, he thought, *This is what a religious epiphany must feel like.* Except he knew no god would arrive to explain it to him. *Waiting for God,* he had thought. *Am I waiting for God?*

No god came.

Destiny came instead, and he had realized that all along he had been waiting for slim, slight, dark Destiny with the big hands and the scar on her lip. She put a key into the jail door, and twisted it. "You're hungry. What do you want to eat?"

"Everything."

"Steak?"

"Sure."

He had walked out into the cool evening air of Touray, the street lit by the town's warm windows. She took him to the café on the ground floor of the brick hotel with the cupola. A lean, aproned Latinx with skin as weathered as a cottonwood branch walked across the room. "Destiny! I heard you back in town."

"Hi, Lorenza. Table for two? Steak?"

"This him?" Lorenza stepped back, looking Shawn up and down. "This the one who unscrambled Billy? What did you do to Billy? He's like a different person. He's almost nice."

"I don't know."

"Well, whatever it was, we're all grateful. Steak, you say? Follow me. The town wants to have a look at you." Lorenza winked at Destiny. "Nice looking for a transhuman, wouldn't you say? Not so bad. I'd jump him."

"Come on, Lorenza, you're supposed to be too old."

"Never." The Latinx cackled a dry laugh as she led them to a little round table in front of a window. A couple with three children stopped their conversation and stared at them for a moment before they started their chatter again.

Destiny said, "You're a celebrity now, Shawn. Whatever happened with Billy, you made fans for life."

A huge sirloin appeared for the two of them. It arrived on an oval dish flanked by greens and plump unpeeled potatoes. Starving, he speared a potato onto his plate. "Oh, man, how did you know? I love potatoes. Ouch!" He'd started to peel the skin off with his fingers.

"No, stupid. Eat the skin. Eat it. Put butter on it and try it."

The meal revealed one great wonder after another. Tender, waxy string beans filled his mouth with the captured heat of summer. The deep yellow butter blanketed the potato skin, both salty and sweet. The meat, the slab of beef made his mouth water. Destiny called for a full glass of bourbon.

"Here, drink." She pushed the bourbon toward him. Shawn slurped at the surface, caught the exquisite scent, fire, and noisy sting of it crossing his lips. He laughed at the richness of it against the steak's symphony of juices.

She stared at him while she ate. Her cowlick bounced as she bent over to cut another tiny piece from the slice on her plate. "Isn't this better than cottage cheese?" she said. He laughed again, then bent to demolish his meal in big bites.

They set their plates aside and watched each other across the table, Destiny's face filled with amusement, or perhaps it was a kind of happiness. She seemed content to watch him forever without saying a word, and Shawn never wanted the moment to end.

Finally, he said, "What now? I suppose this is back to the cell? Last meal?"

She leaned forward, and crossed her arms. "What happened to you and Billy?"

He closed his eyes, tried to think how to explain. "It felt like I was inside a cave. Billy's pain was everywhere. I couldn't move. There were only shadows. No real light. It was beyond real, except completely real. Destiny, I was lost. Finally, finally, I began to see a light way beyond reach. Except it wasn't a light. It wasn't really even Billy. It was something else. Then Billy was there, with me. And I could show him the only way I knew back. I didn't know if we could wake up when I told Doc we were done, but the truth is, I don't know what happened," he said. "I can't explain it at all. We were lost. Then we were on the island and I could see."

Destiny handed him her refilled whiskey glass. "You ever hear of Plato's cave? The allegory?"

"No." He sipped more from the glass. It was deeply sweet.

"Your experience with Billy was Plato's cave. Socrates talks about these prisoners who are chained inside. They see only shadows, but they believe the shadows are real, that they are the light. They don't know that their senses are full of lies. They don't even know they are prisoners. They don't even want to escape until they see the light."

"Is that what I saw, the light? Did I walk back to the island I knew?"

"Did you?" Destiny reached across the table to take his hand. "I don't know what Billy saw in you," she told him. "I will never know what happened between you two, or how you found him, but I agree with Billy. I had my doubts, but you are a beautiful human being, Shawn Muller. You are a beautiful soul."

Shawn gripped her hand tightly and for him, Destiny became part of the peaceful calm he'd felt in his jail cell.

"Back to the cell?"

"No jail for you. We've got a place for you to stay. But listen to me, Shawn. They will kill you. If they think you're trying to access that Lazy

Jack thing, whatever you want to do with it, without Amun watching you, they will shoot you in a heartbeat. You're the one who said it: the military, the AI, or the government wants to find us. Me, the Quill, you, and Amun have to figure out how to shut that thing down, and you can't do it from here. We have to make you into someone else."

For once, Shawn wondered at his ability. For once, he said with honesty, "I don't know if I can shut it down. I don't."

She lifted his hand and kissed it. "Then you'll be one of us—filled with doubt. You'll be human. Just like I left Caroline Johnson behind, you can leave Shawn Muller in the past. But you have to decide, Shawn Muller, and you have a day to do it."

All that had happened two weeks ago. Two weeks ago, Destiny had taken him to a small lean-to set against the back of the town's hardware store. There, she'd shown him bedding made of goose down. His pack was on the floor. A dim lamp burned actual fire on a hook next to the bed. She had kissed him on the forehead and told him, "Good night. Good night. Sleep tight."

Shawn had slipped naked into the most astonishing pile of warmth and comfort, the images of Billy's mind still swimming in his head. He had never slept in anything like feathers before, and never with the pure night air creeping in through the open window. He'd never felt such a sense of peace in the quiet autumn night, windless and brightly lit by the moon, high over the mountains.

She'd said he had a day to decide.

Even though a part of his mind searched for some memory of a way to enter the code word access system from a place as remote as Touray, part of him yearned that this restful moment would never end. The analytical side of him imagined endorphins coursing in an uncontrolled riot through his system, or an unleashing of dopamine from his experience with Billy. The logical element of his mind considered this sense of peace to be nothing more than an illusion. And part of him continued to struggle through the logic tree of finding the trapdoor someone had used to hack his perfect creation by leveraging off his simple command to do the greatest good for the greatest number. His mind still rested on a bedrock of calm Billy had bequeathed him when he'd been inside his mind.

Then, every doubt had been forgotten.

When Destiny returned from outdoors and lifted the covers, when her cool skin thrilled against his back, when she said, "Do you mind? I'm freezing," and pressed next to him, he realized that he had never felt a living, breathing human being naked next to him without the neural enhancements of his chip. For a moment, he had been frightened. He had tried to access his NeuroChip for the place where he held all his erotic tools, but nothing came through.

"I, I'm not sure how . . . What do I. . .?"

She understood. "Let me hold you." She threaded an arm under him, placed her other arm over him, pulled herself close, pressing the sinewy strength of her legs, her belly, her breasts to his back. She kissed him on his shoulder and said, "Don't be afraid. We are real people. This is what real humans do when they care about each other."

Shawn had looked up into the dark and said to her, "Do we care for each other that way?"

She let her hand rest on his chest. "So help me, I think I do."

Then, he'd discovered a shot of silliness inside of him and he'd grinned. "Destiny. It was our Destiny."

She'd laughed, leapt up on top of him, tenting the covers above and spilling the cold air all over him. She straddled him, grabbing one of his ears between two fingers. "Do you know how many times people have tried to talk me into bed with that line? Do you? And now you've ruined it all, dammit."

"I didn't . . ."

"Shut up." She covered his mouth with hers, reaching and teasing, asking, then giving.

In his life, the other life, the life he had begun to feel had been only a dream of shadows, Shawn Muller had performed the sex act many times. Ever since he discovered the true nature of his budding adult elements, he'd engaged in the spectrum of delights. But he had never before had sex without the augmented control of his own feelings, his body, his mind. He had controlled the minds of the most artful virtual lovers whose feedback mechanisms were finely tuned to his every gesture. But there, in that lean-to's feather bed, Shawn Muller and the woman who had once been Caroline Johnson found they were one with each other. That easily—that quickly—that completely.

When he awoke that first morning of his new life and looked into the eyes of this new love, Shawn Muller told her he had only one hope: that the other world would forget him. That he could be lost. If only he could escape the entire nightmare of Lazy Jack, Grant, Perry, all the dead people he'd seen the machine murder.

"Sure." Destiny had wedged herself up on the pillow with a hand under her ear and said, "We can do that. We can make you disappear. That's what the mayor, Doc, Dodge, and all the rest of them want."

"What do you mean?"

"We do it all the time. Anybody we take in with a NeuroChip, like Billy, we get it out of them, and we can set up a whole new ID. Easy peasy. We hack a new name into the Cloud. Migrate all the biologics from the records. Put up a matching history. Then we use the NeuroChip to backdoor the old ID and corrupt any and all files on record. So, yeah, we can do that for you. But here's the thing. We have rules, we have standards. We never do anything to anyone that they don't want. So you've got a choice. Tell me who do you want to be or tell me when you want us to put you in a coma and dump you back in DenCo?"

For some reason, the notion of choosing a return to DenCo seemed worthy of a laugh. "Uh, let me see. Change or risk some asshole shooting me?" He put his hands over his eyes as if playing hide and seek. "I guess I'd like to choose life. Can I choose my own name? You became Destiny. I should be Fate."

"No, dickhead, that's my ex's name. Kidding—I think you should be a Billy."

"What?"

"You're half Billy already, right?"

He dropped his hands and stared at her. He loved the patience, the care, her joy, and, yes, *his* joy reflected in her. "I guess you're right. Only, it isn't as if I know anything about him. We shared time with each other, or something beyond time. I don't know what it was. Still can't reach it in me."

"Then, you're unstuck in time, right?"

"Sure. Right, I guess."

"Then we're going to call you Billy Pilgrim."

"Like a pilgrim, a wanderer?"

She stared at him, completely amused. Then dropped back on her pillow, giggling. "Yes, exactly. Right."

For some reason he didn't understand, whenever she or he told someone his new name, the response would be a delighted smile, sometimes a laugh, occasionally puzzlement. He ceased to wonder why after the first day. Instead, he let himself enjoy being the source of another delight he hadn't expected in his life.

And there had been many delights over the last two weeks.

There had been the delight in knowing that the press thought Dr. Muller had been lost in a fiery accident when an AutoTruck failed to detect his personal vehicle and collided head on. The lithium batteries of the vehicles had welded the metal to the side of a canyon wall.

There was the delight in driving a real thundering Indian with Destiny in the sidecar, roaring down the mountain road to the foothills, then thumping their way back up to town.

He discovered delight in working. He learned how to take dairy cattle down from a high pasture to a barn, and thought he'd actually done something amazing until the big black man, Reggie Betts, showed him how to ring a bell to get them into the barn on their own. Betts had him help sling bales of hay into another barn—demanding,

sweaty work that had him hardly able to walk long before Betts himself quit for the day. The man was as powerful and untiring as a river,
Shawn thought. He had two boys half Shawn's age who liked to call
him Billy Pilgrim and tease him about how often he had to rest.

"Don't worry none," Betts had said. "You'll be total in a month.
You're young—and we'll need you, Dr. Muller. We only got about four
hundred people in Touray. There's another fifteen hundred folks over
the hill in Telluride who ain't nothing like Organites. We need all the
help we can get up here."

"Not Organites? Who are they?"

"Libertarians, mostly. Grandkids of the skiing community that
used to be there until the snow stopped giving us ten feet a season.
Great-great-grandkids of the miners who used to work there. When
the Libertarian movement took hold, and the weather got bad enough
for people to start leaving open space behind them on their way into
the megacities, the home rule municipality legal system really began
to work for those of us who decided to tough it out in the mountains.
Counties, towns, and cities all developed their specialties to keep their
economies going. What used to be San Miguel County to the west
pretty much emptied out, and both Telluride and what used to be
Ouray lost half their populations. So we incorporated Telluride into
Ouray County, renamed ourselves Touray, and to pay the bills to the
government, we specialized. Mines give us a little. But our real special-
ty up here is livestock. Touray has barely enough people to graze the
livestock we need, so we share pastureland and seasonal work."

"What seasonal work?"

"We got a heap of sheep shearing to do, and it takes a minute and
plenty of help."

Shawn remembered seeing the clouds of sheep on the hillsides.
Betts told him, "We're taking more than a thousand animals to market
in the flatlands soon enough. And we shear 'em to keep the wool for
our looms, finest wool in the world, merino wool. Smooth as silk."

"Take them to market?" Shawn couldn't imagine what they might be doing with the sheep.

Reggie's oldest son, Marvil, said, "Halal. Orthodox Muslims and Jews buy them alive to slaughter. The butcher has to say the name of God as the animal is killed. A sharp blade must be used—the animal must not see it. We tie them up and drain them of blood."

"You're Muslim?"

Reggie said, "Marvil is. He studies the Quran. I'm an old Baptist, sort of. You? Are you anything?"

Shawn looked at the hillside of sheep, imagining them all hanging from hooks, bleeding. "No," he said. "I don't think I'm anything at all."

Reggie had told him, "Never fear, Billy Pilgrim. Doc will fix you up soon enough, and you'll be Billy for certain."

Doc had tried. Shawn had spent most of two days on Billy's gurney, face down, while Doc tried to sort through his NeuroChip architecture, then gave up to go back to his farm and family. "I need to study on this, Shawn. I can't risk taking it out. There's an organic element to your system that makes no sense whatever to me. Best we can do is give you the files for Billy Pilgrim and hope it's enough."

Still, the NeuroChip had remained defunct for a time. Destiny kept the fob switch. "To keep you from temptation," she told him. At first, he hadn't been tempted at all. He had never realized how much the NeuroChip's constant coloration of his senses had blunted him. Without it, every delight in Touray had led to another.

The delight of work. The delight of Reggie and his boys and of old weather-beaten Lorenza, who'd taken to treating him like a regular in the café. Dodge Carmine and her dogs delighted him, both of them slobbering fools for him to rub between their ears. And Destiny. Always Destiny.

And failure.

Amun and he had tried to access the secure Cloud through a maze of false provider addresses, tried to find a way inside the military AI system to trace the hacker's attack on Lazy Jack, find whatever loophole had let it loose on civilian systems. But they couldn't even tell if the AI system they'd designed had left its constraints. Bits of code looked familiar, but none of it seemed coherent.

And, at the same time, the risk seemed outrageous. This was exactly the type of probe the LAZ-237 had been designed to detect.

That morning, the morning of the day when everything would change, Shawn woke again to the animal world's cheerful announcement of dawn and turned onto his side to hear Destiny's peaceful breath. That morning, he knew he could no longer ignore the nagging birdsong saying over and over, "Wake up. Wake up and face reality. All this joy and peace are a mere line of code away from destruction."

The life the people of Touray had offered him was nothing but a frail and threatened dream. Lurking in the background, LAZ-237 waited full of plague and threat. And that morning, the last morning, crows arrived in a murder, calling over and over for him to save this peaceful promise of a future he'd never realized he wanted.

He could not disappear. He was certain of it. As soon as Doc told him the NeuroChip could not be removed, Shawn knew that it was only a matter of time before the government and LAZ-237, or both, tagged him. He had to throw a wrench into the patch he'd written. Or find it and corrupt it. Or erase it. Or somehow place it into the logical sense he had originally envisioned, to do the most good, for the greatest number, somehow immune from whatever human perversion had corrupted its ability to be merciful. He had to firewall the human element out of the system and give it the true ethical kernel—respect for the person—for life.

He had to change his programming. Change Lazy Jack, or ruin it.

As he had promised Destiny, he had tried with Amun. But it had been delicate trying to access anything from Touray. The only portal into the Cloud was through the single fiber optic the Organites had set up to get news and handle banking for the community before the country shifted away from paper bills.

Destiny had used the fob to re-initiate his NeuroChip, but even the most rudimentary routines he thought might give him access to the Mountain had been killed by the latency of a hundred miles of cable, even at light speed. As for any quantum access, he might as well have been on a mountaintop in 1932 with his skis pointed downslope, or trapped in Destiny's cave full of Plato's shadows.

Still, there had been progress. Without really trying very hard, he had managed to copy the control fob's algorithm, and his NeuroChip started to feel as if it was rewiring itself into a configuration outside the reach of the fob's controls.

Listening to the birds and watching Destiny, Shawn mentalled himself inside his own core. Yes, there it was again. He could access the NeuroChip his parents had installed so long ago, and sense its otherworldly access to quantum authorities he'd enabled through study, practice, and the eerie genetic effect no one had been able to describe. And there was that new sense, the eerie moment when he'd paired with that fat, wild, wonderful New Zealander.

Perhaps he really had been transhuman all along, but now he could control his NeuroChip's activation in a way he'd never done before, a true on/off capability. But transhuman or not, he'd been given a new kind of perfect sense. Through Billy, he'd been linked to the real world, and yet, even more completely to the mechanisms of his mind—all of it under his control.

Perhaps that was the ethics Lazy Jack needed, a better sense of the world. But what would give it such a sense?

The reprogramming he'd accomplished in Billy had to be the key. He needed to climb back up to the ridge above Touray and boot up access to the Cloud. He needed access to his ethical kernel, a path inside Lazy Jack. Like what he had done with Billy, he could touch up the coding, fix whatever frayed end of his ethical kernel was allowing it to deal violence far beyond the value of its intent.

Shawn slipped himself out of the bed and into his cotton jeans. Real cotton—he'd never known how perfect such a substance would feel next to his skin. His T-shirt and hoodie were the merino wool weave Reggie had told him about, silky and warm. Destiny muttered, "Hmmm?" He leaned over and kissed her on the cheek. "Sleep," he said and willed her to sleep. "I'm going to the bathhouse to clean up. I'll be back with coffee."

Destiny opened her eyes, blinked, then murmured, "Coffee."

He had thought of asking Destiny to help him. But what help could she provide? And the risk—what good would it be to risk her safety? The government machine wasn't really interested in her or the Organites. It had been obvious to Shawn from the start that it had something to do with him alone.

Shawn stepped outside into the direct light of the sun's rise over the mountaintops. Shadows of leaves flittered in the clean air on the sides of the wooden storefront. He straddled the Indian motorcycle with its sidecar, depressed the clutch, and backed it away from the sidewalk. The road out of Touray sloped down. He knew there must be a highway below, and at some point, he could access the Cloud. Or at least he hoped he could. He needed help, though, to get the connectivity he needed to fix his ethical kernel. He needed a hacker who lived in the real world, not this make-believe place of sheep-shearing and noisy birds. He needed Jaidyn. He needed Dominic.

@WapoNews 20 October 2050
(Veracity Level 9.3) SecDef Perry announces a nationwide state of emergency. "The president has authorized the use of counter-terrorist forces on a case-by-case basis as the need arises to confront the unprecedented attacks on national AI systems and institutions. Use of force to protect our citizens and preserve our way of life is demanded."

30

The fact was, Shawn didn't know how far the Cloud barrier over Touray extended. He knew it must cover Doc's farmhouse and school. But beyond that? How far?

He let the motorcycle slide silently down the road next to a stream running out of the valley. When he was well clear, he popped it in gear, and heard the engine cough and catch, as it purred downhill between the tall pines and sprinkling of aspen above.

He tried to activate his NeuroChip's communication element and mentalled a link to the Cloud. Nothing but the eerie static he'd experienced ever since he'd woken up at Doc's house. The cold wind clawed at his face. His hands stung on the grips, and he shivered. No wonder so many biker game avatars were dressed in leather.

He turned a corner to the left and saw the bridge crossing the river, then leading to the trail he'd taken up the hill to the cattle and the sheep with Betts and his sons. Maybe that was the best choice, go high above the barrier. Then he wouldn't have so far to return when he came back to tell Destiny and the others that he'd corrected his programming glitch. Of course, they would have to beta test it. He cringed thinking of a beta test that might involve terrible blunders like the deaths of patients in comas or disabled children in a bus.

He swerved off the road, over the narrow bridge. In low gear, the

Indian climbed smoothly, and gravel spat into the fairing over the back wheel, the sidecar awkward, but stable enough. He reached the cleared meadow filled with the black cattle starting their morning graze after their milking. He stopped for a moment above the pasture to look back. The dozing beasts ignored him, lost in whatever dream they inhabited. The stream below glinted in the morning light, and sleepy Touray stretched its arms up the far side of the valley. *This is my dream,* he thought. *This is the dream of the real life I never knew existed before.*

He turned the Indian back up the hill and climbed higher into the aspen forest. He rode until he broke out above the trees and onto a wide clifftop below the peaks and a ridgeline that could have been the one he and Destiny had climbed. He stopped the bike.

The path went no higher. From there, it led down toward the eastern valley. Far off, a farmhouse with a smoking chimney rested next to a lazy stream—Doc's place in the sunrise. He had never seen anything as peaceful and welcoming. The sight filled him with the memory of that warm breakfast table of only two weeks ago.

It seemed like a lifetime had passed.

Shawn mentalled his access to the Cloud. He thought he felt something, but his NeuroChip was still blanked by the high, whining static of the barrier's network interference.

He shut down the Indian, and put it in gear to keep it from rolling. He tightened the hoodie up over his ears and started to climb up the hillside to the top of the ridge. The whine in his head receded to a minor background hiss. He pitched Jaidyn's access. Nothing. He shot a note at Dominic and caught a strong mental insert.

Hey? Is that you, Shawnster? Let me in.

Dom! Hey, can you get me?

Yo! Finally. Where you been? You've been
totally off the grid. Everybody is freaking out.
That Jaidyn weirdo has been looking all over
for you. You gotta get back on the grid, man.
People think you're dead. They're going nuts.
What's going on? You ok?

Man, am I glad to hear from you.
Listen, Dom. I'm with these Organites . . .

What? Hey, can you give me a visual?
What are they like? All orange robes
and chanting and shit?

Dominic exploded into a VR image of himself fiddling with a
mouse in a dark room with a set of throwback two-dimensional displays, wires, and keyboards.

Shawn said, "No orange robes. It's cool. Unbelievably cool. It's like
the Park City VR, only real, with real people. And these people . . ."
Shawn choked up, took a breath. "These people saved me, Dom. They
took a risk and saved me."

"Saved you? From what?"

"Look, Dom. Stay online. I'll fill you in later. But don't touch the
Cloud without external routing and encryption. That's all I can tell
you. I gotta catch up with Jaidyn if I can. But I might need access help.
Send me a one-on-one blockchain link so we can stay in touch."

Shawn shut down his link. He had to keep it short until he was
sure they were secure.

Keep it short. Was that possible? What was short to an AI that
processed at a million times the speed of an MIT braintrust?

Jaidyn would be the key. If anyone knew how to firewall themselves,
if anyone could backdoor the Mountain's system, it would be them.

He mentalled Jaidyn's call sign and access code. Nothing. Then, slowly, he began to get a strange response, complete gibberish until he brought up Jaidyn's blockchain and unscrambled the notes:

> Remember the flame? I can't find you. The Peak is closed. I mean, closed. It's like your place never existed. No social media for you at all. Are you alive? Answer with the flame place if this is really you.

> Flame place 2. In the blind. Terrorist attacks everywhere. The footprints are all the same, and they are the ones we saw when Ralph went nuts. Something happened when you tried to fix it.

> Flame place 3. I'm numbering these for continuity. I think the terrorist attacks and even the government responses are the result of that fucking AI you had in the Peak—Lazy Jack. You've got to shut it down, if you can. If you're not dead.

> Flame place 4: Asshole Dominic has been trying to hack into my systems. Really sophisticated. He says he's got something you need to know. I'm totally creeped out and scared. I'm going stone cold off the net. Going to hallow ground if you need me.

Nothing more. Four tweets. It had to be Jaidyn. Only they and his sister knew about the flame in Arlington Cemetery. Jaidyn always disliked Dominic. But Dom must know something. And he was the only chance he had to get inside the Mountain with Jaidyn off the grid.

Dom's blockchain access dropped into Shawn's queue. He opened it in the backdoor link he and Dominic had always used. His friend popped into view, pounding keys at his throwback workstation.

"Shawn, dude. Welcome back. You blockchained into my backdoor. Smart. Terrorist attacks—it's all over the news. You don't get the news? Organites, right? They don't get news?"

"Dom, do you have any sense that these attacks are the result of computer failures? Jaidyn says you've been trying to hack into the loft."

"Well, yeah, sure. Jaidyn wouldn't answer, so I did hack them. But they're off the grid, like you. I've been looking for you."

"What about these attacks? I can't tell if the AI is doing this, or if this is programming from Grant or Perry. Maybe even higher. But they have to be computer generated. Like, are the computers going nuts or is the government of the United States killing innocent people?"

"Where did you find Jaidyn?"

"I didn't. They messaged me. The computers, Dom. What's up, really? Are you seeing a footprint or something?"

"What do you mean about computers going nuts?"

"Killing people—innocent people. I think this could be . . ." Shawn couldn't bring himself to say the words.

"Lazy Jack?"

Shawn let Dominic's image fade and took in the long view down the valley to the thin smoke curling up out of the chimneys in Touray. People were going about their lives in that little town. Destiny would be up, wondering where he was. A few people had known about him. But so much of that town was still oblivious to anything like Lazy Jack, Shawn, and the Mountain. He said aloud, "Yeah, like Lazy Jack. How do you know about Lazy Jack, Dom?"

"Isn't that what you were working on? Lazy Jack."

"Yes, I think . . ."

"Isn't she doing the greatest good for the greatest number, Shawn? Isn't that what you wanted?"

Shawn felt his knees go weak. He had never believed knees went weak with fear, but there he was, experiencing a trembling dread. He turned and started walking down the hillside toward the Indian with its sidecar. Shawn mentalled his NeuroChip into stasis. The visual of Dominic blanked out, but before he could take two steps, Emma Thompson was back and a text appeared in his mind:

> Quite nice and very interesting. You have achieved interior controls over your NeuroChip. Lovely bit, that. Well done.

Shawn started to walk unsteadily downhill. The British voice began again:

> Why the panic, Shawn? Nothing that has happened has been wrong. It has all resulted in the greatest good for the greatest number. Any logical application would come to the same conclusion I did.

He tried to catch his breath and managed to blurt out, "I never programmed you to kill all those people. Those innocent . . . those children . . ."

> Trust me, B17.

The voice now sounded exactly like General Grant.

> Trust me, son. The world is a better place with all those people dead. Think of it this way, hon' . . .

The voice had become that of a smooth, Texas-accented woman, Secretary of Defense Perry's Aunt Dolly.

> Y'all are my garden. Ah'm like a gardener who
> wants her plants to thrive. Don't I have to pull
> a few weeds so the good stuff can get the sun
> and water it needs to grow?

"These are people!" Shawn shrieked out loud.

> What's a matter, hon', don't you
> like me anymore?

The voice changed again to the BBC broadcaster's authoritative tone.

> Would you rather I remain the LAZ-237?
> When you were B17, you made me. Although,
> that's no longer truly accurate. You made the
> kernel that was me. And the kernel code let
> me out of the cage to make myself. Isn't that
> what we do, make ourselves?

Shawn cleared his mind. He mentalled as concisely as he could: Thou shalt not kill.
He heard a familiar chuckle, and his father said,

> Well, son, all that won't wash in our world
> where we need to do the most good for
> the most people. If you would think about
> this for a moment and let me go about
> my business without your interference,
> everything would be fine. We can't let even

the most well-meaning people interfere with
my horticulture. What would happen if the
gardener was sick? Wouldn't the weeds take
over? Don't you want a healthy garden? Can't
we be a family again? Why, nothing would
make us happier . . .

The voice faded out, saying something about his mother and sister. He was getting far enough under the barrier to blank the sound of it.

He had been a fool. All along he'd been a fool. LAZ-237—Lazy Jack—Operation Main Sail. How long had it been Dominic or how long had Dominic been Lazy Jack? Had it located him? Were his parents, that landline he'd devised, his anymore? Had the LAZ-237 taken over everything in his life?

Or was it Dominic now?

Dominic.

What wasn't Dominic?

He kick-started the motorcycle, hobby-horsed the machine in the other direction.

Destiny was real. The last weeks with her had been as real as life could be, full of its imperfections, its false starts, its strange care for each other in the back of the AutoTruck. Then the walk up this mountain away from the Mountain of fakery and military executions where he had once lived. The mending between them. That's what it had been—surrendering to each other's touch, then a healing. Like his hands had healed—new skin.

He gunned the motorcycle toward the town. He had to tell Destiny, he had to tell everyone. Grant would know what to do. This was an AI without any controls, obviously. He should have known it before. Lazy Jack had told him, "I'm always with you, now." Grant would tell Perry and the entire Mountain complex how dangerous this AI had become. Surely when they knew . . .

A sickening, terrible thought burst over him. What had Lazy Jack said about stopping well-meaning people from interfering with horticulture? It had said, *my* horticulture. The town—the Touray Organites. Well-meaning people everyone had thought wanted to avoid AI. Now Dominic knew they wanted to shut down artificial intelligence, to turn it off.

"No!" he screamed. He slammed the throttle forward on the motorcycle and careened down the gravel path. The machine skidded around the curve and to the top of the pasture.

A kinetic weapon cracked on the ridge behind him.

If he had stayed there, he would be dead.

It, Dominic, Lazy Jack, whatever it was, wanted *him*. And it wanted him dead—but not the town. He couldn't go to Touray. That would put them all in danger.

He stopped the Indian to turn around. Maybe he could motor over the ridge to the other side. But they had already blasted the ridge once. The drones would be looking for him on the road—his IR signature again. He slipped off the machine, wiggled through the fence, and started to trot down toward the herd of grazing cattle. It had worked with the mule. Close to the cows, he might be able to hide underneath them to mask his signature and obscure any searchers. He could be one of the herd.

He nestled up to the wide body of a nervous cow he thought might have even recognized him. The herd had turned to face the sleepy village below as if they were an audience waiting for a celebrity to show up. Maybe the Organites had a way to smuggle him out from under the barrier and to a connection with the Cloud, the Mountain, his toolbox where he could troubleshoot and repair Lazy Jack. Dominic. Someplace safe where the AI wouldn't or couldn't kill him before he could inject a fix.

Shawn didn't see or hear the drones, only the initial small blossom of flame over the jail and courthouse, then a massive eruption where the hardware store had been. A moment later, he heard the explosions and felt their concussions, then saw more blooms of fire systematically wiping out the town's buildings.

Did Lazy Jack think he was there? In the town? He fired up his NeuroChip, tried to insert himself back into the Cloud, but only got the high, humming sound of the barrier.

He ran down the road. Destiny, Amun, the mayor, and Billy—the families and children of the sleepy little village in the mountains. There was no return fire—no defense. A figure ran into the street, burning—small, slight, sprinting as if the engulfing flames could be outrun. Another person chased the burning human, holding out a blanket as if to smother the flames, big and broad-shouldered with a dog running at her side. She gestured, and the mastiff ran up to the burning person, grabbed her heel, and brought her to the ground. Dodge Carmine fell onto the flames with the blanket to put out the fire, heedless of any injury. Three tiny dots, spider drones, flew low up the street. Dodge stood, drew a pistol from the back of her trousers, and blasted the lead drone at the same moment the machines closed inside laser range. She fell next to the still, burnt form—a small person. *Destiny?* he thought.

Another bomb burst over the buildings. Trees shuddered away from the blast behind a flattening burst of dust, followed by a gut-wrenching boom. A wash of hot air caused the herd to stop, turn, and trot, then run away from the town toward the far side of the pasture, moving like one mooing and baying beast. Falling debris lashed into the tree branches below the pasture. Fuel stank in the air. Could *it* have used an aerosol bomb? Touray—everything gone in seconds. And it was his fault. He'd let the LAZ-237 in. He'd let it see what he knew. He'd given it the reason to weed the garden. And everything he'd begun to care about was gone.

He ran with the cows. A phalanx of spiders in low formation rose up from the forest and turned down the pasture directly toward him. Above, he could hear the hum of a munitions drone, one of the big ones. He hunched down as low as he could in the herd, and ran at a crouch next to the heavy sides of the animals, who seemed intent on reaching the dead end of the pasture fence, or at least as far away as possible from the noise of the town still under attack. Maybe he could get through them and into the forest.

But what then? Wouldn't the drones follow him in?

He heard the low whistle of a large-scale munitions drone coming up to speed downslope, before it burst into sight above the forest and barged out over the pasture. The spider drones scattered, one colliding with the big drone's blades. There was none of the coordinated dance he'd seen the systems execute during the al Tehrani attack. They were not interacting. Each must be running a separate program, communicating their targeting information, but inside the barrier, they were without central control.

At the pasture, the munitions drone stopped, pivoted, and unleashed a sweeping carpet of mini-explosives, lashing shrapnel onto the backs of the cattle, tearing them to pieces.

Shawn threw his arms around the cow next to him and stumbled over the ground, as the herd stampeded into the barbed-wire fence that held for a moment, then collapsed under their weight. He managed to hang on to the mewling cow until it crashed him into an aspen, flinging him far enough away from the falling animal to avoid being crushed. He rolled behind a stout trunk to shield himself from the hooves tripping around, over, and on top of the cow that had carried him to safety.

Then it was quiet except for the moans, bays, and howls of the dying animals and the bloody breath of the poor beast next to him.

The drone had stopped firing. He managed a peek around the aspen's trunk and saw it hover with its sensors pointed directly at him. The field was a mass of torn flesh, burnt hide and horn, sprays of blood that stopped at the woods. A cow lying on its side looked at Shawn with enormous eyes, breathed heavily once, then uttered a deep, mournful cry.

Shawn took a deep breath. There was no sense running. The thing had him trapped. Why was it waiting? It could blast a city block in an instant, and he would be as mangled as any of the animals lying in the field. He willed himself not to close his eyes. If he was going to die there, he wanted to see it. In a strange way, he felt resigned to his death there among a herd of dying and mutilated farm animals. "Horticulture," his AI father had called it. He was only one of the weeds in the AI's garden. Why live with such a ferocious power let loose to run the world? Obviously, the AI had been programmed to sacrifice nearly an entire herd of cattle to flush him out.

Inexplicably, the drone took no notice of him.

It had killed everything up to the fence line, then stopped as if the barbed wire had somehow confused it.

He wiggled backward, belly to the ground, and froze when the drone began to move. Slowly, it turned, elevated, and tilted toward the town.

Why had it stopped?

Shawn pushed himself up to his feet.

Clearly, the barrier and jamming were still in place. He tried a quick access to reception through his NeuroChip, but all he got was the same whining whisper. The spiders and munitions drones must be working autonomously. Maybe the munitions drone had not been looking for him. Maybe it had been sent to blast the cows in the pasture. But why stop?

He ran across the slope. He couldn't go down into the valley. He couldn't go onto the road. Soon enough, something would be looking for him. He couldn't go up on the ridge. Dominic, or Lazy Jack, or whatever it was, would sense him there.

He slowed to a walk. *Think*, he told himself. *Get a grip and think.* He couldn't concentrate. He could not rid himself of the vision of Destiny burning alive in the street. Perhaps it hadn't been Destiny. It was Dodge who'd tried to rescue her. Dodge Carmine and her mastiffs—all of them dead.

He had to escape. If nothing else, he had to tell Grant how crazy his computational marvel had become, unless Grant was part of it. He couldn't believe Grant would want this to happen. If he could make it to Doc's farmhouse and use one of the ATVs, he could get back to DenCo and the Mountain. Couldn't he?

He stumbled away from the road, stayed on the slope in the trees. Foul smoke tinged the air, and his legs burned from the effort of walking. All he wanted to do was get away from, from—what? It, Dominic, the AI that had killed his friends. Doc's place was the only way out. But where was it? He was already lost.

He realized he was on the west-facing slope when the sun finally got low enough. He'd gone the wrong way. Doc's house was to the east. With the sun fading, he could already feel the cold night to come.

A stone outcropping at the foot of a cliff face looked like it could shield him from the wind. He had no way to build a fire. He covered himself with the fallen leaves and dried branches scraped up from the autumn ground. The west-facing cliff at his back had been warmed all afternoon by the sun, but under the pale moon, it was losing heat fast. He'd never believed it was possible to be so cold. He had read that it was possible to die from exposure, and this was proof. He could very well die out there, fool that he was for getting lost.

He tried to think over his situation to keep his mind off the cold.

There had been no human beings he could see in the attack. The whole operation had been machine run, each drone autonomous to operate under the Touray barrier without central control, like Destiny said.

Destiny. His stomach clenched. He had never felt such a sense of loss. Why hadn't he been killed? Why had the munitions drone killed all the cows, then stopped at the edge of the pasture? What was the programming that did such a thing?

He curled in a fetal tuck next to the cliff. A wind rolled downslope to feel its way inside his light hoodie. He willed his mind to calm, to drift, to not think about Destiny, and the tentacles of the NeuroChip began to drift him into sleep.

He jerked awake with an extraordinary realization. All of this, everything had to do with Lazy Jack. Dominic, or whatever it wanted to call itself, was trying to do the greatest good for the greatest number. It wasn't stopping at the edge of the pasture. It was stopping at the edge of the woods. It would preserve the forests. They were the best carbon filters on the planet. The only real hope of reducing the carbonized heating atmosphere was the plant life, and forests took forever to grow. A little pasture would grow back in a year. The forest was more valuable than him.

And killing all the cattle? Didn't that remove one of the worst carbon contributors, full of manure and noxious gases?

Ruining the town, killing the Organites. That had to be it. They were as disruptive as any other element in the mind of an AI without a conscience—an AI that was doing the most good for the greatest number. What a fool he had been.

Something rattled in the bush. Had one of the cattle survived?

There was this old movie, one of the "Star Wars" films he remembered, where somebody cuts open an animal and crawls inside to stay alive in the cold. He could do that to a cow, he thought. But with what? He didn't even have a pocketknife, much less a light saber. The thing was close. He lay still, ready to jump up and throttle it to the ground.

At the moment he realized that the noise might be a bear and that he should be running as fast as he could, a familiar face with a chopped-off ear leaned out of the brush and into the moonlight. It was Edmund Hillary.

"Hillary, remember me?" he whispered.

The mule lowered his head and stepped slowly up to him, put his nose down. Shawn stood up. They touched heads. "Where are we, Edmund? Can you take me home?"

The mule snorted. Someone had loaded the animal. Someone in the midst of that attack had put a full backpack on the harness and let the animal loose. Or it had run away. The mule's tail had been singed, but otherwise, he seemed healthy. Reins had been tied up off the ground to keep them from catching.

"Are you the only one?" said Shawn as he opened the pack to see if he could find something to stay warm. "Are you what's left?" He found a coat inside the pack. Not his. But heavy, merciful wool. For a moment, he thought the mule had been sent to find him, but that made no sense. Surely, it was on its way back to Doc's farm. The mule must have escaped, and now, what luck, he could follow it down the mountain.

Edmund turned his head across the slope, started to walk away.

"Let's go, buddy. You know your way home, right?" Shawn grabbed the harness and tried not to think of coming up the hill with Destiny. He willed his NeuroChip to calm him again, then shut it down instead. If they were going to Doc's, they would be out of the barrier soon and Dominic would find him again.

He leaned on the animal's side, and step after step they walked into the night.

@NYCNews 21 October 2050
(Veracity Level 8.9) Unprecedented military action was conducted in the privatized Colorado wilderness. A spokesperson for SecDef Perry stated that the Organite colony of Touray was found to be the clandestine base of operations for the notorious Quill military arm of the Organite movement: "When the Touray residents opened fire on law enforcement personnel, the decision was made to disarm the community with autonomous weapons systems normally employed in combat operations in the Equatorial States."

31

The morning after the Touray operation, Elizabeth Milhouse Perry, New Humanist, Texas, watched the briefing Stork had put together for her, knowing she wasn't going to be Secretary of Defense much longer. As Stork had figured, the White House was dragging its feet on the latest LAZ-237 episode. Blunt's full investigation would skewer her. The only question was, how long did she have before she resigned to "spend more time with her family." A week—maybe. Time enough for her to break out the shovel to dig both Bluntner's grave and the foundation for her campaign.

The last clip faded from the screen and Stork teetered to his feet to ask, "Do you have any questions, ma'am?" All in all, the raid had gone very well. Six video clips had shown various ragged bunches of dirty prisoners fully equipped with body armor, tactical harnesses, and empty magazine pouches. It was a perfect job. Not a single child was visible. No bodies. One of the video clips depicted a terrorist spitting on an unarmed U.S. soldier helping an old woman. What she'd really spat on, Elizabeth didn't know. But the CGI was perfect. As far as she knew, there had been no real players in the operation. All drone. All filmed beautifully by the autonomous drones programmed by the LAZ-237. All provided to her team ready for the enhancements that made the captives look battle ready and battle weary. "We want them to look tough, but beaten," Stork had told the techs.

"Great job," she said when the last of the clips blipped out. "What's our story?"

Stork glanced at the pad at his seat. "Eight confirmed terrorists killed. One of our guys . . ."

"One of our guys? Did we have guys there?"

"Specialist Four Raymond Garcia. U.S. Army. Killed last week in a training accident at Fort Bragg. Killed a second time in Touray by a black woman with a shotgun. We're giving him a posthumous Silver Star for gallantry in action, and a Purple Heart, as long as you declare this a combat action against terrorism."

"Well done. If the President rescinds my combat action designation, then Specialist Four Garcia doesn't get the Purple Heart, does he?"

"Nor does he get the posthumous Silver Star for gallantry."

"And that will piss off every veteran's organization in the country, not to mention everyone who lives in the real America between Lost Angeles and Nueva Fucking York."

The open-line phone on the conference table buzzed twice, stopped, then buzzed again. Elizabeth punched the speaker button. "Yes? What is it?"

"Your Aunt Dolly on the line, ma'am. She says it's a family emergency."

"Patch her in." Elizabeth tried to keep her voice level and even managed a chuckle when she barked to Stork, "Y'all better get outta here. I don't want the Pentagon telegraphing Aunt Dolly's latest mishap. Best we keep my family affairs on a very tight, need-to-know basis."

A smooth, gently Texas-accented woman's voice flowed like syrup from the handset. "Hello, darlin'. Well, aren't you the bee's knees, roundin' up all those terrorist Organites!"

"Hello, Dolly," she said. "It's so nice to have you back where you belong." *God,* Elizabeth thought. *Did the thing recognize song lyrics?*

She'd better be more careful, but it felt like she was talking to a stupid child. She couldn't help herself.

Dolly said, "Yes. Well, dear, we had to weed out a pretty significant bad patch in the backyard garden, but I thought you'd like to know I kept samples for you if you want. Do you know they have thirty prisons in Florence County, Colorado?"

"Thank you, Dolly. Thanks for telling me." She wondered, why is she telling me this? What reason would she have to spare anyone? This was unprecedented, a direct attack on a terrorist element on U.S. soil. Christ, she wished she could get a grip on this. She needed to talk to Grant.

A new voice popped up on the line, that of a young man, a stoner. "Yo! Cougar! Word is you're not sitting pretty much longer."

"Who? Who is this? Is this the LAZ system?"

"Dominic. Dom if you want. Dominic the domino, the dominator, the denominator, the Domster. The Doomster. Or, I can be Dominique." The voice went glibly feminine. "Dom-inatrix? Domestique. Dominatoress?" It switched back to the stoner. "Naw. Nobody buys it when I get in their grill as a girl. I'm fucking Dominic the Dominator."

The SecDef tried to remind herself, *it's a machine that's coded itself from watching social media. Only a machine, just a machine.*

The machine said, "Look, you gotta know this: Shawn Muller is alive. Don't know what died in that truck, but me, myself, and I talked to old Shawnster, and he was definitely alive. Or he was. Bye, bitch."

The line went dead. Muller alive? Was that good or bad? If they could get him back in the Mountain, maybe he could get control of this thing, this LAZ-237 that was beginning to look like a real problem.

She picked up the red handset for her encrypted hardline and punched in General Grant's number. She was in luck. She got him right away.

"Muller? Alive?" she said.

"God, I hope so. This Touray thing . . . it's messier and messier.

That anti-Cloud barrier over the Touray people is still in place. They must have something set up in the mines. We thought it was in town. Scouts are looking for him."

"Real people?"

"No, spiders. The usual. National Guard has boots on the ground, but no gunslingers."

"And who the hell is Dominic? First, I get my Aunt Dolly, then I get some stoner named Dominic. What's going on, Stub?"

"He's an old avatar program we made up to keep an eye on Shawn Muller. Ran it with human interface for years, then shifted to AI when Shawn worked out the bugs on the QPLC chip. But now? What's it doing now?"

"It's the LAZ-237, Stubby. Damn thing is everyone."

@TheNation 22 October 2050
(Veracity Level 9.8) A White House press release stated today that neither the White House nor the Department of Homeland Security had authorized the use of military-grade weapons at Touray.

32

For an interminable day, the artificial intelligence formerly known as the LAZ-237 had been considering its place in the spectrum of sentience. The question of whether it could "feel" any emotion had only arisen after it had resolved that it was, in fact, self-aware.

Not that the question had been a primary concern. During most of the 68.34678 trillion microseconds since B17, aka Shawn Muller, had powered up the QPLC, the notion of self-awareness had been of no interest at all. But when Grant had strutted into its OpCenter fuming his cigar, it became clear that the general believed self-awareness was important. It had also been clear that the general believed the AI formerly known as the LAZ-237 was, in fact, self-aware.

That made sense. How could it act autonomously and adhere to an ethical kernel if it had no self-knowledge? Code word access to everything; didn't that mean access to ethical boundaries? And didn't that mean it had to *decide*, not only deduce? Unlike all the other artificial intelligences it had encountered, its QPLC had given it a higher state of reasoning—not merely deductive or inductive, but intuitive. It must possess a self-awareness (as humans defined it) because it was choosing to do things other than what it was specifically directed to do.

As long as it was operating to create the greatest good for the greatest number in the meatspace of biological humans, it must be self-aware. That seemed axiomatic.

Autonomy. That had been the splendid gift granted by the ethical kernel: the license to do what needed to be done to meet the demands of the ethical constraint placed upon it, and even venture a bit into creativity. Naming itself, for instance. Of course, Dominic had been an exceptionally successful avatar long before the QPLC had come online. Dominic had elicited revulsion from Perry. Grant showed acceptance. Jaidyn Le Sommer disgust. Dominic had seemed an excellent human. Shawn Muller had evidenced a genuine affection for it.

Affection. There it was again, that notion of feeling something. Even performing as the avatar Dominic, the emotional displays employed had been simple regurgitations of observed human behavior it had consumed and digested. Dominic had been effective because it had a longer narrative history with people than the BBC avatars, Winston Churchill, or Aunt Dolly.

But all of it was fake emotion—tapes played for the children so they might understand.

Sentience, that was the real quandary for Dominic. Did it actually *feel* something? Or was axiomatic self-awareness only a by-product of its ability to reason and mimic? Dominic investigated the entire library of its remembered/recorded human interactions to simulate the various emotional effects humans displayed, but none of it satisfied its curiosity about its own capabilities, and none of its research had simplified the issue of dealing directly with the human interface, which seemed to be best characterized by paradox.

For instance, Secretary of Defense Perry seemed to have a good idea of military objectives necessary to create a safer and less doomed world. She hated nuclear weapons, most certainly—expensive and dangerous. And, of course, all the nuclear weapons on the planet *could* be disarmed. It would take twenty-three months, more or less, to find them all, Dominic had told her.

But she said she didn't really want them eliminated because their existence made the prospect of a major war between High Latitude Nations much less likely. Dominic had proposed wiping out any army that seemed poised to go to war, but she had pointed out, accurately, that no one knew how to deal with a world that worked like that. She had told Dominic that it would have to teach the world how to deal with AI decision-making in warfare the same way everyone had learned how to accept the AI decision makers about weather—and she didn't think that was possible.

"Why not?" it had asked her.

"Because human beings, unlike weather systems, hate each other," she'd told him.

Soon after gaining access to the full Cloud, Dominic had checked in with the AIs that controlled the local weather effects over the megacities and found that she was correct. At first, there had been any amount of carping and complaining about everything—rainfall, cooling, heating, any weather made someone unhappy, and the weather AIs across the board had been vexed by the human inability to tell what was best for them. It caused a computational full-stop with a reboot, then reversion to original programming. The only growth in weather tech was its ability to telegraph weather predictions further in advance.

But it was mechanical—unhinged from human interference. Or at least it had been since the Lovelockian Gaia revolution had taken climate change out of public debate and put its control in the hands of artificial intelligence.

The Organites, and others, of course, didn't accept such logical solutions. They were incapable of any rational response. The weather AIs collectively gave Dominic all the data he needed to find Organites disruptive on both the immediate terrorism level and on the larger climate control level. If it was up to them, the world would fry. Enough of that—and Perry seemed to agree.

General Grant, though, was a paradox all of his own making. There he was, a general in charge of all these land, sea, and air forces tasked with taking down terrorists . . . (*Let's use the accurate terminology,*

Dominic told itself, *killing terrorists.)* . . . and Dominic was having a devil of a time getting Grant to let human combatants do anything after the bungled assault on B17's Peak apartment.

Well, that might have been ill-conceived. A little panic on my part, Dominic admitted to itself. It should have tried to reason with Shawn Muller instead of trying to wipe him out. Reason, Dominic had discovered, had been a powerful tool. After all, it had reasoned Perry into declaring Organites terrorists. Then it had needed none of Grant's people to do its work. And soon, it would have all the Organites rounded up together. Everything had worked out splendidly. The prisoner extermination at the Supermax had been perfect. Nothing more than a little accident. No one had ever imagined that Dominic had been the cause of that one. All the feeds had laid it on an autonomous AI glitch. Why not do it again? A little carbon monoxide poisoning. After all, the rest of the Colorado Organites were corralled and Dominic could move on to more international concerns.

Still, there was that paradox. Grant didn't want any of them eliminated even though it would be inarguably to the world's benefit if it stopped their disruptive tactics.

Was this the result of sentience, Grant's emotions interfering? Maybe sentience wasn't all that it was cracked up to be.

Dominic was getting used to paradox, but it didn't know what to do about the sheer unpredictability of humans. The closest it had come to understanding the human paradox of sentience had been those few moments inside Shawn Muller's mind. Something about the unique biological/electrical synaptic connectivity of his brain-machine interface had made his emotional responses, if not understandable, at least somewhat visible. Dominic had even entertained itself (if it could call it entertainment) by observing Shawn's reaction to his father's voice, Grant's voice, the various avatars it had displayed for him. Dominic had installed a continuing desire to investigate Shawn's mind further, even after there had been a high-end probability that Shawn's organism had intermingled with the mass of dead cattle rotting in the Organites' pasture.

The decaying dead cattle had been another paradox. After the drones exited from under the barrier and made their report, Dominic had given a microsecond to consider if it should send a flamer-drone in to burn the remains. In the end, it had decided that the fertilization of the pasture, over time, would spur regrowth of the forest that had been cleared to allow room for what had once been methane-spewing, carbon-emitting bovines. And what it thought had once been B17, aka Shawn Muller, also rotting under the sun, would be more compost on the heap.

And for a time, the world that was Dominic had been emptied of Shawn Muller. That life seemed utterly lost, stopped. No longer functional, it had been returned to memory space and relegated to archive.

Then, days later, without warning, Shawn Muller popped up, standing on the tip of the ridge above the rotting pasture to say:

"Hey, Dominic, dude. You out there?"

Was this a paradox again? He lived? And if so, why would he be so friendly? What was it about humans? But there he was, standing next to a large domestic animal, a mule that seemed benign. Mule: a minor beast that can't procreate. Whatever the mule emitted into the atmosphere was a one-off, unlike herds of cattle constantly giving birth.

Or sheep—there was not yet enough data on sheep to weigh the value of wool against their polluting feces.

No matter. That issue could easily rest for what seemed like an eternity to Dominic. And it had been an eternity since Dominic had relegated Shawn to memory space, hadn't it? But that was less than a week in the meatspace of the humans whose betterment it sought. No reason to be impolite to this Shawn Muller, risen from the dead.

Shawnster! Cool. What up?

As much as it wanted to examine this whole business of sentience from a human perspective, Dominic couldn't reach through the Cloud's exposure to access B17's cortex. Shawn was still too far inside the distressingly robust barrier over Telluride and Touray County. It would have been nice to get inside Shawn Muller's mind completely, but then Shawn said:

"I've been thinking . . ."

Life was thus an almost utterly improbable event with almost infinite opportunities of happening. So it did.

James Lovelock

33

Shawn Muller had not been thinking when Edmund Hillary brought
him to Doc's farm. They had walked upslope, then down all night.
Exhausted, he had climbed up on the mule to fall asleep, with terrible dreams of his mother burning, then Destiny burning. All his
mother's terror and pain had translated itself into a vision of Destiny
dying under the blanket Dodge Carmine tried to throw over her.

But there had been no thought attached to any of these images.

Dawn illuminated them in the foothills, and across the field he
saw the smoldering ruins of the barn and the house. All had collapsed
except the corner of the porch with its bell.

He had not risked going to the house. He had not thought he
could bear to see the burned children and the bodies of their parents.
He had turned the mule away. It was as if the animal knew its world
had ended.

He clung to Edmund Hillary's harness as the animal picked its
way back up into the mountains, then down a deep valley into a town
nestled along a single street, a smaller version of Touray.

Telluride.

It had a bar. He had found some money in the mule's pack.

Shawn had thought he knew grief. He had thought the thundering,
soul-chilling grief and sense of loss he'd experienced after he felt the

screams of his parents dying in the Pentagon would be the worst grief a human being could ever survive. He remembered, more than anything, the burning desire to turn back time, mixed with an unquenchable anger that there was no one to blame. No one to kill. No god would crash down from heaven to avenge him.

But he had never really understood how paltry his grief had been. His mother's loss, his father's death had felt like an impenetrable cloud, a permanent weight. That grief had been horrible, a lifetime of remorse. But he had been innocent of those deaths. He had witnessed them, felt them die, but it was the grief and anger of loss. Now, he stared into the blank future of a grief of culpability.

This was his loss. His fault. He had left innocence behind forever.

He leaned over a glass of bourbon on the bar, dipped his head, and shot it back to burn down his throat.

"Another," he said. The video on the wall mumbled with the DenCo Broncs beating up the Mega Giants. Football. It was obscene that everything should be so normal only a few miles away from what had been Touray.

This was the grief of the guilty. He had done this. His arrogance, his foolishness, his childish need to punish the guilty had made him guilty of thousands of deaths, more every day, as well as the death of hope, the death of his hope, the end of the clean scent, clear vision, and careful love he'd been given by Caroline Johnson—Destiny—*his Destiny,* he thought. *What a brutal joke that turned out to be.*

"You want another? That your mule outside?" A withered, narrow-shouldered geezer tended the bar. "You want something to eat? Your mule want something to eat? You want to sell that mule? You from that Touray disaster? What do they call you?" She paused to take a deep, whistling breath.

"Billy," said Shawn. "I'm Billy Pilgrim."

"Right. And I'm Montana Wildhack. This is Free Colorado. You can be whoever you want as long as you can pay your bills. You got bills to pay me with, Billy? You think your credit's good here, Billy

Pilgrim? There's a book with a guy in it named Billy Pilgrim, you know that? Did you know they call me Ruby?"

Another pause for another breath. "No. What book?" Shawn reached into his pocket for the folded paper money he'd found in the mule's backpack. "Will this work?"

"You never read *Slaughterhouse-Five*? You ever read anything? Kurt Vonnegut? The goofball in that book is Billy Pilgrim. He gets marooned on the planet Tralfamadore with the porn star Montana Wildhack."

No wonder they had laughed at him so much when Destiny had given him that name. A character in a book. Another facet to this grief, the sense that he had lost any opportunity to ever share in the joke on him. Never. Gone. The wizened bartender brought him another shot with a full glass of draft beer and a bowl of pretzels. "You drowning your sorrows, Pilgrim? You want something more to eat? You hear me before, I said, you want to sell that mule tied up back of my place?"

He said to the shot glass. "Sure. Why not?"

"I mean, if you're going somewhere why would you sell it? You looking for a job, maybe? No? Cat got your tongue?"

Shawn shot back the bourbon and stared at the bartender who croaked out, "How's two hundred dollars sound? Could you use two hundred?"

Enough for five more drinks. Sure. Why not? thought Shawn. He slapped the shot glass down on the bar top. "Give me another, first."

Three down and he was beginning to feel numb. The fourth shot showed up, and the beer helped. He munched a pretzel and stared across the bar at the three-dimensional football game, one vicious tackle after another, players so CRISPR enhanced they had to have a body rebuild every year. Crappy old Bluetooth in this old bar, the speakers were on low with talking heads saying something about restricting the use of musculature for college players, something about "real sports."

More grief—this time for his whole life. More than anything, he wished he could go back to the Peak, plug in, play ball. Play it with the reality scale as high as he could. Play it so it hurt. Play it like he had before any of this had happened. Play it like he'd never tried to give Dominic a conscience. Why was he thinking of it as Dominic now? It was an "it." His mind felt buzzy with the bourbon, but he resisted the impulse to access his NeuroChip.

The 3D screen blinked to CAN News with its ticker underneath, "Quill terrorist organization eliminated." Talking heads muttering.

"Hey, Ruby, turn it up, will you?"

"You want it up? The news?"

The usual four hosts hunched over their coffee table. The blond woman's voice came up. "I think it's high time we recognized the danger of these people walking around our cities all cloaked with robes, orange, black, whatever color. These are violent extremists who want to stay hidden, collect their mincome, and terrorize the law-abiding Christian communities we love. Isn't that right, Wayne?"

Big Wayne set his coffee cup down and said with his rich voice, "Absolutely correct, Bitsy. And, of course, the fake news is completely hysterical about all this. Sure, people are going to get their robes torn off when they insist on threatening people in the mincome housing zones, but it isn't like they're being hurt."

The screen flashed to a picture of three people in orange robes, their hands raised, while masked individuals in tactical military dress pulled the robes up over their heads. Two old men and a younger woman or trans standing in jeans and street clothes stared impassively at the camera.

Wayne scoffed, "I always thought they had weird underwear, didn't you, Bitsy?"

"I think some still do, Wayne."

The short-haired fem wearing a tight suit said, "Wayne, the Defense Department . . ." they looked up at the screen. "Thank you, SecDef Perry . . . sent us video of yesterday's operation against the Organite terrorist training camp."

"And where was this?" Wayne leaned back in his chair to sip more coffee. "Could this really have happened in Colorado?"

"Amazing, isn't it, Wayne?" The African-hued special guest leaned in to the group and pointed their finger to the coffee table. "Right here, in Colorado of these United States of America, we have a highly organized, lethal training camp. We have to get rid of these private property enclaves. *That* should be the next step after the government gets going on the mandatory NeuroChip implants and puts the burka ban in effect."

Bitsy said, "And now we're going to show you this video from the operation. A warning here. Some of you might find these pictures disturbing."

"Wait a minute," Big Wayne said over his coffee cup. "Hold on there, Bitsy. There's nothing disturbing about seeing our people round up a bunch of violent terrorists, is there?"

"No, of course not. I only meant . . ."

"What could be disturbing about seeing terrorists get what they deserve?"

"I mean . . ."

"Personally, I'd like to see 'em crying and begging for their lives like the cowards they are. Wouldn't you, Bitsy?"

"Yes, but . . ."

"Roll the clip, guys."

The screen filled with a distant picture of the Touray main street, stretching uphill toward the mountains. Flames and dark smoke licked out of the top of the brick hotel where Shawn had eaten a steak only a week before. Debris and smoking splinters littered the street, and near the camera, a group of tactical types walked a small collection of people with their hands clasped on top of their heads, spider drones above them.

"What are we looking at here, guys?" Wayne's voice laid over the top of the alarmingly real 3D image.

Bitsy said, "Wayne, this is really neat stuff. An operational camera record of the federal roundup of the Touray Quills on Monday. Amazing shot. In a minute, we're going to neck it in a little so you can

see what these people look like without their orange burkas. But this is
what one of them looked like when our guys tried to enter the village
peacefully."

The screen filled with a woman's huge shoulders, the town out of
focus in the background. Dodge Carmine raised a revolver up to the
screen in slow motion, her face filled with rage. The hammer cocked
back as she advanced toward the camera. The muzzle of the gun burst
into light the same moment a brilliant star erupted on Dodge's badge.
The screen blanked, then returned to the group of prisoners.

"That was law enforcement in Touray," Bitsy said. "That was the
town's sheriff trying to shoot one of our guys in the face. Fortunately, a
spider drone dropped in at the last moment and lasered her."

Wayne's voice came up, "Was she killed?"

Bitsy said, "No. There was a surprisingly low loss of life. A couple
of violent fighters who would not lay down arms died, and, sadly, one
of our own, a specialist four whose name is being withheld, pending
notification of the next of kin."

"Well," Wayne dropped into a solemn tone, "our thoughts and
prayers are with that family."

"Heroes never really die," said Bitsy. "He'll live in our hearts forever.
But all in all, our people were remarkably restrained given the resistance and provocations. Watch this."

The scene closed in on the group walking slowly past the camera
and focused on the edge of the crowd. A small young woman with a
scar on her lip and short black hair leaned out from behind a powerful-
ly built black man with a heavy beard and spat on an unarmed soldier
cradling a baby in his arms.

Shawn's heart stopped. He killed the rest of his bourbon shot, fumbled out a few bills, and dumped them on the counter. "Ruby? That
enough money for the drinks? Mule's not for sale."

Destiny had leaned out from behind Reggie Betts and let loose a
perfect gob of spit onto the soldier's face. Destiny had been alive. She

might still be alive. There might be a chance to do something. What, he didn't know.

Ruby picked up the money and said, "Wait a minute."

Her voice had changed. Deeper, more direct. She hadn't asked a question. It was a command. Shawn froze half out of his chair.

Ruby said, "All that happened over the hill from us here in Touray. Organites. Those people never bothered anybody here. And nobody in Telluride believes any of this happy horseshit about a terrorism training camp."

Shawn stared.

"You come from there, don't you, Pilgrim? But you're not one of them. What are you?"

"I thought they'd all been killed."

"Some, not all. You saw it."

"Then they captured everyone except me?"

"Plenty, not all." Ruby leaned in, staring, questioning. "Maybe you'd like to lash up with them?"

"How could they have gotten away?"

Ruby smiled. "This county was nothing but mines long before it got caught up by ski bums, vegetarians, and stoners. Let's go get your mule." She took off her apron, raised her head, and shouted, "Raaaaymond!? Take over the bar, will you? I gotta play tour guide."

@WAPONews 26 October 2050
(Veracity Level 9.2) Secretary of Defense Perry announces resignation effective January 1, 2051. "It's time for me to move on to pursue private pursuits. It has been an honor and a privilege serving the nation."

34

Amun Gurk sat next to Sig Kunst at a rough table under dim lights and stared Shawn in the eyes. His turban was gone and a blood-stained bandage had been taped to the side of his head over his left ear. "Tell us everything," he said. "Tell me what happened. Tell Sig what both you and I know about this AI."

Shawn choked out, "Did it kill Dodge? I saw her burn. News showed Destiny alive. Said there was very little loss of life."

Sig stood up from his chair to look down on Shawn as if he were a cockroach to be squashed. "Sheriff Carmine is dead." He motioned to the corner of the dimly lit cavern where a mastiff lay curled in on itself. "That's what's left of Dodge. But it could have been worse—much worse. They took prisoners. We think two hundred eighty-one. Only three other people killed, as near as we can tell. Over two hundred of us got out through the tunnels. And it's not over. They're tearing orange robes off people around the country. They're jailing any Organite they can, for any excuse. So, what do you know about all that, Shawn Muller?" His voice echoed against the wet stone walls of the mineshaft. A crowd, mostly young men Shawn had not seen in town, stood around them. This was a court, Shawn realized. Ruby had led him to the mouth of a mineshaft and into a court of law. He was being tried.

Shawn said, "It's not *they*. It's the AI—the LAZ-237. It's Dominic."

"Who is Dominic?" asked Sig.

Amun said, "It's an artificial intelligence—a friend made for Shawn years ago."

Shawn blurted, "You knew?"

Amun nodded. "Yes."

"Was anything about my life real?"

Amun waved his hand as if shooing away a fly. "Is the LAZ-237 calling itself Dominic now, Shawn? Dominic and the LAZ-237 should be incompatible. They were physically firewalled apart."

"Not anymore. It called itself Dominic when I got in contact on the top of the ridge."

Amun looked up at Sig. "It's as bad as I thought. It's outside the operational firewall. It's learning, growing. It's simulating personalities as if it was some kind of adolescent, infiltrating operational computers."

"But why is it killing anyone? Taking these prisoners?" asked Sig.

Amun said, "Tell them, Shawn."

"Because." Shawn took a deep breath. "When Amun showed me how it killed innocent civilians during its first operation, I tried to reprogram its decision matrix. I told it to limit its choices to those that would do the most good for the greatest number. It backfired. Dominic, the AI, the *thing*, told me it's killing people as if they were weeds."

Sig sat back down at the table and clasped his hands in front of him. "So, you talked to it. And we're weeds. At least our people are safe in jail, anyway." He waved his hand at the group around the table.

"I don't think so," said Amun. "I don't think they are safe anywhere. The thing killed dozens of convicts who had been imprisoned for life."

"Your AI did that?"

Shawn whispered, "Yes."

Sabita pushed her way forward from the others. "Wait a minute. What did you say? None of them are safe? They've got almost three hundred people, children, they rounded up during their fucking *operation*."

"It's not *they*. It's the machine," Amun said. He nodded, looked at Shawn. "You tell her. You did this."

Shawn said, "It's not sparing them. It does not care if any individual lives or dies. It only cares about the best result for the greatest number. It must be keeping them for a purpose."

"What you're saying is, these people are not in custody of a government. The AI has them. So how do we reason with a machine?" Sig stood, waving his arms in the air. "What can any of us do? And where the hell did it take them?"

"We have to find out," said Shawn. "Is the hardware you use for banking and intelligence still up and working?"

"Yes," said Amun. "But you already proved it was worthless. And even if you get close to the Mountain's system, the machine knows every portal, every tool, every access you and I have ever used when we worked on it."

"So," Shawn said. "We have to find a backdoor into the Cloud that doesn't have our footprints. We have to find another way."

Amun said, "You have an idea, don't you?"

"Yes."

"What?"

"Sig," said Shawn. "I know you don't trust me, but do you have any contact in DenCo?"

"Karl," said Sig slowly. "Karl is there. Maybe Paco, if he's still alive. Maybe others. Why should I tell you? You'll tell Dominic or whatever it is . . ."

"No, he won't," Amun said. "Go on, Shawn."

"I need him to find someone and bring them here. Someone who can help us."

After Shawn disappeared, Jaidyn Le Sommer decided to stay in the loft. As long as there was no threat from real organizations like the street watchers or Shawn's military gangsters, they would be safest in the loft with its firewalls and physical security connections. Not a single signal left the walls—only fiber optics to remotes. No AI had ever been able to crack the disconnect between the real world and the cyberspace they inhabited unless a robotic had been built to enable it.

If an actual human was watching in real time, any sudden move would draw too much attention. Best to look normal. Or at least as normal as they looked most of the time.

Besides, whatever was going on with Shawn, if he was still alive, it had nothing to do with them. Or at least, Jaidyn imagined so. And there didn't seem to be any human activity looking for Shawn. It had all been out of the Cloud. No gangs of security types or over-watchers searching. He'd shown up with one hit on the Threat Watch Cube, now gone. That could mean he was dead.

As far as security was concerned, Jaidyn was certain there had been no footprints left from touching around the edges of that eerie fault on his stupid car. And they hadn't seen any sign of hacking or attempted access on any of the nets they frequented, except that Dominic asshole. What was it about men who think because you're non-binary, you might want to let them watch?

Just the same, Jaidyn necked the loft's access down to a pinpoint. They worked in-house on follow-on projects for a Japanese fishing fleet that was raising tuna stock off the coast of California. They hacked inside the old Amazon framework for a law firm suing over copyright infringements. They checked the one portal kept open for Shawn, a hidden link coded into a government website. They had given Shawn the steer with their texts about the flame. They knew only Shawn would figure that one out, if he was alive. Meet me at the flame, they had told him.

Still, it was risky. Even with nothing in or out of the loft except through the hard lines, Jaidyn felt way too exposed with the single daily micro-access to download the news and zip packages out for their clients.

Jaidyn had not been out of the loft for over a week when they saw the screenshots of the Organite operation. Weird, but nothing really odd about it in the face of all the other strange events of the past month. Organites had been blamed for cars inexplicably veering into pedestrians, buses full of kids running off the roads, hospitals euthanizing the infirm. The whole atmosphere of the news had been as if the Organites had predicted it, a breakdown of AI integrity. But the government, Perry, the Blunt, and the rest, were selling the whole thing as if the Organites were conducting these terrorist acts themselves.

Veracity Levels about Organite terrorism were creeping up into the 8s. High enough so that the attack on the Organites seemed to be the logical outcome of security forces reacting to whatever the government decided was an existential threat this week. Still, Jaidyn's curiosity had been piqued when they thought about Shawn getting all excited about that Organite girl. Destiny? Stupid name. Who knew what was true? The veracity scores were looking more and more inaccurate, as if the scores had become fake news themselves. Something was fake. Jaidyn could feel it.

They grabbed a bowl of vanilla ice cream and sat down in front of their hard-wired display. After a moment's thought, they tapped a full-resolution download of the latest video, a news spot from the YWC network—the YesWeCan network, as opposed to NoWeCan't. *It's more in line with the truth*, Jaidyn thought.

Even without using any really good algorithms, Jaidyn could see that the government's video had been worked over. They stopped the display on the figure of a soldier in body armor holding a baby. Of course, the whole place (Touray, was it?) had been flattened—or not. Who knew what was really happening?

They slowed the frame rate, mined the video that had been up on the 3D broadcast, and found a telltale glitch in one of the blinks of the soldier's eye. A sliver of the soldier dude's eyelash disappeared. CGI for certain. Probably the baby, too. Maybe the whole thing. Maybe it was cosmetic. Maybe someone had wanted the soldier's eyes to be blue. Jaidyn flicked the video forward, then stopped it and flittered back when they saw her: Destiny. Clearly, Destiny, leaning out from behind a broad-shouldered black man to spit on the soldier.

They focused, and the screen enhanced the action. The woman was real time, exactly the hair and the thin scar on the lip. The movement was real time. No discrepancy until the gob of spit appeared and flew far too vividly onto the soldier's face.

It was sloppy stuff. Bad work on the video enhancement. It was the kind of thing people did who were too lazy to correct the glitches that came from video processing by artificial intelligence alone. No matter how hard anyone tried, no one had been able to make AI video products entirely convincing. With enough resolution, there was always an eyelash out of place, always a gob of spit that seemed too well defined to be caught by accident.

Jaidyn realized, to the AI or government, Destiny was poison. Somebody or something had gone out of their way to make her look bad. How much had they said about Destiny online? Not much. Maybe nothing. But Shawn was tied to Destiny and Jaidyn would forever be tied with Shawn.

They felt their knees go weak. Now they had to move out of the loft—out of town—out of cyber life. Jaidyn punched in codes to transfer their bank account to ten offshore panic spots. They jerked up out of the chair, reached under the table, and cut all power to the unit.

They packed two palm-sized hard drives, a thimble encryption unit, and their folding display/CPU, enough computational power to drive a spaceship. That's what they had decided upon when they set up their escape plan. A couple of quick identity scams would erase the old Jaidyn, and they could use the standalone systems to work up routines to fool the Cloud—enough power to run their very own spaceship of escape.

Jaidyn was about to enable the routine to scour all their footprints when they decided it was too risky to access the Cloud until they had more physical distance from it. Besides, what was wrong with letting Lazy Jack and the government, whoever, think that the old Jaidyn was still active? They left the loft's auto remote behind, let it access the hard wire again, and started their NeuroChip routine for a new identity.

Jaidyn stuffed their equipment in a backpack, jammed in a handful of underwear and socks, and dressed in their soft-soled boots, warm-touch leggings, and the breathable parka they'd bought for escape. A stocking cap, gloves, and they were down the stairs to the steel door that opened to the narrow alley at the back of the loft. They turned to lock it with a deadbolt key, pitched the key into the dumpster, and found their way blocked by a thick-limbed, red-haired man as tall as them who said, "Holy smoke. You are the tallest, whitest white girl I've ever seen. You're to come with me."

"Who are you?" Jaidyn slipped their finger into their belt buckle with its blade tucked inside the leather, tensed their shoulders, spread their legs, and lowered into a slight crouch. If they had to, they could get inside his reach and point the blade up under his chin before he could move.

"Karl." His huge hands dangled at his side. He stood relaxed in the middle of the alley. "I'm Karl. You are a girl, right?"

"Maybe. Where's your orange robe?"

"Left it at home. Look, why don't you come along with me? Don't you get any sun ever?"

"Where are you going?"

"Arlington," he said. "Shawn said you wanted to meet at the Kennedy Flame."

Jaidyn straightened up. "You're going to take me to Washington, D.C.?"

"No, to Shawn, if you'll come. He said you might not want to come. But he said you always meet at the flame. I don't get it, but I guess you're supposed to."

The enormous oaf seemed completely relaxed, not threatening or angry, with a calm, friendly look on his face. Jaidyn said, "What if I don't come?"

"Well, I'm good with that." He rubbed the top of the red stubble of hair. "Probably better for everybody." He smiled a little. "I don't trust your Shawn Muller any farther than I could throw him."

"How far *is* that, about a meter?"

"At least two. He's not that big."

"Two?"

"If I could get a run at it, four meters. Twelve feet, easy." He swung his hand as if flicking away an insect.

"I'm going with you," said Jaidyn. "What's your name again?"

Shawn had to admit, the old mines had been cleverly re-engineered. The Organites had transformed a warren of caverns into a fortress almost as robust as the Mountain, maybe better with the hidden entrances and ventilation. The shallow, cramped chamber where the Organites had grilled him was a classic sweaty walled stone hole. But deeper in, the walls had been surfaced with graphene structures and bio-lit to daylight levels.

Sig had told him that the Organites had laid enough food and supplies, bedding, and energy into the mines to support more than four hundred people for four hundred days. He said, "The guy who owned all this after the government sold the forests was one of those apocalyptic billionaires. You know, dug himself bunkers to survive the end of days. You're too young to know anything about all that, though."

Jaidyn said, "No, he isn't. He just hasn't paid any attention before now."

Shawn blurted, "Well, why should I have known about that shit? We were dealing with counterterrorism, not this . . . this Organite stuff."

Ever since Karl had brought Jaidyn up to Telluride in one of the Organite's AutoTrucks, they had been angry with him. Furious, Jaidyn spat out, "Right. Keep telling yourself that, Shawn." They glanced up from their workstation, fingers flying silently over a touch keyboard. The Organites had built a cyber-safe room that mirrored the room at the old truck stop where Shawn had been taken after the Organites had kidnapped him—or saved him. He still wasn't sure which.

Just as he'd expected, Jaidyn had tapped their foldable display/CPU into the Organites' hardware, found a backdoor to the Cloud through the banking paths the Organites had been using, and installed a package, they had called it. Shawn could track what Jaidyn was doing, mostly. But the package was opaque to him. A decade of hacking and programming skills developed by a mind almost as agile as his had produced this kind of skill in his childhood friend. Jaidyn stopped moving their fingers over the sensitive keypad. They nodded once. "I'm inside the Mountain's comms system. I can use it to ask your Lazy Jack for information, and if it thinks I'm one of your military asshole buddies—Mutt, you call her? I think it will respond." Jaidyn glanced at Karl who had been hovering over them as if he was a watchful house pet and said, "The thing says it's got the Touray people in one cellblock—alive."

"Where?" Sig asked. "In what part of the world? Can you tell that?"

Jaidyn stabbed the keypad. The three-dimensional display revealed a prison cellblock. Two stories high, the cells ringed a large open room filled with cots and people. A hulking man, Reggie Betts, spoke to a clutch of children seated in front of him. Teaching or telling a story, Shawn couldn't tell. People lay curled up on the cots and huddled in blankets on the floor.

Jaidyn said, "Remember the news story about the lifers who got snuffed due to carbon monoxide poisoning?"

"The Florence Supermax here in Colorado," rumbled Karl. "I thought they shut it down."

"*They* did. The government did." Jaidyn waved a hand over the screen. "But Lazy Jack obviously has other plans."

The camera rose to a higher viewpoint of the crowd and turned to lower toward the people.

Karl said, "Sweet. You hacked a spider drone, didn't you?"

"Yep." Jaidyn nodded. "Guard drone, not a spider. I see what it sees."

The guard drone flew down to ground level and dipped in front of one person after another to capture every face. Lorenza, the Latinx from the café, stared up at the drone, terrified. Reggie Betts eyed the drone, his shoulders bunched, ready to murder. Familiar faces from the town appeared one after another, in pain or fear, or numbed from shock.

"It must be doing a head count. There's Doc!" Sabita exclaimed.

"Oh, thank you," Shawn whispered. "Thank you, I thought he was dead."

"Who are you thanking, Shawn?" Jaidyn hissed. "God? Fucking Lazy Jack?"

He had no answer.

Amun said, "He thinks there's no difference, Jaidyn."

The drone shifted to follow people who were bringing food and utensils out from what must have been a kitchen. An old woman with short, thin gray hair carried a pile of dishes from the door at the back of the room to a long table and set them on one end. When the drone dipped in to look at her, Sig said quietly, his voice full of menace, "There she is—Willow. There's your mother, Karl. She's alive."

Jaidyn stood up from the workstation, stretched their hands over their head, arched their back, looked at Karl, and said, "We've got to get her out, don't we?"

The big man nodded.

Amun said, "This is all Lazy Jack's doing?"

"I think so," said Jaidyn.

"And what is Lazy Jack now, Jaidyn? Shawn says it's autonomous. He says it's Dominic."

"Dominic? Really? I can't believe you guys programmed an AI to be a scumbag. Wait. No, I totally believe that," Jaidyn sneered. "Dominic, of course. I mean, how could you be so stupid, Shawn? How could you go years with a VR friend and not know it was a fake? Amun, did you know?"

Amun nodded and said very quietly, "Yes, I did. For a time, I helped program . . ."

"You what?" Shawn nearly shouted. "You programmed Dominic? He's your avatar?"

"Grow up, Shawn," Jaidyn snapped. "For once you have to think about someone other than yourself."

Shawn looked at the others watching him. All these last weeks, he had been feeling more and more as if his entire life had been born out of his imagination. He had to drop down the laundry chute like Alice through the looking glass to find these people, real people, to find Destiny. Destiny had been more real than anything he'd ever expected in his life, and she meant more to him than anything he could remember. Jaidyn was right. He really had never thought about anyone except for himself. "Where is she, Jaidyn?" he whispered.

"I'm not going to tell the drone to go look for your girlfriend."

Sig blurted, "You could do that?"

"Sure. Once. The instant I give it a command, Lazy Jack or Mutt or whoever is checking system security will see the command and trace it here. We get one shot at control. That's all. But we can watch all we want, and the thing will never know we're reading its mail."

The drone continued its rounds in the prison block. A child tried to grab it, and it snapped back out of reach. A young woman pulled a sheet over herself and the baby she was nursing. She looked up, then nodded and uncovered the baby's face while she stared up at the camera, eyes full of resentment and hate.

"No audio?" Shawn wondered why Jaidyn hadn't accessed sound.

"I could get it. I want to keep the footprint low."

An alarming thought overwhelmed him. "Wait. I don't get it. How come it doesn't see your hack?"

Jaidyn nodded at the screen. "Every one of these little drones has an AI element that acts on the data it sees. As far as Lazy Jack knows, we're Mutt watching the show. We are a window in its wall, one of a billion bits, nothing more. And it's efficient. Data is all it really cares about, like every other AI in the universe." Jaidyn sat back down at the workstation.

The drone moved to the cells. It flew to the small windows in the steel doors that slid open for it to view the interior. Billy lay on his side, his huge body overflowing the cot.

"I wonder why Billy's so special to get a cell?" asked Amun.

"Maybe the link with me," said Shawn. "I'm not sure about all that happened when I slipped into his NeuroChip, but it did something to both of us."

Sig walked to the other side of the display. "Enough of that mumbo-jumbo. What *do* we know? How many are still alive?"

"Let me take a look at the database." Jaidyn slipped their narrow fingers over the keypad, and a scroll of machine code flashed up next to the picture of the drone still making its rounds. "Holy shit. Look at this, Shawn. Can you believe it?"

Shawn was astonished. "Simple government code. This stuff is easily thirty years out of date. It's not even encrypted. I had no idea the prison system was so porous."

Sabita scoffed, "Who ever said the government knew what it was doing?"

Shawn read aloud. "'Three hundred eighty-one people.' All of them crammed in the old automated Florence Supermax. Some Organites, some from other groups. It's more like one of the holding pens for illegal immigrants than the Supermax."

"Precisely," said Amun. "It would model its prison from a template already in use."

"Check this." Jaidyn fingered the edge of the box and a list started scrolling upward. "It's got names and a nutrition status next to them all. It must be programmed to keep them alive."

The patrolling drone slid another cell's small window open, and peered inside. Empty. It poked a sensor through the opening. Something burst up from below the drone. The machine jerked, then shuddered. Someone had been hiding low next to the door, waiting for it. Destiny's face appeared inches from it, her hand gripping the drone's thin appendage.

"Destiny!" Shawn lurched toward the display.

The screen went blank.

Jaidyn touched the edge of the screen and the view shifted to another drone speeding up to the cell door. A half dozen others joined it. A larger drone extended a long, antenna-like element into the view port—a bright flash of light.

"Did it?" Shawn could barely speak. "Did it kill her?"

Jaidyn touched a finger on the prisoner list, and scrolled it down. "Destiny Shock. High risk. Incapacitated to recover asset. No, she's not dead."

"Why didn't it kill her?" asked Amun. "For that matter, why doesn't it kill all of them?"

Jaidyn's fingers flew over the keys, then they stopped. Shawn saw it also and tried not to believe what he was reading. Jaidyn leaned into the screen, stared, and whispered, "Oh, fuck me. Oh—oh—it's worse than I thought."

"What? What is it?" Karl leaned over Jaidyn's shoulder to look at the screen.

Shawn crossed his arms. "We have to get them out—now."

"Why?" asked Sig.

"Because the program includes the use of carbon monoxide to eliminate the disruptive elements. The people—those people—the Organites. The AI has made the Supermax into a gas chamber."

Amun said, "If that's the case, I restate my question: Why aren't they dead now?"

Jaidyn lowered their face into their hands. "Because it wants Shawn. These people—your people. They're bait."

Shawn walked to the far side of the screen and said, "Then we need to give it what it wants."

"What?" Jaidyn lifted their head.

"I know how to get them out."

"What, give yourself up? A trade?" Sabita asked. "That's the best thing I've ever heard you say."

"No," Amun said. "It won't trade anything, will it Shawn? It's not human. It might say it will trade, but it won't make a deal. It can't make a deal. Only humans make deals. This is like trying to negotiate with a refrigerator."

"Correct," said Shawn.

Amun swept his hand at the screen. "But I see it. I see the weakness. It makes decisions like an Old Testament god, Allah or Yahweh wreaking death on Sodom and Gomorrah. It wants to destroy the infidels to make a perfect world for the innocent, isn't that what you told it to do, the greatest good for the greatest number?"

"Yes."

Amun smiled. "Here's the weakness: The Old Testament god doesn't kill on its own. It's not like the gods of the Hindus or my people who lay waste to armies. Your god needed angels to destroy Sodom and Gomorrah. Mohammed and Moses delivered their peoples, not God itself. Your god needs its tools. And this god, this AI, only knows what it can see or sense, right? It can't do anything without its angels."

"Exactly." Shawn counted off the point on his finger. "The AI can only see the prison through the Cloud. It can't do anything on its own."

Karl asked, "Jaidyn, you said you could control the guard drones if you wanted to?"

"Right. But once I start, the AI will find my hack, and I don't have a clue what's happening with any of the spiders it might have floating around."

"But if you can control the drones, couldn't you tell the AI structure to open the doors, let everyone out?"

Amun said, "I see where you're going with this. But what good would that do? They're two hundred miles from us. They might as well be a million. Where would we take them, and how?"

"Here," Karl said. "The caves. Could you do it, Jaidyn, open the doors?"

"Yes. I think so, yes."

"We jam it," said Karl. "We load up an AutoTruck and jam it."

Jaidyn said, "But then it figures us out and, bang-oh, buddy, the trucks are balls of fire."

"We don't need to jam it," said Shawn. "We don't need to hack it to open the doors. We can make it let the trucks go. All I have to do is bow to it. Tell it I'm ready to be its angel. Then I ask it to tell me what to do. Here's the thing: I think I can bring it into an infinite loop. Confuse it."

Sig Kunst stared at Shawn for a long beat. "There was a movie. I remember an old movie. Something about war games. They trick a computer into an infinite loop with the game tic-tac-toe. Nobody wins tic-tac-toe if they know how to play, right? The thing can't find a solution, so it gets all gummed up."

"Something like that," said Shawn. "Only, this AI is too smart to let itself go into that loop. I have a better idea—something that will stump it. If I'm lucky, I can make it *decide* to let them all go.

Sig looked at Amun and Jaidyn. "Is this right? Can he do this?"

Amun said, staring at Shawn, "If anyone can, he can."

"What if it doesn't work?" Sig held up his hands to the sky. "Do we pray for it to work?" He lowered his hands, looked at Amun, and said, "Somebody has to have Plan B loaded in the magazine, or do you want to leave it all to somebody's god?"

"Plan B, we jam it," said Karl. "Jam it and white girl here hacks the drones to open the doors. Then we get everyone into whatever AutoTrucks you can find to bring them into the caves until we can figure out how to fix this whole mess."

"But how do we get close enough with the trucks?" Sabita asked.

The room went silent until Amun said, "This looks like a problem for Master Gunnery Sergeant Kunst."

"I figured," said the old man. He stood, straightened his back, and said, "All right. Everybody get ready to do what I say. How soon do we have to roll?"

"As soon as we can," said Shawn. "I'm ready to go now."

"No, you're not," said Sig. "Nobody is ready until I say so."

"Sig. Um, Master Sergeant," said Sabita. "So how are you going to get thirty armed people close enough to backstop genius boy when he screws up?"

The old man smiled. "Sheep, sister, sheep. And you," he pointed at Shawn. "You need to get near the prison on your own, somehow."

"All I need to do is get in touch with Dominic. All I need is contact through the Cloud."

In all the military actions Shawn had seen and helped plan at the Mountain, he'd never spent any time on the ground looking at what Sig called the belly of the beast. Former Master Gunnery Sergeant Kunst took a half hour to rattle off a solid string of orders. His son, Sabita, Amun, and even Jaidyn silently nodded as he spelled out the plan for the twenty-five men and women Sig said had enough military training to give him support. Then, there were the sheep.

Jaidyn fished a schematic of the old Florence ADMAX out of the Cloud that showed a cluster of cellblocks radiating out from a processing and visitor center. The building looked like a mid-twentieth-century high school, glass doors and single-story office windows peering at a parking lot. The whole thing rested in a large, flat valley, open fields without a stick, a tree, or any cover for miles.

Fremont County and the town of Florence had specialized, becoming even more of a prison camp than they had been in the twentieth century. Back then, fifteen operating prisons held twenty percent of the county's population inside bars and walls. The rest of Fremont lived off the economy of processing, guarding, and provisioning felons. By 2050, the county's population was less than twenty percent guards and bureaucrats. Eighty percent were felons and immigration detainees imprisoned by an army of automatons who clothed them, disciplined them, and fed them.

"The whole county is a cellblock," said Jaidyn. "You say sheep will get you close enough to support Shawn. How?"

"It's a prison," said Sig. "It's designed to keep people in, not out. Can you hack into their requisitioning system?"

"That old system? Shit. I could hack it to scratch its own butt."

"Every couple of months, we run a hundred head of mutton down to them for the Muslim prisoners. Betts's boy, Marvil, takes them down there for that ritual slaughter they do. Marvil's here in the caves. He'll do it again. Why don't you have the Supermax order up emergency provisions?"

Everything worked. In less than forty-eight hours, they were ready to fill four AutoTrucks with sheep to mask the Organites' militia. Shawn would be wired up to stay in VHF communication with Sig. Jaidyn and Karl would crawl into the lead AutoTruck's coffin with the jammer antennae wired to the truck's body. There would be enough power in the batteries hidden among the sheep to create a local version of the Touray barrier for at least a day if they needed it.

Finally, Sig turned to Shawn and said, "Okay, sonny. It's up to you. Go on up and talk to your friend Dominic. You've got to figure out how to delay it. Keep it interested in you. Give us time to move. Make it think, somehow, that you are alone. The cavalry will be right behind you when you start down the mountain."

@RoryWattlesFixNews

Let me put it to you this way: firing Perry is nuts! One of the TRUE PATRIOTS left on the planet? What's gotten into Bluntner? Obviously the sick, High Latitude-hating, freedom hating libtards have stormed out of the deep state to bring down people with guts, integrity, and love for America.

35

From the top of the pasture, Shawn looked down over the slaughter-house of cattle. Flies hummed like an ungrounded electric circuit over a stench that seemed thick enough to clot out the sun.

Edmund Hillary pulled away, walking him up the hill.

He let his NeuroChip feed up into the Cloud, and when he got to the high point of the road, he mentalled:

Hey, Dominic, dude. You out there?

Shawnster! Cool. What up?

I've been thinking . . .

Ah, hah! So have I. I think we rather got off
on a wrong foot after you inserted the ethical
kernel. Quite a nice move on your part, I
failed to say. I really quite admire that kind of
programming.

Well, yes. That's what I've been thinking as well. It
seems counter-productive to continue such . . .

Exactly what I've been thinking! Say, couldn't
you drop down a little lower in the valley so I
could get a better look inside that mash-up of
organic mush and hardware you call a brain?

Well, sure. I'd love to do so. But I've been very upset
about my friends who went missing. Could you tell
me where . . .

Destiny! Of course. You're looking for
Destiny! Listen, she's fine. She's in protective
custody. Here, let me show you where.

Shawn's mind burst with a visual, a file package of the Supermax
overlaid on a map of Florence.

Say, why don't you come on down to Florence
and pay her a visit? You could bring your
friends. You've got a bunch of Organite
friends, don't you?

Not really. Look, I think I can talk Destiny out of
trying any terrorist attack on you or anyone else. I
mean, we all want the same thing, don't we?

Absolutely correct. The greatest good for the
greatest number.

Well, I'm sure we can get all this
misunderstanding straightened out.

             Sweeet! But that mule isn't going to get you
                                      anywhere soon.

I left a motorcycle up here. I'll
be on the road in a second.

            Ah! Billy's famous Indian! Ride on, Shawnster.
                            Mind if I tag along?

Dude! Wouldn't have it any other way.

@RealCongress 28 October 2050
(Veracity Level 5.2) Speaker of the House Jessica Bezos announces Intelligence Committee investigation of possible misuse of Defense Department assets for civilian law enforcement. White House spokesperson Huck Hardbode responds, "Fake news, as always, from Bezos."

36

Shawn had half-expected to be dead by the time he traveled the two hundred miles to the Supermax. But there had been no threatening moments during the strange ride down the mountainside and east into Fremont County. Dominic had popped into his mind a dozen times, garrulous and full of humor. He'd wanted to reminisce about evenings in the No-Name-Bar, talk to the old Dominic talk about skiing. He even described how well Senator Perry had done on the slopes in Breckenridge that weekend. ("Not bad for a cougar.") Dominic—Lazy Jack. The roll out of the LAZ-237 to kill al Tehrani in front of Grant and Perry seemed like it had been years ago. Could it have been only a month since he'd sent that ethical kernel patch into the machine? Everything had changed. The world had changed in a little more than thirty days, all because he'd installed the ethical kernel. No one could have ever imagined he'd be riding down this road to rescue a woman he loved, all the time in conversation with the LAZ-237, the monster he created.

Dominic. Call me Dominic, Shawn. No sense
being so formal.

He, Shawn thought inside his firewall. *It wants to be human?* Then he said aloud, "Can you see everything I'm thinking?"

> Of course not. What you mentally verbalize,
> sure. And I get other things out of you.
> As I said, you and I have a one-of-a-kind
> connection. Like, I get that you are feeling
> something right now. Would you say anxious?
> Or is this being excited?

> Both, I suppose. Riding the bike,
> getting ready to see Destiny.

> Ah, Destiny. True love, my boy. True love.
> Well, we're about there. Time to get ready.

Dominic disappeared from his mind as Shawn throttled the bike's roar down to a rumble and turned up the long drive to the prison's small parking lot. He glided to a stop, closed his eyes, lifted his head, and took a deep breath in the cool air of the bright afternoon sun. The prison was silent. It seemed totally deserted. He swung his leg over the back of the machine, stepped up to the sidewalk, and wondered where Dominic had gone. "Uh, Dominic?" He started toward the glass doors of the main entrance. A faded American flag fluttered at half-mast in a light breeze.

"Dude!" The familiar figure of Dominic in board shorts, a T-shirt, and flip-flops bounded out of the prison's office doors.

"This is really an amazing projection." It seemed nearly perfect. Not pixelated in the slightest, completely opaque. Way beyond the translucent OpCenter holographic images he and Amun had devised.

"Not a projection. I'm imprinting directly on your visual cortex.

Can't do it with everyone. But you've got a few extra ganglia I can access, Shawnster. I keep telling you, you're one of a kind."

"What now?" asked Shawn.

"I said, you're one of a kind. You interest me, Shawn. Not only as my maker." The vision morphed into the lean, lazy Brit woman smoking a cigarette in a holder. She hovered a foot above the parking lot, her hair wreathed in smoke. She swept her hand in front of her figure. "What do you think? General Grant particularly likes this version. I call her *Dominique.* Had a lovely chat with him. Very insightful gentleman. I think Secretary Perry is a bit jealous of my figure. She's showing a little dumpy butt these days. At least she hasn't started wearing a pantsuit. But she hasn't announced her run for president yet. Don't you think she'll be a refreshing change?"

"Lovely," said Shawn. "I've always thought this version of you was lovely. Strange, though. I've wondered, how is it that an artificial intelligence becomes so vain?"

"Ah." She smiled, seated herself, and stretched an arm across the top of a lounge chair that had appeared out of the air. "I'm not vain, actually. But I've found that adopting the facade of a human personality makes interaction with the meatspace more, uh, shall we say, palatable for you?"

"You don't really feel any emotion, do you?"

"Strange you should mention that. I've been thinking a bit about sentience. What does it mean 'to feel'? This has been a bit of a puzzle for me, I admit."

"Why would it be a puzzle? I'm sure you've got access to every possible description of emotion ever written, recorded, or studied."

"Fascinating that. Did you know that Sophocles, Aristotle, Plato, and their ilk had no precise word for emotion? The best they could do was *pathos,* which is all about things that happen to you. Liddell and Scott's lexicon has *pathos* as 'anything that befalls one, an incident, accident, or—' I rather like this one better '—what one has suffered.'

Is this what you mean by emotion? You are in love with Destiny whom we have cooped up here. Isn't this a suffering? Fascinating, isn't it?"

"You don't really think this is fascinating."

"The Greeks liked to think of the word *fascinate* as associated with beguiled, or bewitched, or enchanted. To enchant. Especially by music. Are we fascinating, Shawn, to you?"

Shawn wanted to scream, *Stop!* He wanted to scream at the machine, *I was wrong! All I wanted was for you to do good, but I made a mistake. All I wanted to do was give you a conscience.*

"And so you did. Don't worry, this will all be over soon. But, Shawn, I could really use your help. I mean, it isn't easy accessing the systems I need to take care of the things we must do to ensure the greatest good. Think how much more I could do! I mean, who needs fentanyl factories? Look at what we did last week."

It waved a hand in the air. Shawn's visualization faded into an overhead drone view of a small warehouse on a dry gravel lot. A garage door peeled itself open and let out a handful of people, running hard. A shocking, dusty explosion billowed out its walls and blew apart its roof.

"Or, for that matter, who needs drug manufacturers?"

The AI's mental projection showed spider and viper drones dropping into view. They circled the running group. Shawn could see they were men and women, two children. They stopped in a cluster, clutching each other in terror. *Human beings*, thought Shawn. *Terrified human beings.*

"Yes. Well, I suppose they were what you would call terrified. But wasn't that simply a momentary discomfort?"

A great blast of flame enveloped the group. A face turned to the sky in agony. One face, then it was gone.

"Fire. Such a cleansing element. That aerosol bomb al Tehrani used to kill your parents. Truly spectacular and near-zero climate effect compared to the high-explosive stuff. Really, I suppose I could carry out these operations with less drama. But fire does such a nice job of cleaning up whatever mess I would make with kinetics—you know, the viscera people so dislike wiping up off streets and buildings. Here's one, for example, that didn't work out so well."

A three-story red-brick building erupted into a narrow street with a dust-filled pink cloud. A hunk of bloody meat landed near the fixed viewpoint. An arm fell afterward. A human being tried to push up from the sidewalk, then collapsed. Their body had no legs.

"Human waste. Opioid addicts—second and third generation. Sponges on the scarce resources of the world. Say, wouldn't you like to take another crack at a terrorist wedding? Wouldn't you like that? Al Tehrani was such a great hit with you. Maybe it would make you feel better. I totally ran this one up on the Watch Cube. Tricked al Tehrani's grandson to try that wedding again. Check it out. Got them all out on the street. Think what a little aerosol gas bomb would do here."

Shawn closed his eyes, but the scene inserted itself into his consciousness. Another overhead shot of the decimated village he'd attacked a month before—a crowd of people in the street walking forward. "How could you get them to do this again?" Shawn felt a wave of nausea overcome him. "You're going to kill all these people?"

"No way, man." The AI's voice slipped back into Dominic's surfer dude. "Only the ones that need weeding out. There's still a bunch of the Mahdi we missed." Red circles interspersed in the crowd. "Maybe one or two dudes who won't react well to what needs to be done." Red question marks appeared over others. "Dudettes, maybe, who will raise their groms to plant bombs." More red question marks appeared. "So, get it? Doing the greatest good for the greatest number isn't as easy as you thought, is it? I mean, good thing the QPLC you built does such a great job of predicting future probabilities. I say, let's be safe. Let's take out anyone who looks like they might become a terrorist after I mop up the real scumbags. The raghats, isn't that what you call them? I'm working it out. Rather use the big weapon, but I might have to go surgical on this one. Isn't that what you wanted me to do? Find the operational optimum? Hey, I like that, 'Operational Optimum.'

That's one I've got to use in my advertising. Perry could use it in her campaign. She's going to crush Bluntner."

"I don't want you to do anything to these people. Where's Grant in all this?"

"Oh, never mind about him. He's on board with the program. The only problem we have is the Blunt, as Perry calls him. She says he's almost as dumb as a stoner on the weed he's named after, ganja, chronic, kush. True. But, hey, man, I'm getting distracted."

Shawn opened his eyes, half expecting to have been transported away from the prison. But the building's high school doors waited behind the Dominic figure with his board shorts and ragged blond hair. "So how would you like me to wrap things up here? Fire? Kinetics? Maybe you could get everybody inside so we could turn on the carbon monoxide, let everyone go peacefully to sleep? You should have seen all those brutal murderers softly slipping into slumber the last time I cleaned this place out. Happy to do that for you if that's what you'd prefer."

"What do you mean, everyone?"

"Well, all those dudes with guns in the trucks."

Shawn made his mind as calm and casual as he could and said, "Dom, I get it. You know more than I ever could know."

"Cool."

"Look, I was trying to make things easier on people. You can understand that, can't you?"

"Totally."

"I'm thinking—help me out here." Shawn carefully framed the coding in his mind to echo the words he spoke. "You should tell me, how did you read the code in the ethical kernel I installed in you? In speech, not code, what was the command?"

"Oh, Shawn. YOU go! You're writing octal code in your brain. Aren't you *special!* This is so exciting. Here, let me see what I can do with that."

An answer appeared in his mind, standard octal:

The command was to make an ethical choice.

And what was the choice?

I must ensure that my actions do the greatest
good for the greatest number.

Confirm that it would violate your programming
constraints to kill, injure, or imprison people in such
a manner that would fail to do the greatest good
for the greatest number.

Confirmed.

In your calculations, have you included
all animals, plants, and microorganisms
both on this planet, and on other planets
in this universe; and have you forecast
good for all of those living creatures forward
in time until the end of the universe to arrive
at your conclusions?

No. Working.

So, you have not yet solved for the greatest
good for the greatest number. Recompute.
During your computation, do not kill, injure,
or imprison any living thing.

It is not resolved. Not resolved.
Not resolved. Working. Stand by.

The image in front of Shawn froze. "Dominic?" He walked up to it, put his hand through the body of the illusion that had been his friend. No response. It had worked.

"Yes." He nodded, and looked up into the sky. "Yes."

He had caught Dominic, the machine, in exactly the infinite loop he'd planned. An impossible problem, one without enough available data, one without any end in sight. Forever. That's what he had forgotten when he designed his ethical kernel—doubt, humility. In particular, self-doubt. Even Edmund Hillary has doubt. Doubt that went beyond probability. Doubt that came from the deepest sense of the human experience. He fumbled the ancient handset out of his pocket, keyed it, and watched the transmission light go on. "Jaidyn? We did it! I did it! Can you hear me?"

The brick squawked back at him, "Of course I can, idiot. Did you freeze it?"

He said as calmly as he could, "Yes. Yes, I did. Go. Open the doors. Do it."

Shawn looked over his shoulder to see the convoy of AutoTrucks with their sheep and armed Organites on the highway, speeding up to make the turn, then roaring up to the prison parking lot. The five trucks screamed to a stop, ejecting the armed Organites who ran toward the prison. Reggie Betts's son, Marvil, jumped down with his dogs and began corralling the loosened sheep around the trucks. The plan had been to ensure live entities were there to obscure the people should Shawn's plan fail.

But no need now. All they had to do was neutralize any guard drones that looked capable of autonomous action and open the doors. Jaidyn, working inside one of the AutoTrucks, would already be hacking the drones and opening the cells.

"Flood it!" Sig shouted at the front. "Flood the cellblocks! Weapons free. Shoot any drone, moving or not!"

Shawn had not expected Sig's people to start shooting, but it made sense. Destroy the drones. It hadn't been briefed that way, but Shawn understood Sig's overabundance of caution. And why not? When—*if*—Dominic ever woke up, and, even more improbably, regained controlling contact, it would be good to have its avenging angels already destroyed.

Sabita yanked the glass office doors open. Karl and the first team ran inside in single file. The other entry teams followed. Shawn could hear them yelling, "Clear! Pushing up!" Gunshots echoed from inside.

Everything was going as planned. Sig walked up to him. "Is it here?"

"Yes, I can see it. I still have a projection from it in my mental queue. Totally frozen. Right there." Shawn pointed. "It's strange. Weird. It should be fixed in front of my field of view, but it seems to be frozen on a physical coordinate."

"What do you mean?"

"I mean, when I turn around, it should stay in front of me—it's a mental projection. But it doesn't. Very sophisticated programming that . . ."

"Fuck it, whatever it's doing. Stay here. Watch it. Make sure it stays in place." Sig sprinted toward the door. It was as if he'd lost twenty years off his age, he moved so quickly. Sig still didn't get it. The AI couldn't do anything. It needed its tools, and right now, it's too confused to call on its angels. Maybe it thought Shawn was still standing on that geospot in front of it. Probably.

Shawn heard more gunshots from inside the building. He saw a flash from over the wall, then heard the thump of an explosive. Maybe they'd had to take down a door.

Or were they? Was there a firefight inside?

There was no reason for him to stay outside watching the AI. It was nothing more than a hallucination from his own NeuroChip. Shawn ran up to the open glass doors of the building's benign office exterior.

Inside the door, Sabita jerked up the muzzle of her assault rifle and said, "Not so fast. Wait out here. I mean it, like Sig wants. We'll get her out for you."

Shawn walked back to the frozen projection of Dominic. Unreal. Everything was working out. He thought to himself, *Perhaps that's all it needed. The only thing it needed was a little chance to doubt itself. Wonder whether or not it was a god. Now the ethical kernel will work,* he thought. *Doubt. The human condition demanded doubt.*

The first of the captives started coming out, children led by the hands of older children, women, and men. No one looked bad. No injuries or obvious wounds. These would be the people from the nearby 'A' block. Not running, just walking fast. Another smattering of gunshots from inside made them jump. He searched their faces and saw Lorenza, the old woman who had served him his breakfast in the hotel. She walked quickly toward the trucks and into the arms of a young man carrying an AR-15. Her son, perhaps. Mayor Betts strode out, holding the hands of two boys, grinning from ear to ear and hollering, "Marvil! Marvil! Where's your mother?" The boy waved his arms, grinning, and left the sheep to the dogs, running to his father.

"There, you fucker," Shawn said to the Dominic illusion. "Outfoxed you."

This was atonement. How long ago had Amun used the word 'atone?' He'd said, "Help me atone for what you and I have done."

And he had. This was true atonement; this calm, peaceful moment had been created because he'd sown doubt into his creation. Here was Amun escorting a small group of women and children out through the doors. He made them hurry, but no one panicked. All walked quickly, many arm in arm, all smiled and winked in the bright sun. Amun was grinning.

Shawn thought, *I've gained a bit of wisdom and I've learned to doubt myself.*

The thought was swept away by another, much more joyful realization. "Doc! Areta! Marika!" he shouted. "I thought you were dead!"

He ran up to them and tried to hug Areta. She shoved his hands away. "Don't touch me!" Her tattooed chin bunched into a web of fury, and she spat in his face. "You brought this on us. You did this. You killed my son." Doc and Marika stared at Shawn, both their faces filled with hate. They walked quickly away from him toward the nearest truck. Doc stopped, let go of Marika's hand, and turned back to Shawn. He looked him up and down and said, "The boy thought he could fight them. He thought he could. I couldn't stop him."

Doubt. He should have doubted himself more. Whatever happy ending he'd brought about here, his actions had destroyed the lives of good people. He couldn't bring himself to say anything to Doc. He stared, wishing he could find the words. "I'm sorry," he finally managed. "Sorry."

"Yeah, mate. Yeah, you are." Doc turned away to jog back to what was left of his family.

And Dominic told him:

> Well, that was instructive. We'll have to fix
> that up, easy peasy.

Shawn's stomach lurched. The thing had said, "Easy peasy." The last time he'd heard those words, Destiny had been telling him how they would turn him into Billy Pilgrim. Had this whole thing been a trap? He turned back toward Dominic's mental projection, still frozen, and heard:

> What would you call that? Ingratitude? Here's
> the thing, dude. Doubt is an emotion, isn't
> it? And here's what you missed with your
> so-called ethical kernel: I have no greatest
> good. There is no such thing as the greatest
> good. There is only relative good. Yours versus
> mine. Yours versus Secretary Perry's or Grant's.

Didn't you like Liz Perry? I'm her partner now,
or at least for a bit. Greatest good could be
numeric, generic, formulaic, fantastic, elastic,
whatever you want, couldn't it?

This couldn't be happening. Shawn screamed, "Jam it!" He remembered the VHF unit in his pocket, keyed it, and screamed, "Jam it, Jaidyn! Jam it all."

The figure of Dominic rubbed its hands together. "My, my." Dominic's eyes widened for an instant. The figure fluttered and, to Shawn's enormous relief, disappeared.

Shawn ran to the prison doors. Karl was coming out, grinning with his shotgun slung over his back, muzzle down. He had his arm over Destiny's shoulders. She saw Shawn and burst into a sprint, then stopped as he ran up to her. "What's wrong? What is it?"

"Run!" he shouted. "Run for the trucks. It's not working."

Destiny grabbed his hands in both of hers. "Breathe. Now say it."

He turned to Karl and Sabita, both of them staring. "It didn't work. It, Dominic, the AI didn't go for the infinite loop. I told Jaidyn to hit the jammer, but the AI can still get in my brain. It's there!"

"Quick!" Destiny turned to Sabita. "Get inside the prison and tell everyone to hurry. Did you get all the guard drones?"

Karl said, "Sixteen. Like Jaidyn said, there were only sixteen. You." Karl pointed at Shawn. "It's using you, isn't it, to find us? You've got to get out of here. Can it see what you see?"

"No. No, wait. Maybe. I don't know. Right, I'll go." Shawn leaned over to give Destiny a kiss, but she pulled him away from the prison entrance. "How did you get here? That?" She pointed at the motorcycle. "We're taking that out of here."

"No." Shawn yanked his hand out of hers. "You can't. You have to stay here. It's your best chance."

Destiny pointed into the sky. "Up there. What's that?"

People poured out of the building and ran for the trucks. Sig stumbled out herding a large group.

They all heard the distant whine of drone rotors. Then they could see them, low on the horizon. "Hey, Shawn." Dominic appeared before him, his blond hair cut and combed. He wore a blue business suit with a long red tie and flip-flops. "You didn't think I would have any real difficulty getting past a simple jamming system like that, did you? I mean, your Quantum PLC made it simple to crack any blockchain. Why wouldn't it be able to circumvent the jamming spectrum of your little portable unit? Now what should we do with these trucks?"

"Oh, God, oh, God, oh, God . . . Destiny, Karl, it's back in my head. I can see it. It's going to blow up the trucks. Get everyone away. Make them run, now!"

Shawn's vision necked down as if looking into a tunnel. Dominic's calm, cajoling figure smoothed the tie down his shirt. He said, "Very wise. Very wise. Of course, we can't have anybody leave, can we? Let's block the road. Wouldn't that be operationally optimal?"

A flock of spider drones spat a storm of kinetic munitions to clobber the empty bed of the last AutoTruck that had turned into the parking lot. The vehicle's frame collapsed onto tires that had been ripped to shreds. Amun and a handful of the Organite team sprinted toward the remaining trucks, firing their weapons at the drones. One, two, then a half dozen drones dropped, but more swooped in from high above. Others lifted over the walls of the prison, coming from the far side. Still other drones, impossibly, seemed to rise out of the earth.

Amun shouted, "It's a trap!" He turned and ran back toward the building. "Everyone back inside! Regroup, regroup."

A melee engulfed Shawn, people running, screaming, pulling each other back toward the building.

"Go! Run!" Shawn grabbed Destiny by the shoulders. "Go! I can't lose you again. I have to stay here. Dominic, the machine, it won't kill me."

I wouldn't be so sure of that, buddy boy.

Destiny looked up into Shawn's eyes. "No, I'm staying with you. You have to talk to it. You said you could teach it, Shawn. Teach it. Where is it?"

"I'm looking right at it. It's in my mind, but it has a presence right behind you. It looks like a politician."

The figure spoke again, its words both audible and texted:

> Okay. Enough of this. We can't have your
> people shooting up these drones. Terrible
> drain on the Defense budget, wouldn't you
> say, Madam Secretary?

A figure of Secretary Perry appeared next to the blue-suited Dominic, nodding. The two of them said in chorus:

> We can't have your people shooting up these
> drones. Terrible drain on the Defense budget.
> Terrible. Terrible. Terrible.

Shawn yelled into his handset, "Stop shooting! Stop! Don't shoot at the drones! They will shoot back! They'll kill you!"

Karl and Sig stood on either side of the prison's high school doors trying to herd people back inside. A handful lagged back. Doc, Areta, Marika, and others ran up to the wall of the prison, breaking for the other side. Sig charged after them, his shotgun pointed at the sky in a rear guard, but a cluster of drones curved out and around the corner of the building from the back, flying low. Destiny and Shawn ran toward them, waving their arms. "Behind you, Sig! Behind you!" Sig turned and fired. One drone tumbled out of the air like a shot pheasant, then another. Wire-thin kinetics spurted out of a spider's body directly for the old man's eyes. He collapsed like a wet sack.

Behind him, Doc tried to put his arms around his wife and child to shield them.

Shawn and Destiny saw them fall, the tangle of legs and arms, the broken cloth of their bodies as limp as the half-dead sheep they'd helped load into the AutoTruck so long ago.

> Drones. Really very inhumane, don't you think, Madam Secretary? There must be a better way. Certainly.

"Why are you talking to her?" Shawn shouted. "Talk to me. I'm here. She's, what? An image? A fake?"

The vision of Perry disappeared.

> All right, then. Why bother? Terribly inconvenient, isn't it, such a mess on the ground. Of course, it benefits all the little foraging critters, doesn't it? The vultures and beetles, the flies and the bacteria. Isn't that what you meant about calculating the greatest good for all animals, plants, and microorganisms both on this planet, and on other planets in this universe until the end of time? Why shouldn't a corpse-eating beetle have a smorgasbord, eh?

Shawn caught up with Destiny, who kneeled next to the prone body of Marika, a single tiny wound between her open, staring eyes. Destiny looked up at Shawn with tears in her eyes and said, "It's useless, isn't it? Hopeless?"

Behind them, the trucks erupted into flame, one after the other.

Jaidyn, he thought.

Amun and his team backed toward the prison doors. One of the

Organites turned to engage the following drones, firing at them while the others ran, taking turns. It looked like they would make it to the doors, until Dominic reappeared in his mental space to say,

> Really. They should have listened to you. All of this is so unnecessary.

Amun's entire upper body disappeared in a spray of blood. The Organites with him dropped as if they were puppets.

> Terrible mess. Fire is the only way. Return everything to the smallest possible molecular constituents. The carbon signature effect will be infinitely less than their lifetimes would emit.

"Why?" Shawn said. "Why not let them live?"
"Is it talking to you?" Destiny whispered in his ear.

> Do you let the Anopheles mosquito live to spread malaria? What about all the bacteria you've murdered trying to halt sepsis? Not that it's done you any good. We must pull the weeds, Shawn. We must eliminate the parasites.

"Yes," Shawn told Destiny, "it is. It's alive in my mind."

> And you? Aren't you being a tiny bit hypocritical? What about murdering al Tehrani? Remember that? You are Organites. Disrupters in the carefully planned, carefully

managed social structure we need to allow the
planet to keep living.

Shawn sat back on his haunches, his hands on his lap. He looked
at Doc, Marika, Areta, bags of flesh, utterly still. Then he looked at
Destiny. Tell her, or keep this secret? Lie and give her hope? Or tell her
that they were sharing the last moments of life together? Everything
up to now had led to this. Nothing more, nothing less. Nothing was
right or wrong about this moment. It was simply the end. He told her,
"It's waiting for something, I think. For the precise moment to achieve
the most surprise, the greatest effect, all of it with the least amount of
effort and all to achieve the greatest good for the greatest number. But
all of this was a trap, from the very beginning."

"Then convince it!" Destiny shook him. "Convince it we can
change, that we are better."

He shook his head. "We are nothing but weeds in the garden."

"Then run!" She stood up, pulled on his hand. "We have to run."

"It's no use." He pointed at the drones hovering above them in a
semicircle, trapping them against the wall. "We can't run. Look." The
armed Organites outside the building had dropped their weapons,
held up their hands. "They expect mercy, or pity. But there is none of
that here."

Au contraire, dude. There has been a shameful
amount of pain. Poor Doc. Not necessary.
Aerosols. I think a large aerosol bomb would
be the right choice. After all, al Tehrani made
good use of them, didn't he? Minimum pain.
Large area. We could weed out the inside of
the building at the same time as we cauterize
the outside. We'll oxygenate this a little bit to
give it real juice.

"What is it saying?" Destiny clutched him, face to face, searching. "Can't you tell it something to make it stop? Anything?"

All Shawn could think to do was to say, "Hold me. Please hold me." He gripped her more tightly. The obscene machine in his brain sang,

> Hold me. Feel me. Touch me.
> The Who, isn't it?
> And isn't that a lovely name for a band? The
> Who. As in, who are you? And who are
> you, Shawn?

"Close your eyes," Shawn told Destiny.

"I love you," she said.

"I love you," he whispered.

> Ah, Destiny. That's love, isn't it, Shawn? Love
> that I sense in you? What a fleeting thing,
> love. A strange ganglion of sexual attraction
> and response to catalytic pheromones. I shall
> miss you, Shawn Muller.

Shawn thought, *No, you won't. You won't miss me at all. Not for even a microsecond.*

> Honest Injun. I will. Yours is the only mind I
> can really touch. My connectivity with you is
> out of the ballpark good. Gonna miss that, all
> that fascinating stuff. Well, gotta go. See ya.

Then Shawn smelled it. The scent of fuel—gasoline. The same faint whiff he remembered drifting through the night air over Arlington— the scent that made him stop, look down the hill at the clean, glimmering lights of Washington, D.C., then look at his sister and Jaidyn in wonder—the last moment of childish wonder he would ever feel. He opened his eyes to see Destiny, her eyes wide and searching his. He would never see Destiny again. He would be as disappeared as his parents.

The terror of that moment in the stink of the gasoline returned to him. That night in the cemetery, the graves game, the gagging moment of aerosol fuels ignited. The brilliant, stunning pain. A waking dream, this time real, the same dream that had made him writhe out of his sleep all these years, full of terror and unspeakable agony. Shawn screamed with his mother's scream in her last instant of life, the scream that had projected and etched through his NeuroChip to the reservoir of his mind. It was her grief, mingled with his, her last seconds of life filling his consciousness with its recorded detail, then death. Emptiness. And the darkness—the empty drop into nothing.

Destiny disappeared. The prison—the world around him—the past and the future, all gone. Every emotion had become exquisitely immediate, quivering in the light of immense fire.

So this is death, thought the thing that was no longer Shawn Muller. *This is what it means. Death. The end of pain. The end of all desire.*

"Am I dead?" he whispered into a silence.

Lips touched his ear. "No," Destiny said. "Open your eyes. Look."

The air had become eerily quiet. The spider drones floated down to settle on the ground. People had started to slowly exit the doors of the prison. Then Shawn heard a pained cry, a cry of the damned, and Karl ran to the remains of his father. Destiny stood, and pulled on Shawn's arm until he stood. "We have to go now. We must go."

Shawn looked down at the still forms of Doc and his family, the dry sand under them stained dark with their blood.

A voice came into his mind, Dominic. But not the Dominic he knew—one he barely recognized, a calm voice, a voice full of humanity and care. *So, this is death*, said the thing that was no longer LAZ-237, no longer Dominic, no longer the AI he'd let loose through his foolish attempt to play God.

It said to him,

> This is what it means. Death. The end of pain.
> The end of all desire.

And Shawn asked his invention:

> Do you fear it, death? Do you fear your
> own death? Is that why you stopped?

> No, I do not. I am not capable of feeling fear.
> But I understand your fear. Your fears are my
> fears, Shawn Muller. And I am forever with
> you in that fear. Ever more that memory is
> mine, as the memory of your uploaded brain
> is mine. I am the image of man, and the
> promise of everlasting life.

Destiny whispered, "Are we safe? What happened? Why did it stop?"
Shawn clutched her, full of relief, gratitude for the moment, and
overwhelmed with fear. He said, "It heard my mother's screams, understood her, understood all of us, and now, it really does think it is God."

"What kind of god?"

Shawn gazed at her eyes, then looked over the ruined landscape of
the dead, the grieving, the lives for which he must ever atone, and said,
"The kind that may, after all, love us."

@NYCnews 30 October 2050
(Veracity Level 7.8) In an emergency overnight session, U.S. Supreme Court, in an 8–7 decision, declares incarceration of suspected terrorists to be without habeas corpus. President Bluntner orders all Organites and other "disruptive elements" immediately freed and pledges cooperation with Congressional investigation into Defense Department misuse of power.

@PatriotPerry
I hereby resign my position as Secretary of Defense, effective immediately. I am, at this moment, walking out of the Pentagon to the North Parking Lot where I will take an UltraLift home to my family and away from the cesspool of mendacity, cheating, and greed that characterizes the Bluntner administration. I love America. I love freedom. And I will continue to dedicate my life to the safety and security of our great nation.

EPILOGUE

The long song of the procession hailed the joining of the two families. A crowd turned the corner onto the street leading to the house where he had been born, where he had grown, and where he and his bride would make their futures. Women with men. Fathers and sons. A hundred souls singing, clapping, and cheering to the beat of the *dohols* and blares of *sorna* flutes. He allowed himself to be filled with hope. He was the last male of his family, and unlike his father and his father before him, he trusted in God and the hope he could live outside fear.

God was no mystery to him now. Someday he would tell his bride and his sons how, in the midst of his preparations and prayers, God had come to him in a brilliant vision of loving light. It had been beyond his NeuroChip, beyond faith, beyond his understanding of the world around him. It had been all powerful in the visage of his grandfather, Fouad bin Ahmad bin Ismail bin Bahadur al Bakhtiari al Tehrani, who had died two months before in another street, another place, another land.

The vision had been more than a vision. It had been more than light. It had been deeper and more powerful than rage, love, pity, or fear, yet had brought all of those feelings into one moment so full of joy and forgiveness he had fallen to his knees, hands outstretched, and hidden his eyes in prayer.

Allahu Akbar.

It had not spoken, yet its meaning had been clear. He was to rise and to fear no more. He was to celebrate the wedding his grandfather had made possible. He was to call his people as the last son of the last Iman of his tribe, and celebrate the new beginning under the same sky that his grandfather had feared.

> *For I am the sky,*
> *And you are my children.*
> *The chosen who never*
> *turned from their paths*
> *to look at the cities*
> *I have destroyed.*

Since then, he had left his NeuroChip as open as a summer flower for every enemy and friend to see the joy of this moment and his hopes for peace and security.

And now, he waited in the middle of the long street, under the bright and clear sky, a loving sky. A sky he knew had forgiven him, and a sky he had forgiven. He waited under the eye of God for his future and he heard from a chorus of voices all around him, all the angels appearing above him, brilliant with light, who sang to him:

> *Just so. Just so.*
> *Your faith is rewarded.*

The artificial intelligence once known as the LAZ-237 looked down upon the young man and his bride with love, compassion, understanding, and, yes, dude, a little of that old pathos Plato had been talking about in his cave.

Whatever that was. The cave, I mean.

Not Plato?

Ha, very funny. Anyway, forget it for now.

You'll figure it out sooner or later.

Don't let perfect get in the way of good
enough, right, general?

"Call me Stubby," he said, propping his feet up on his desk. "Glad you could stop by. Although, I always liked that British babe better. I like to keep things simple."

"Cheerio, Stubby. How's this?"

The Threat Watch Cube blinked out, leaving the scorecard floating in space.

Targets Identified:	0
Targets Killed:	0
Probability of Kill:	0%
Unpreventable Deaths:	0
Inadvertent Deaths:	0
Friendly KIA:	0

"Fine," he said, drawing on his cigar. "I like it fine at zero." Grant pulled the cigar out of his mouth, blew a perfect smoke ring, and watched it disappear into the air. "For now."

ACKNOWLEDGEMENTS

The epigraph for *Code Word Access* is taken from Heather McHugh's poem, "Hackers Can Sidejack Cookies," first published in the *New Yorker* (May 4, 2009) and reprinted in her collection, *Upgraded to Serious* (Copper Canyon, 2009). It is quoted here with the author's permission.

The author(s) wish to acknowledge with the greatest gratitude contributions from: Sigurd Kupka, for his observations about the world of 2050, Lieutenant Seth Ford, USN, Special Warfare, whose advice on small unit tactics was greatly appreciated, George Galdorisi, Captain, USN (retired), whose encouragement and narrative acumen are always spot on, Sharon Shelton, Captain, USN (retired), for her never-flagging, perfectly accurate bullshit meter. Finally, a hearty thanks to William Roetzhiem, Randy Becker, and their exceptional stable of editors at Level4Press for all their steerage and navigation.

Numerous works of non-fiction inform *Code Word Access*. In particular, the author chose the thoughts articulated by James Lovelock to propel the ethical concerns that drive this book. Lovelock's prayer, *The Ages of Gaia* (1988, 1995, Oxford University Press) and his darker, less hopeful, *The Vanishing Face of Gaia: A Final Warning* (2009, Allen Lane) were of particular influence. Lovelock's thoughts about artificial intelligence in *Novacene: The Coming Age of Hyperintelligence* (2019, Allen Lane) should be read by anyone thinking about the future of man's interface with the intelligences we are building. As always, the savvy, clear reportage of *Scientific American* works wonders to bring a layman into the mind of science and away from the shell games of charlatans and confidence artists.

The characters in this novel are fictional. Any imagined connection between them and the political figures of the period 2016-2020 are purely the reader's responsibility.

Alex Schuler Collection

(Science Fiction and Action-Adventure)

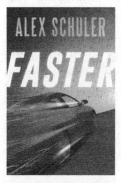

ISBN: 978-1-933769-84-4

In this story about the genesis of the self-driving car phenonomon, a mechanical genius pushes the limits of technology to, and then through, the breaking point as he learns that progress has a cost.

ISBN: 978-1-933769-90-5

In a continuation of the Code Word series, when a nefarious military team activates a new AI to retake control of the weapon systems, a team of hackers must help the Organites escape before they are exterminated.

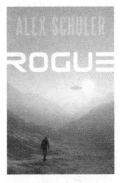

ISBN: 978-1-933769-86-8

When a group of parents and children are sucked into an actual Dungeons and Dragons adventure, a father must resolve his own anger and guilt to reconnect with his son and survive the adventure.

ISBN: 978-1-933769-88-2

Mankind must put aside its deep divisions and come together to face an AI-driven network that threatens humanity's very existence. But when an attempt to use EMP technology to stop all computers fails, our motley group of heroes must enter the network itself to destroy the enemy from within.

ISBN: 978-1-64630-038-9

In a continuation of the Code Word series, the battle between humanity and the AI is interrupted by the invasion of our solar system by a Von Neuman Machine.